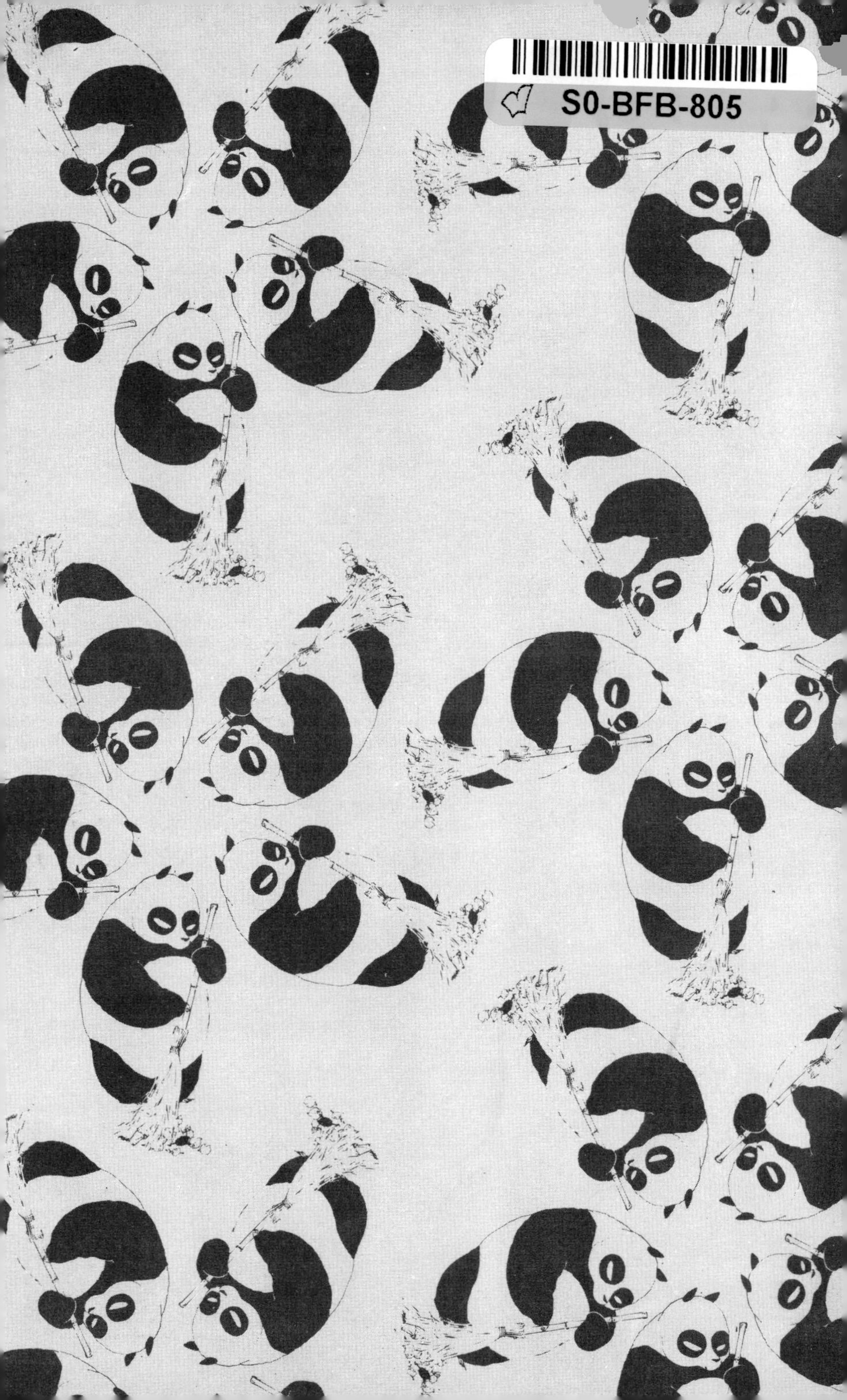

VIZ GRAPHIC NOVEL

# RANMA 1/2™

7

This volume contains RANMA 1/2 PART FOUR from the second half
of #6 through #11 in their entirety.

Story & Art by Rumiko Takahashi
*

Translation/Gerard Jones & Toshifumi Yoshida
Touch-Up Art & Lettering/Wayne Truman
Cover Design/Viz Graphics
Editor/Trish Ledoux
Assistant Editors/Annette Roman & Toshifumi Yoshida
*

Editor-in-Chief/Satoru Fujii
Publisher/Seiji Horibuchi
*

First Published by Shogakukan, Inc. in Japan
*

Printed in Canada
*

Published by Viz Communications, Inc.
P.O. Box 77010
San Francisco, CA  94107
*

10 9 8 7 6 5 4 3 2 1
First printing, September 1996

VIZ GRAPHIC NOVEL

# RANMA 1/2

STORY & ART BY

## RUMIKO TAKAHASHI

# CONTENTS

# PART ONE

# WHEREFORE ART THOU, ROMEO?

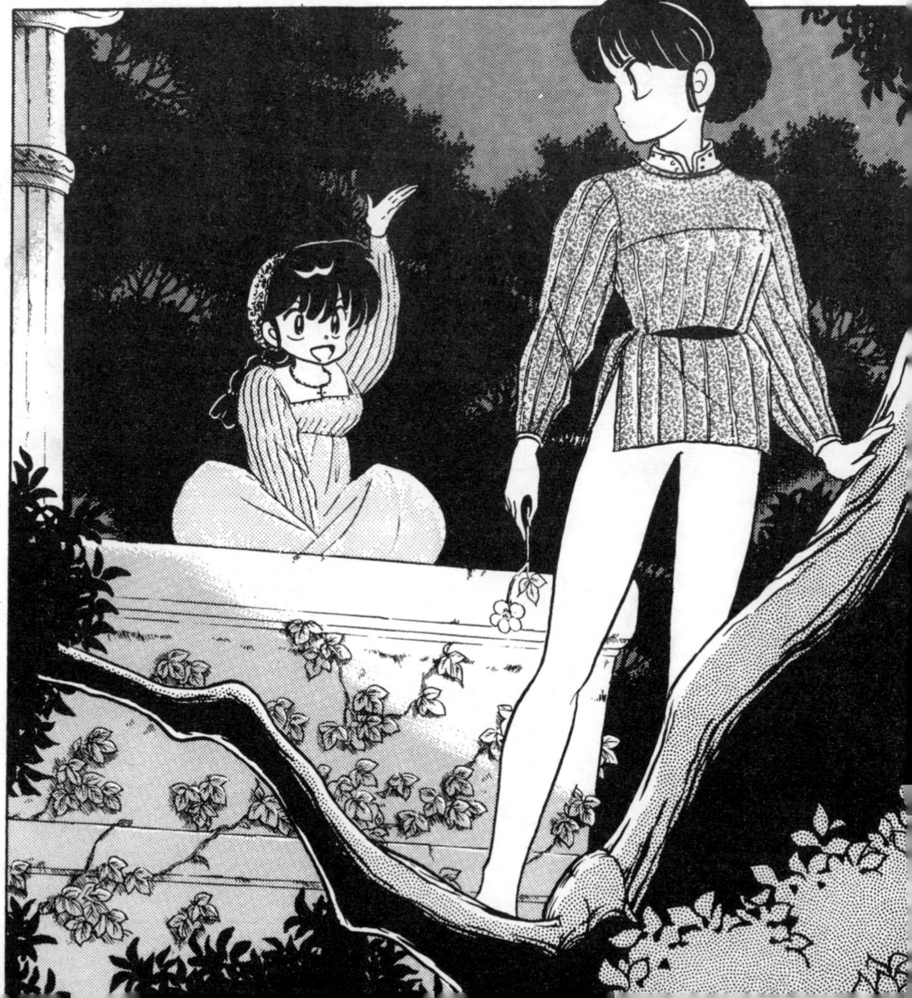

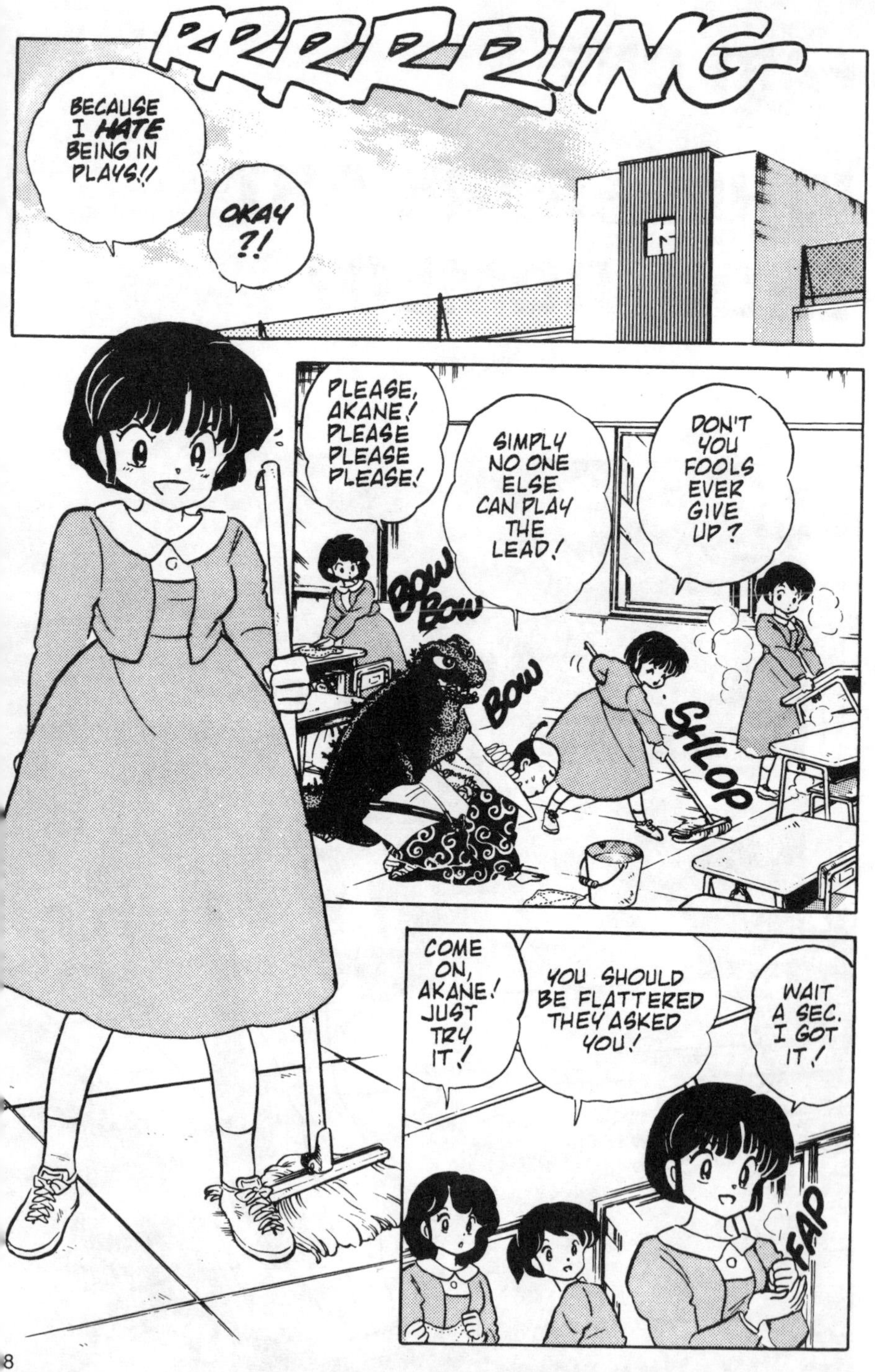
RRRRRING
BECAUSE I HATE BEING IN PLAYS!!
OKAY ?!
PLEASE, AKANE! PLEASE PLEASE PLEASE!
SIMPLY NO ONE ELSE CAN PLAY THE LEAD!
DON'T YOU FOOLS EVER GIVE UP?
BOW BOW
BOW
SHLOP
COME ON, AKANE! JUST TRY IT!
YOU SHOULD BE FLATTERED THEY ASKED YOU!
WAIT A SEC. I GOT IT!
FAP

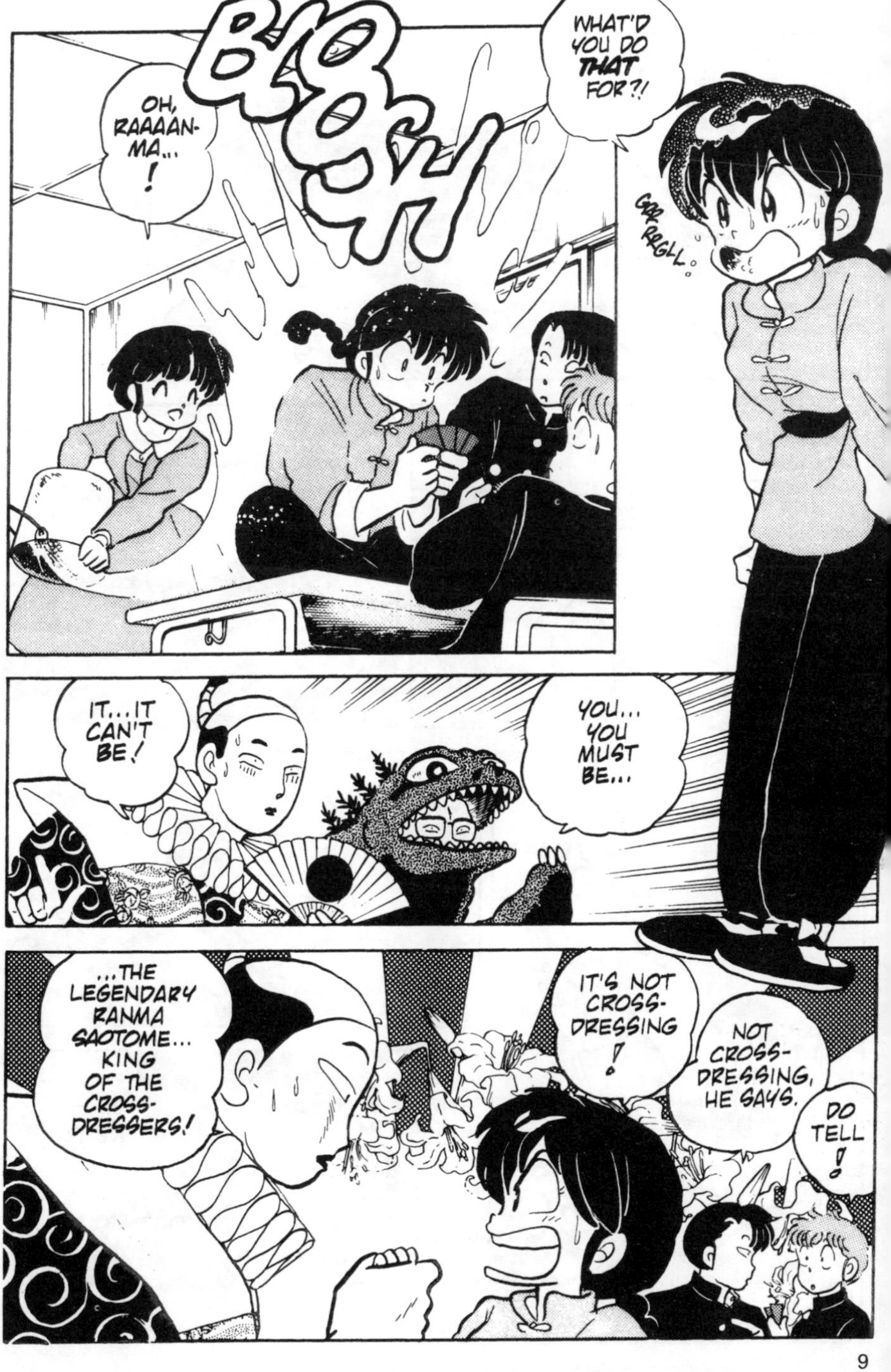
OH, RAAAAN-MA... !
BLOOSH
WHAT'D YOU DO **THAT** FOR?!
GRR RRGLL
IT... IT CAN'T BE!
YOU... YOU MUST BE...
...THE LEGENDARY RANMA SAOTOME... KING OF THE CROSS-DRESSERS!
IT'S NOT CROSS-DRESSING!
NOT CROSS-DRESSING, HE SAYS.
DO TELL!

HE DOES AERIAL FLIPS.

CRUSHES ROCKS BAREHANDED.

AND HE LEARNS NEW TRICKS EVEN QUICKER THAN LASSIE.

HEY!

WHY DON'T YOU WANT THE ROLE, AKANE?

IT'S THE LEAD! IT'S...

LET ME GUESS.

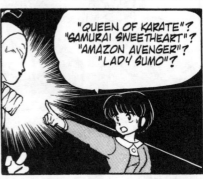

"QUEEN OF KARATE"? "SAMURAI SWEETHEART"? "AMAZON AVENGER"? "LADY SUMO"?

GO FOR IT, AKANE! YOU WERE BORN FOR THE ROLE!

WHISH

WHOA!

BUT, AKANE, IF YOU'D ONLY LET ME--

BOOM

BOOM

I SAID **NO** AND I MEAN **NO!**

DO WE HAVE A CHOICE?

I THINK WE DON'T.

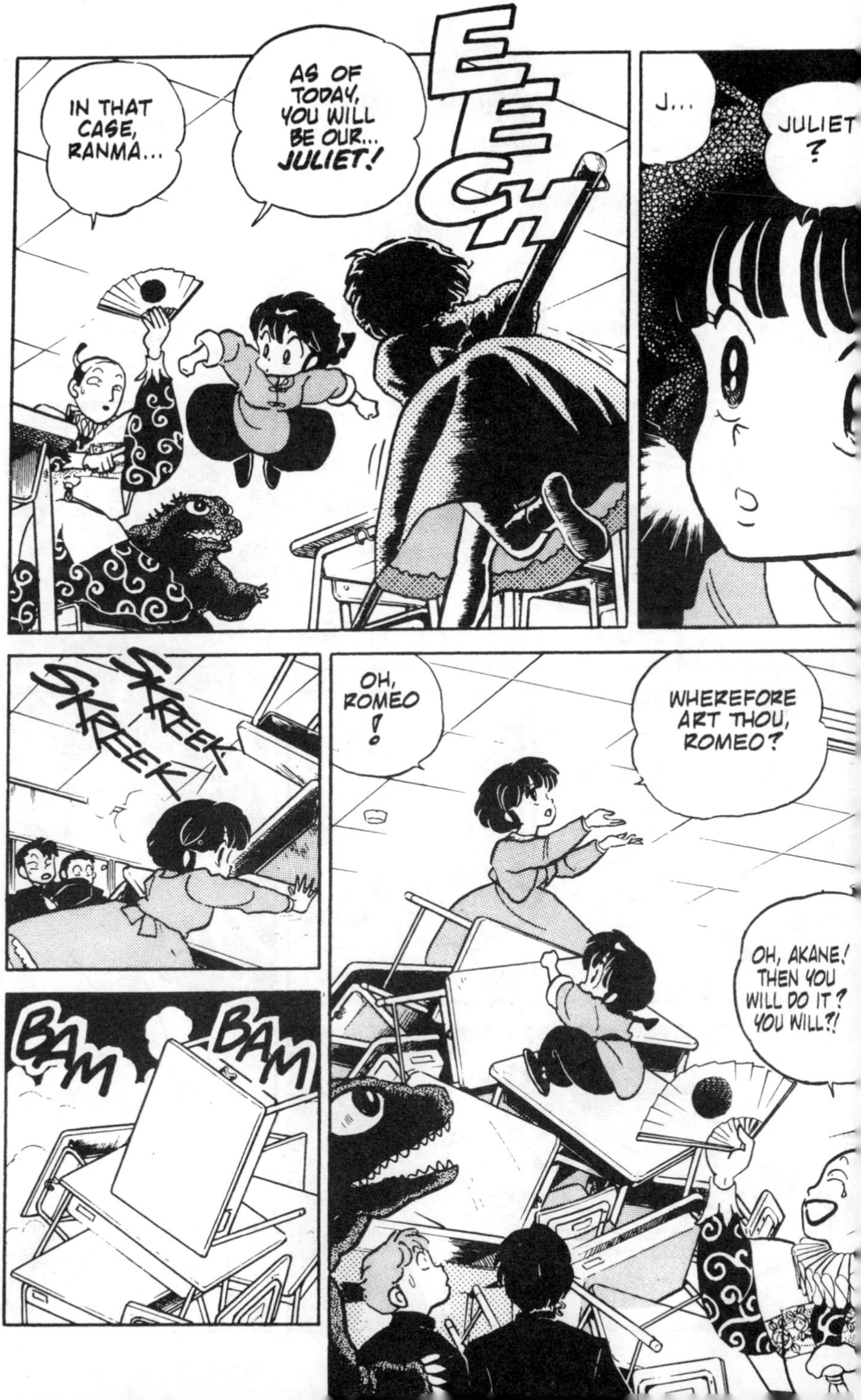
IN THAT CASE, RANMA...
AS OF TODAY, YOU WILL BE OUR... JULIET!
EEECH
J...
JULIET?
SKREEK SKREEK
OH, ROMEO!
WHEREFORE ART THOU, ROMEO?
OH, AKANE! THEN YOU WILL DO IT? YOU WILL?!
BAM BAM

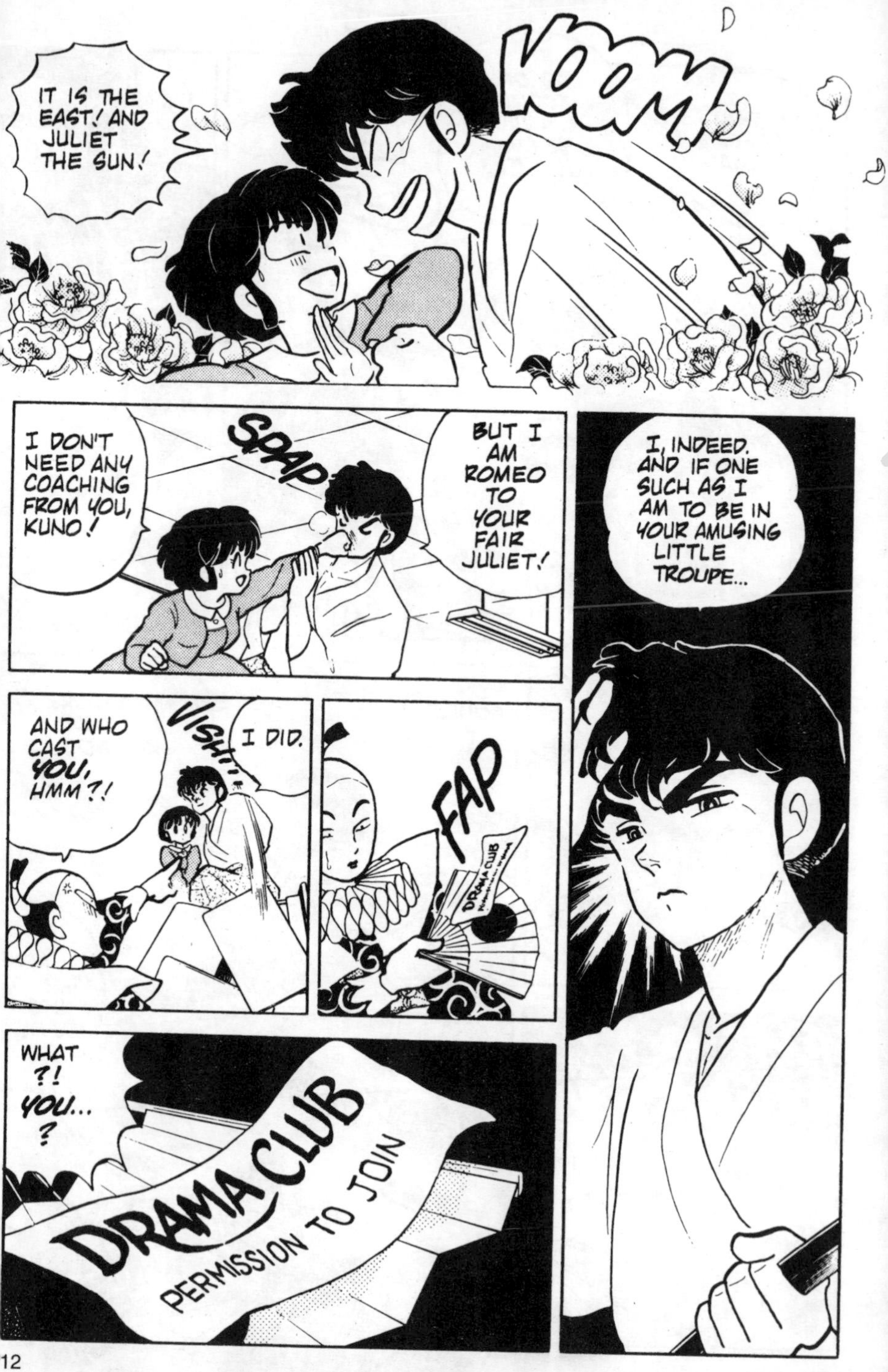
IT IS THE EAST! AND JULIET THE SUN!
VOOM
I DON'T NEED ANY COACHING FROM YOU, KUNO!
SPAP
BUT I AM ROMEO TO YOUR FAIR JULIET!
AND WHO CAST YOU, HMM?!
VISH!!!
I DID.
FAP
DRAMA CLUB
WHAT?! YOU...?
DRAMA CLUB
PERMISSION TO JOIN
I, INDEED. AND IF ONE SUCH AS I AM TO BE IN YOUR AMUSING LITTLE TROUPE...

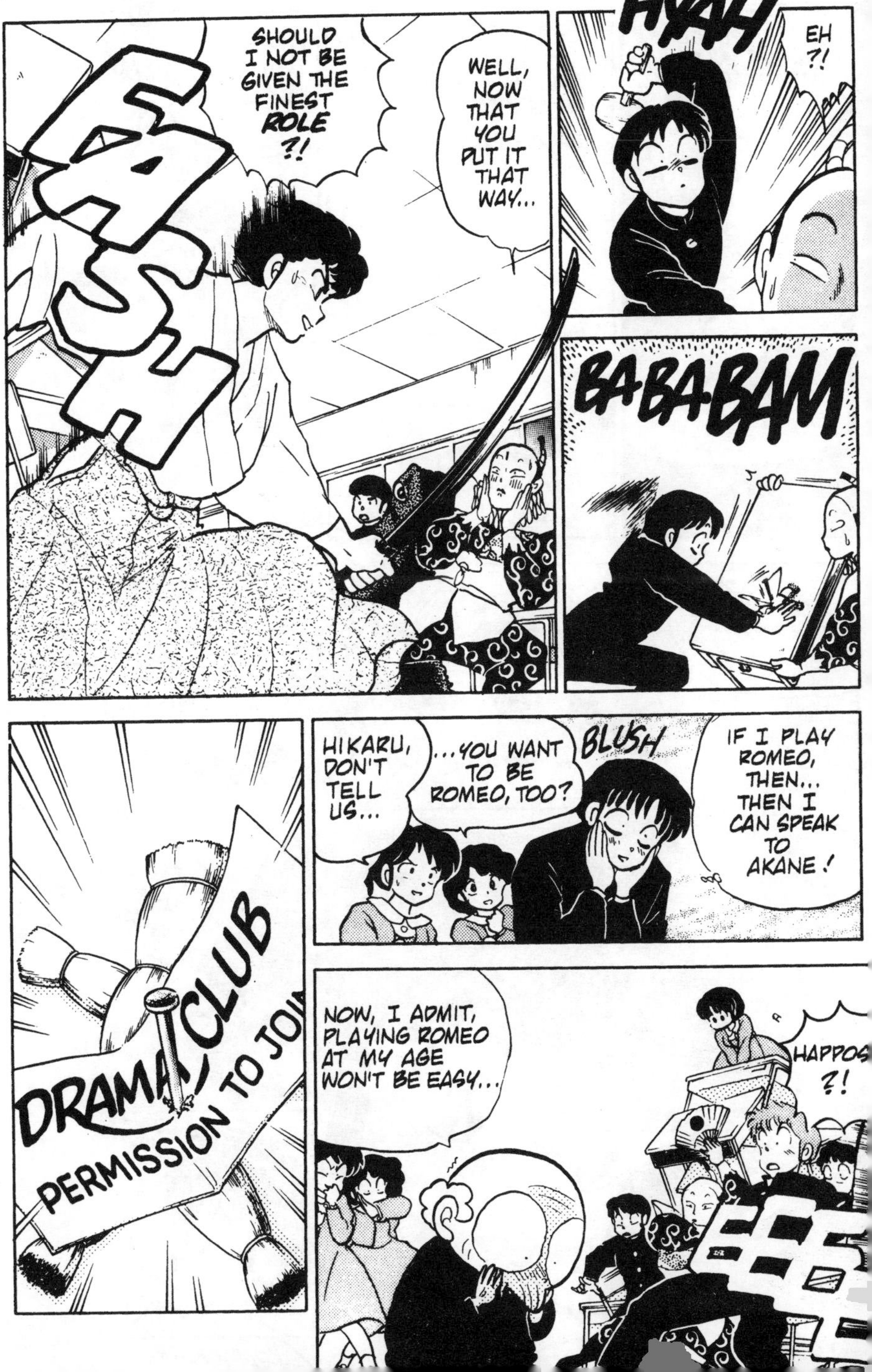
SHOULD I NOT BE GIVEN THE FINEST ROLE ?!
WELL, NOW THAT YOU PUT IT THAT WAY...
FASH
HYAH
EH ?!
BA-BA-BAM
DRAMA CLUB
PERMISSION TO JOIN
HIKARU, DON'T TELL US...
...YOU WANT TO BE ROMEO, TOO?
BLUSH
IF I PLAY ROMEO, THEN... THEN I CAN SPEAK TO AKANE !
NOW, I ADMIT, PLAYING ROMEO AT MY AGE WON'T BE EASY...
HAPPOS
?!

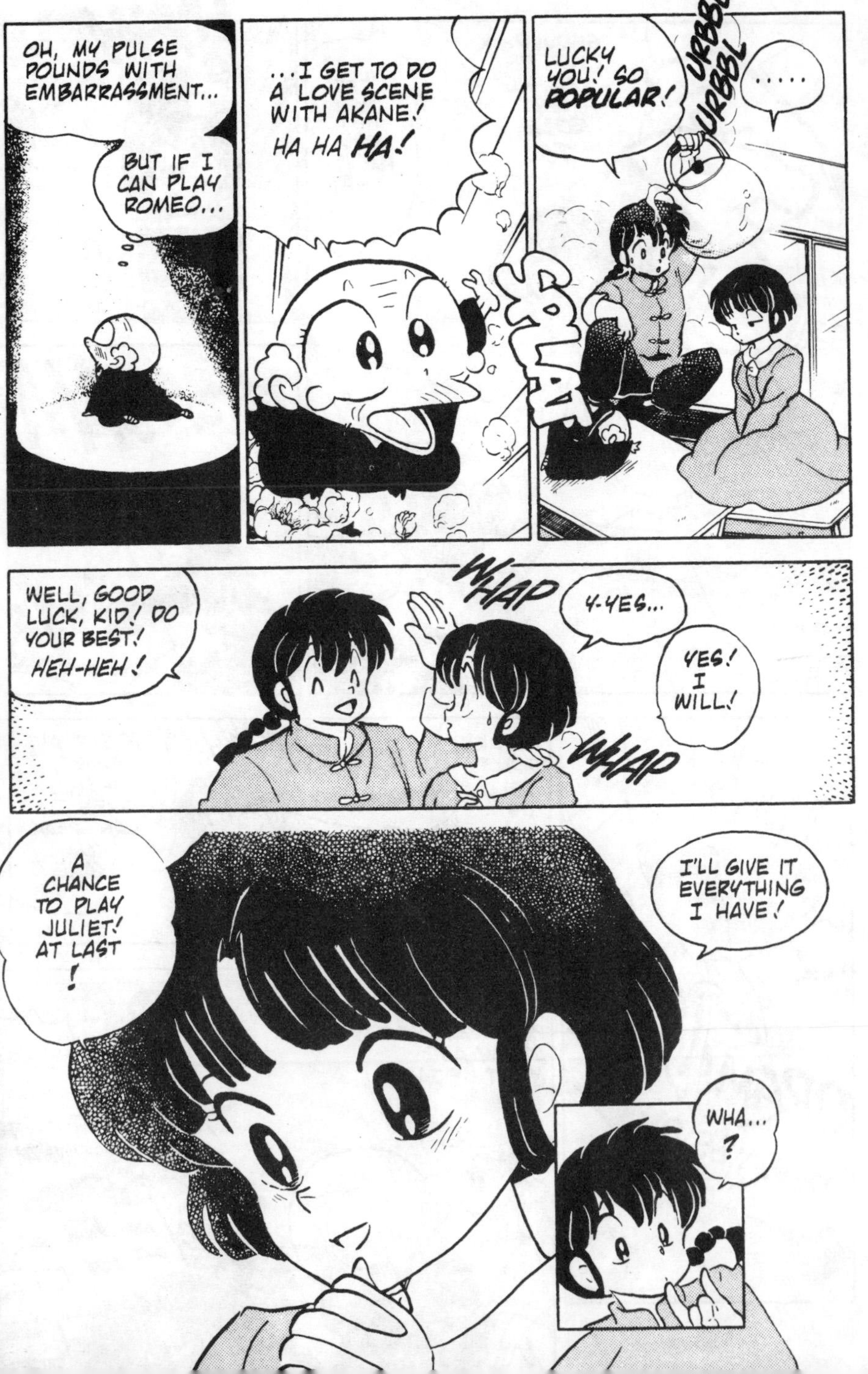
OH, MY PULSE POUNDS WITH EMBARRASSMENT...
BUT IF I CAN PLAY ROMEO...
...I GET TO DO A LOVE SCENE WITH AKANE! HA HA HA!
SPLAT
LUCKY YOU! SO POPULAR!
URBBL URBBL
......
WELL, GOOD LUCK, KID! DO YOUR BEST! HEH-HEH!
WHAP
Y-YES...
YES! I WILL!
WHAP
A CHANCE TO PLAY JULIET! AT LAST!
I'LL GIVE IT EVERYTHING I HAVE!
WHA...?

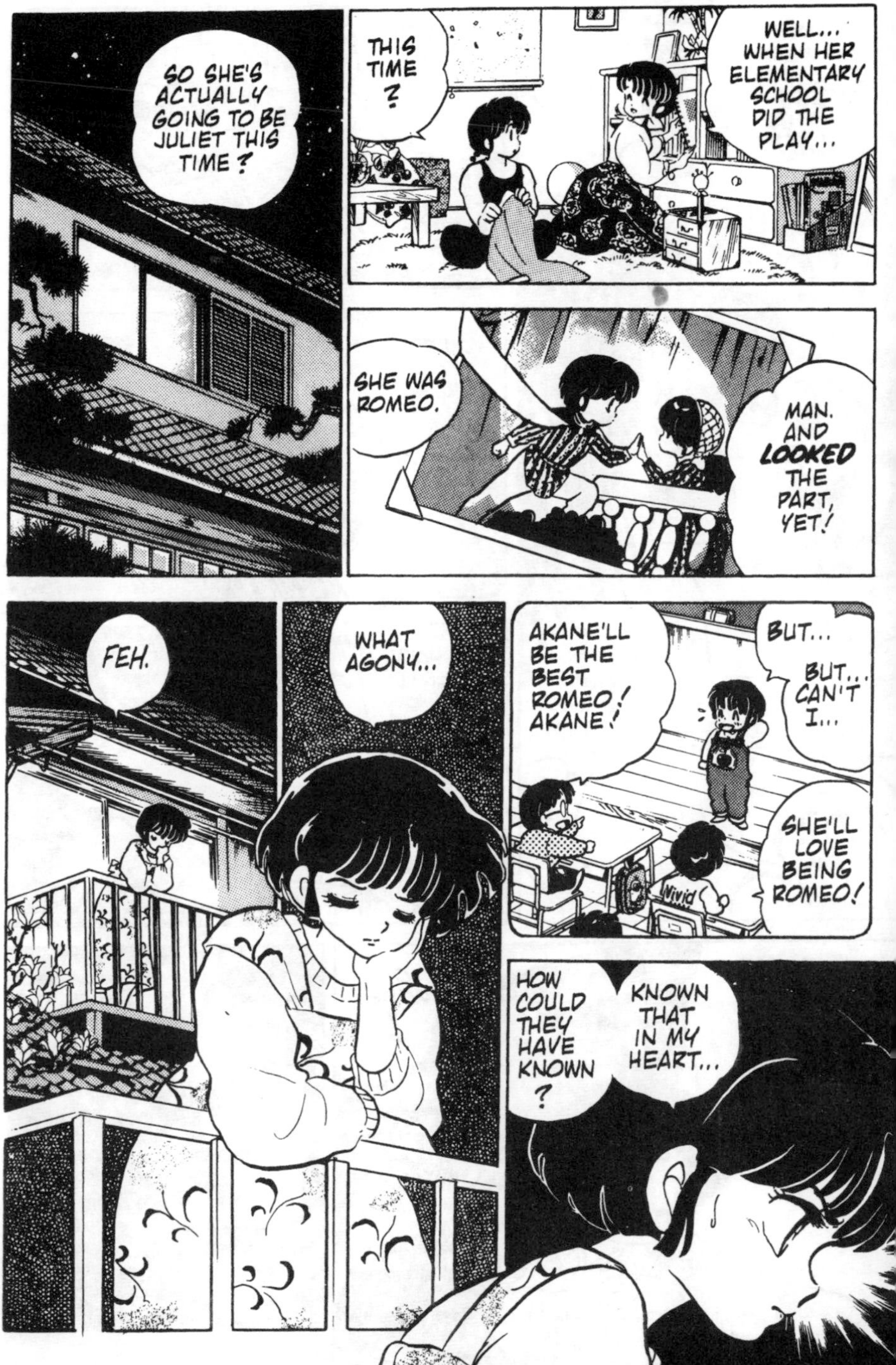
SO SHE'S ACTUALLY GOING TO BE JULIET THIS TIME?
THIS TIME?
WELL... WHEN HER ELEMENTARY SCHOOL DID THE PLAY...
SHE WAS ROMEO.
MAN. AND LOOKED THE PART, YET!
FEH.
WHAT AGONY...
AKANE'LL BE THE BEST ROMEO! AKANE!
BUT...
BUT... CAN'T I...
SHE'LL LOVE BEING ROMEO!
HOW COULD THEY HAVE KNOWN?
KNOWN THAT IN MY HEART...

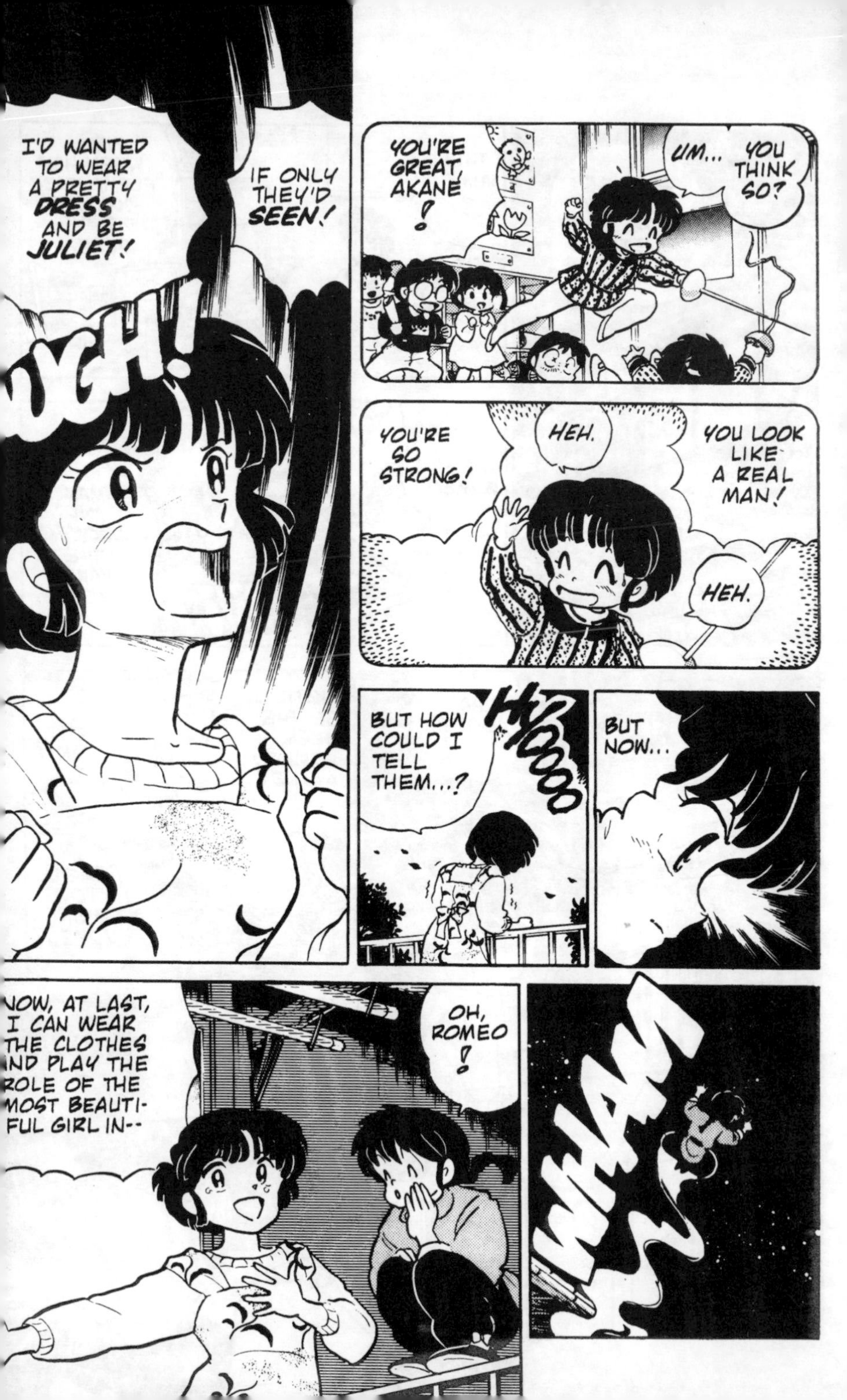

I'D WANTED TO WEAR A PRETTY DRESS AND BE JULIET!
IF ONLY THEY'D SEEN!
UGH!
YOU'RE GREAT, AKANE!
UM... YOU THINK SO?
YOU'RE SO STRONG!
HEH.
YOU LOOK LIKE A REAL MAN!
HEH.
BUT HOW COULD I TELL THEM...?
BUT NOW...
NOW, AT LAST, I CAN WEAR THE CLOTHES AND PLAY THE ROLE OF THE MOST BEAUTI-FUL GIRL IN--
OH, ROMEO!
WHAM

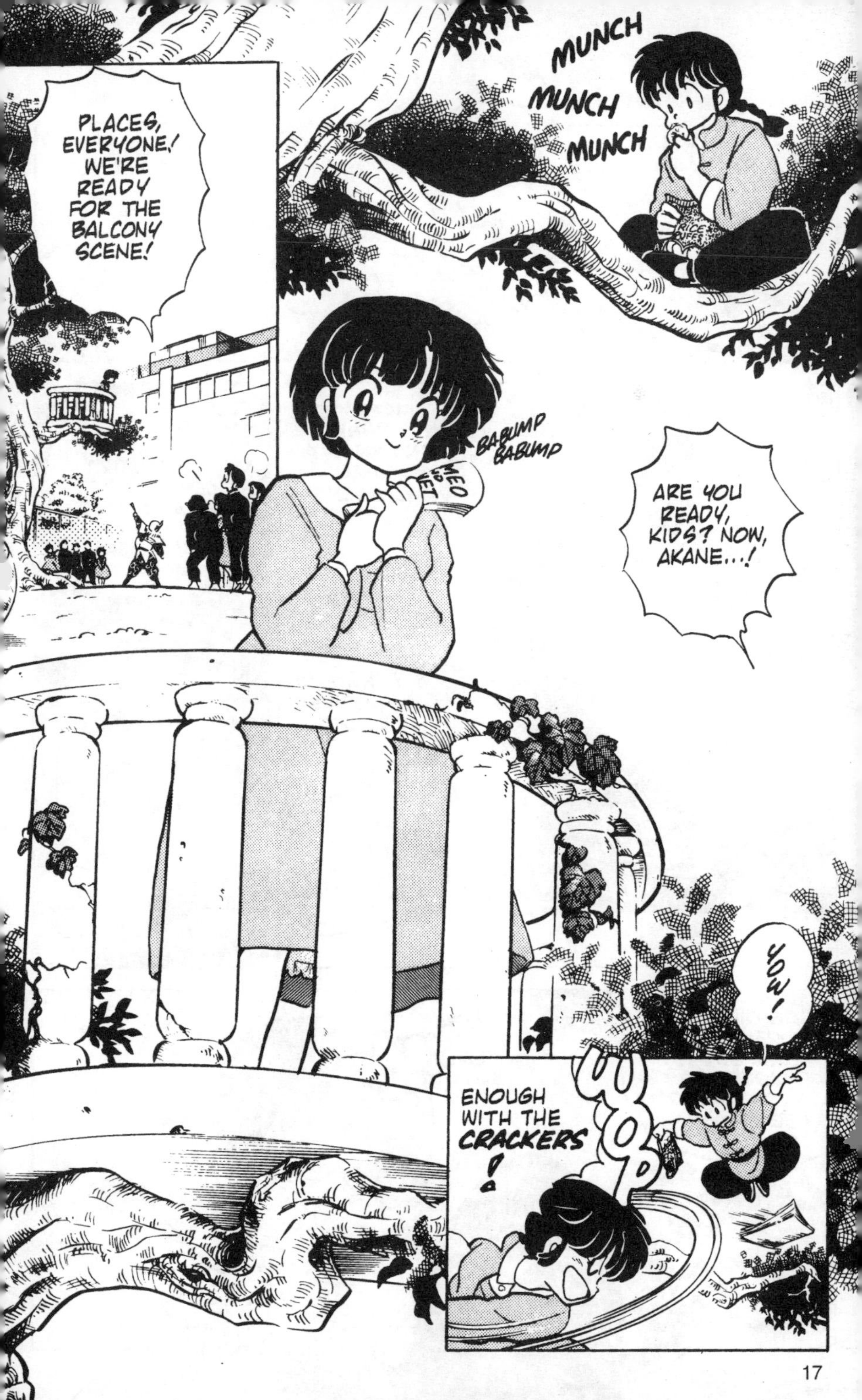
PLACES, EVERYONE! WE'RE READY FOR THE BALCONY SCENE!
MUNCH
MUNCH
MUNCH
BABUMP BABUMP
ARE YOU READY, KIDS? NOW, AKANE...!
YOW!
WOOP
ENOUGH WITH THE CRACKERS!

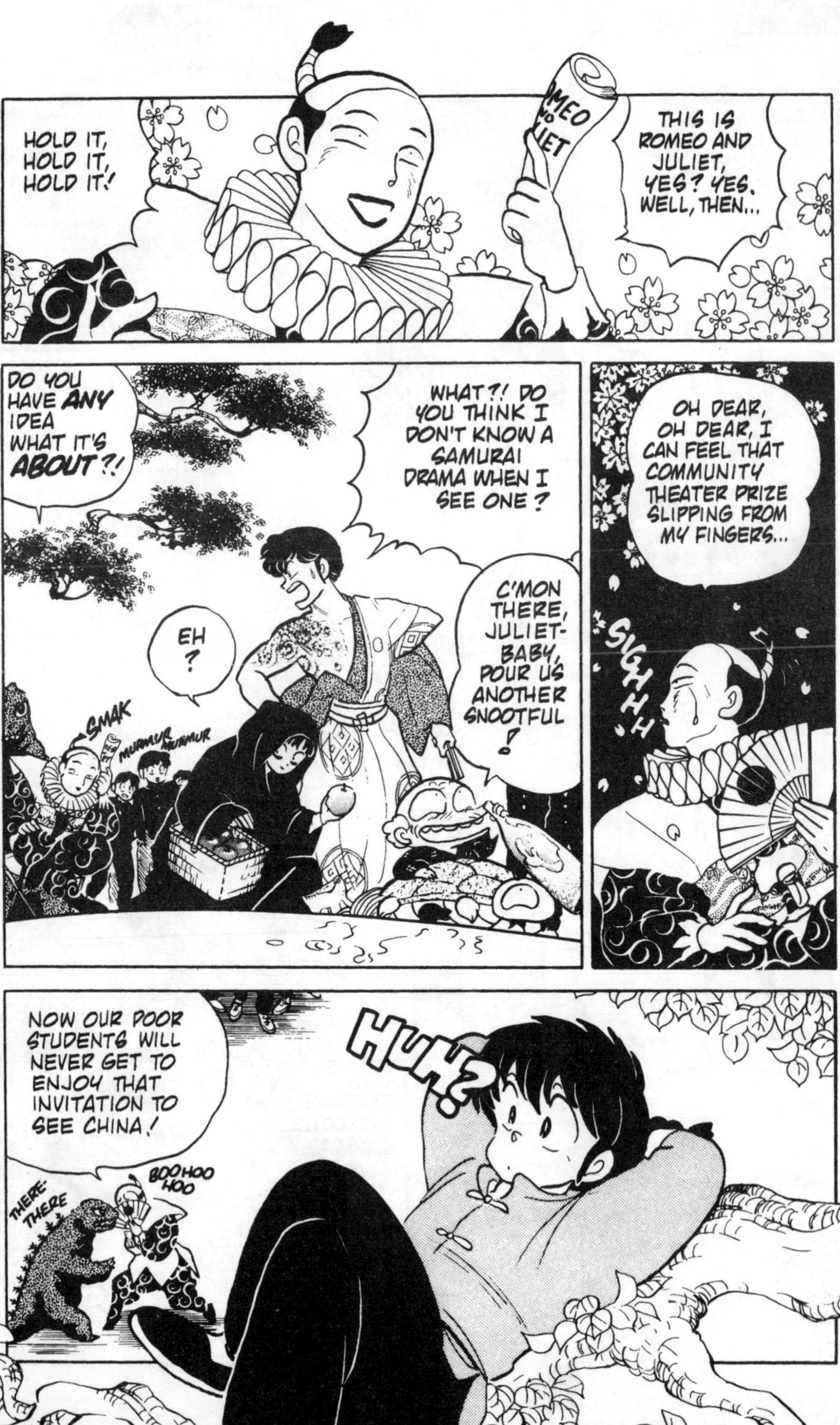
HOLD IT, HOLD IT, HOLD IT!
ROMEO AND JULIET
THIS IS ROMEO AND JULIET, YES? YES. WELL, THEN...
DO YOU HAVE ANY IDEA WHAT IT'S ABOUT?!
WHAT?! DO YOU THINK I DON'T KNOW A SAMURAI DRAMA WHEN I SEE ONE?
EH?
SMAK
MURMUR MURMUR
C'MON THERE, JULIET-BABY, POUR US ANOTHER SNOOTFUL!
OH DEAR, OH DEAR, I CAN FEEL THAT COMMUNITY THEATER PRIZE SLIPPING FROM MY FINGERS...
SIGHHH
NOW OUR POOR STUDENTS WILL NEVER GET TO ENJOY THAT INVITATION TO SEE CHINA!
HUH?
THERE THERE
BOO HOO HOO

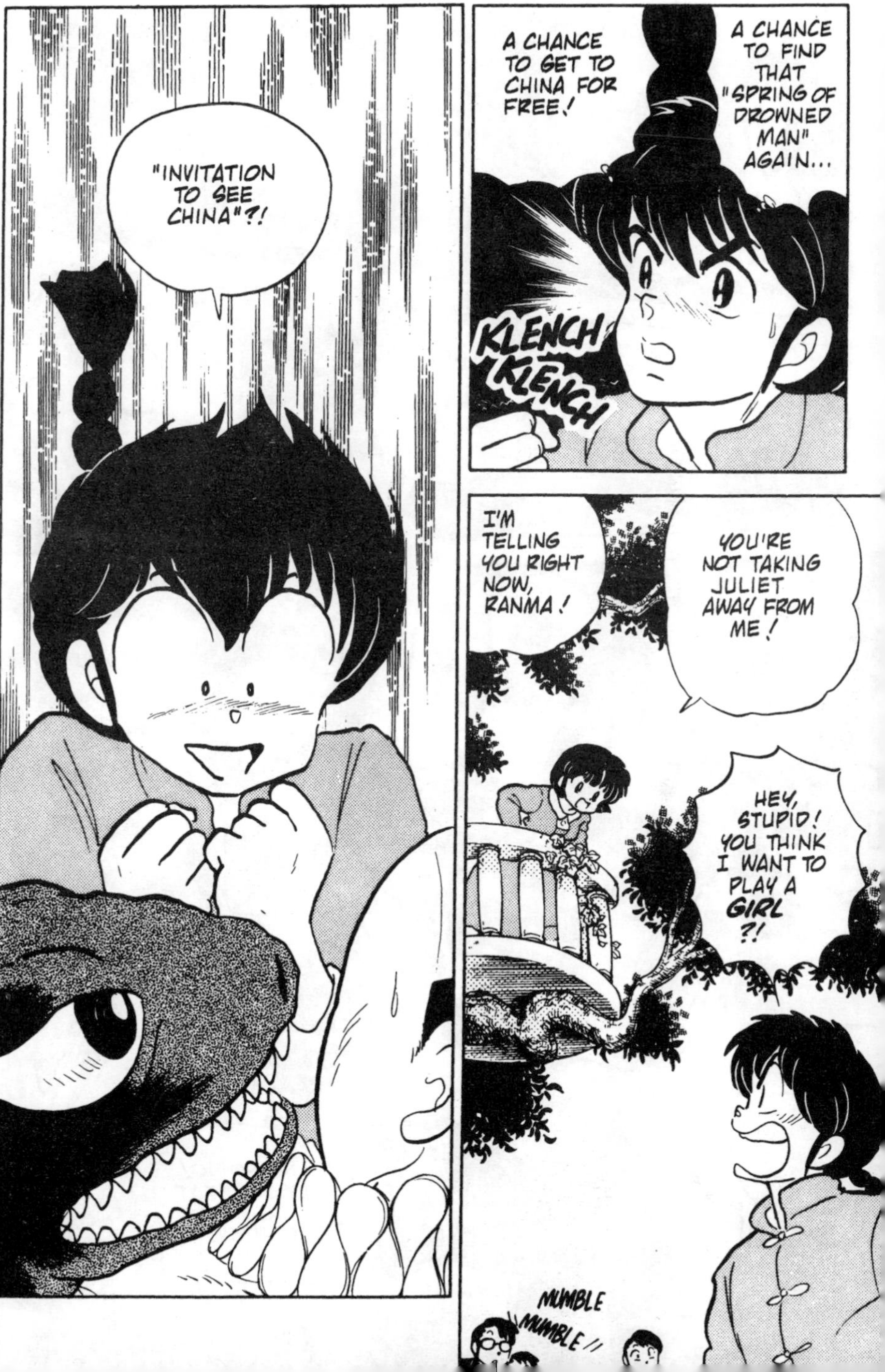
"INVITATION TO SEE CHINA"?!
A CHANCE TO GET TO CHINA FOR FREE!
A CHANCE TO FIND THAT "SPRING OF DROWNED MAN" AGAIN...
KLENCH KLENCH
I'M TELLING YOU RIGHT NOW, RANMA!
YOU'RE NOT TAKING JULIET AWAY FROM ME!
HEY, STUPID! YOU THINK I WANT TO PLAY A **GIRL** ?!
MUMBLE MUMBLE

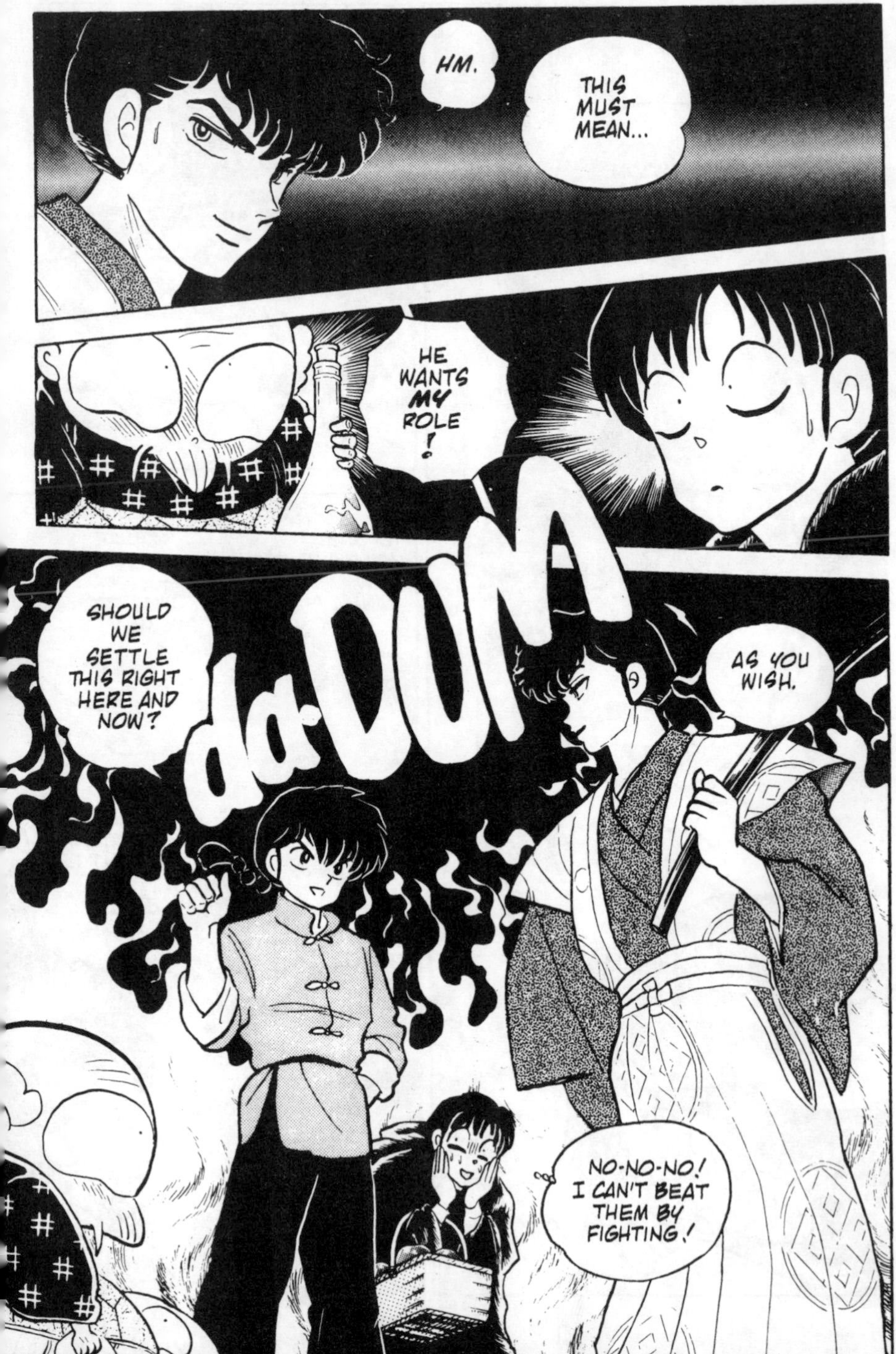
HM.
THIS MUST MEAN...
HE WANTS **MY** ROLE!
SHOULD WE SETTLE THIS RIGHT HERE AND NOW?
da-DUM
AS YOU WISH.
NO-NO-NO! I CAN'T BEAT THEM BY FIGHTING!

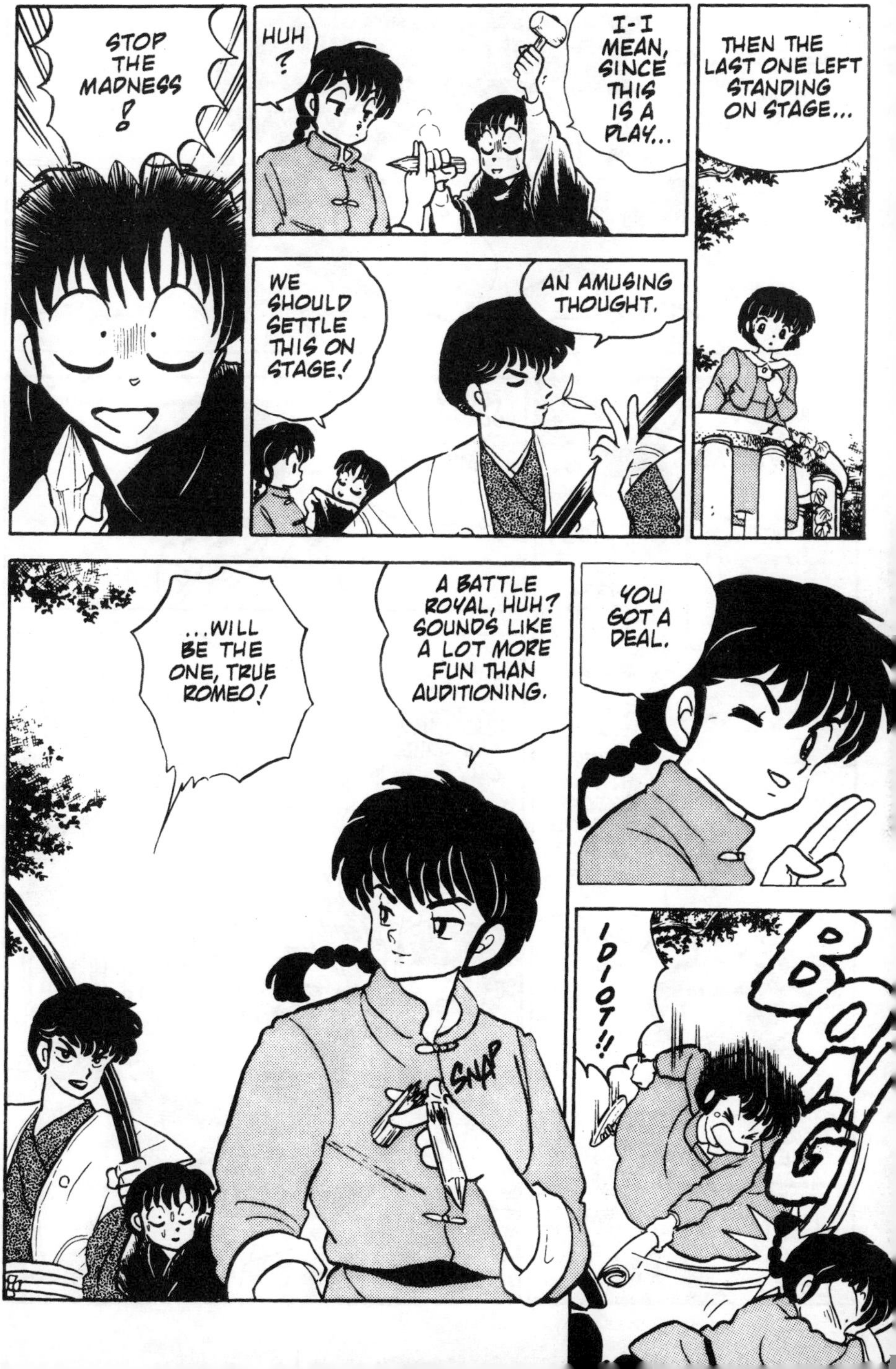
STOP THE MADNESS!
HUH?
I-I MEAN, SINCE THIS IS A PLAY...
WE SHOULD SETTLE THIS ON STAGE!
AN AMUSING THOUGHT.
THEN THE LAST ONE LEFT STANDING ON STAGE...
...WILL BE THE ONE, TRUE ROMEO!
A BATTLE ROYAL, HUH? SOUNDS LIKE A LOT MORE FUN THAN AUDITIONING.
SNAP
YOU GOT A DEAL.
IDIOT!!
BONG

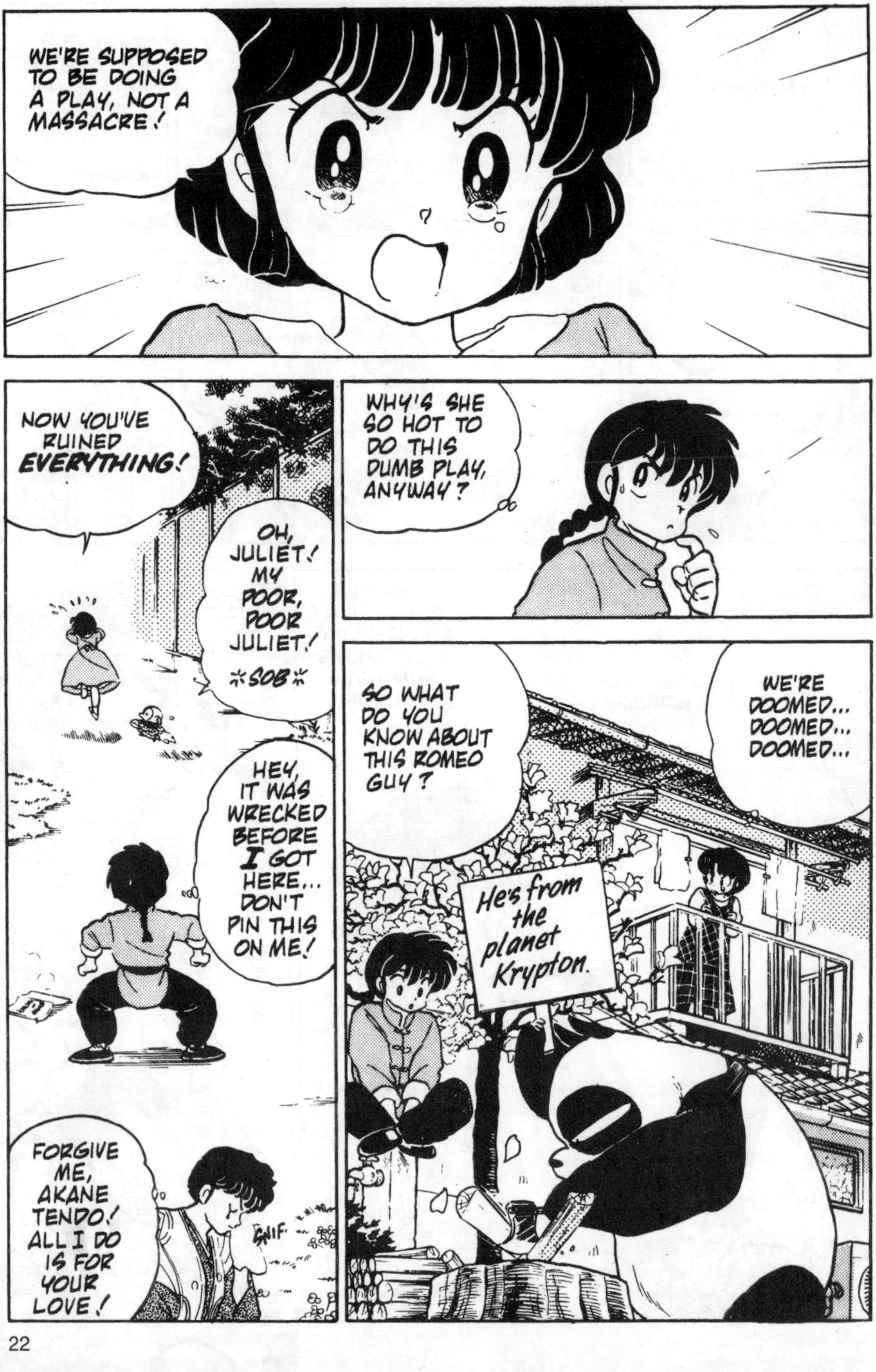

WE'RE SUPPOSED TO BE DOING A PLAY, NOT A MASSACRE!
NOW YOU'VE RUINED **EVERYTHING**!
OH, JULIET! MY POOR, POOR JULIET! *SOB*
HEY, IT WAS WRECKED BEFORE **I** GOT HERE... DON'T PIN THIS ON ME!
FORGIVE ME, AKANE TENDO! ALL I DO IS FOR YOUR LOVE!
SNIF
WHY'S SHE SO HOT TO DO THIS DUMB PLAY, ANYWAY?
SO WHAT DO YOU KNOW ABOUT THIS ROMEO GUY?
WE'RE DOOMED... DOOMED... DOOMED...
He's from the planet Krypton.

# PART TWO

# ROMEO? ROMEO? ROMEO!?

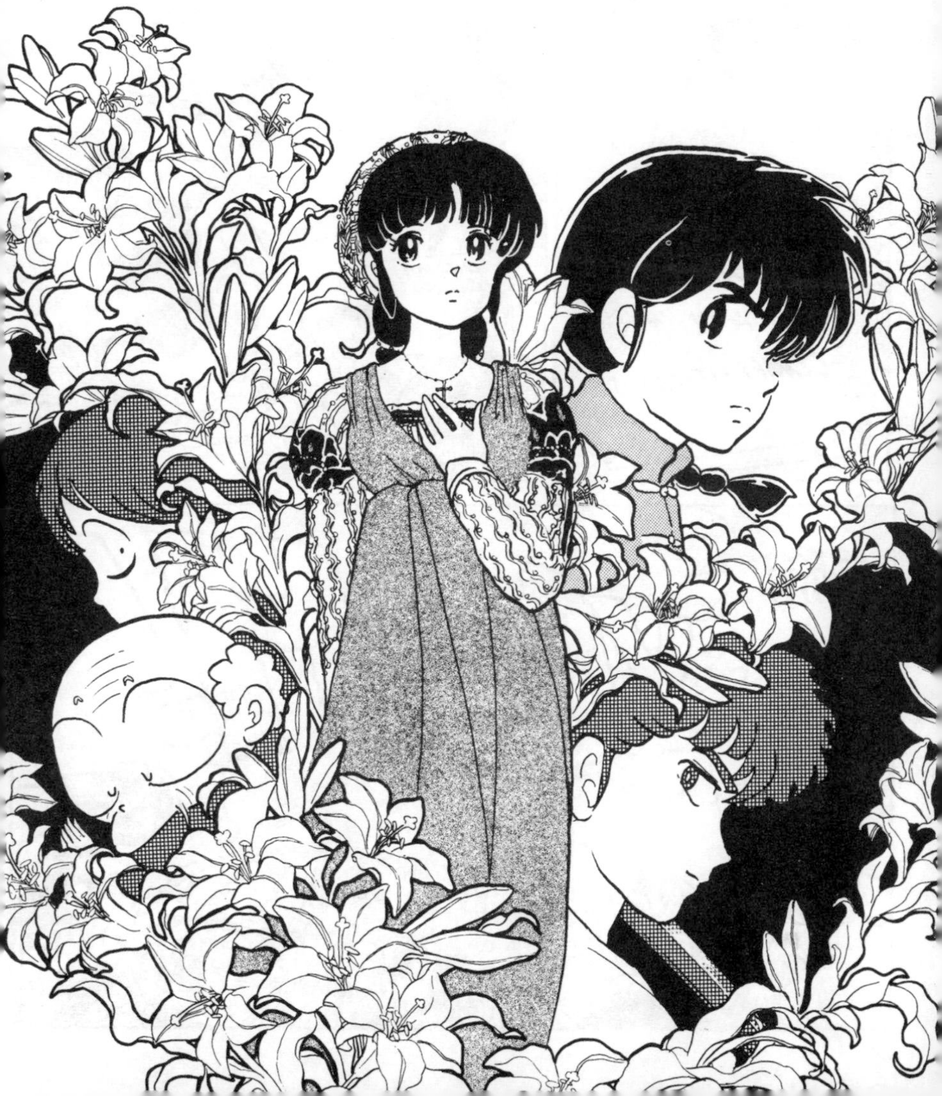

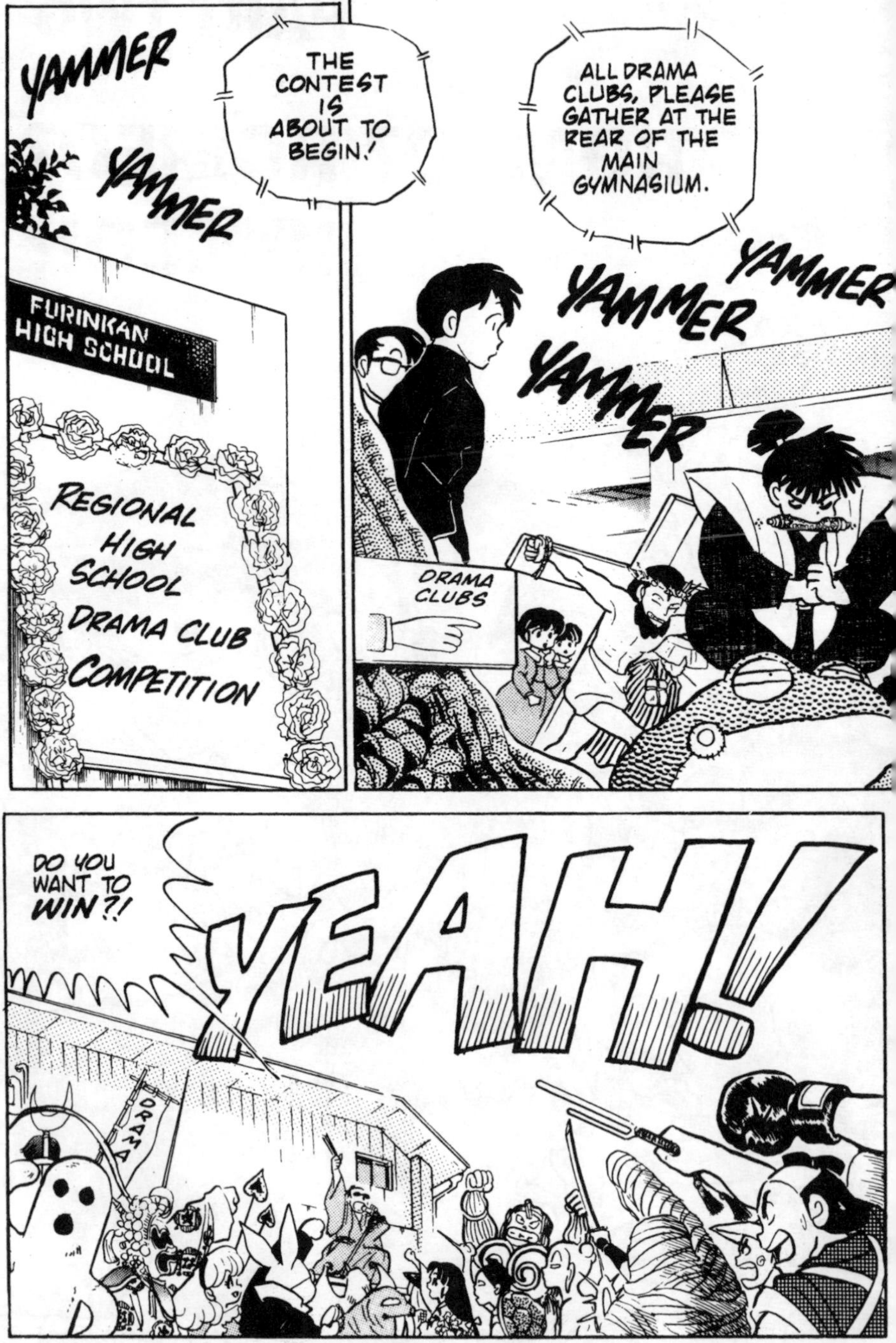
YAMMER
YAMMER
THE CONTEST IS ABOUT TO BEGIN!
FURINKAN HIGH SCHOOL
REGIONAL HIGH SCHOOL DRAMA CLUB COMPETITION
ALL DRAMA CLUBS, PLEASE GATHER AT THE REAR OF THE MAIN GYMNASIUM.
YAMMER
YAMMER
YAMMER
DRAMA CLUBS
DO YOU WANT TO WIN?!
YEAH!
DRAMA

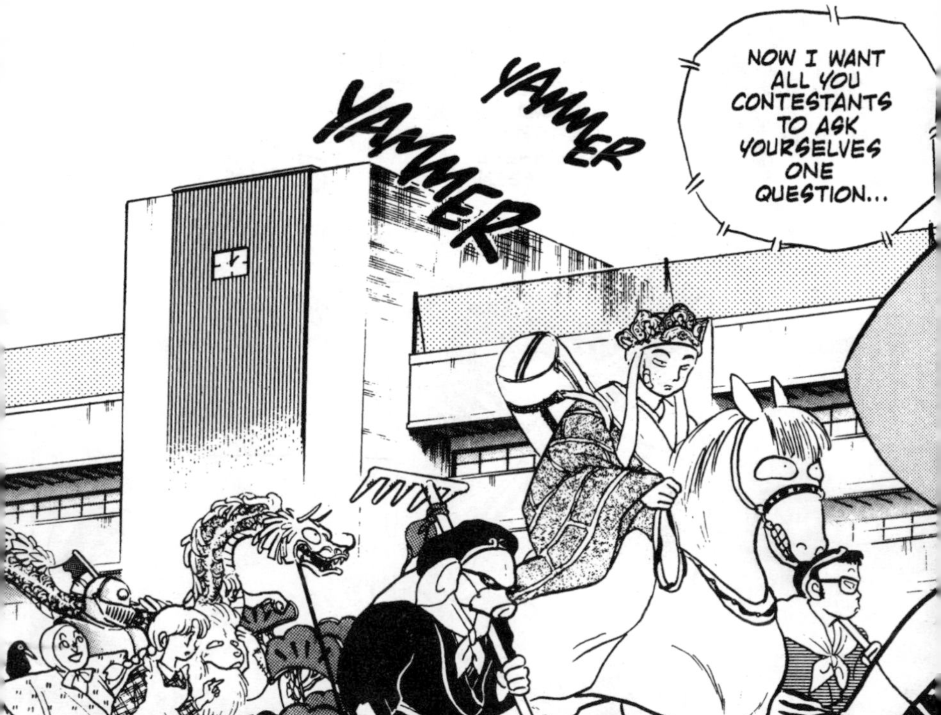
YAMMER
YAMMER
NOW I WANT ALL YOU CONTESTANTS TO ASK YOURSELVES ONE QUESTION...

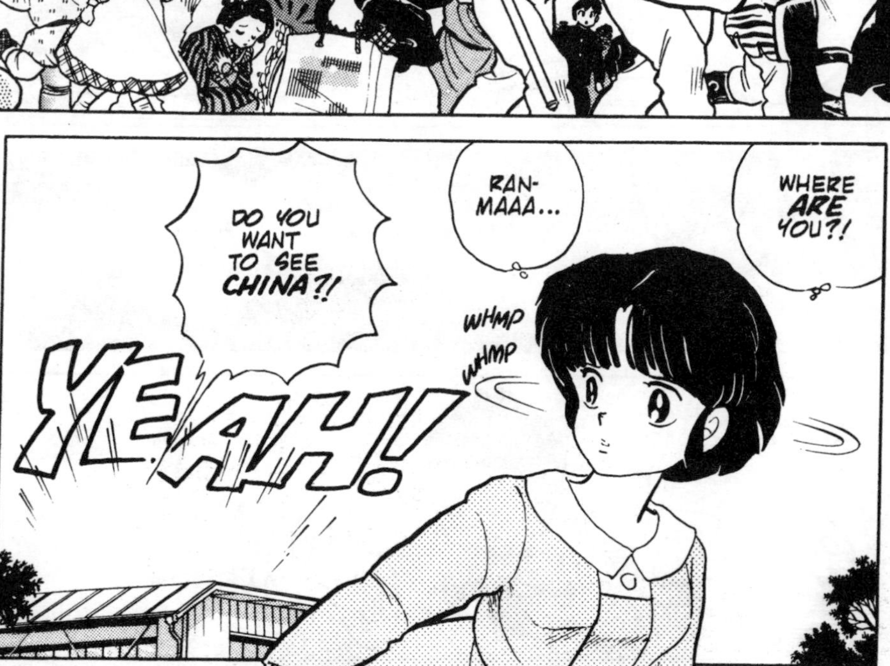
DO YOU WANT TO SEE CHINA?!
RAN-MAAA...
WHERE ARE YOU?!
WHMP
WHMP
YEAH!

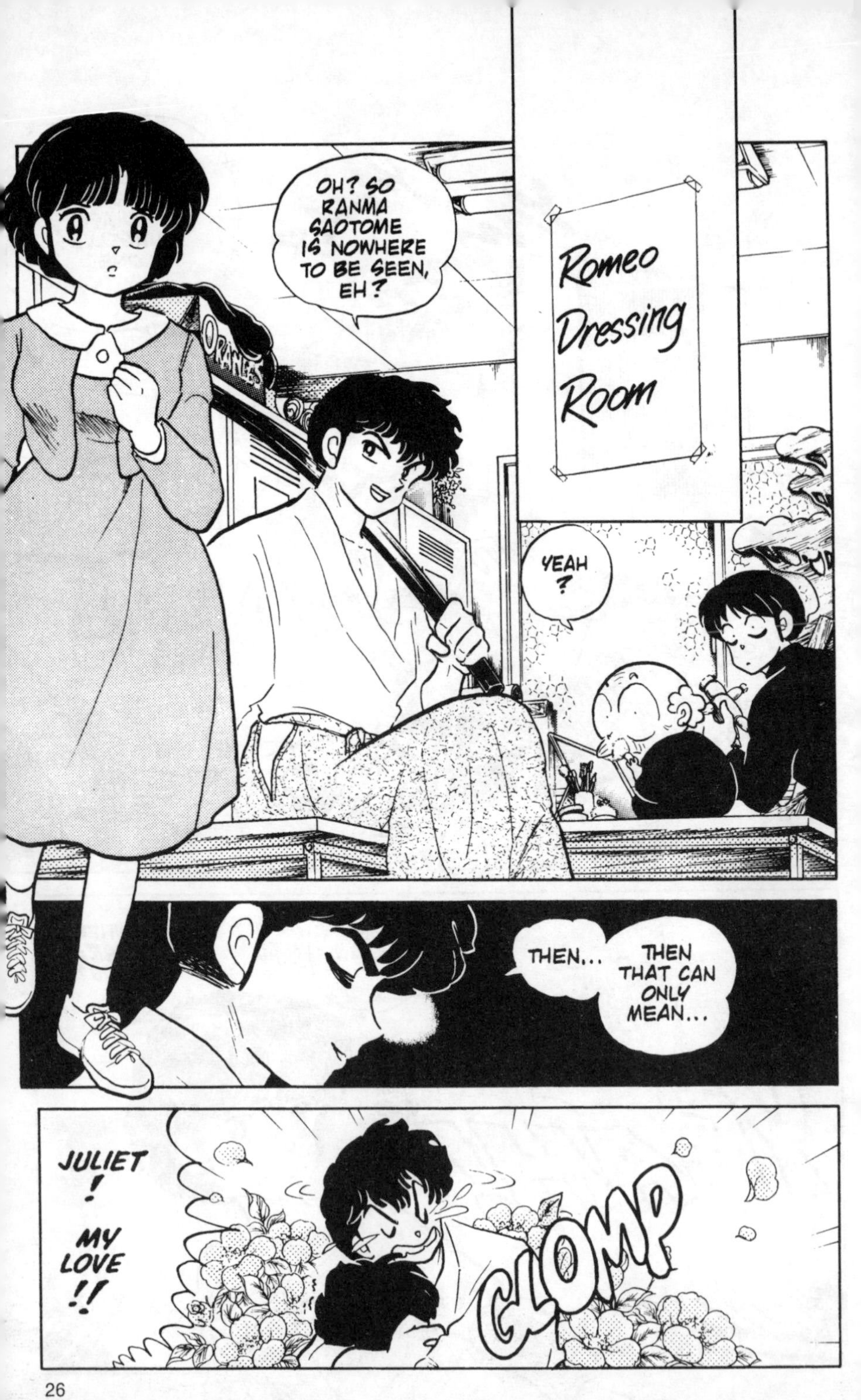
OH? SO RANMA SAOTOME IS NOWHERE TO BE SEEN, EH?
Romeo Dressing Room
YEAH?
THEN...
THEN THAT CAN ONLY MEAN...
JULIET! MY LOVE!!
CLOMP

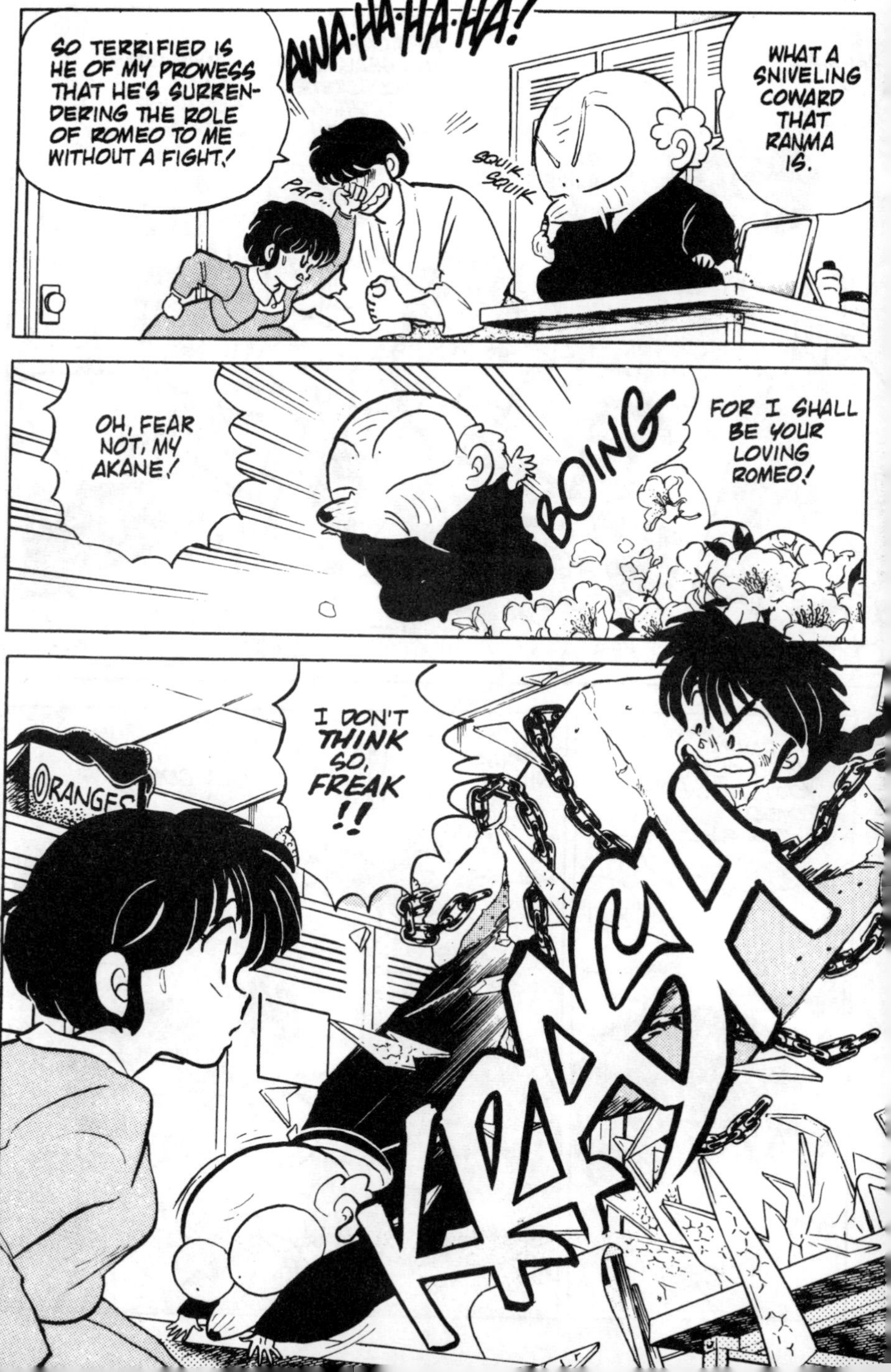
SO TERRIFIED IS HE OF MY PROWESS THAT HE'S SURRENDERING THE ROLE OF ROMEO TO ME WITHOUT A FIGHT!
AWA·HA·HA·HA!
PAP...
SQUIK SQUIK
WHAT A SNIVELING COWARD THAT RANMA IS.
OH, FEAR NOT, MY AKANE!
BOING
FOR I SHALL BE YOUR LOVING ROMEO!
ORANGES
I DON'T THINK SO, FREAK!!
KRASH

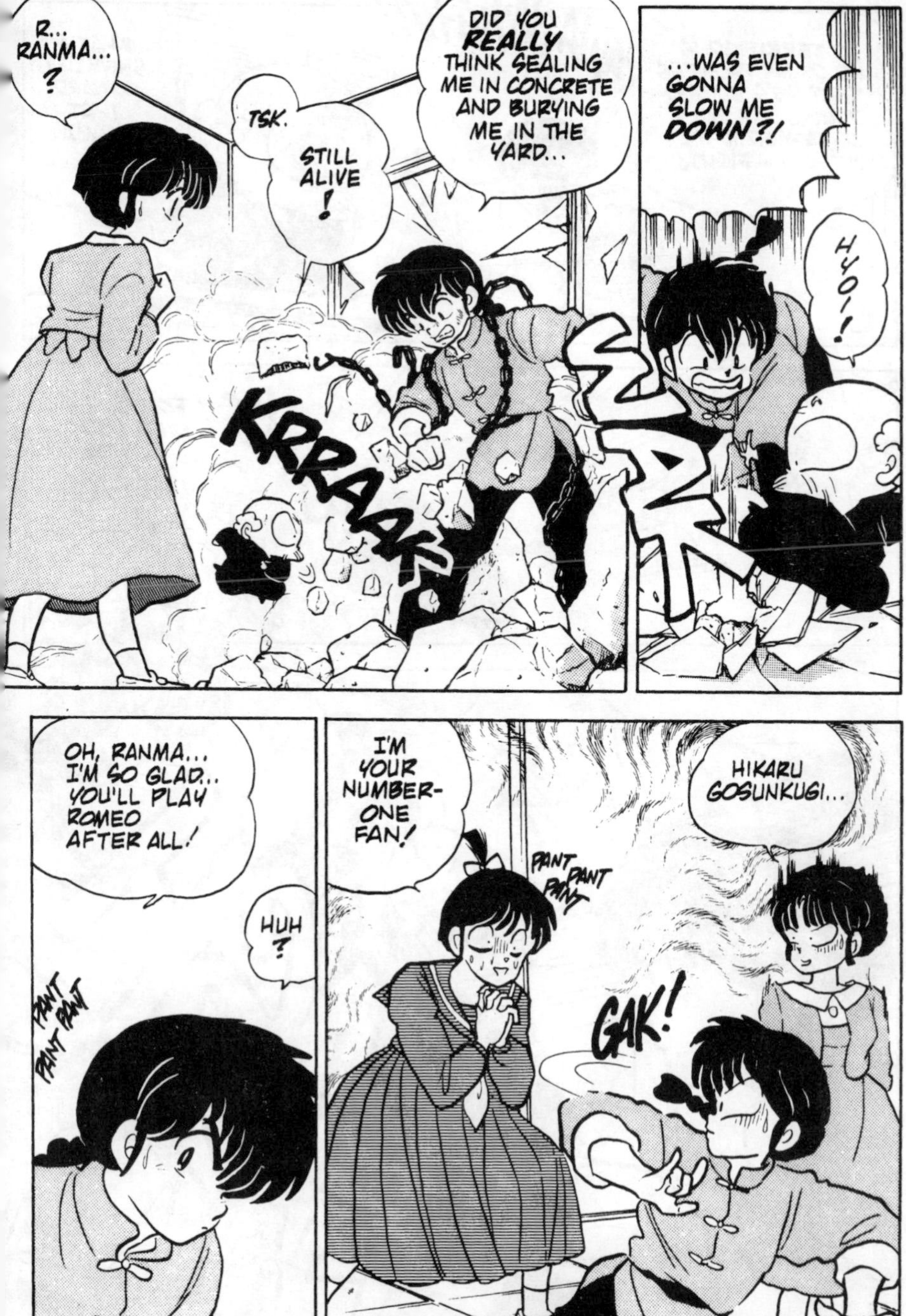
R... RANMA...?
TSK.
STILL ALIVE!
DID YOU REALLY THINK SEALING ME IN CONCRETE AND BURYING ME IN THE YARD...
KRRAAK!
...WAS EVEN GONNA SLOW ME DOWN?!
HYO!!
OH, RANMA... I'M SO GLAD... YOU'LL PLAY ROMEO AFTER ALL!
HUH?
PANT PANT PANT
I'M YOUR NUMBER-ONE FAN!
PANT PANT PANT
HIKARU GOSUNKUGI...
GAK!

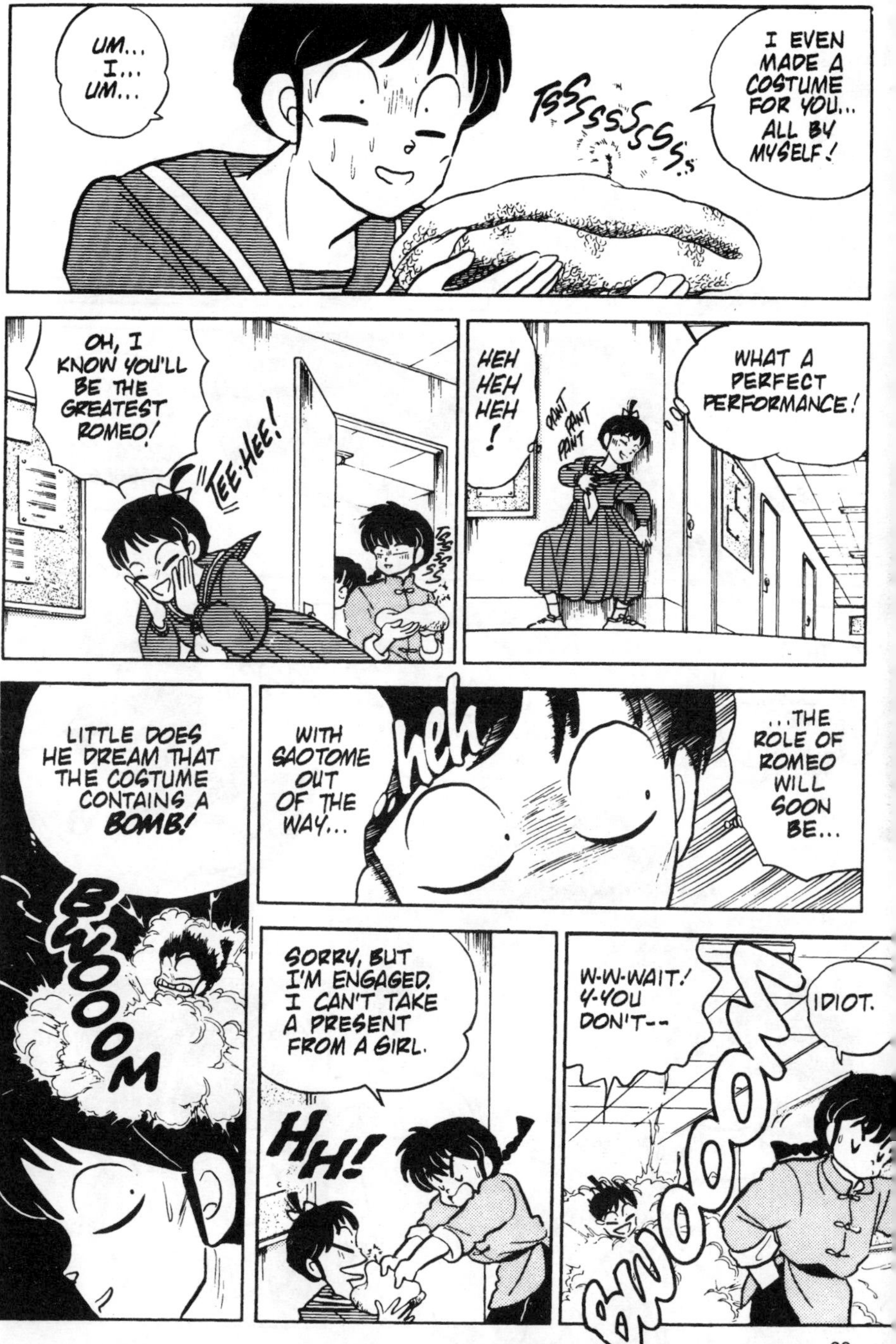
UM... I... UM...
TSSSSSSSSSS
I EVEN MADE A COSTUME FOR YOU... ALL BY MYSELF!
OH, I KNOW YOU'LL BE THE GREATEST ROMEO!
TEE-HEE!
HEH HEH HEH!
PANT PANT PANT
WHAT A PERFECT PERFORMANCE!
LITTLE DOES HE DREAM THAT THE COSTUME CONTAINS A BOMB!
WITH SAOTOME OUT OF THE WAY...
heh
...THE ROLE OF ROMEO WILL SOON BE...
BWOOOOM
SORRY, BUT I'M ENGAGED. I CAN'T TAKE A PRESENT FROM A GIRL.
HH!
W-W-WAIT! Y-YOU DON'T--
IDIOT.
BWOOOM

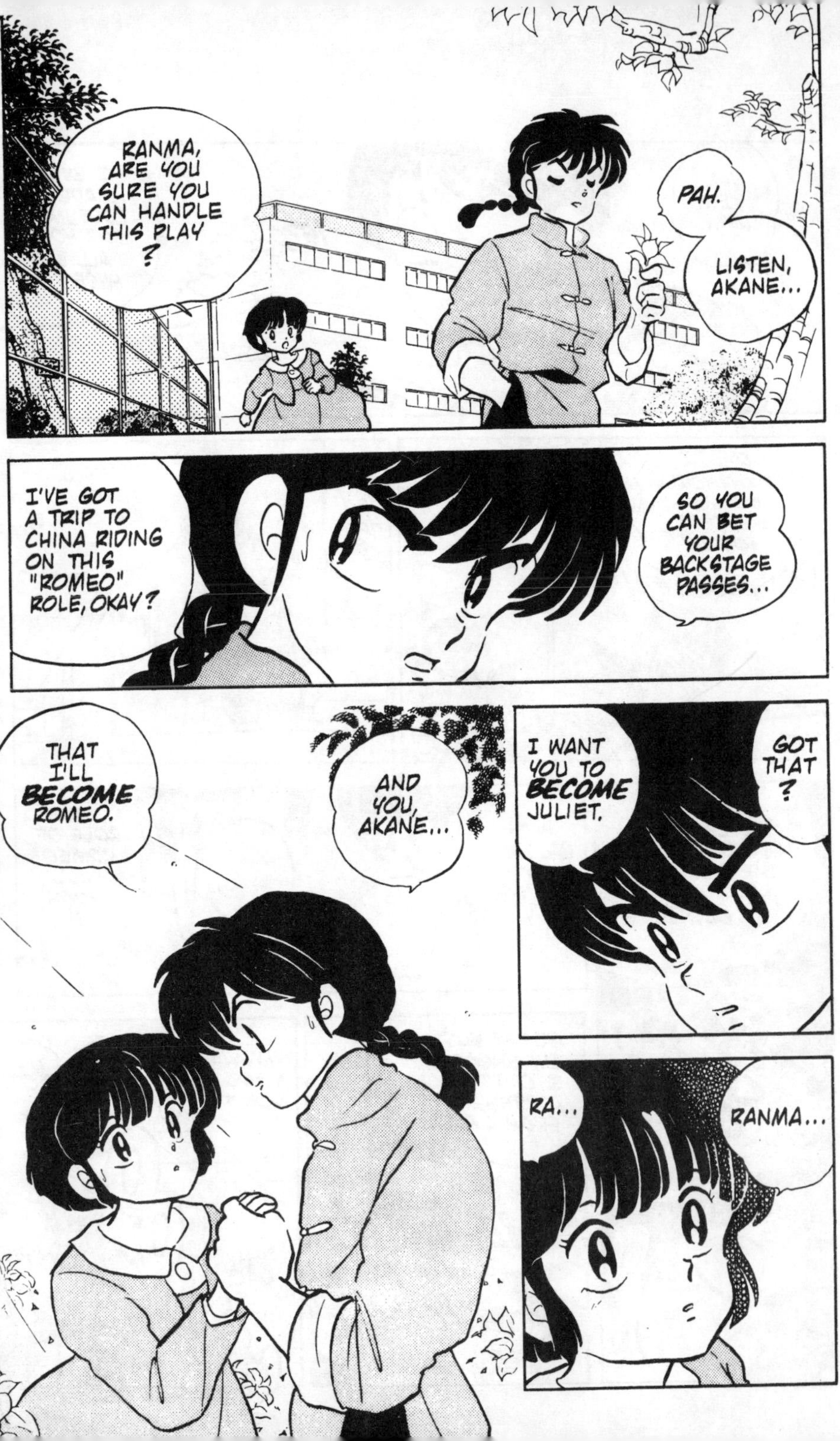
RANMA, ARE YOU SURE YOU CAN HANDLE THIS PLAY ?
PAH.
LISTEN, AKANE...
I'VE GOT A TRIP TO CHINA RIDING ON THIS "ROMEO" ROLE, OKAY?
SO YOU CAN BET YOUR BACKSTAGE PASSES...
THAT I'LL BECOME ROMEO.
AND YOU, AKANE...
I WANT YOU TO BECOME JULIET.
GOT THAT ?
RA...
RANMA...

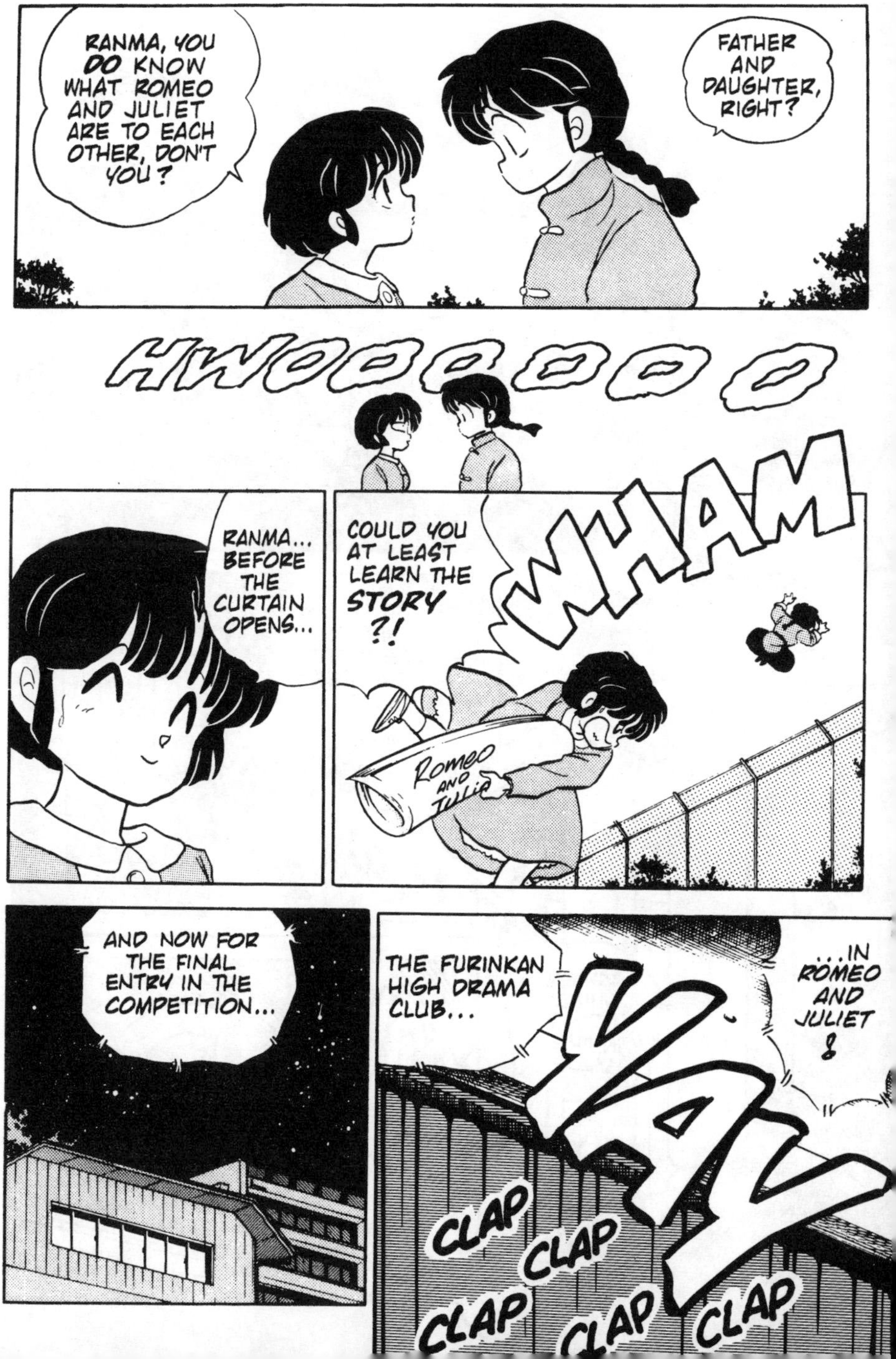
RANMA, YOU DO KNOW WHAT ROMEO AND JULIET ARE TO EACH OTHER, DON'T YOU?
FATHER AND DAUGHTER, RIGHT?
HWOOOOOOO
RANMA... BEFORE THE CURTAIN OPENS...
COULD YOU AT LEAST LEARN THE STORY ?!
WHAM
Romeo and Juliet
AND NOW FOR THE FINAL ENTRY IN THE COMPETITION...
THE FURINKAN HIGH DRAMA CLUB...
...IN ROMEO AND JULIET
YAY
CLAP CLAP CLAP CLAP CLAP

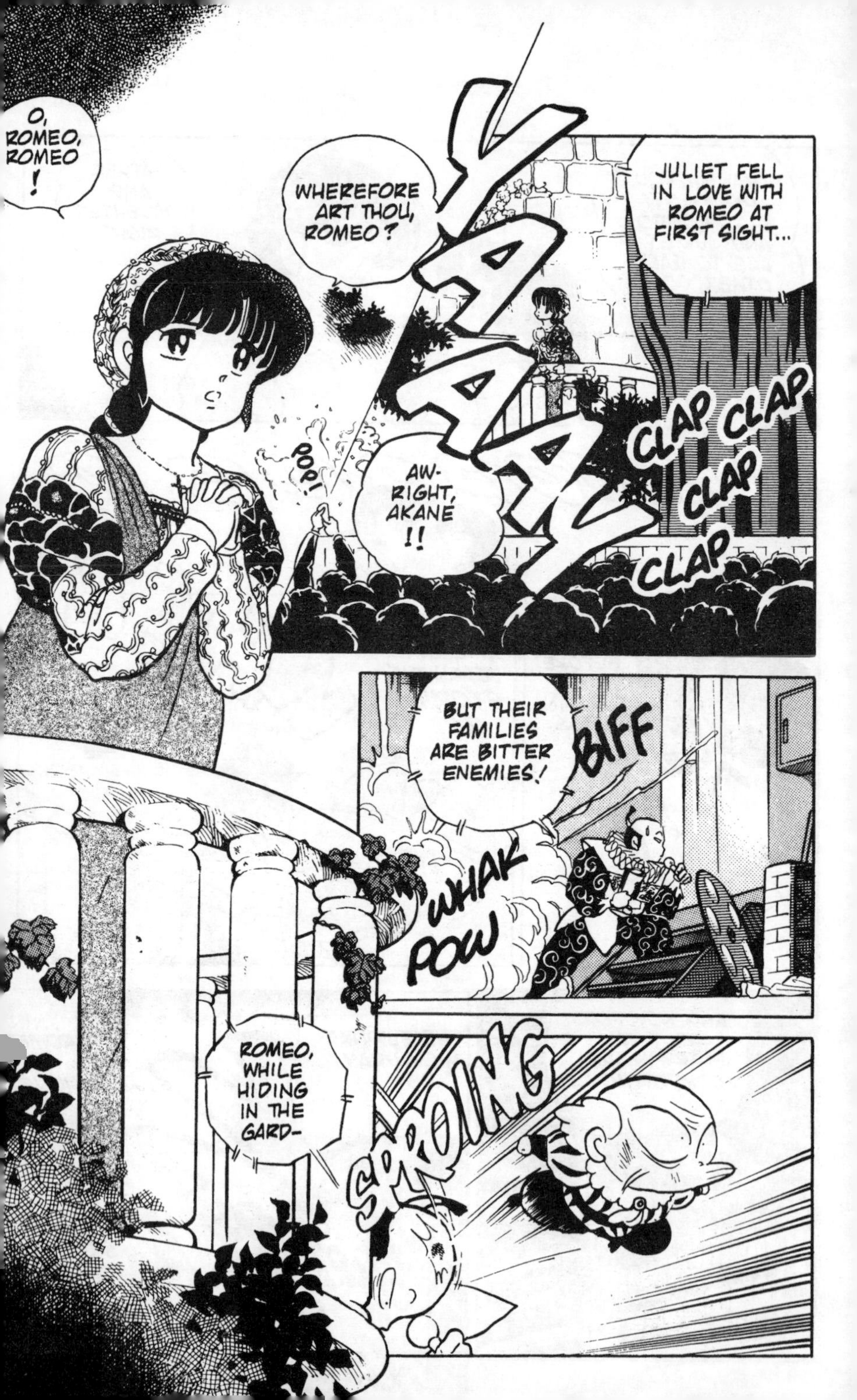
O, ROMEO, ROMEO!
WHEREFORE ART THOU, ROMEO?
YAAAY
JULIET FELL IN LOVE WITH ROMEO AT FIRST SIGHT...
POP!
AW-RIGHT, AKANE!!
CLAP CLAP CLAP CLAP CLAP
BUT THEIR FAMILIES ARE BITTER ENEMIES!
BIFF
WHAK
POW
ROMEO, WHILE HIDING IN THE GARD-
SPROING

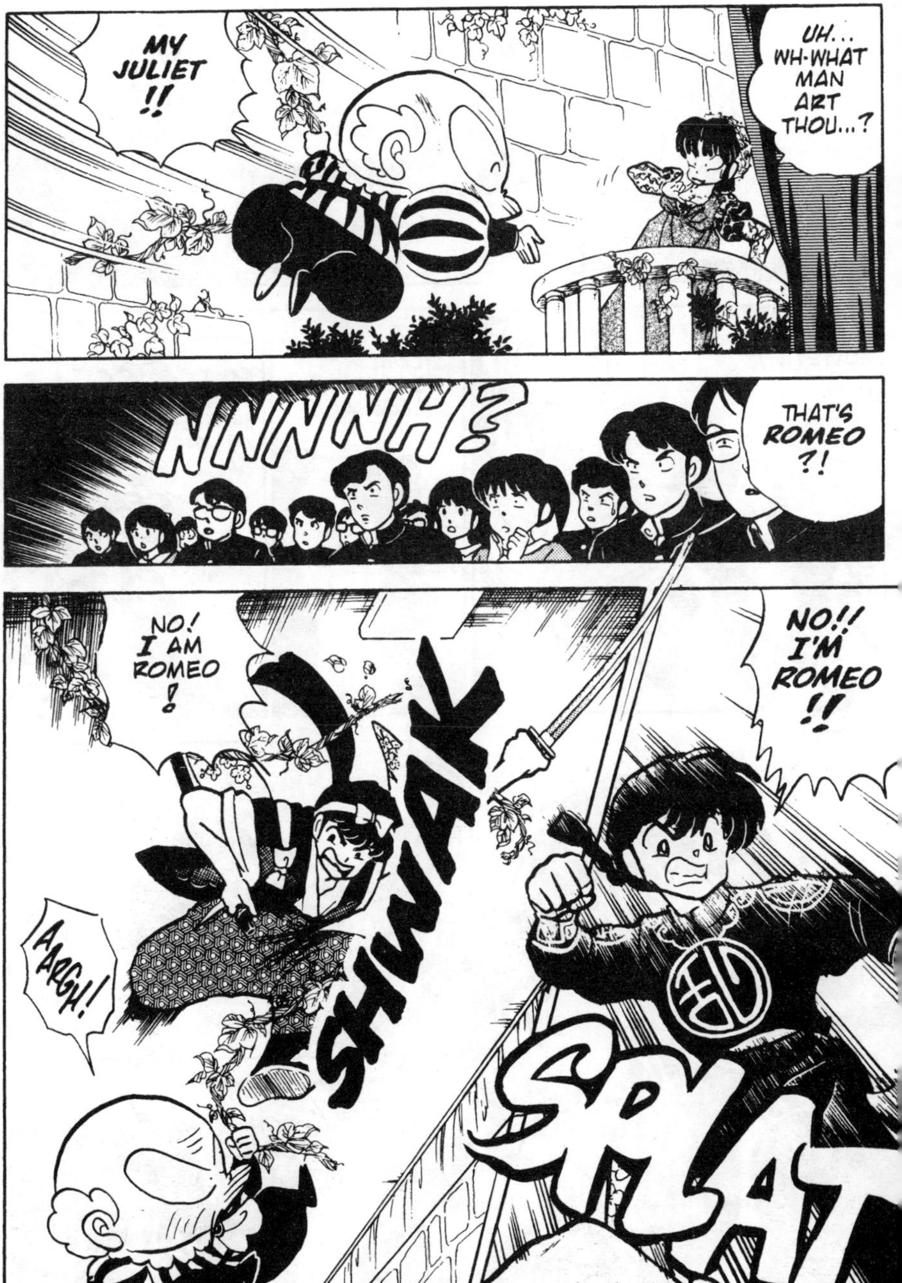
MY JULIET !!
UH... WH-WHAT MAN ART THOU...?
NNNNH?
THAT'S ROMEO ?!
NO! I AM ROMEO !
SHWAK
NO!! I'M ROMEO !!
AARGH!
SPLAT

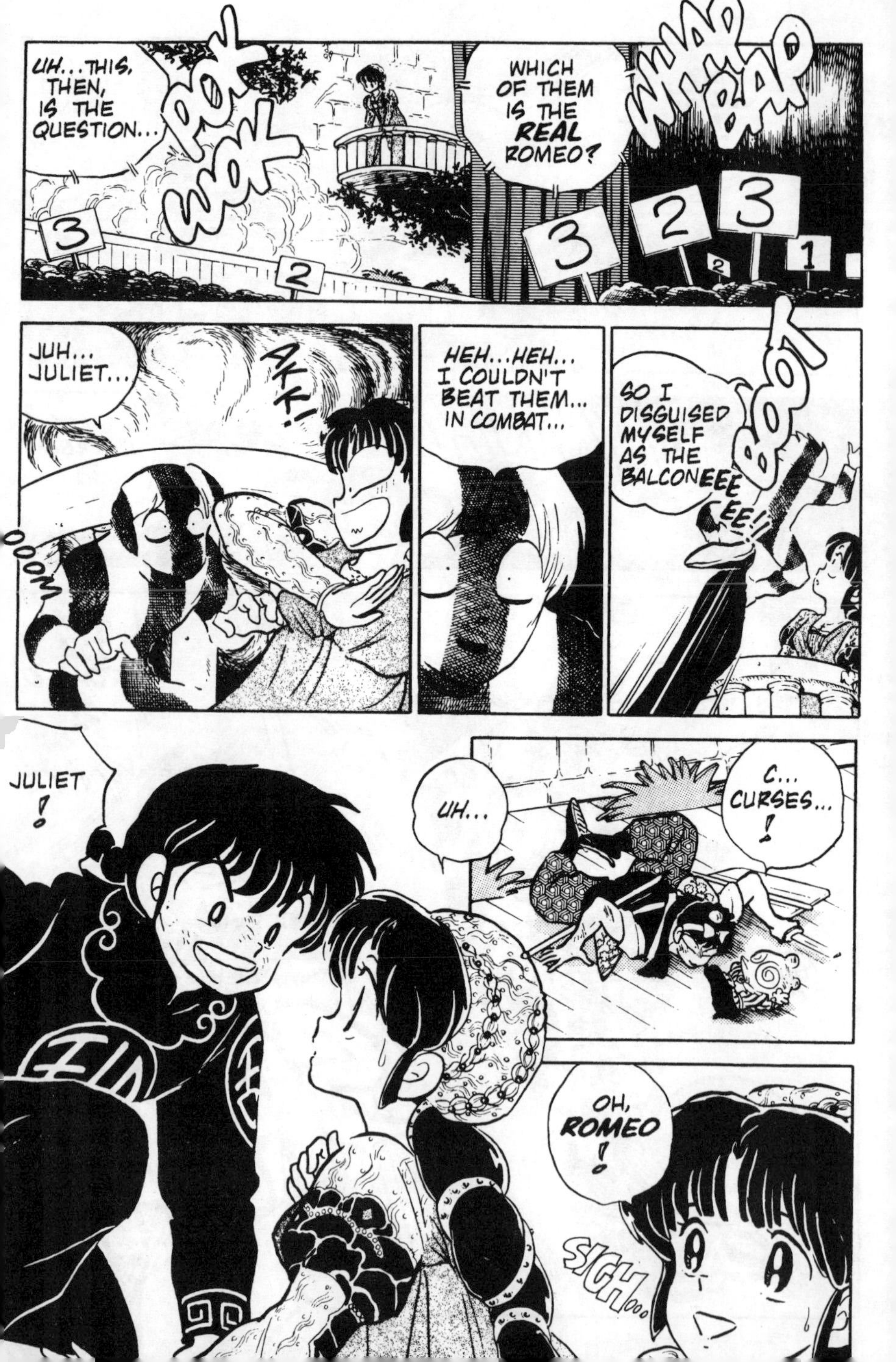

UH...THIS, THEN, IS THE QUESTION...
POK
WOK
3
2
WHICH OF THEM IS THE **REAL** ROMEO?
WHAP
BAP
3
2
3
2
1
JUH... JULIET...
AKK!
WOOO
HEH...HEH... I COULDN'T BEAT THEM... IN COMBAT...
SO I DISGUISED MYSELF AS THE BALCONEEE EEE!
BOOT
JULIET!
UH...
C... CURSES...!
OH, **ROMEO**!
SIGH...

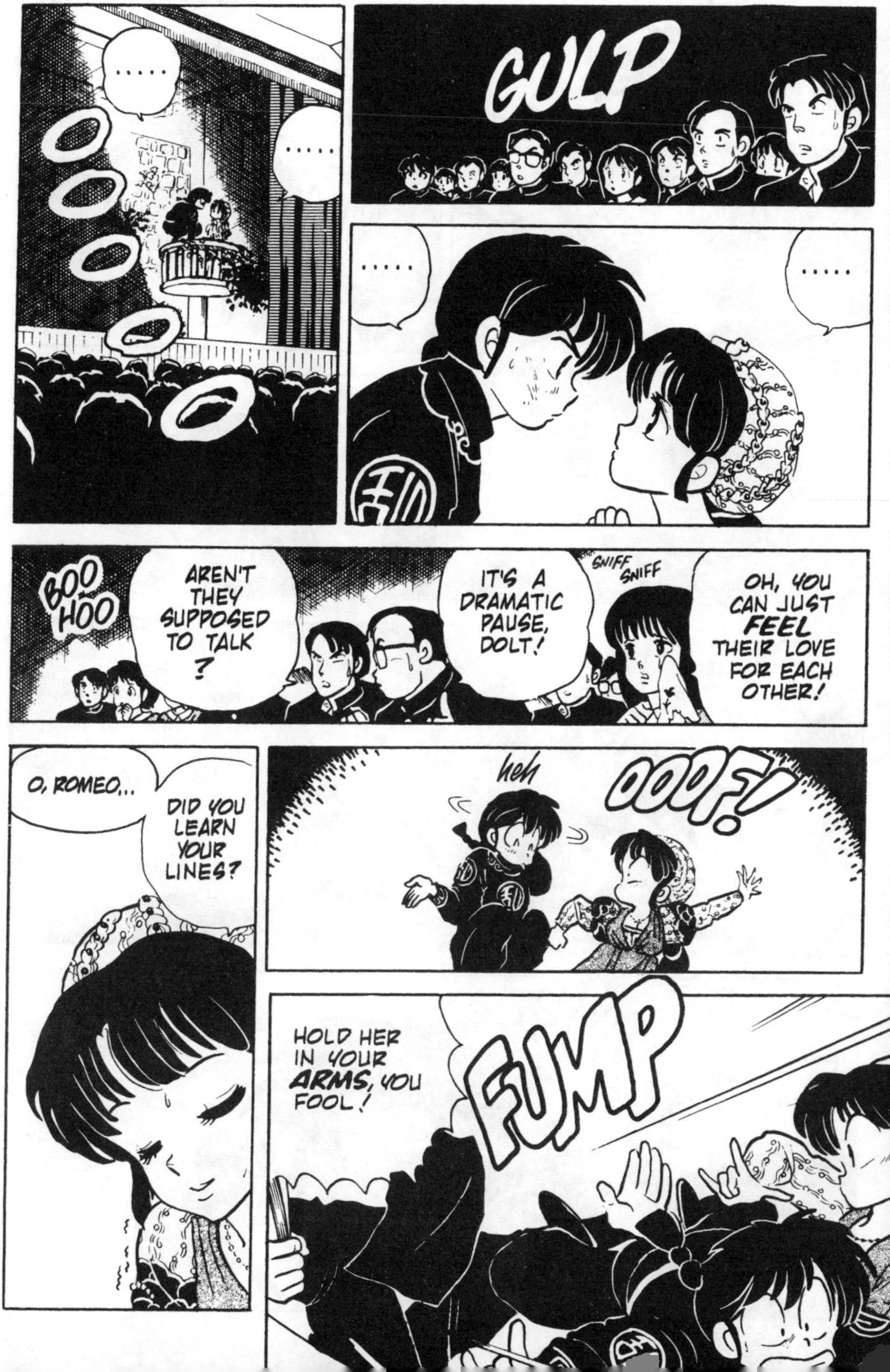
......
......
GULP
......
......
BOO HOO
AREN'T THEY SUPPOSED TO TALK ?
IT'S A DRAMATIC PAUSE, DOLT!
SNIFF SNIFF
OH, YOU CAN JUST FEEL THEIR LOVE FOR EACH OTHER!
O, ROMEO...
DID YOU LEARN YOUR LINES?
heh
OOOF!
HOLD HER IN YOUR ARMS, YOU FOOL!
FUMP

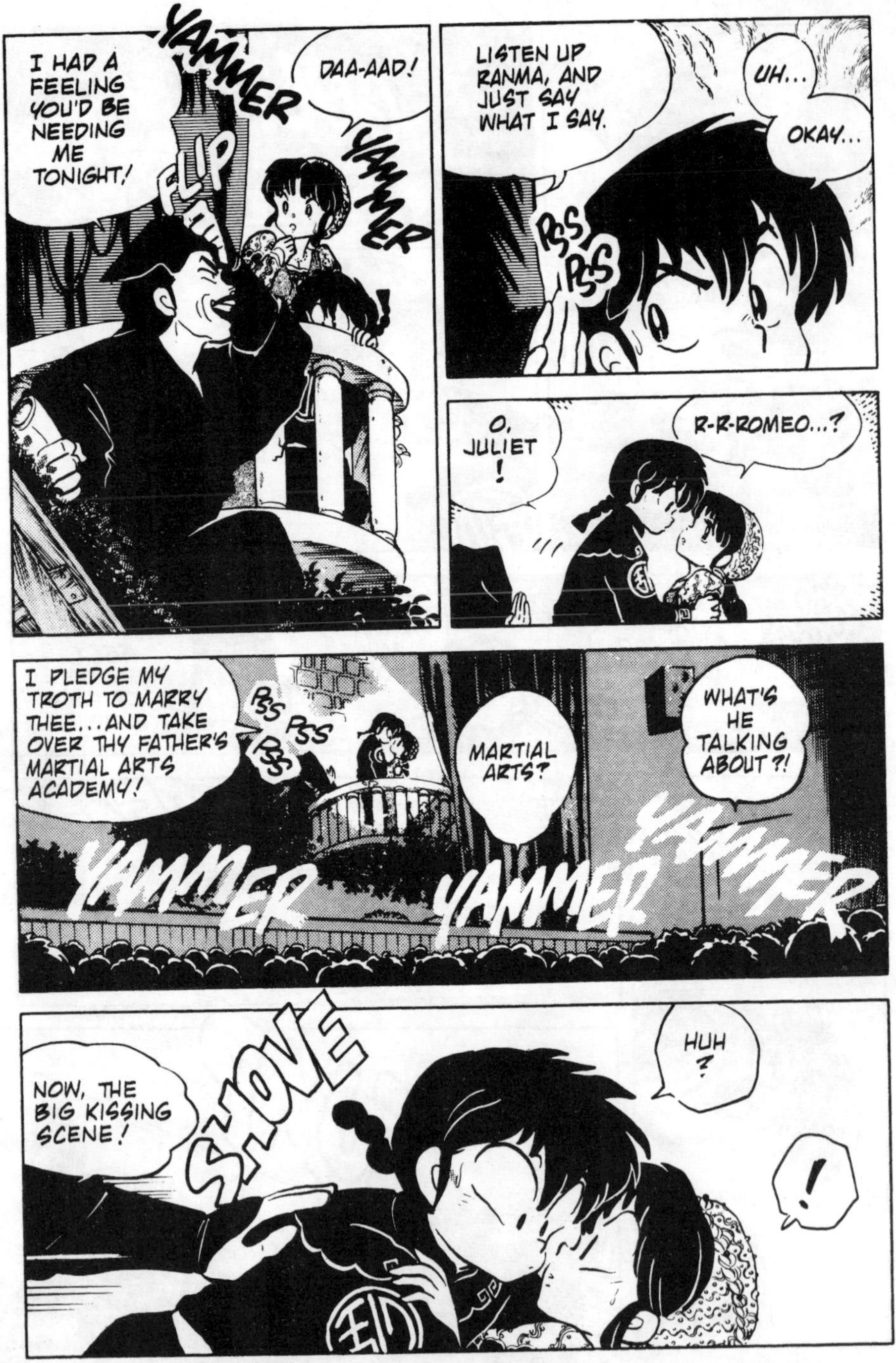
I HAD A FEELING YOU'D BE NEEDING ME TONIGHT!
YAMMER
FLIP
DAA-AAD!
YAMMER
LISTEN UP RANMA, AND JUST SAY WHAT I SAY.
PSS PSS
UH...
OKAY...
O, JULIET!
R-R-ROMEO...?
I PLEDGE MY TROTH TO MARRY THEE...AND TAKE OVER THY FATHER'S MARTIAL ARTS ACADEMY!
PSS PSS PSS
MARTIAL ARTS?
WHAT'S HE TALKING ABOUT?!
YAMMER
YAMMER
YAMMER
NOW, THE BIG KISSING SCENE!
SHOVE
HUH?
!

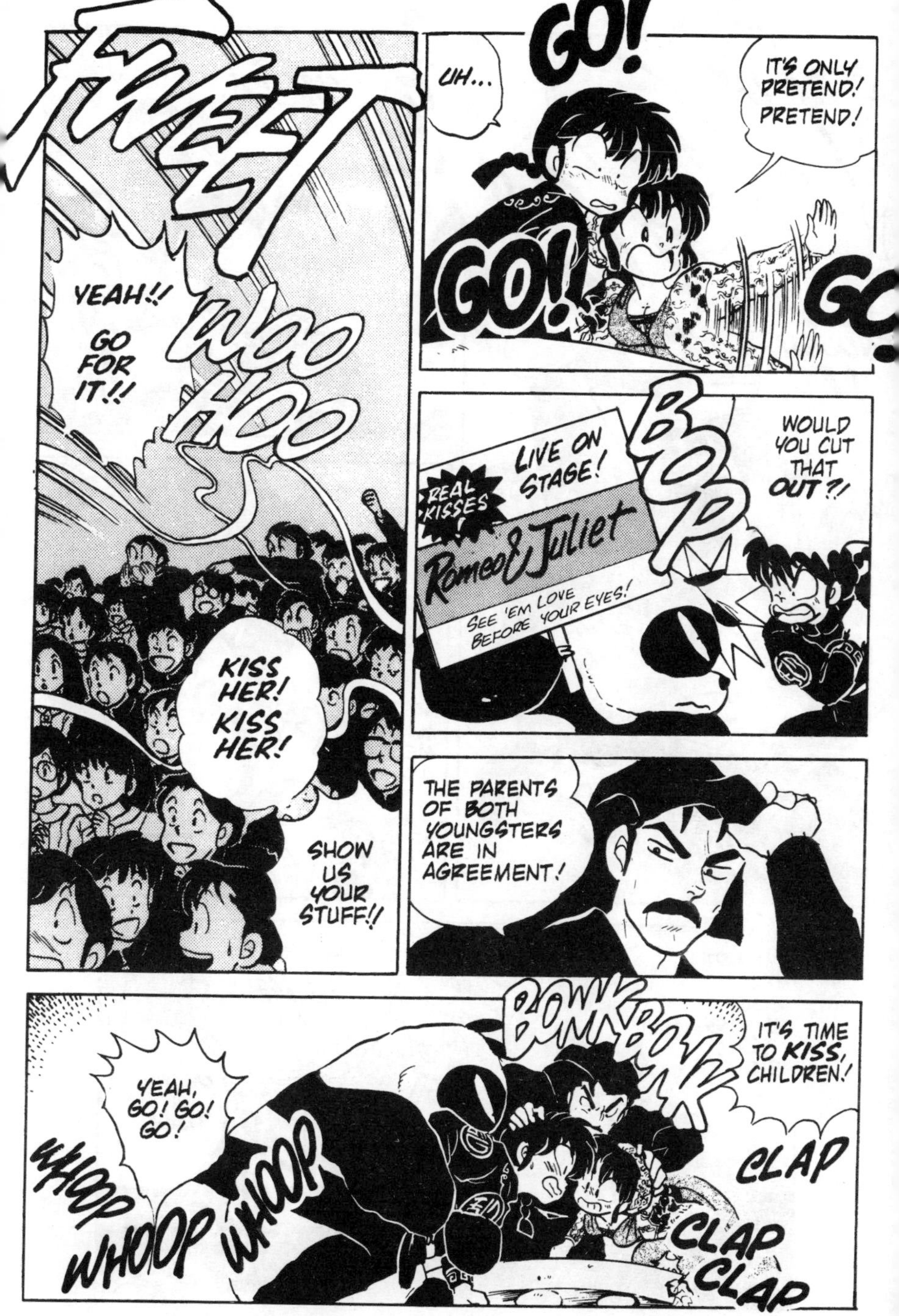
FWEET
YEAH!!
GO FOR IT!!
WOO HOO
KISS HER! KISS HER!
SHOW US YOUR STUFF!!
UH...
GO!
IT'S ONLY PRETEND! PRETEND!
GO!
GO
REAL KISSES!
LIVE ON STAGE!
Romeo & Juliet
SEE 'EM LOVE BEFORE YOUR EYES!
BOOP
WOULD YOU CUT THAT OUT?!
THE PARENTS OF BOTH YOUNGSTERS ARE IN AGREEMENT!
YEAH, GO! GO! GO!
WHOOP
WHOOP
WHOOP
BONK BONK
IT'S TIME TO KISS, CHILDREN!
CLAP
CLAP
CLAP

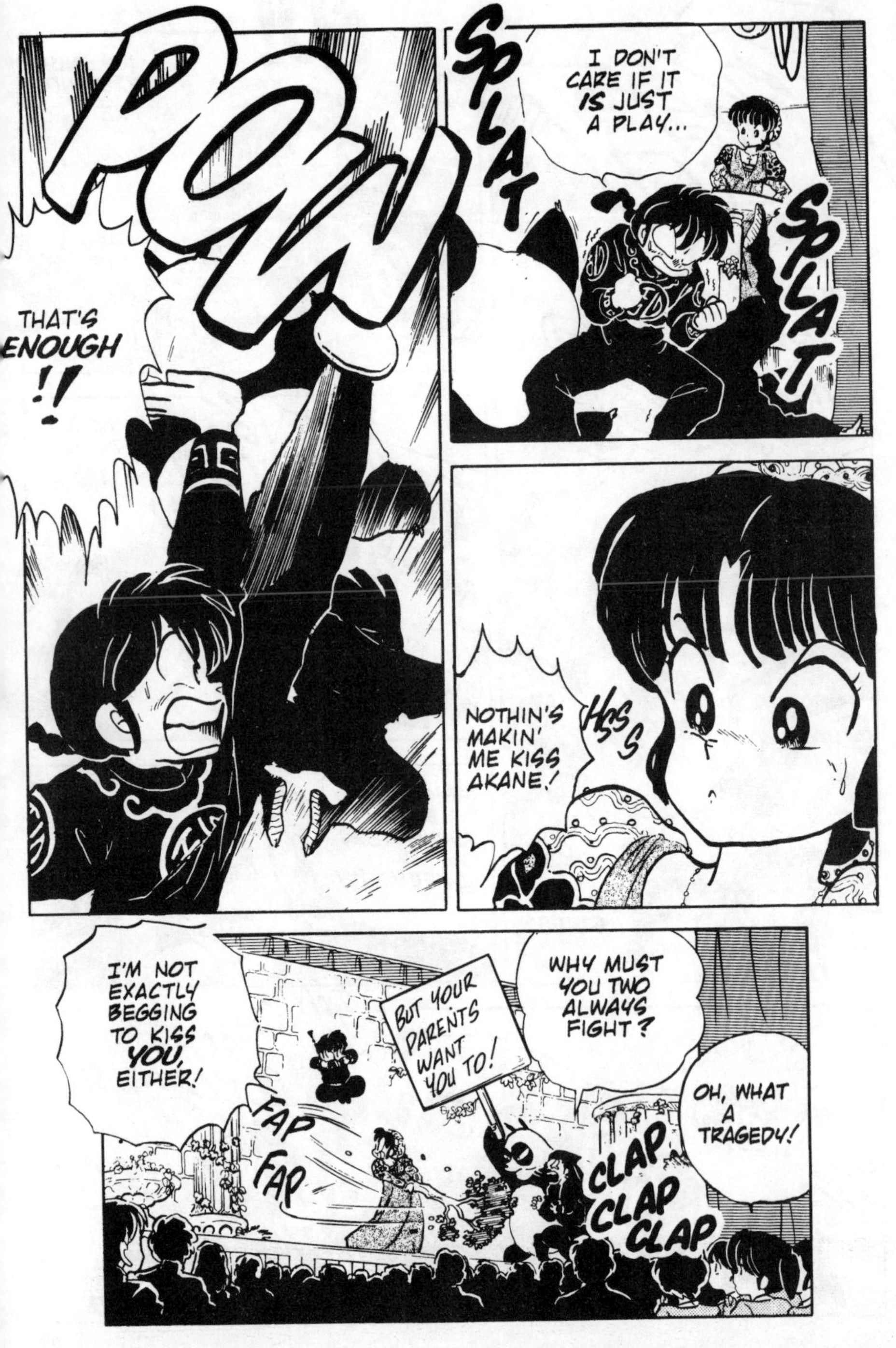
POW
THAT'S ENOUGH!!
SPLAT
I DON'T CARE IF IT IS JUST A PLAY...
SPLAT
NOTHIN'S MAKIN' ME KISS AKANE!
HSSS
I'M NOT EXACTLY BEGGING TO KISS YOU, EITHER!
BUT YOUR PARENTS WANT YOU TO!
FAP
FAP
WHY MUST YOU TWO ALWAYS FIGHT?
OH, WHAT A TRAGEDY!
CLAP
CLAP
CLAP

# PART THREE

# NOT YOUR TYPICAL JULIET

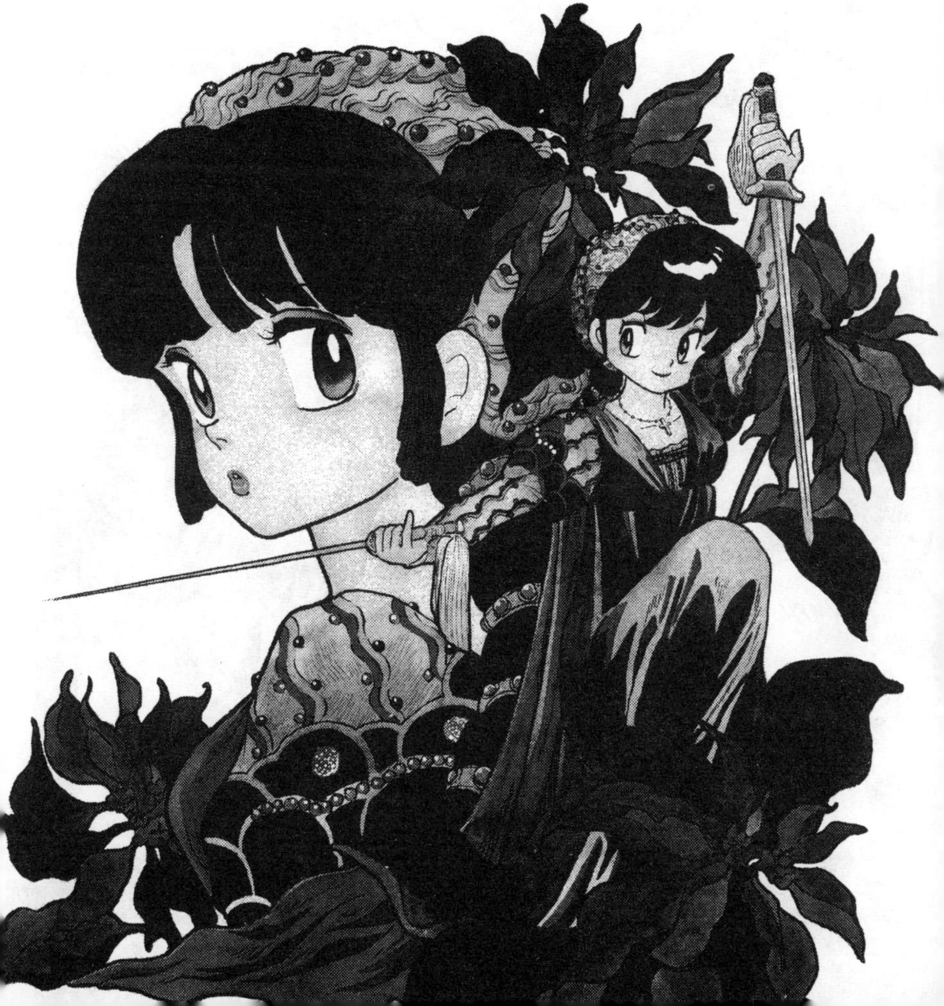

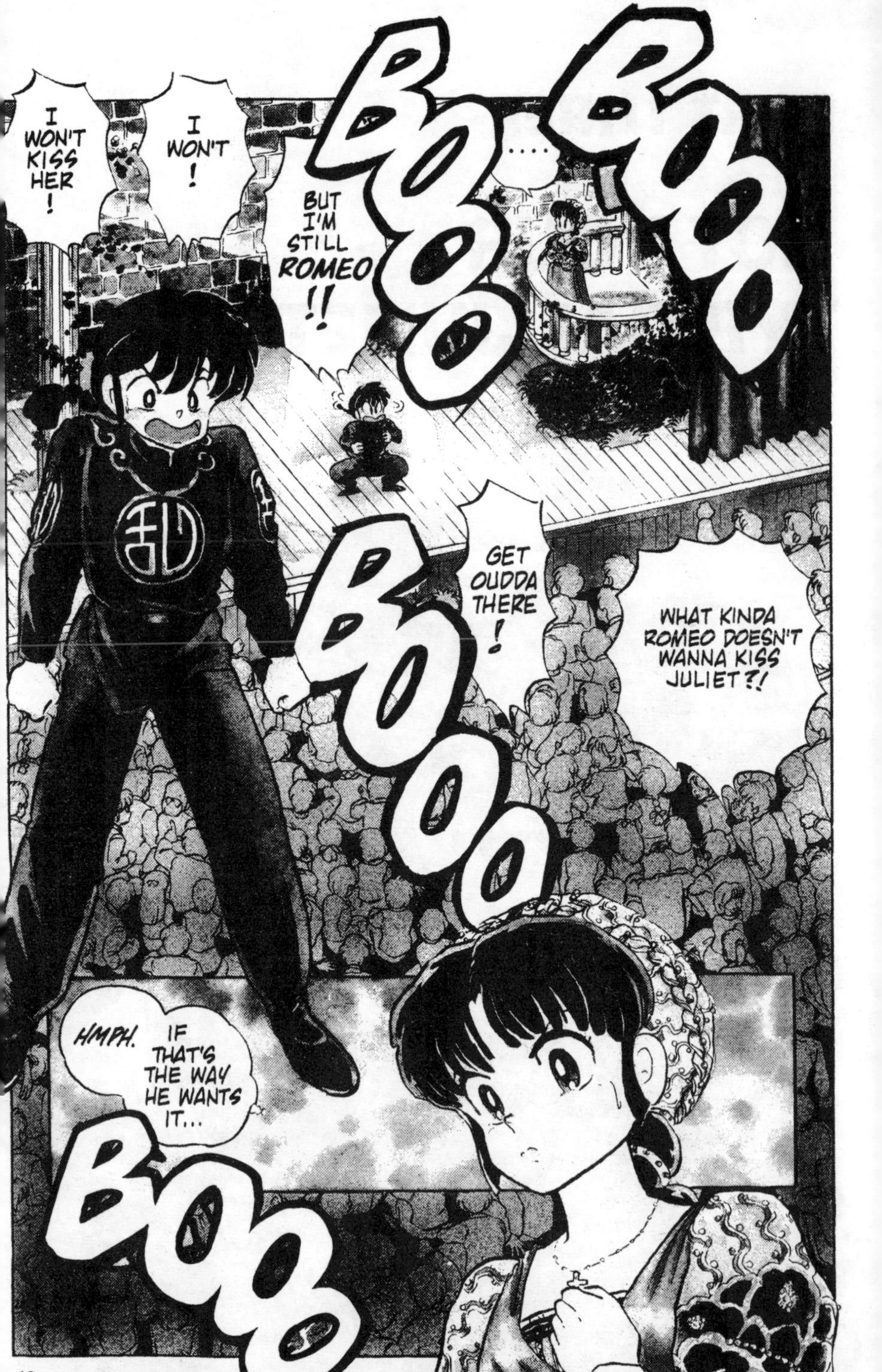
I WON'T KISS HER!
I WON'T!
BOOOO
....
BOOOO
BUT I'M STILL ROMEO!!
GET OUDDA THERE!
BOOOOO
WHAT KINDA ROMEO DOESN'T WANNA KISS JULIET?!
HMPH.
IF THAT'S THE WAY HE WANTS IT...
BOOO

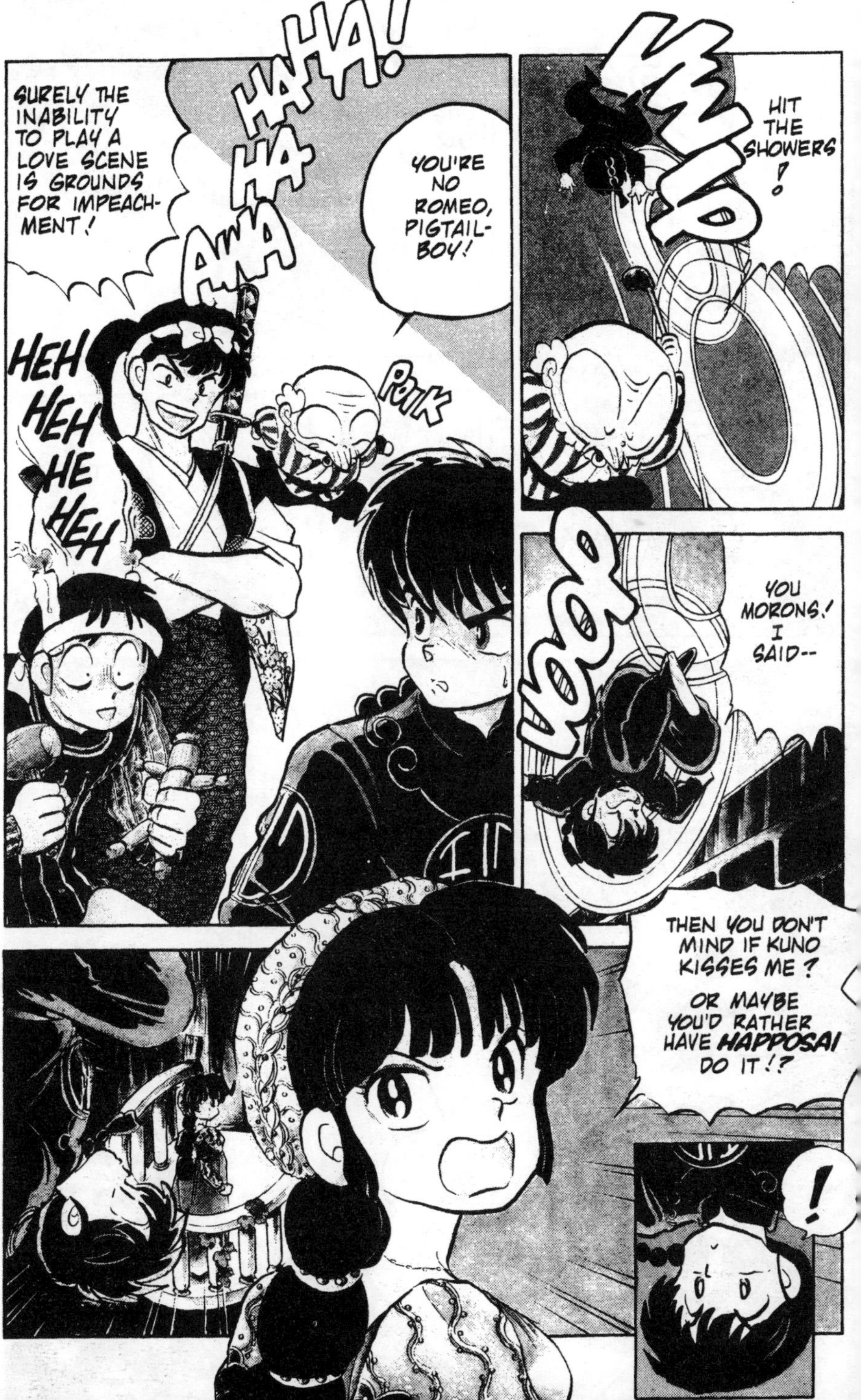

SURELY THE INABILITY TO PLAY A LOVE SCENE IS GROUNDS FOR IMPEACH-MENT!
AHA HA HAHA!
YOU'RE NO ROMEO, PIGTAIL-BOY!
HEH HEH HE HEH
POIK
WHIP
HIT THE SHOWERS!
VOOP
YOU MORONS! I SAID--
THEN YOU DON'T MIND IF KUNO KISSES ME?
OR MAYBE YOU'D RATHER HAVE **HAPPOSAI** DO IT!?
!

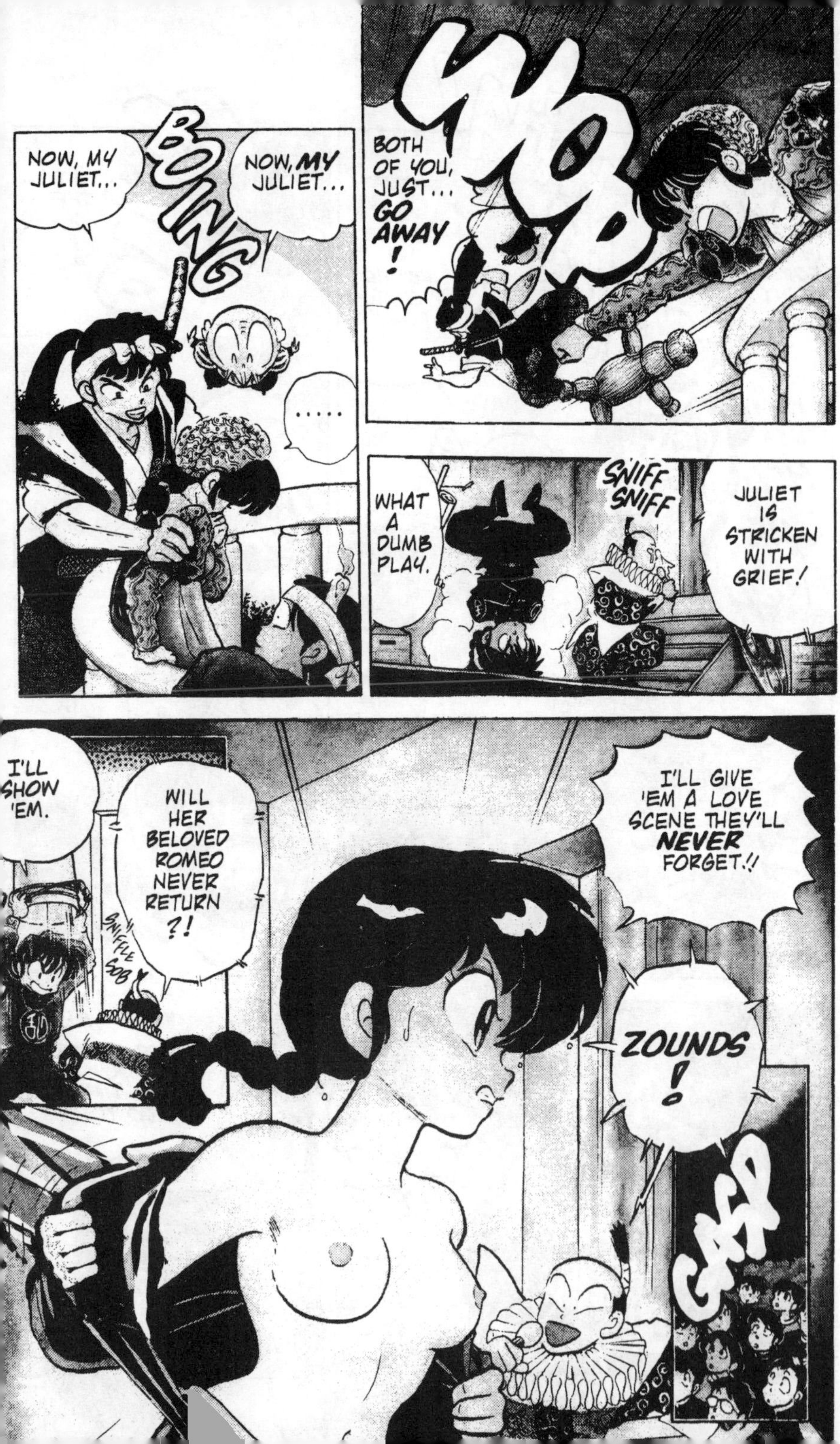

NOW, MY JULIET...
BOING
NOW, **MY** JULIET...
......
WOP
BOTH OF YOU, JUST... **GO AWAY!**
WHAT A DUMB PLAY.
SNIFF SNIFF
JULIET IS STRICKEN WITH GRIEF!
I'LL SHOW 'EM.
WILL HER BELOVED ROMEO NEVER RETURN?!
SNIFFLE SOB
I'LL GIVE 'EM A LOVE SCENE THEY'LL **NEVER** FORGET!!
**ZOUNDS!**
GASP

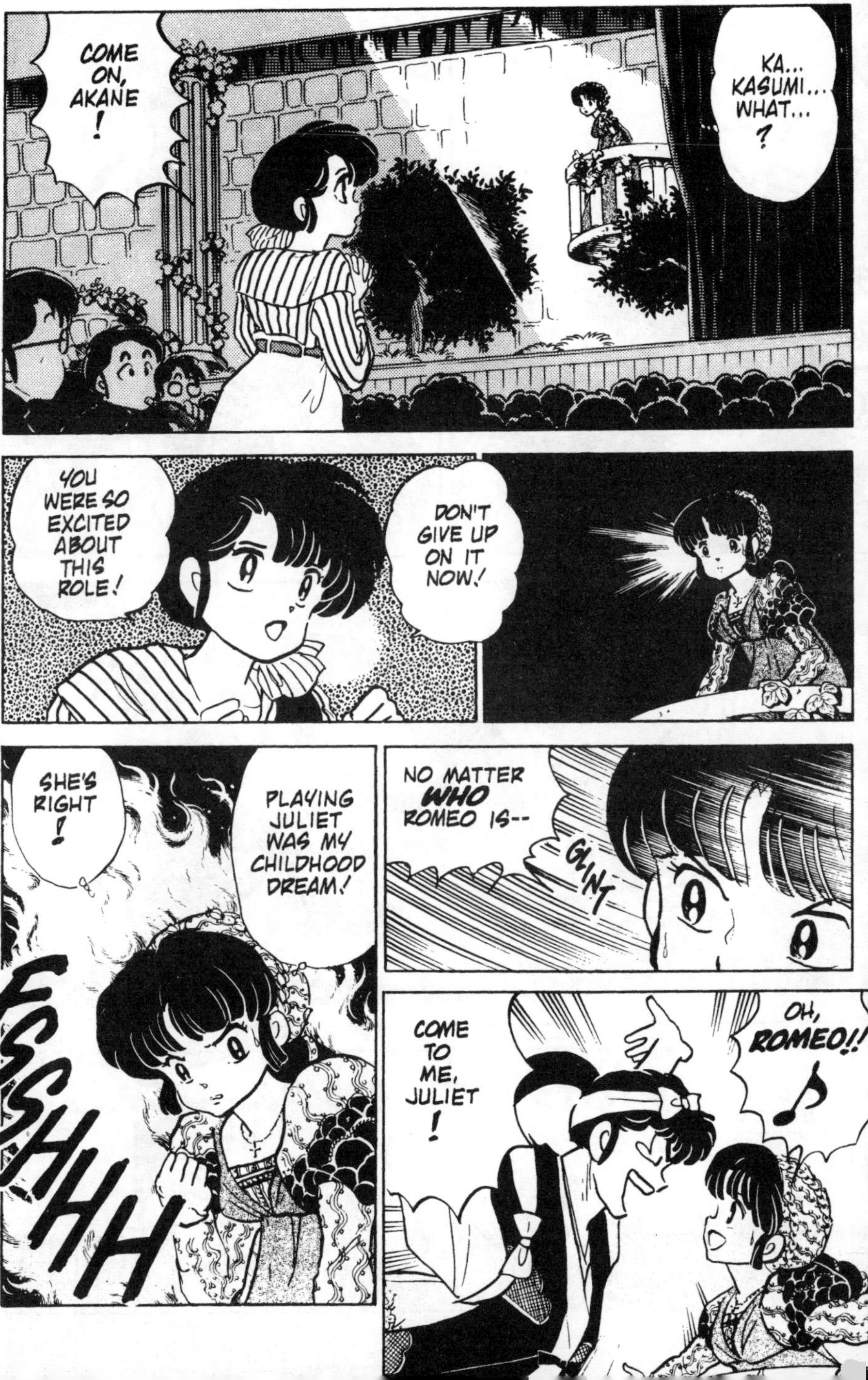
COME ON, AKANE!
KA... KASUMI... WHAT...?
YOU WERE SO EXCITED ABOUT THIS ROLE!
DON'T GIVE UP ON IT NOW!
SHE'S RIGHT!
PLAYING JULIET WAS MY CHILDHOOD DREAM!
FSSHHH
NO MATTER WHO ROMEO IS--
GLINT
COME TO ME, JULIET!
OH, ROMEO!!

NO! I JUST CAN'T **DO** IT!

SHIFF

OHHH!!

TIME FOR THE WEDDING SCENE, THE WEDDING SCENE!

MMPH!

MMPH!

TOIK.

GASP GASP GASP

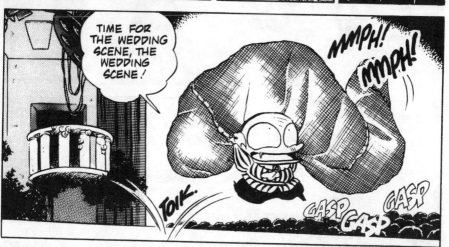

POOR JULIET IS CAPTURED BY AN EVIL BEAST INTENT ON--

DING-DONG DING-DONG

TOK

WHO ARE YOU CALLING A **BEAST**?!

44

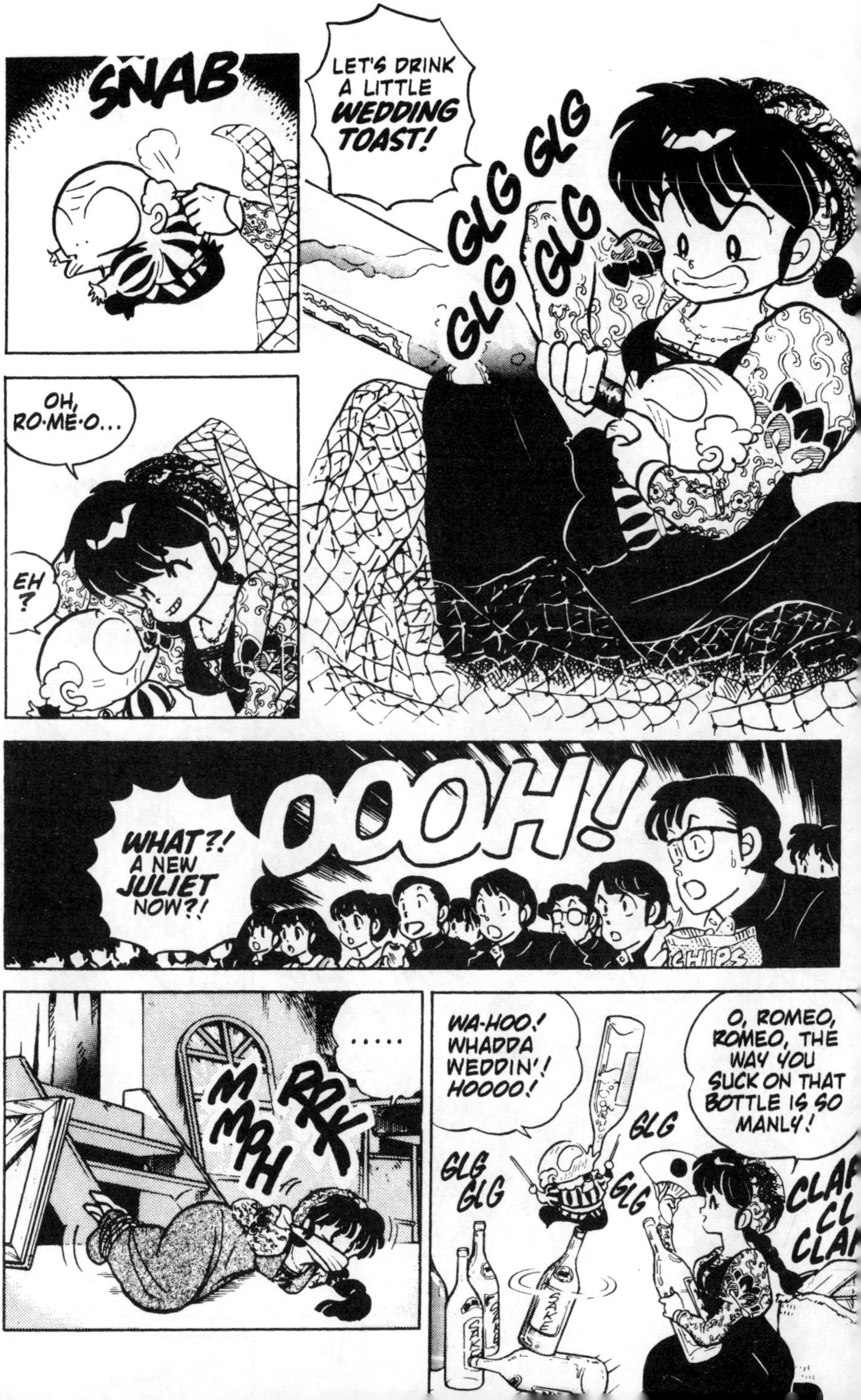
SNAB
LET'S DRINK A LITTLE WEDDING TOAST!
GLG GLG GLG GLG
OH, RO·ME·O...
EH ?
WHAT?! A NEW JULIET NOW?!
OOOH!
CHIPS
.....
MMPH
RRRK
WA-HOO! WHADDA WEDDIN'! HOOOO!
GLG GLG
GLG
GLG
O, ROMEO, ROMEO, THE WAY YOU SUCK ON THAT BOTTLE IS SO MANLY!
SAKE
SAKE

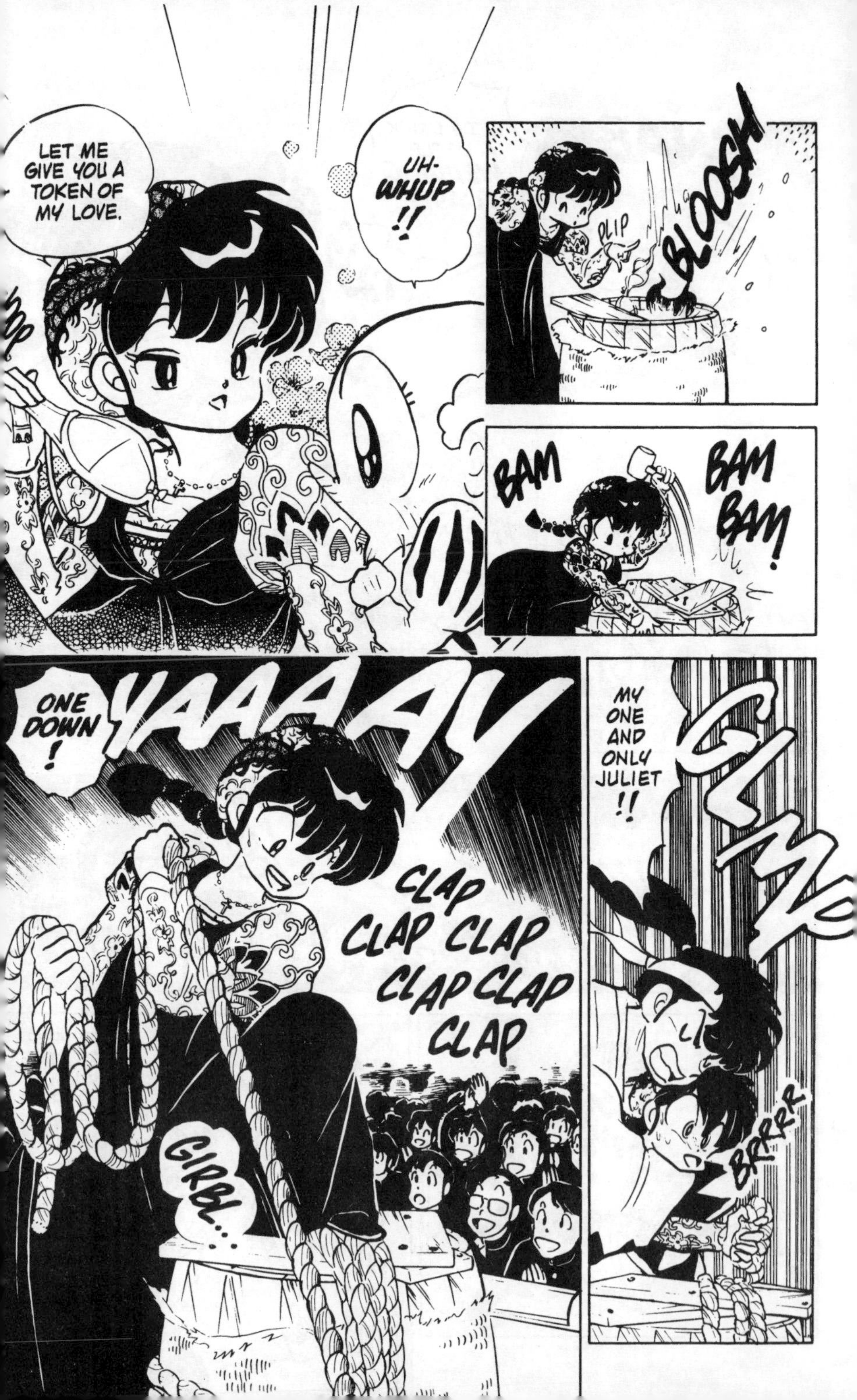
LET ME GIVE YOU A TOKEN OF MY LOVE.
UH-WHUP!!
PLIP
BLOOSH
BAM
BAM BAM!
ONE DOWN!
YAAAAY
CLAP CLAP CLAP CLAP CLAP CLAP
GIRBL...
MY ONE AND ONLY JULIET!!
GLMP
BRRRR

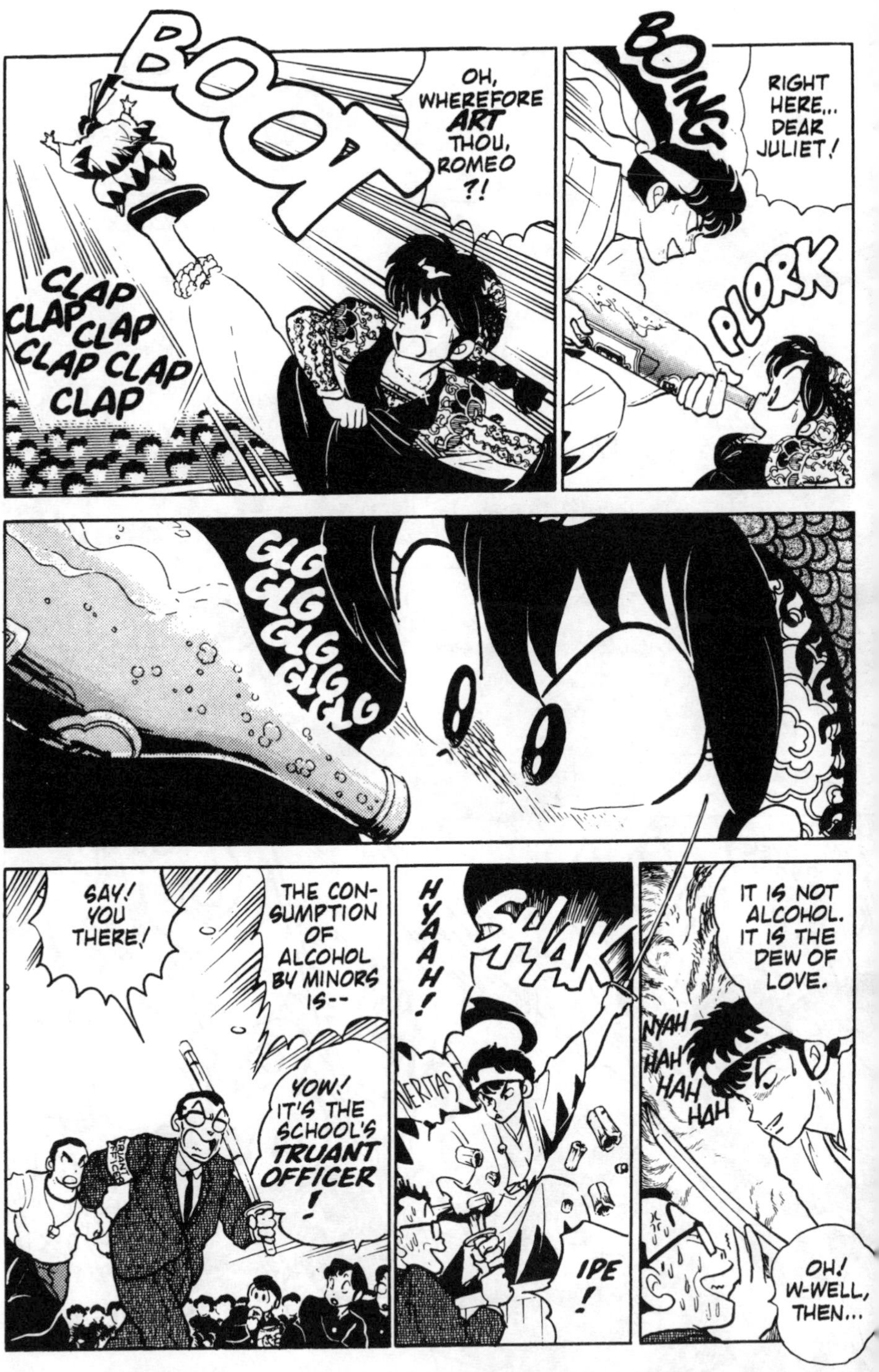
BOOT
OH, WHEREFORE ART THOU, ROMEO ?!
CLAP CLAP CLAP CLAP CLAP CLAP
BOING
RIGHT HERE... DEAR JULIET!
PLORK
GLG GLG GLG GLG GLG
SAY! YOU THERE!
THE CON-SUMPTION OF ALCOHOL BY MINORS IS--
YOW! IT'S THE SCHOOL'S TRUANT OFFICER!
TRUANT OFFICER
HYAAAH!
SHAK
VERITAS
IPE!
IT IS NOT ALCOHOL. IT IS THE DEW OF LOVE.
NYAH HAH HAH HAH
OH! W-WELL, THEN...

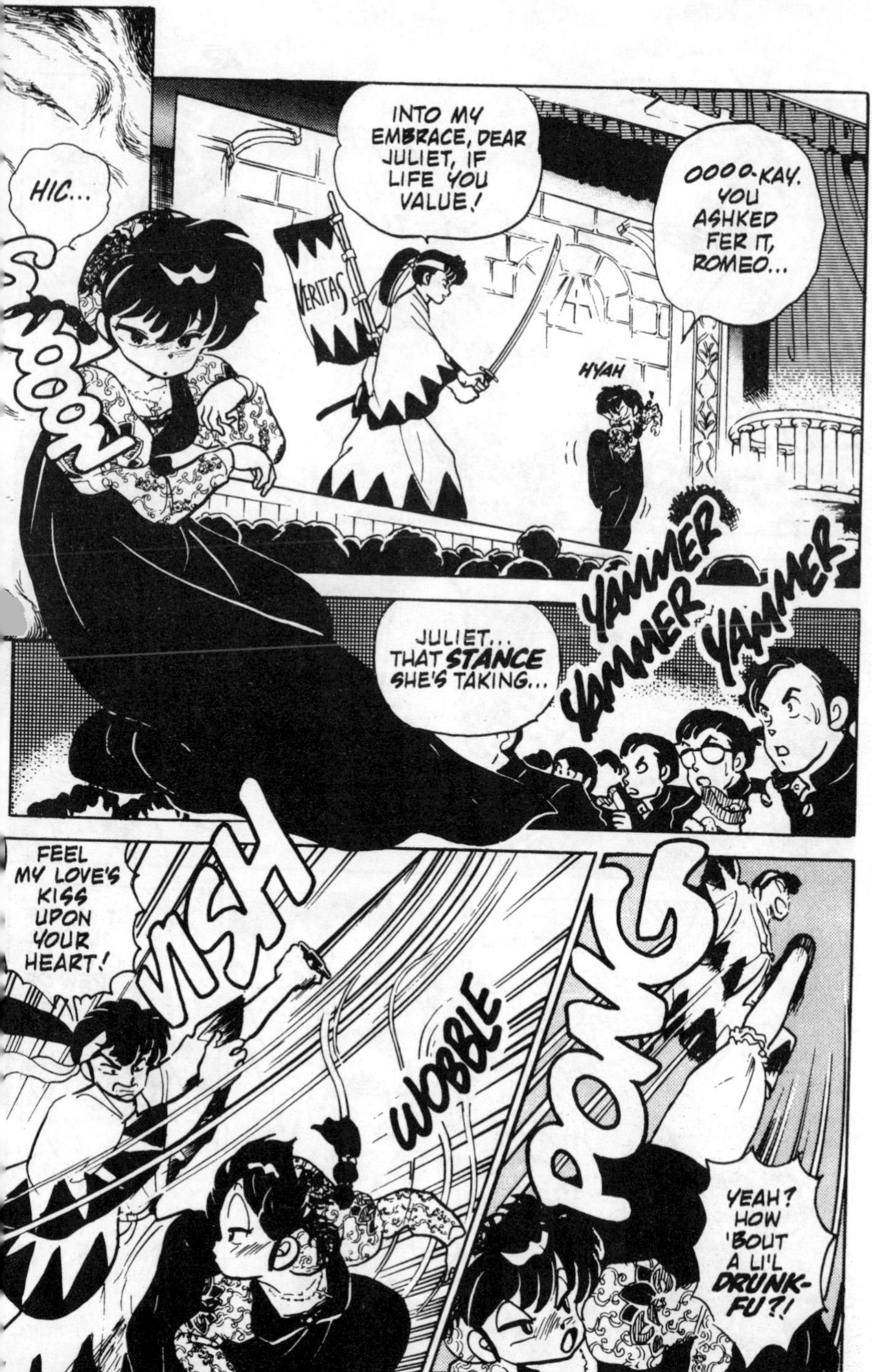
HIC...
GOOON
INTO MY EMBRACE, DEAR JULIET, IF LIFE YOU VALUE!
VERITAS
OOOO-KAY. YOU ASHKED FER IT, ROMEO...
HYAH
YAMMER YAMMER YAMMER
JULIET... THAT STANCE SHE'S TAKING...
FEEL MY LOVE'S KISS UPON YOUR HEART!
WISH
WOBBLE
PONG
YEAH? HOW 'BOUT A LI'L DRUNK-FU?!

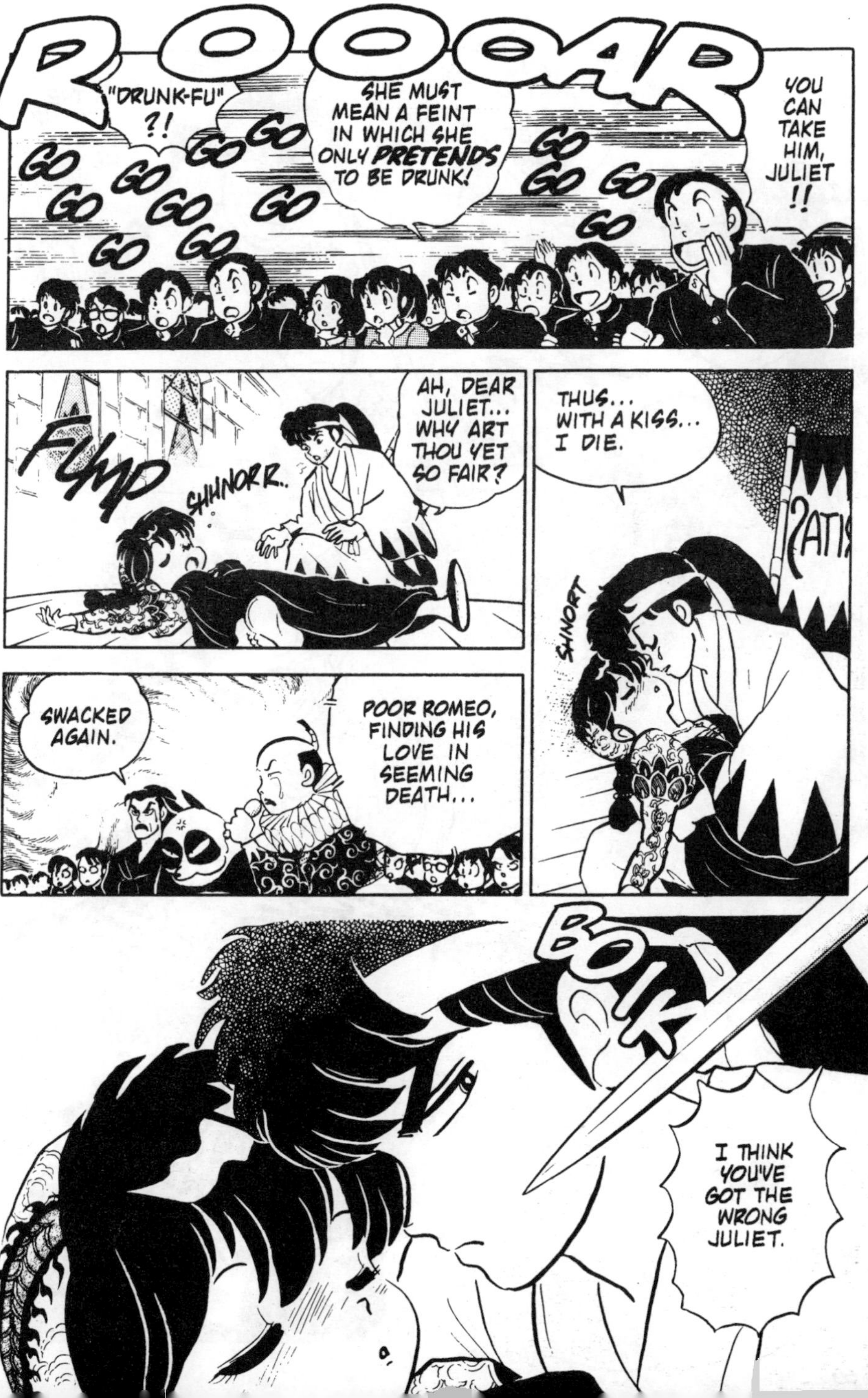
ROOOAR
"DRUNK-FU" ?!
GO GO GO GO GO GO GO GO GO GO
SHE MUST MEAN A FEINT IN WHICH SHE ONLY **PRETENDS** TO BE DRUNK!
GO GO GO GO
YOU CAN TAKE HIM, JULIET !!
FUMP
SHHNORR..
AH, DEAR JULIET... WHY ART THOU YET SO FAIR?
SWACKED AGAIN.
POOR ROMEO, FINDING HIS LOVE IN SEEMING DEATH...
THUS... WITH A KISS... I DIE.
SHNORT
BOIK
I THINK YOU'VE GOT THE WRONG JULIET.

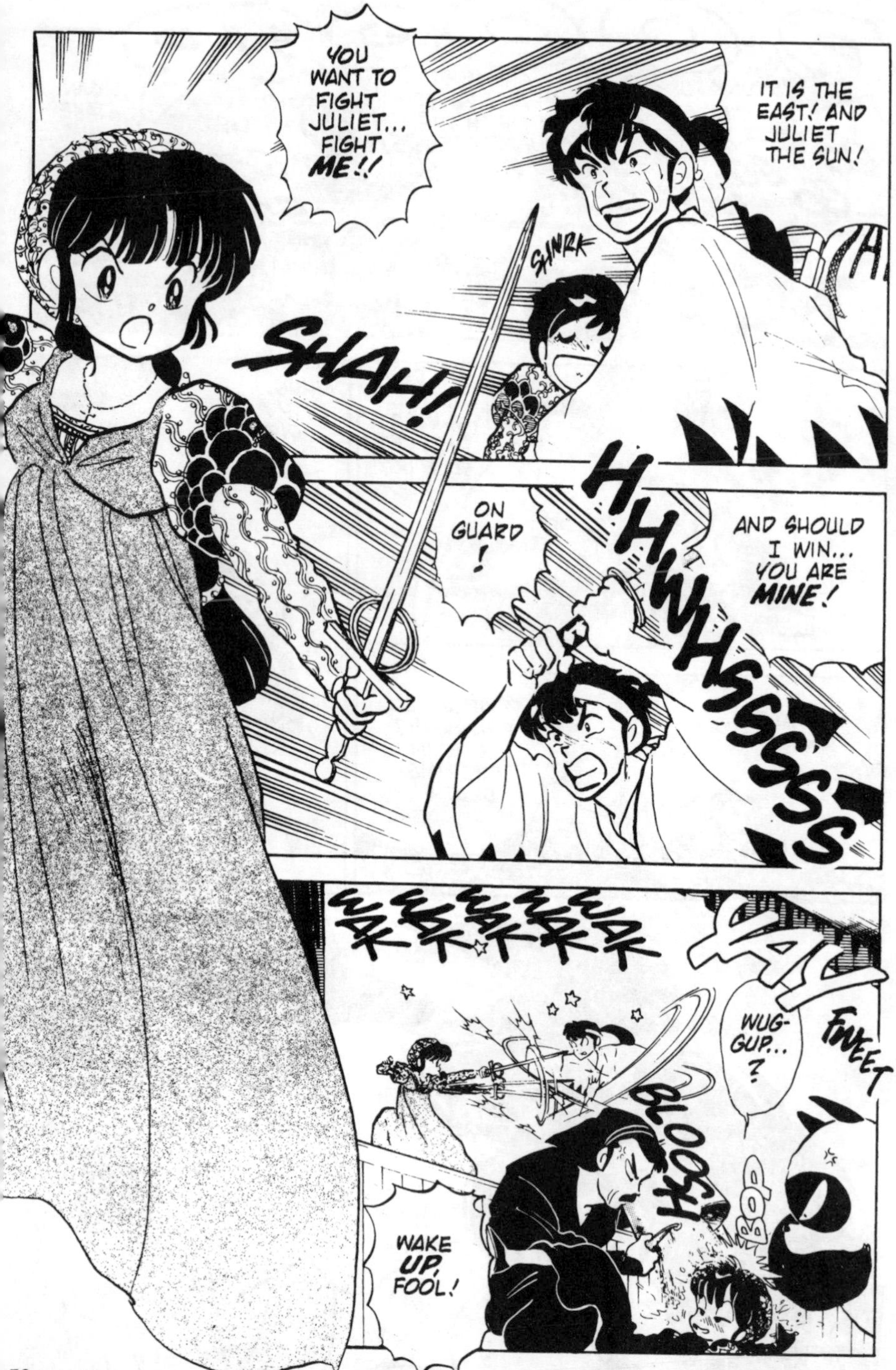
YOU WANT TO FIGHT JULIET... FIGHT ME!!
SHAH!
SHNRK
IT IS THE EAST! AND JULIET THE SUN!
ON GUARD!
AND SHOULD I WIN... YOU ARE MINE!
HHWHSSSSSS
WAK WAK WAK WAK WAK
YAY
WUG-GUP...?
FWEET
BLOOSH
WAKE UP, FOOL!

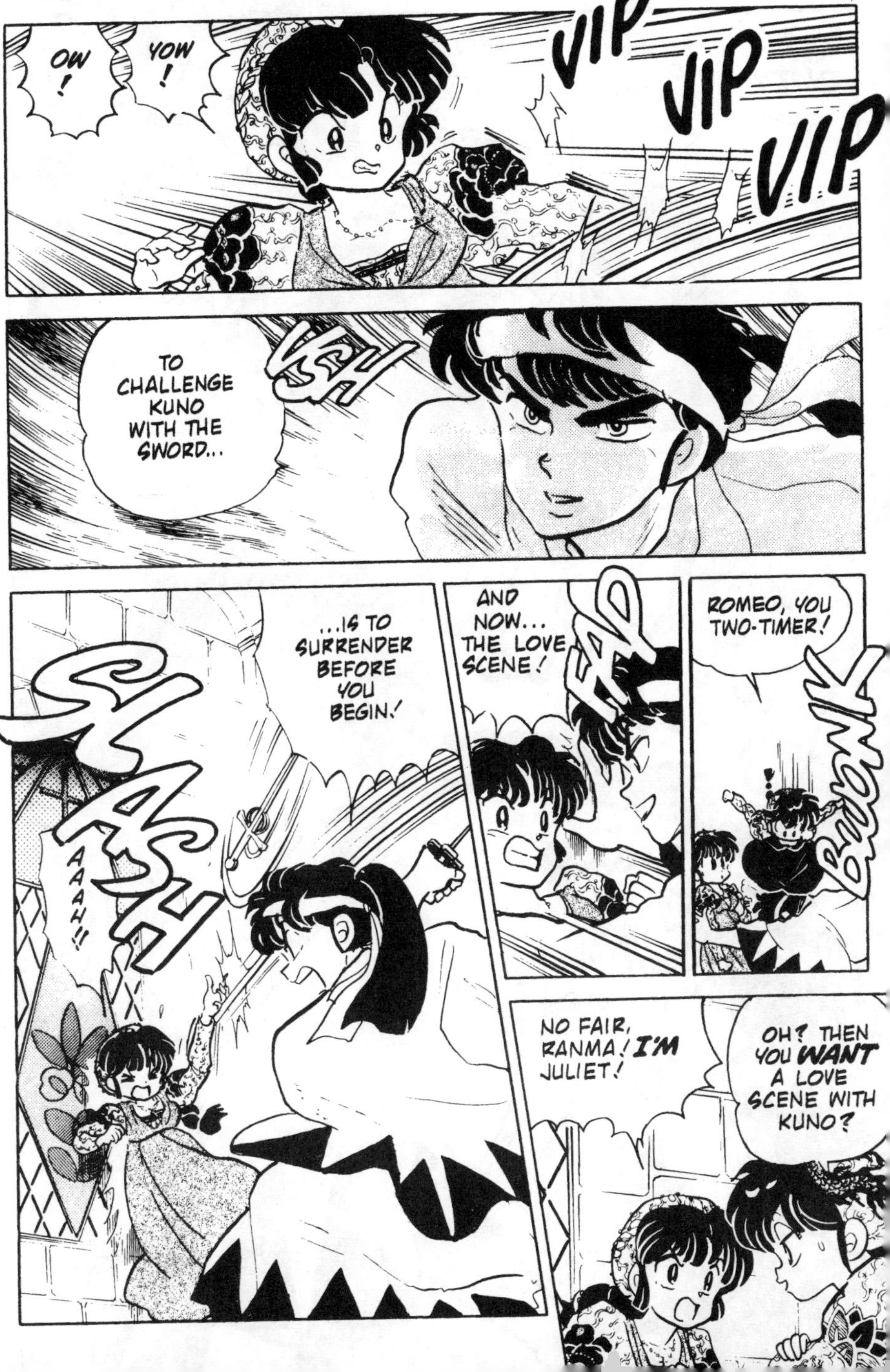
OW!
YOW!
VIP
VIP
VIP
TO CHALLENGE KUNO WITH THE SWORD...
VSH
...IS TO SURRENDER BEFORE YOU BEGIN!
SLASH
AAAH!!
AND NOW... THE LOVE SCENE!
FAP
ROMEO, YOU TWO-TIMER!
BWONK
NO FAIR, RANMA! I'M JULIET!
OH? THEN YOU WANT A LOVE SCENE WITH KUNO?

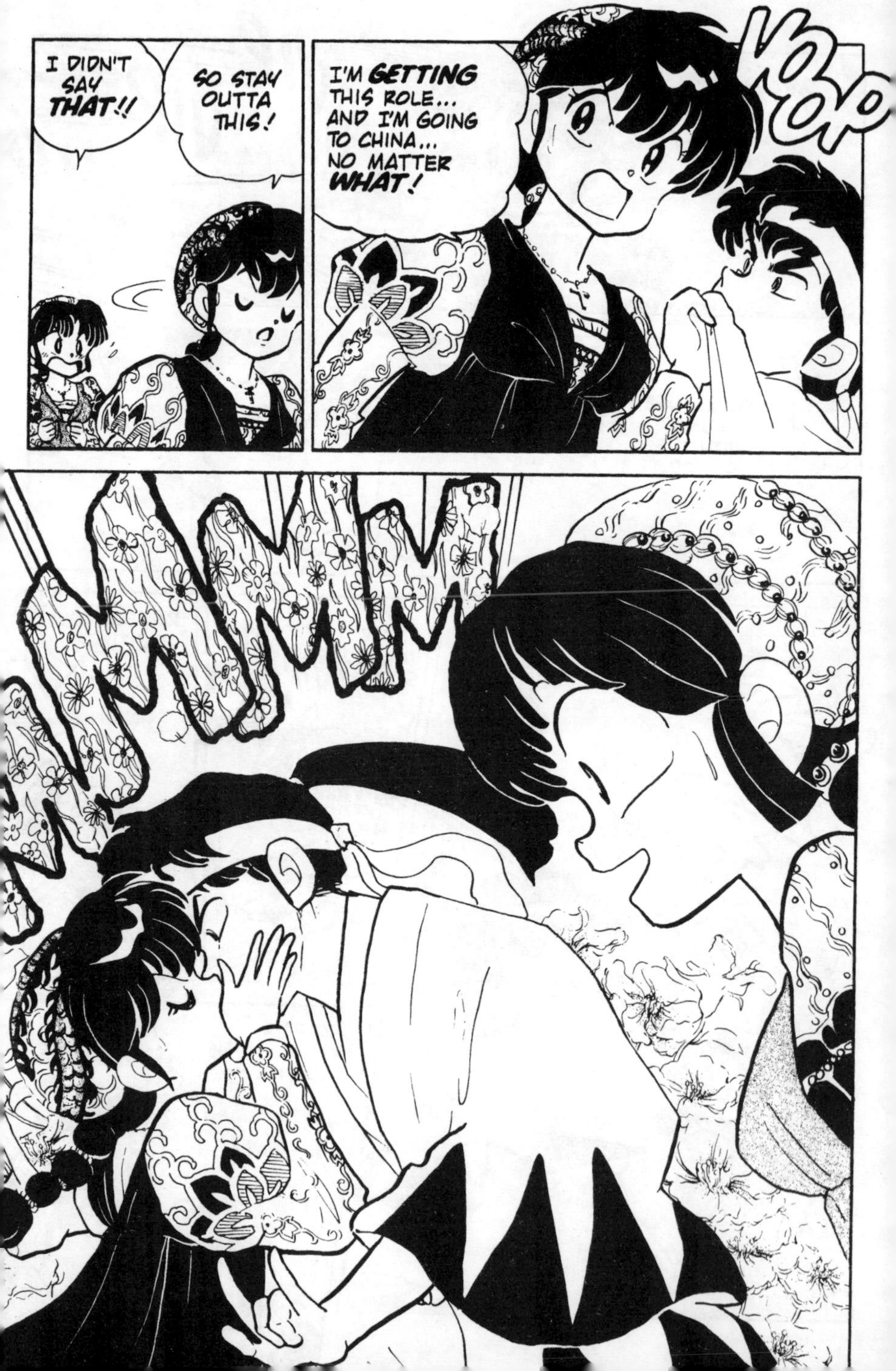
I DIDN'T SAY THAT!!
SO STAY OUTTA THIS!
I'M GETTING THIS ROLE... AND I'M GOING TO CHINA... NO MATTER WHAT!
VOOP

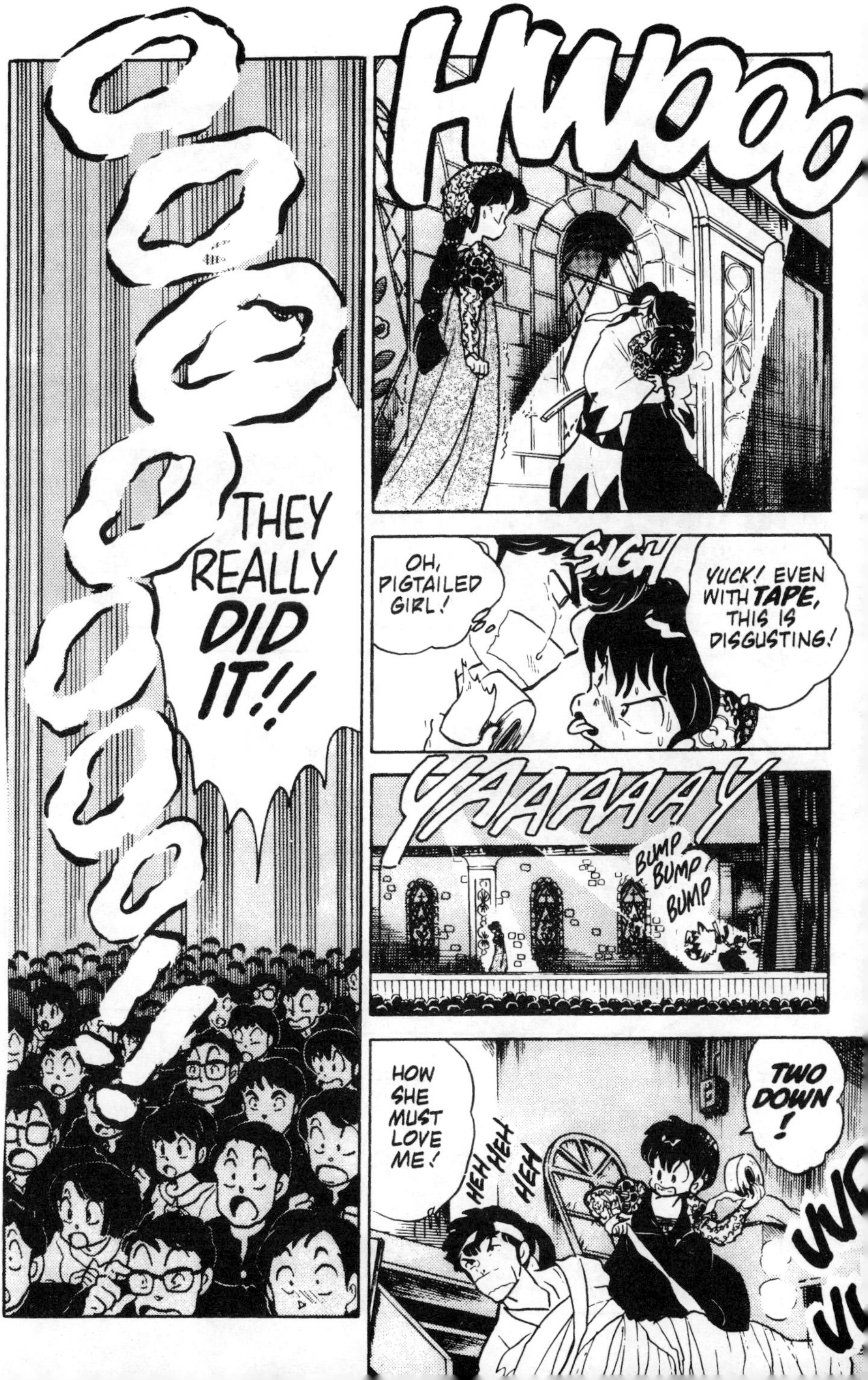
THEY REALLY DID IT!!
HUOOO
OH, PIGTAILED GIRL!
SIGH
YUCK! EVEN WITH TAPE, THIS IS DISGUSTING!
YAAAAAY
BUMP BUMP BUMP
HOW SHE MUST LOVE ME!
HEH HEH HEH
TWO DOWN!

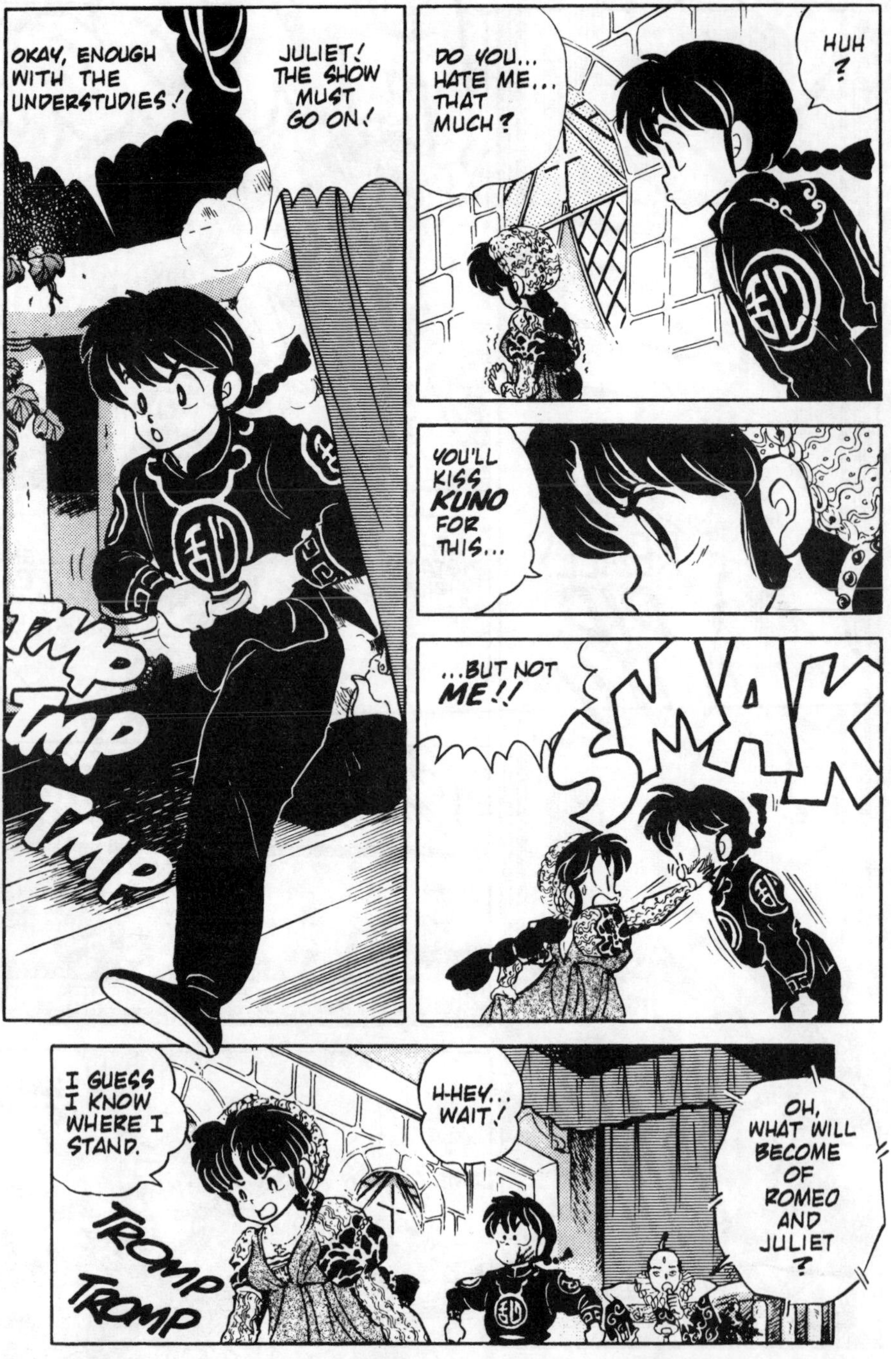
OKAY, ENOUGH WITH THE UNDERSTUDIES!
JULIET! THE SHOW MUST GO ON!
TMP TMP TMP
DO YOU... HATE ME... THAT MUCH?
HUH?
YOU'LL KISS **KUNO** FOR THIS...
...BUT NOT **ME**!!
SMAK
I GUESS I KNOW WHERE I STAND.
TROMP TROMP
H-HEY... WAIT!
OH, WHAT WILL BECOME OF ROMEO AND JULIET?

# PART FOUR

# A KISS TO THE VICTOR

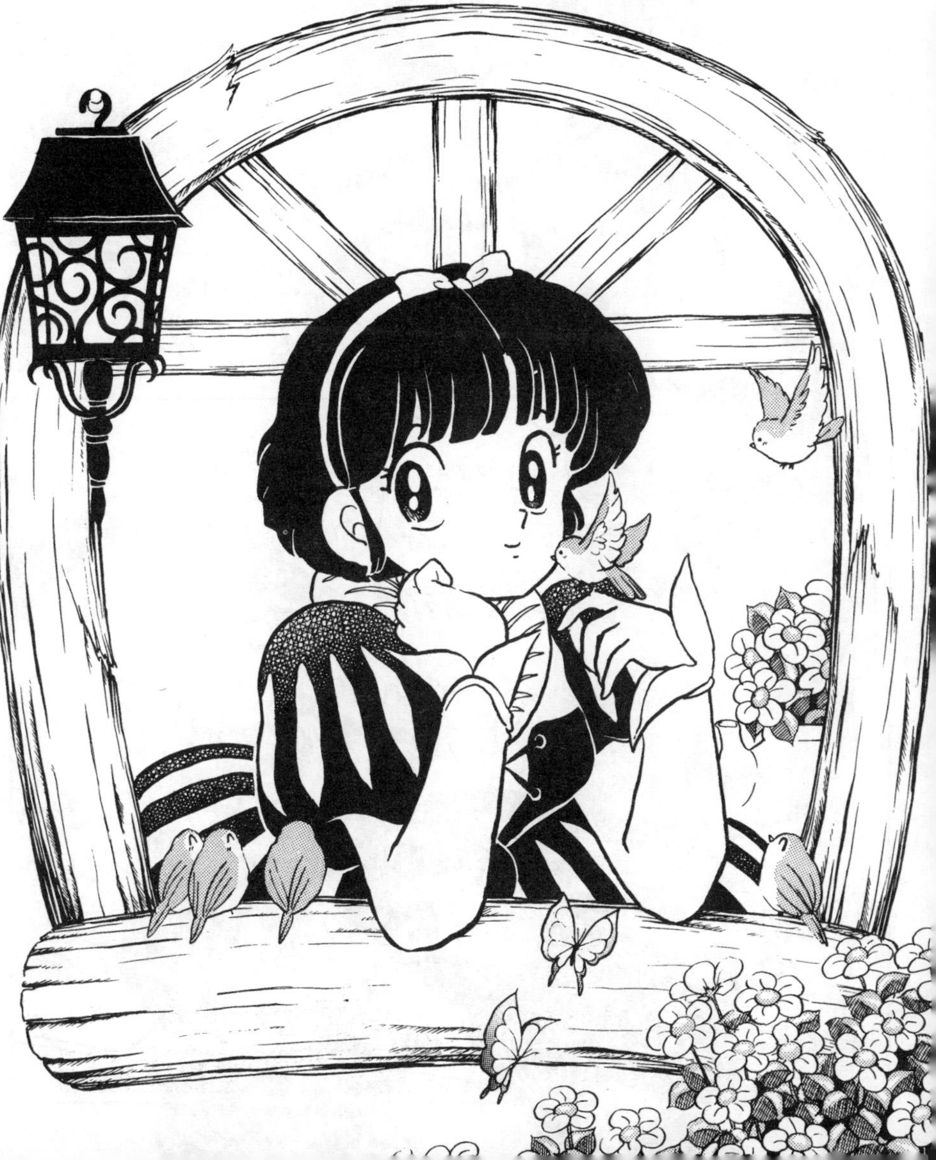

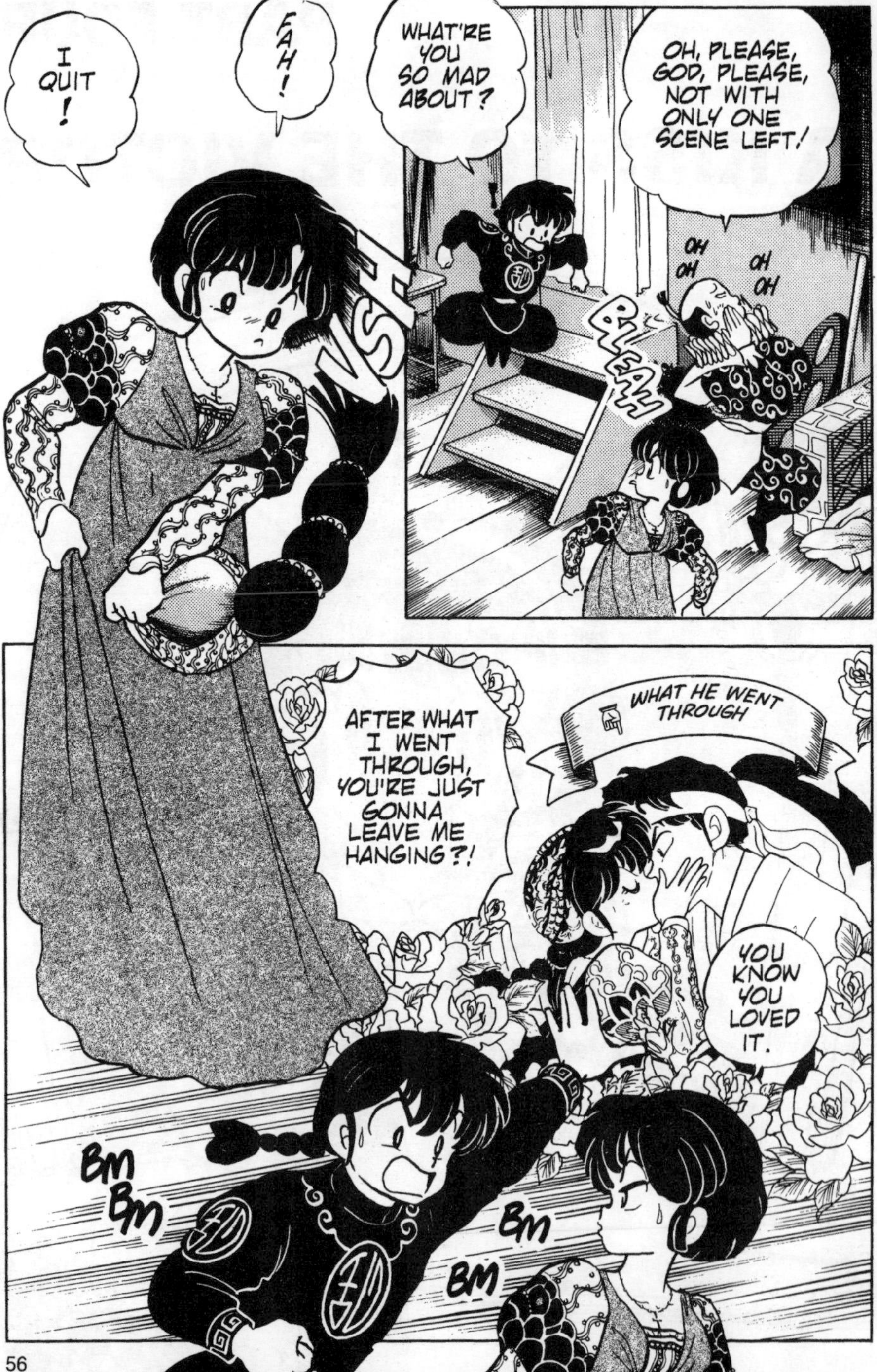

I QUIT!
FAH!
VSH
WHAT'RE YOU SO MAD ABOUT?
OH, PLEASE, GOD, PLEASE, NOT WITH ONLY ONE SCENE LEFT!
OH OH
OH OH
BLEAH
AFTER WHAT I WENT THROUGH, YOU'RE JUST GONNA LEAVE ME HANGING?!
WHAT HE WENT THROUGH
YOU KNOW YOU LOVED IT.
BM BM
BM
BM

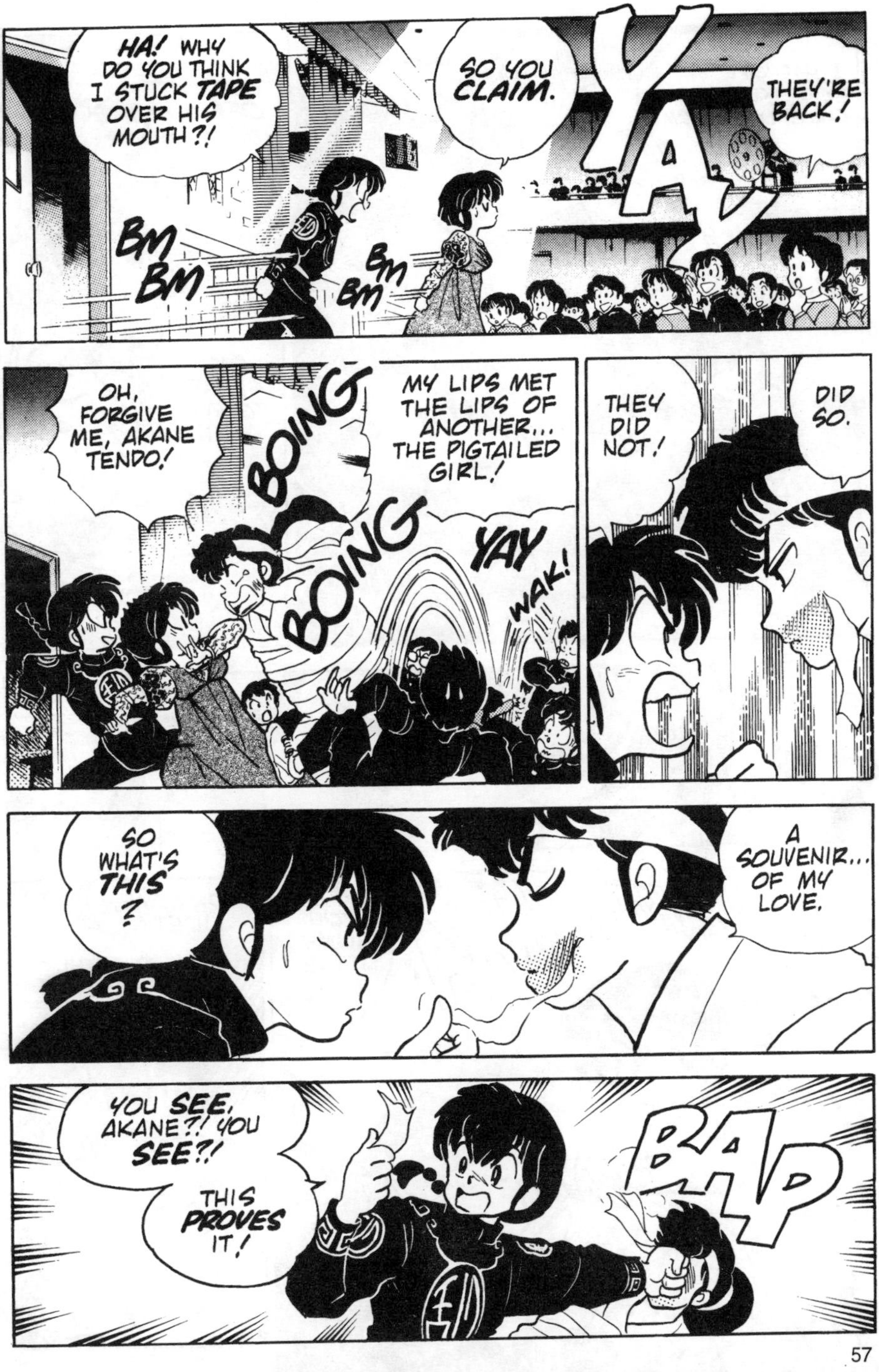
HA! WHY DO YOU THINK I STUCK TAPE OVER HIS MOUTH?!
SO YOU CLAIM.
YAY
THEY'RE BACK!
BM BM
BM BM
OH, FORGIVE ME, AKANE TENDO!
MY LIPS MET THE LIPS OF ANOTHER... THE PIGTAILED GIRL!
BOING
BOING
YAY
WAK!
THEY DID NOT!
DID SO.
SO WHAT'S THIS?
A SOUVENIR... OF MY LOVE.
YOU SEE, AKANE?! YOU SEE?!
THIS PROVES IT!
BAP

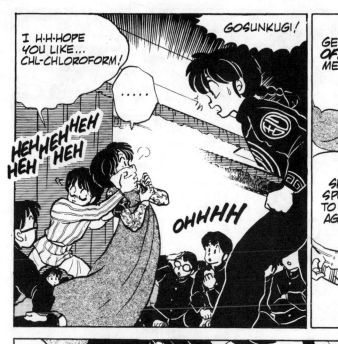

I H·H·HOPE YOU LIKE... CHL-CHLOROFORM!

GOSUNKUGI!

·····

HEH HEH HEH HEH HEH

OHHHH

GET... OFF ME!!

SHE SPOKE TO ME AGAIN...

SIGH

PAP

OH...

WOBBLE OBBLE

COME A STEP CLOSER AND JULIET DIES!

NYAH HAHAHA

YOU SLIMY LITTLE...

FFFMP

NOW COME, JULIET!

TOGETHER, LET US BE OFF, AND...

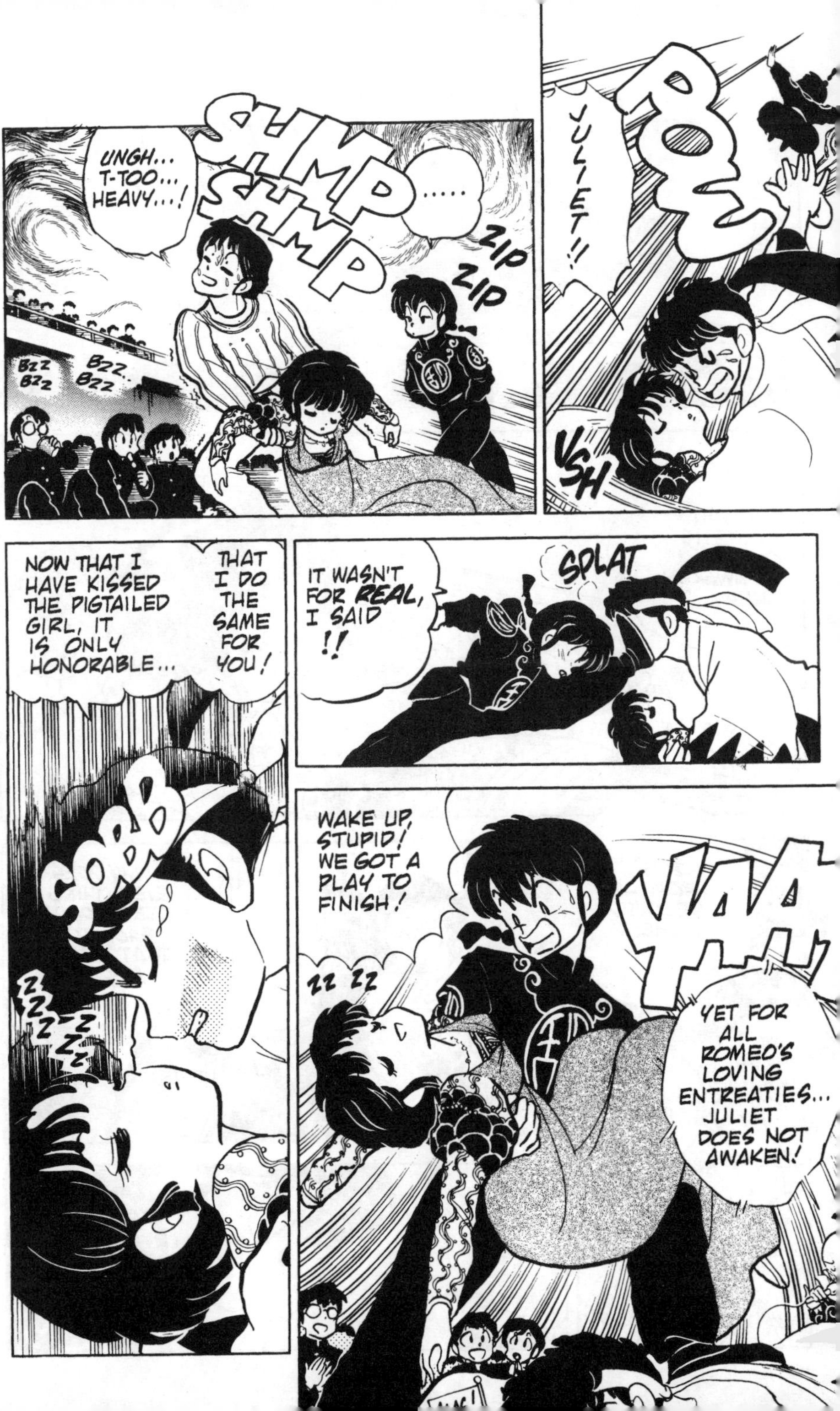
SHMP
UNGH... T-TOO... HEAVY...!
SHMP
SHMP
.....
ZIP
ZIP
BZZ BZZ
BZZ BZZ
BOW
JULIET!!
VSH
NOW THAT I HAVE KISSED THE PIGTAILED GIRL, IT IS ONLY HONORABLE...
THAT I DO THE SAME FOR YOU!
SOBB
ZZZZZZZ
IT WASN'T FOR REAL, I SAID!!
SPLAT
WAKE UP, STUPID! WE GOT A PLAY TO FINISH!
ZZ ZZ
YET FOR ALL ROMEO'S LOVING ENTREATIES... JULIET DOES NOT AWAKEN!

JULIET SLEEPS THE SLEEP... OF DEATH!

YAAAAAY

CLAP CLAP
CLAP CLAP
CLAP

BUT WAIT! THERE IS ONE WAY TO AWAKEN HER!

ZZz
ZZz

HUH?

WHA?

A KISS FROM HER BELOVED ROMEO.!

THAT SOUNDS LIKE SNOW WHITE!

OR SLEEPING BEAUTY !

WHY DOES EVERYTHING KEEP COMIN' BACK TO THAT STUPID KISS!

HIC

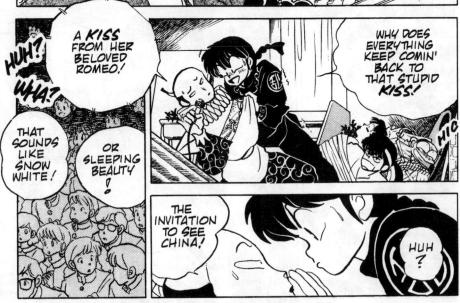

THE INVITATION TO SEE CHINA!

HUH?

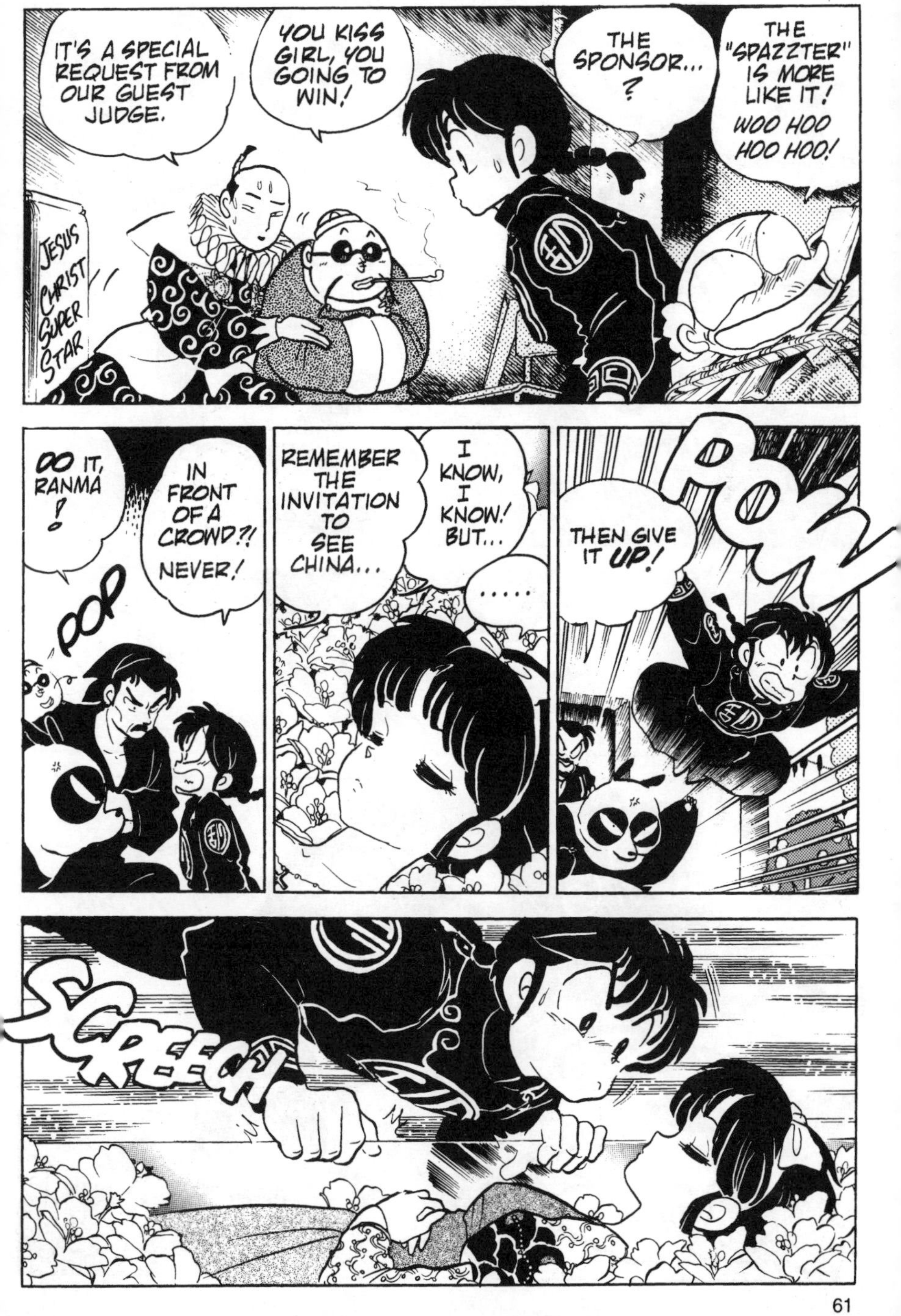
IT'S A SPECIAL REQUEST FROM OUR GUEST JUDGE.
YOU KISS GIRL, YOU GOING TO WIN!
JESUS CHRIST SUPER STAR
THE SPONSOR... ?
THE "SPAZZTER" IS MORE LIKE IT! WOO HOO HOO HOO!
DO IT, RANMA!
IN FRONT OF A CROWD?! NEVER!
POP
REMEMBER THE INVITATION TO SEE CHINA...
I KNOW, I KNOW! BUT...
......
POW
THEN GIVE IT UP!
SCREECH

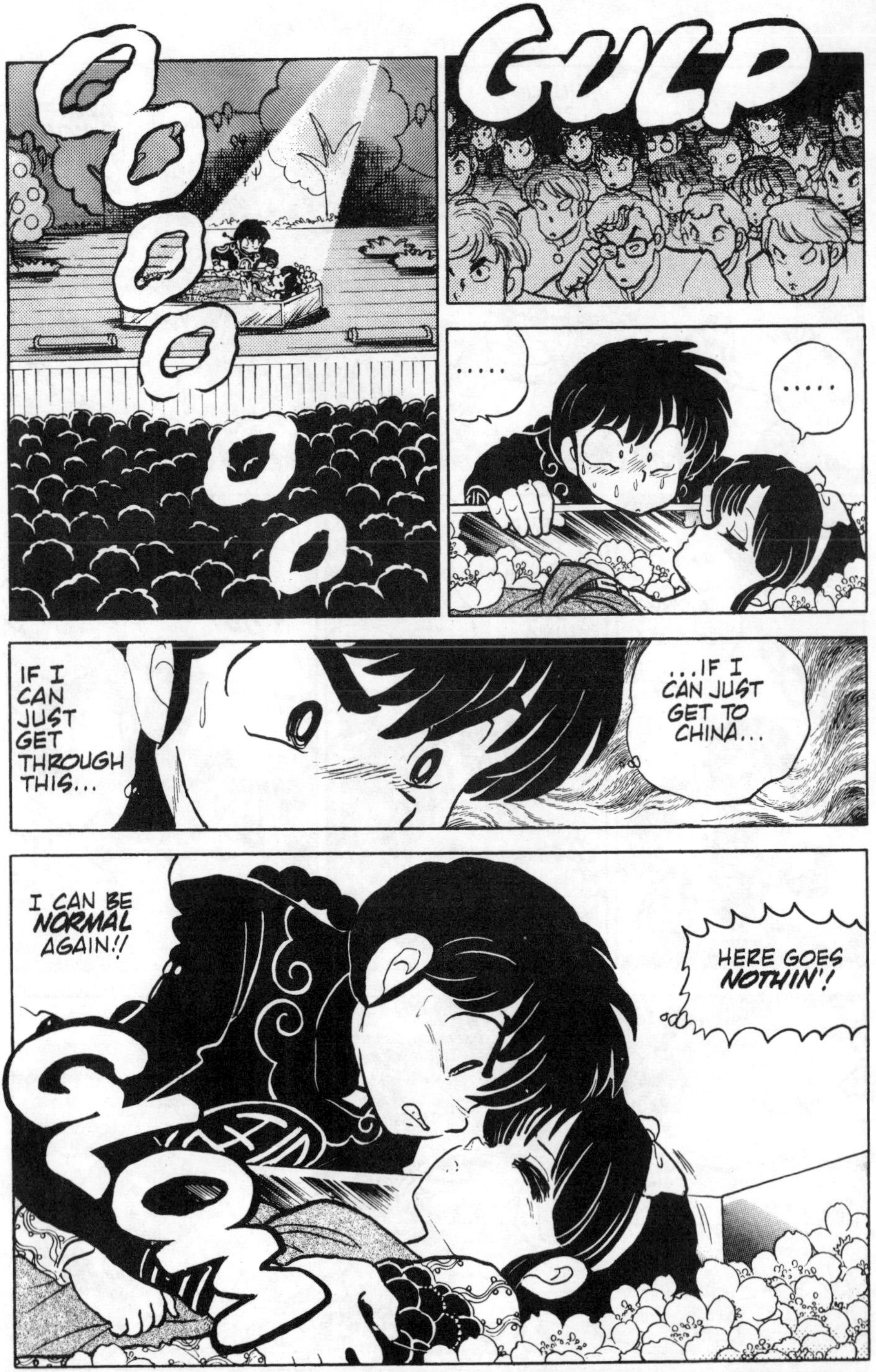
GULP
.....
.....
IF I CAN JUST GET THROUGH THIS...
...IF I CAN JUST GET TO CHINA...
I CAN BE NORMAL AGAIN!!
HERE GOES NOTHIN'!
GLOM

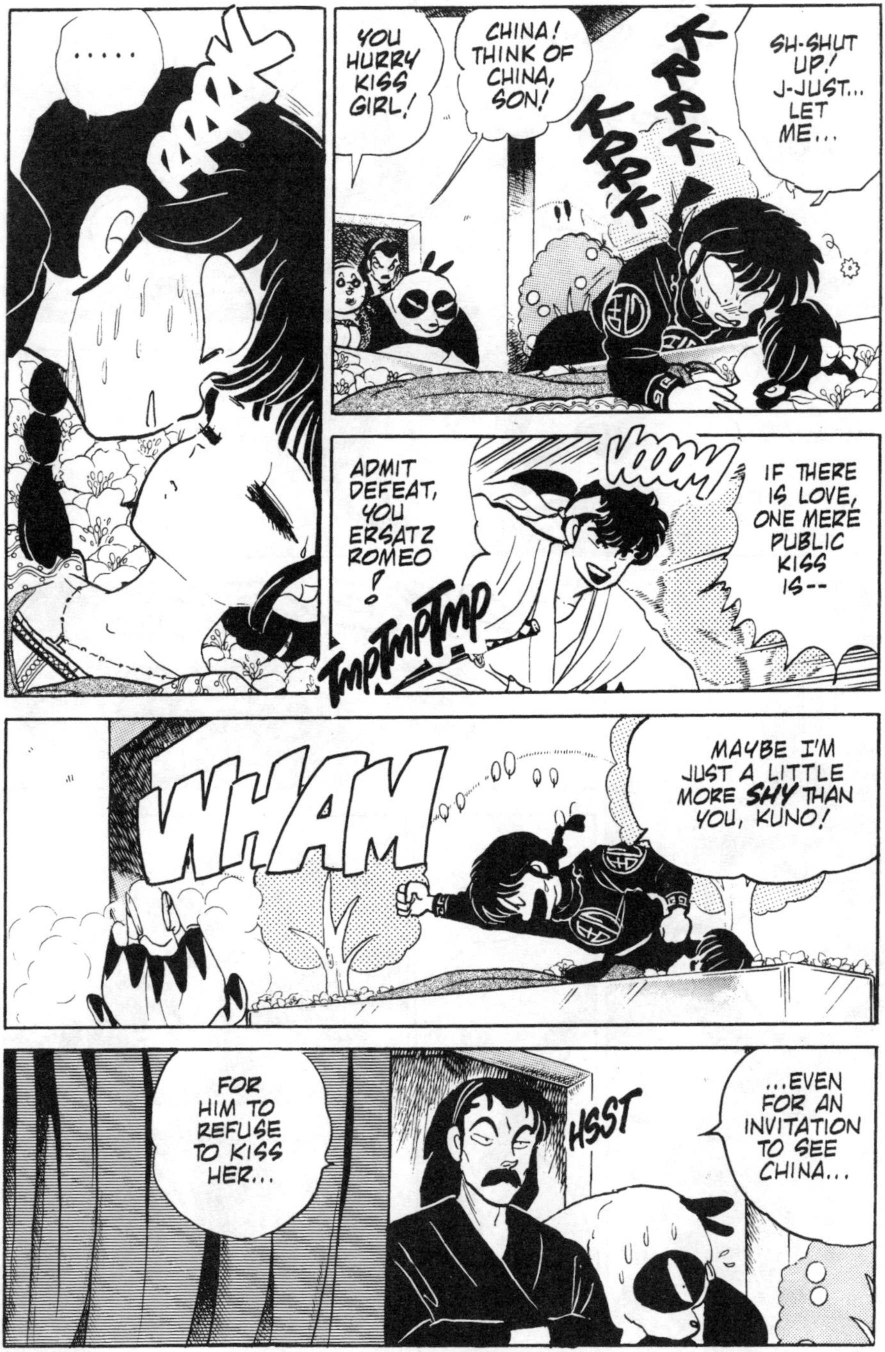
. . . . .
RRRK
YOU HURRY KISS GIRL!
CHINA! THINK OF CHINA, SON!
KRPK KRPK
SH-SHUT UP! J-JUST... LET ME...
ADMIT DEFEAT, YOU ERSATZ ROMEO!
VOOOM
IF THERE IS LOVE, ONE MERE PUBLIC KISS IS--
TMPTMPTMP
WHAM
MAYBE I'M JUST A LITTLE MORE SHY THAN YOU, KUNO!
FOR HIM TO REFUSE TO KISS HER...
HSST
...EVEN FOR AN INVITATION TO SEE CHINA...

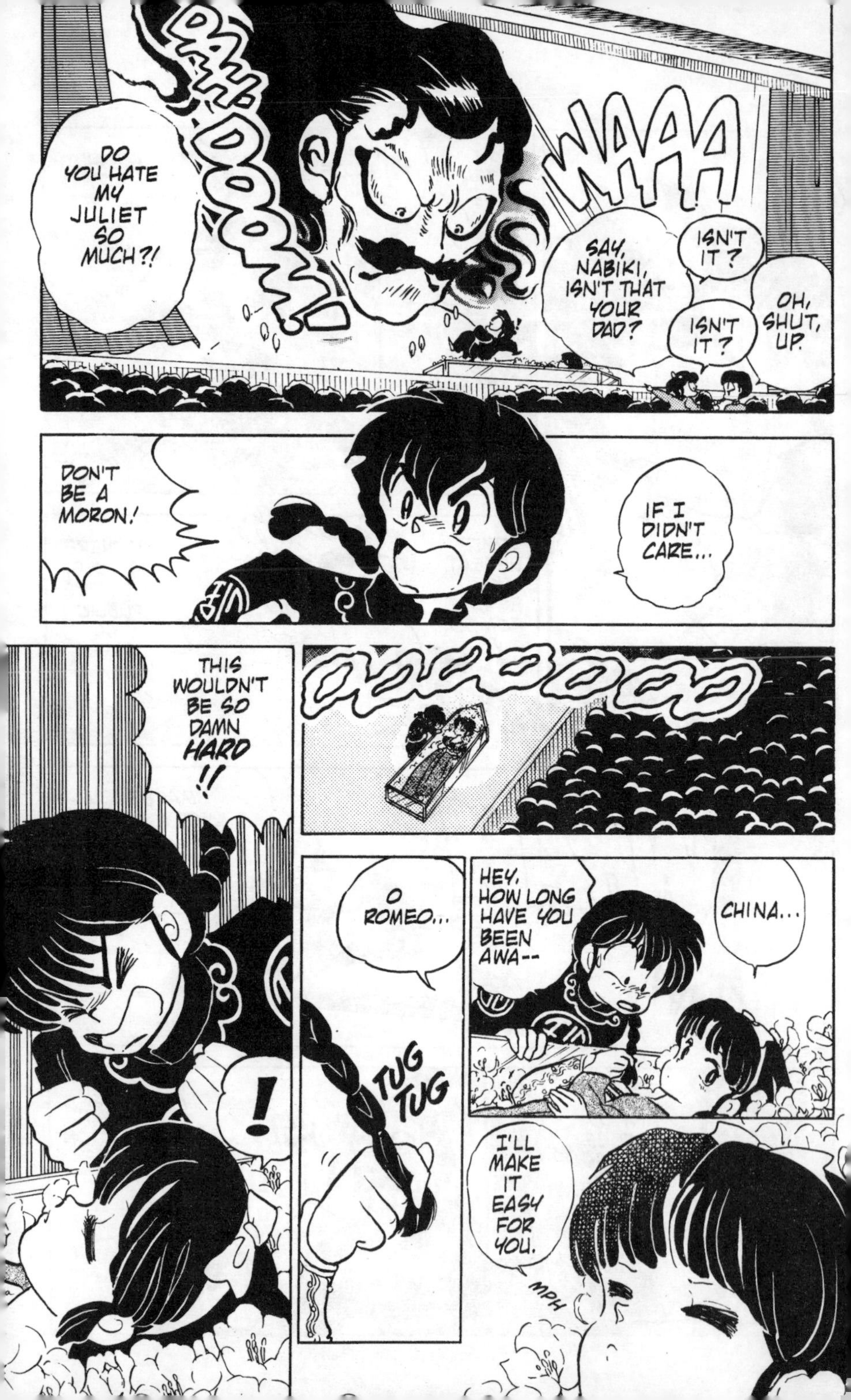
DO YOU HATE MY JULIET SO MUCH?!
DAH-DOOM!
WAAA
SAY, NABIKI, ISN'T THAT YOUR DAD?
ISN'T IT?
ISN'T IT?
OH, SHUT UP.
DON'T BE A MORON!
IF I DIDN'T CARE...
THIS WOULDN'T BE SO DAMN HARD!!
OOOOOOO
!
O ROMEO...
TUG TUG
HEY, HOW LONG HAVE YOU BEEN AWA--
CHINA...
I'LL MAKE IT EASY FOR YOU.
MPH

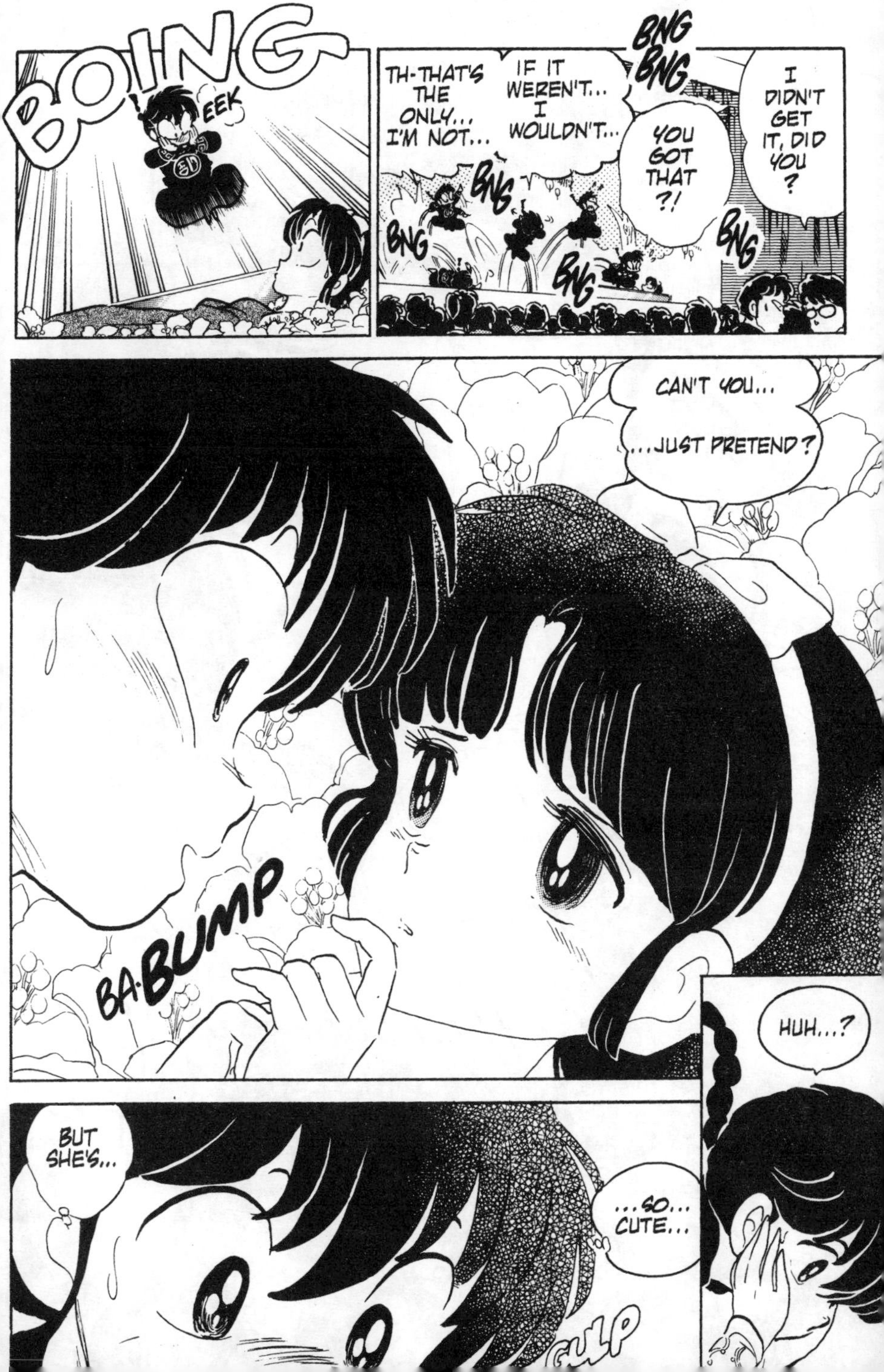
BOING
EEK
TH-THAT'S THE ONLY... I'M NOT...
IF IT WEREN'T... I WOULDN'T...
BNG BNG
YOU GOT THAT?!
I DIDN'T GET IT, DID YOU?
BNG
BNG
BNG
BNG
CAN'T YOU...
...JUST PRETEND?
BA-BUMP
HUH...?
BUT SHE'S...
...SO... CUTE...
GULP

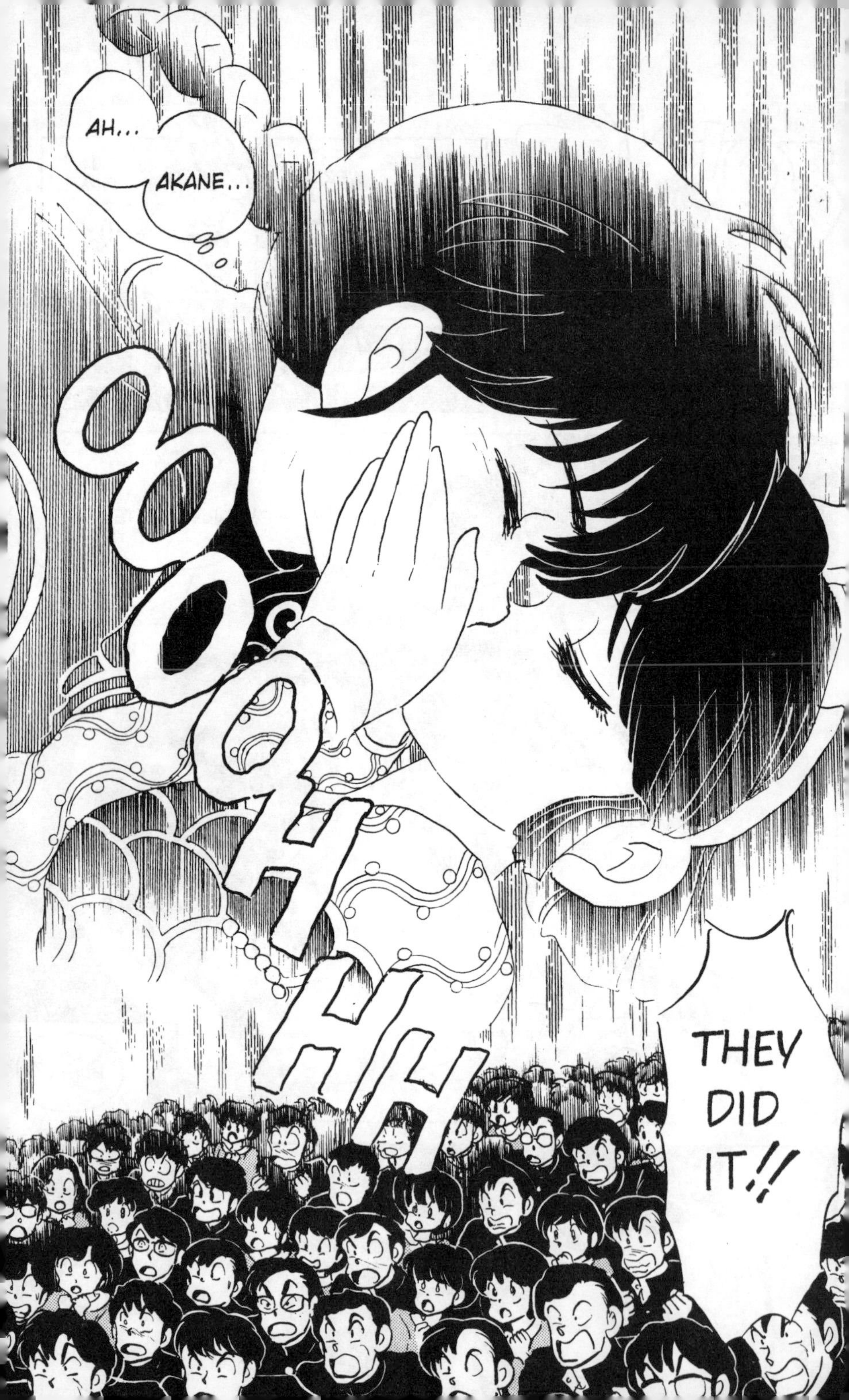
AH... AKANE...
OOOOOHH
THEY DID IT!!

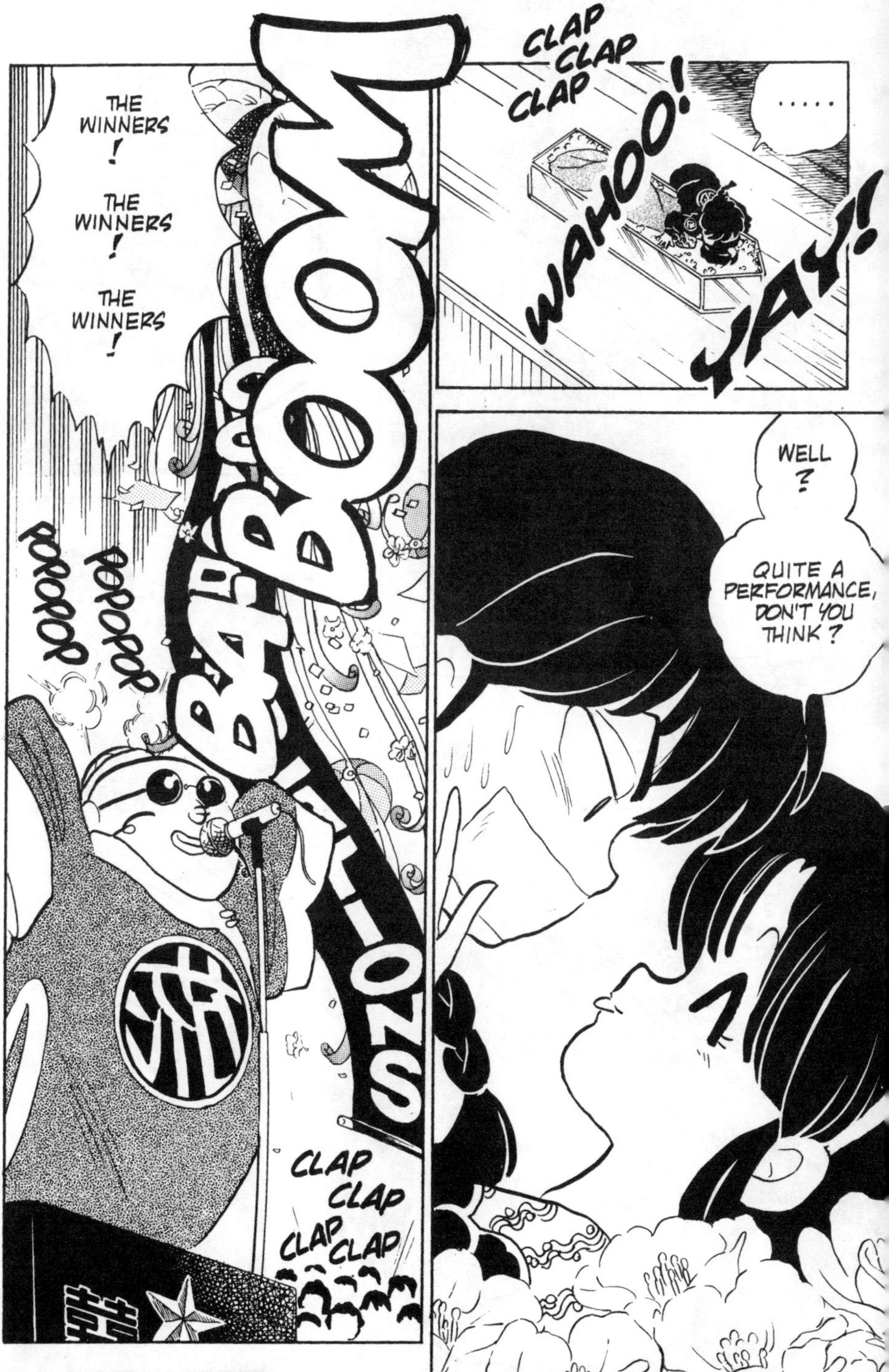
THE WINNERS!
THE WINNERS!
THE WINNERS!
BOOM
POPOPOP
POPOPOP
CLAP CLAP CLAP CLAP
CLAP CLAP CLAP
WAHOO!
.....
YAY!
WELL?
QUITE A PERFORMANCE, DON'T YOU THINK?

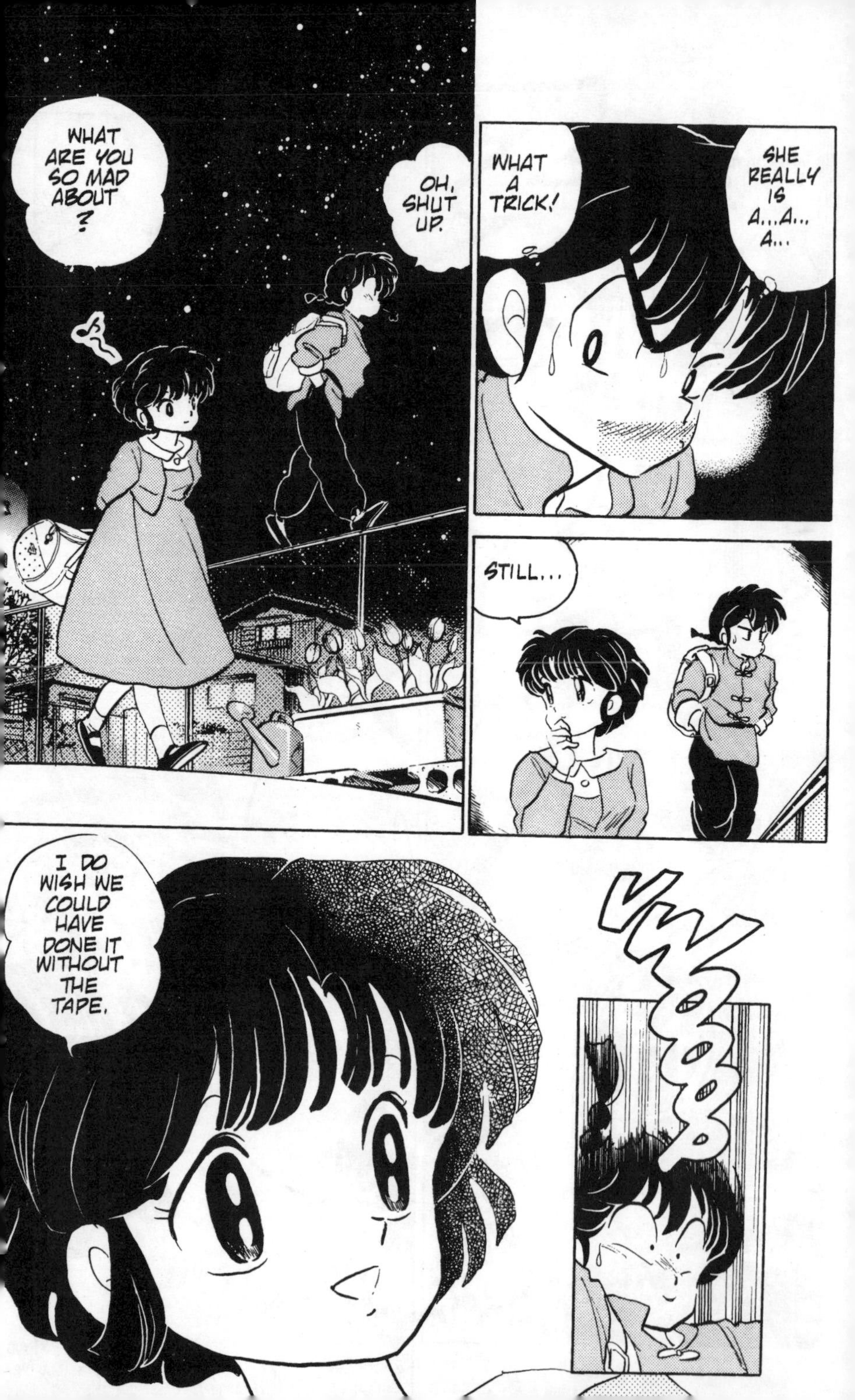
WHAT ARE YOU SO MAD ABOUT?
OH, SHUT UP.
WHAT A TRICK!
SHE REALLY IS A...A... A...
STILL...
I DO WISH WE COULD HAVE DONE IT WITHOUT THE TAPE.
VWOOOO

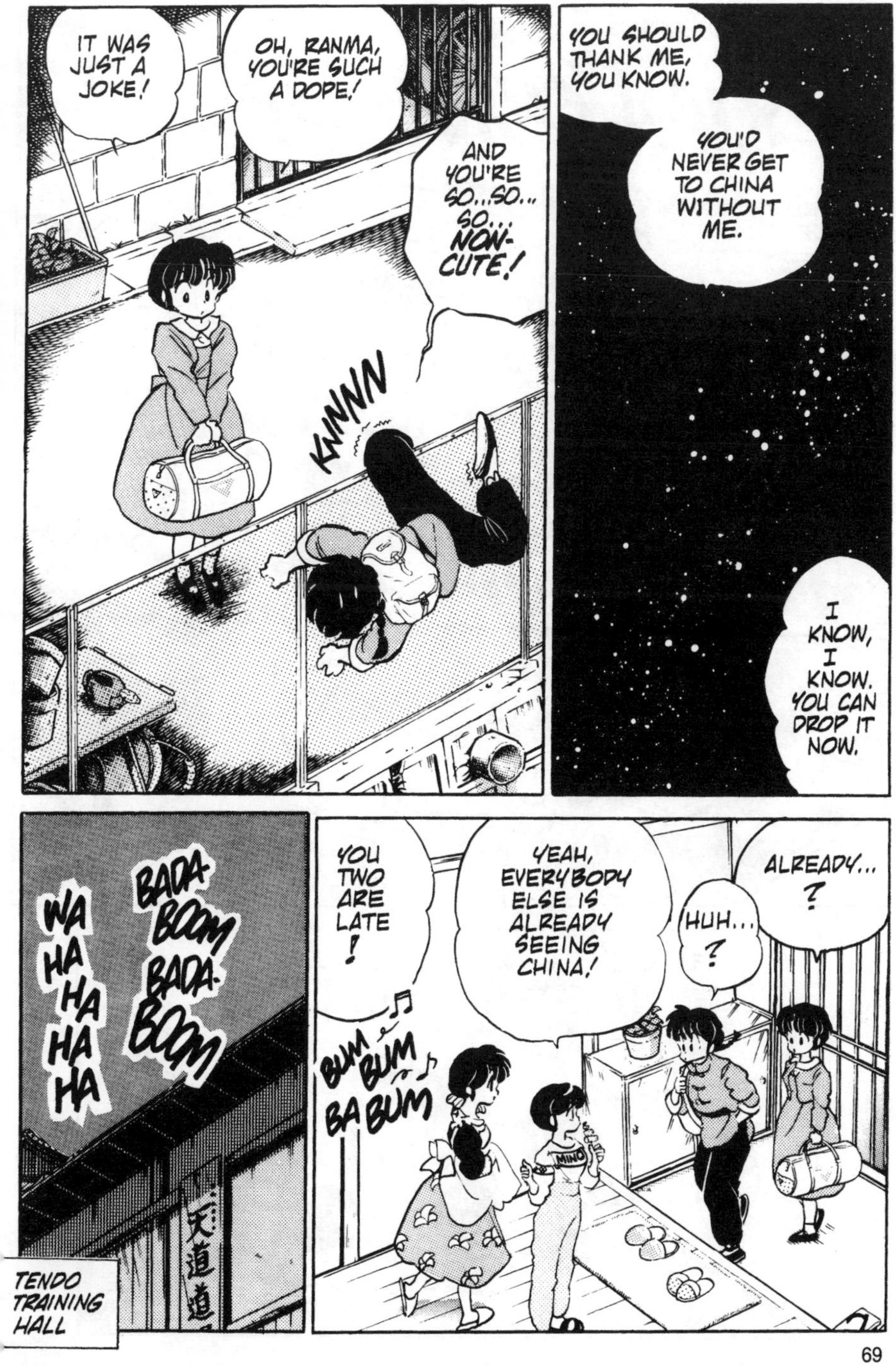
IT WAS JUST A JOKE!
OH, RANMA, YOU'RE SUCH A DOPE!
AND YOU'RE SO...SO... SO... NON-CUTE!
KWNNN
YOU SHOULD THANK ME, YOU KNOW.
YOU'D NEVER GET TO CHINA WITHOUT ME.
I KNOW, I KNOW. YOU CAN DROP IT NOW.
WA HA HA HA HA
BADA-BOOM BADA-BOOM
TENDO TRAINING HALL
YOU TWO ARE LATE!
YEAH, EVERYBODY ELSE IS ALREADY SEEING CHINA!
HUH...?
ALREADY...?
BUM BUM BA BUM
MINO

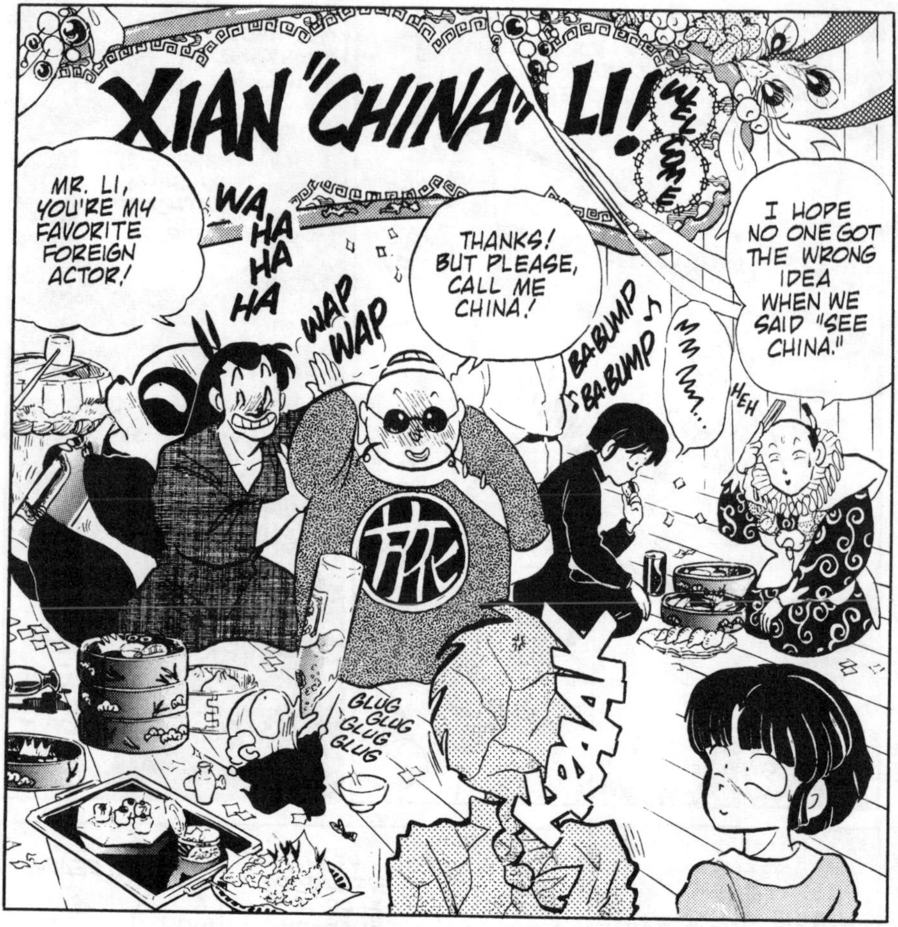
XIAN "CHINA" LI!
WELCOME
MR. LI, YOU'RE MY FAVORITE FOREIGN ACTOR!
WA HA HA HA HA
WAP WAP
THANKS! BUT PLEASE, CALL ME CHINA!
BA-BUMP BA-BUMP
MMM...
HEH
I HOPE NO ONE GOT THE WRONG IDEA WHEN WE SAID "SEE CHINA."
GLUG GLUG GLUG GLUG
KRAAK

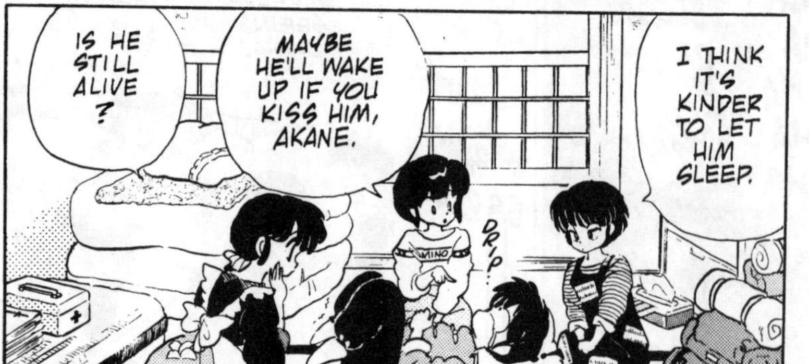
IS HE STILL ALIVE?
MAYBE HE'LL WAKE UP IF YOU KISS HIM, AKANE.
I THINK IT'S KINDER TO LET HIM SLEEP.
DRIP...

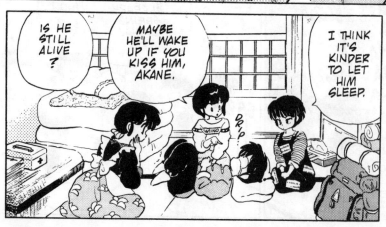

# PART FIVE

# QUEST FOR THE HIDDEN SPRING

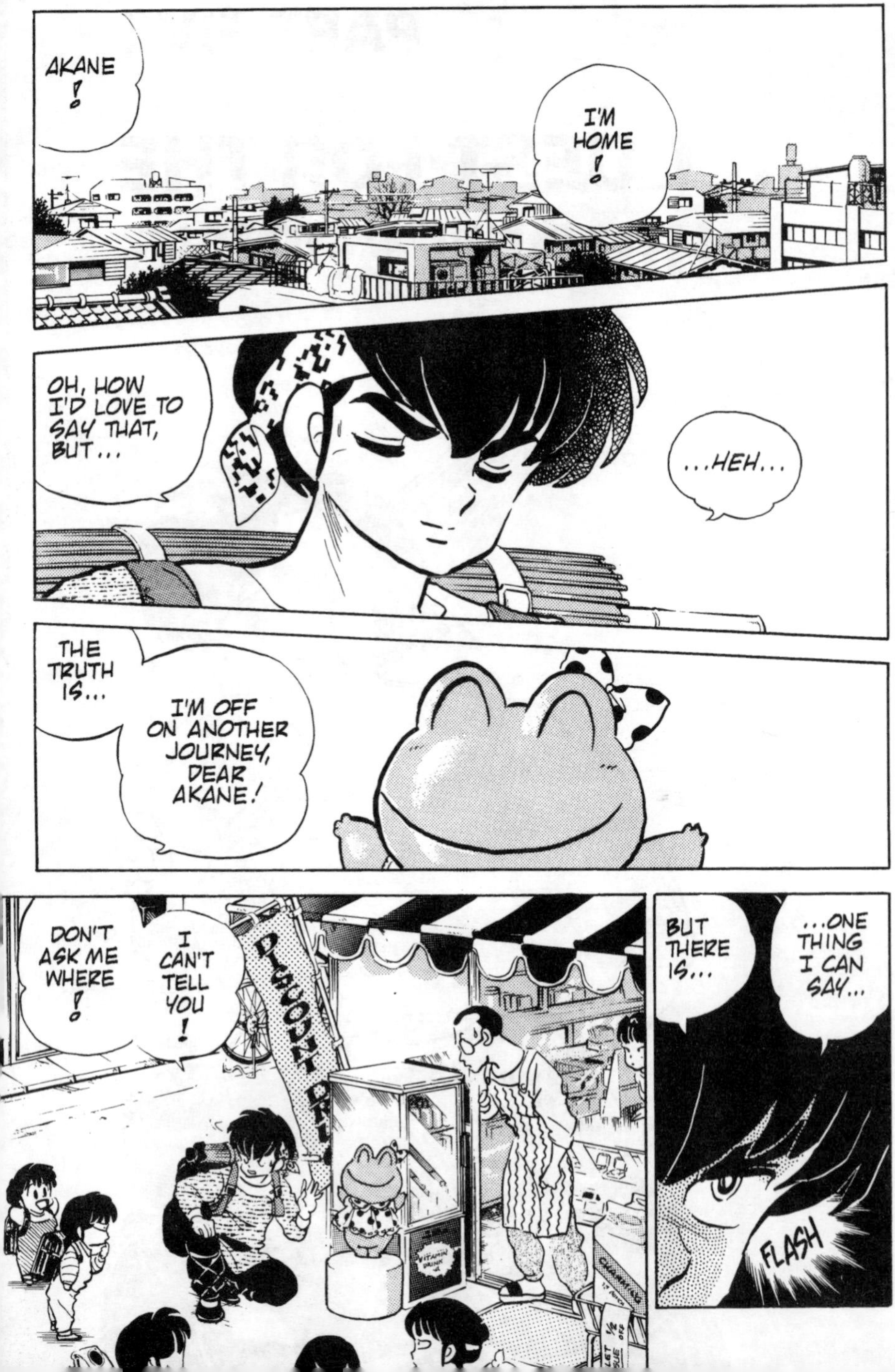
AKANE!
I'M HOME!
OH, HOW I'D LOVE TO SAY THAT, BUT...
...HEH...
THE TRUTH IS...
I'M OFF ON ANOTHER JOURNEY, DEAR AKANE!
DON'T ASK ME WHERE!
I CAN'T TELL YOU!
BUT THERE IS...
...ONE THING I CAN SAY...
FLASH

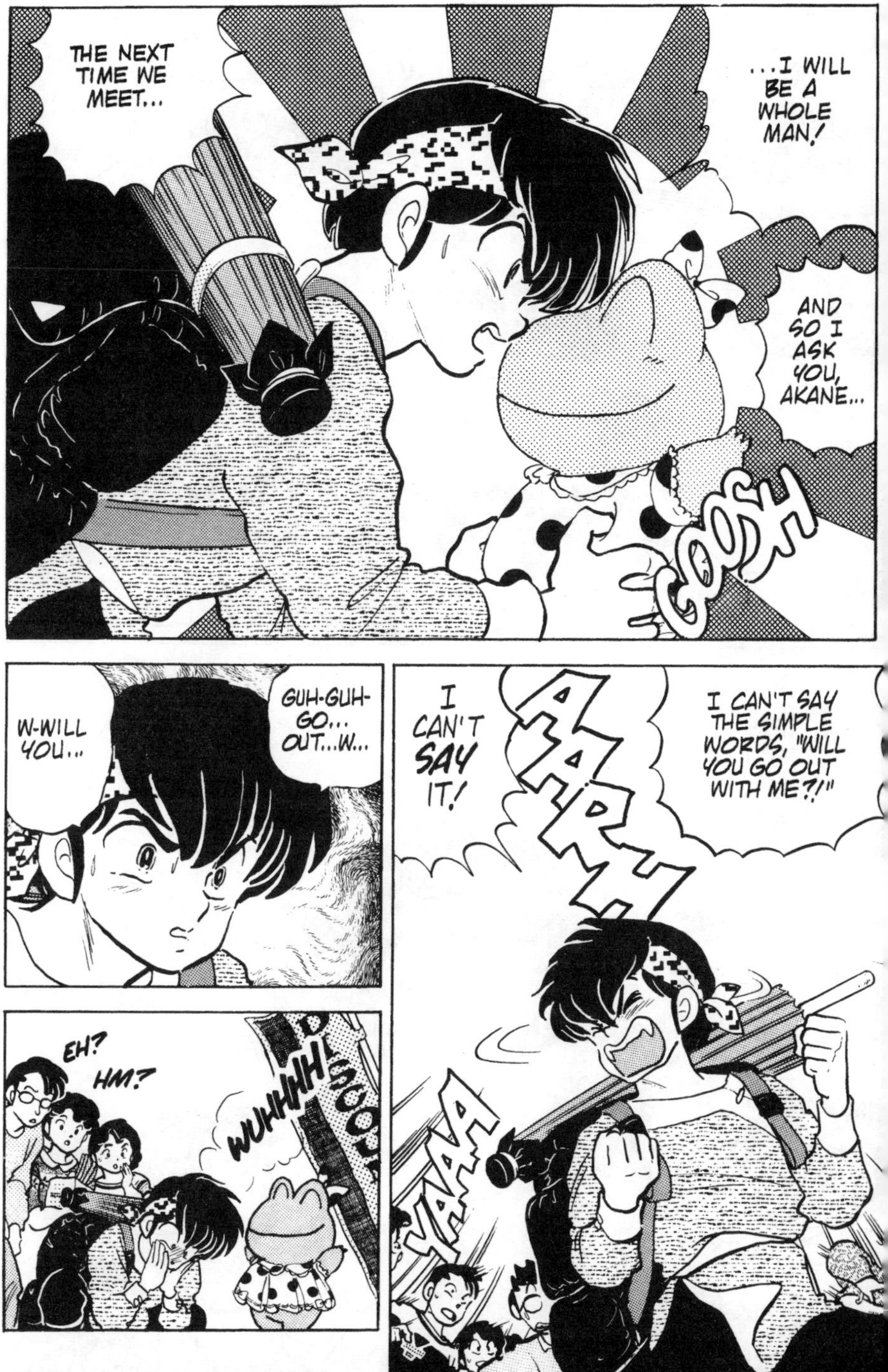
THE NEXT TIME WE MEET...
...I WILL BE A WHOLE MAN!
AND SO I ASK YOU, AKANE...
GOOSH
W-WILL YOU...
GUH-GUH-GO... OUT...W...
EH?
HM?
WUHHHH
I CAN'T SAY IT!
AARGH
I CAN'T SAY THE SIMPLE WORDS, "WILL YOU GO OUT WITH ME?!"
YAAA

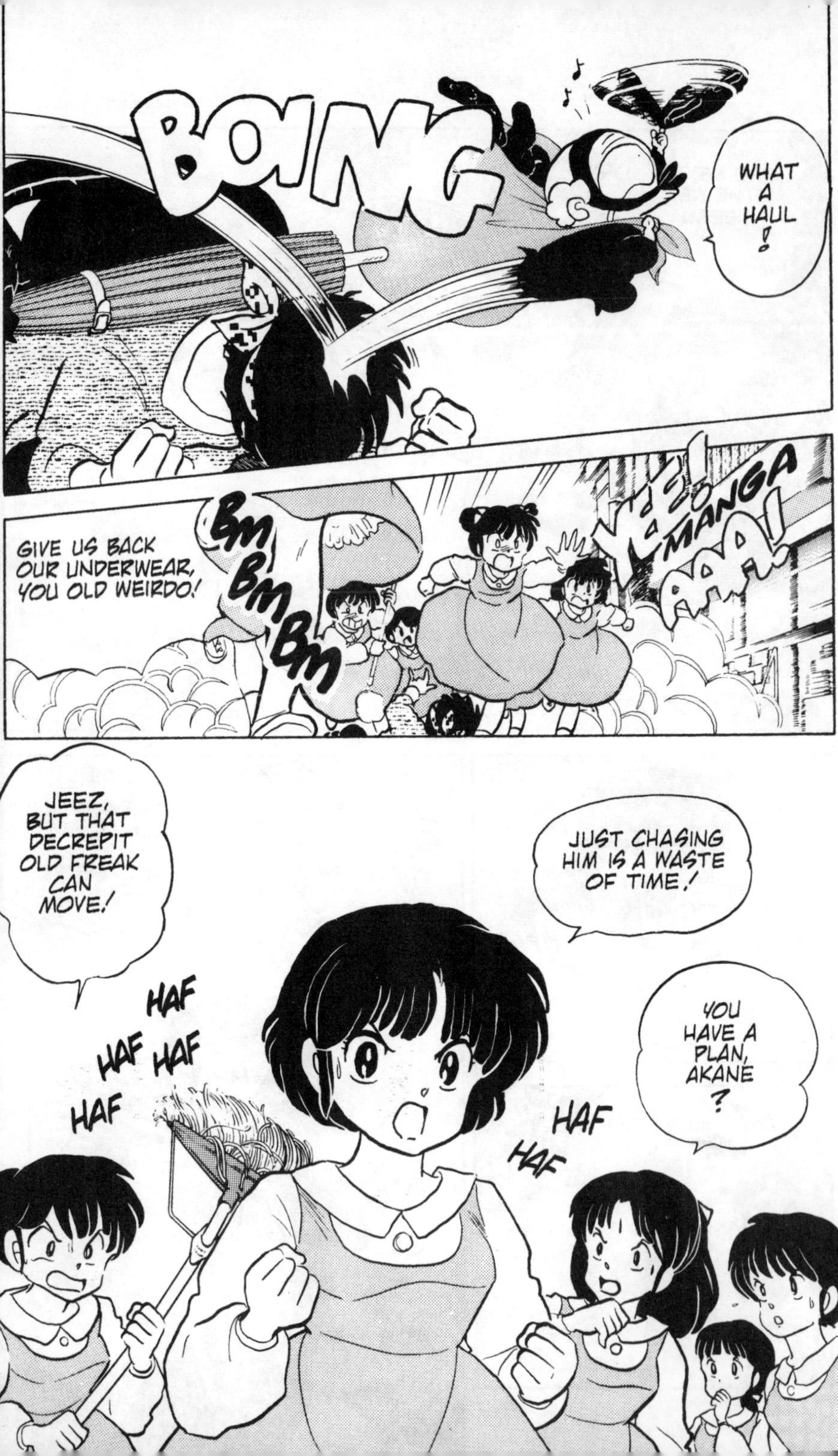
BOING
WHAT A HAUL!
GIVE US BACK OUR UNDERWEAR, YOU OLD WEIRDO!
BM BM BM BM
MANGA
AAA!
JEEZ, BUT THAT DECREPIT OLD FREAK CAN MOVE!
HAF HAF HAF HAF
JUST CHASING HIM IS A WASTE OF TIME!
HAF HAF
YOU HAVE A PLAN, AKANE?

WE'VE GOT THE MANGA FOR YOU!

HOW ABOUT THIS...?

PSST PSST PSST PSST

VVVIP

HM?

SQU...

WHAT ARE YOU DOING THERE?

R-YOGA!

H- HI.

OH, THEN YOU'RE LEAVING AGAIN, RYOGA?

YES.

WHY DON'T YOU STOP BY AND SEE RANMA? IT'S BEEN A WHILE.

I DON'T WANT TO SEE RANMA!

AKANE, THERE'S SOMETHING I MUST ASK!

YES?

FWIP

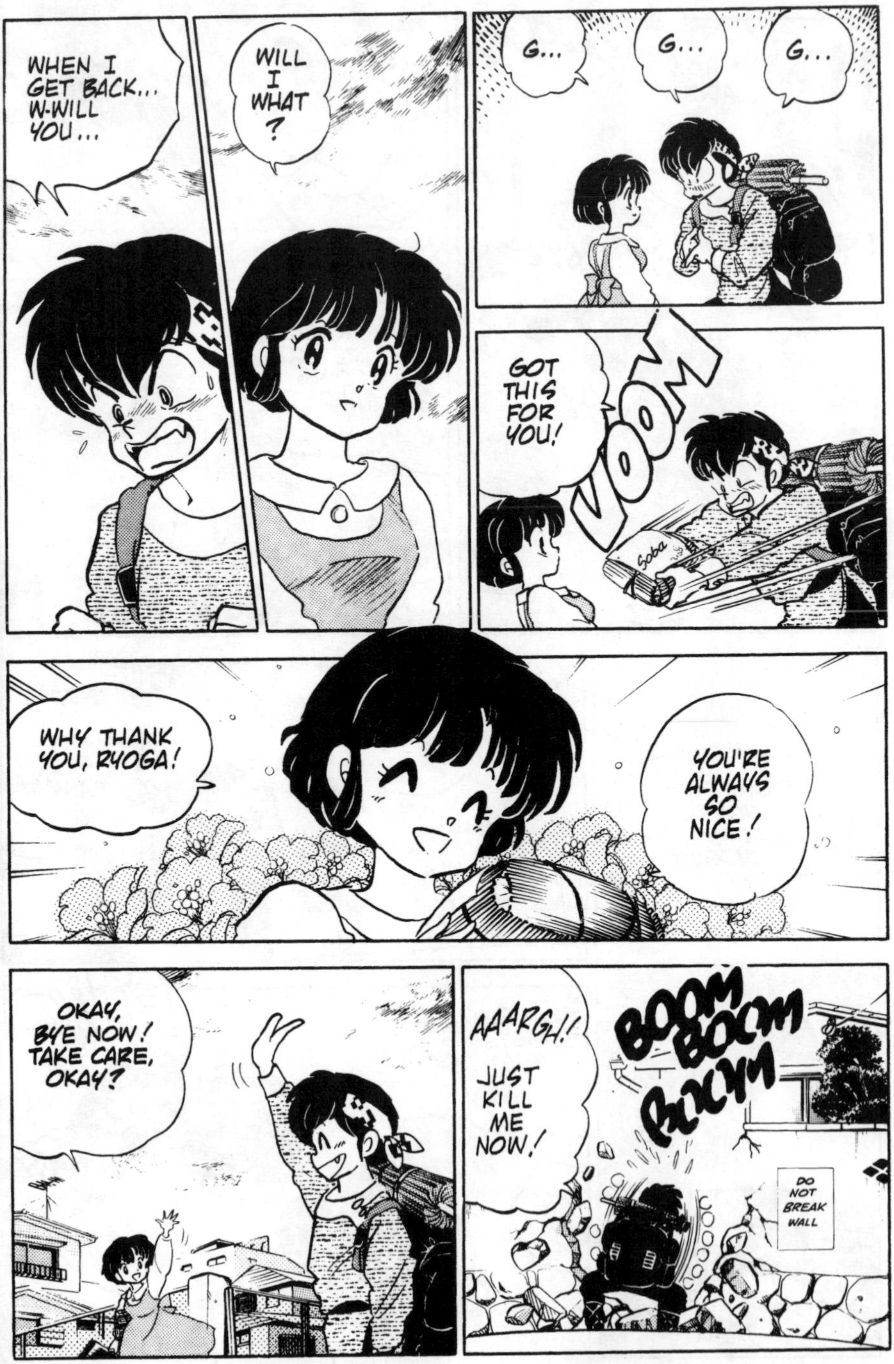
WHEN I GET BACK... W-WILL YOU...
WILL I WHAT?
G...
G...
G...
GOT THIS FOR YOU!
VOOM
Soba
WHY THANK YOU, RYOGA!
YOU'RE ALWAYS SO NICE!
OKAY, BYE NOW! TAKE CARE, OKAY?
AAARGH!! JUST KILL ME NOW!
BOOM BOOM BOOM
DO NOT BREAK WALL

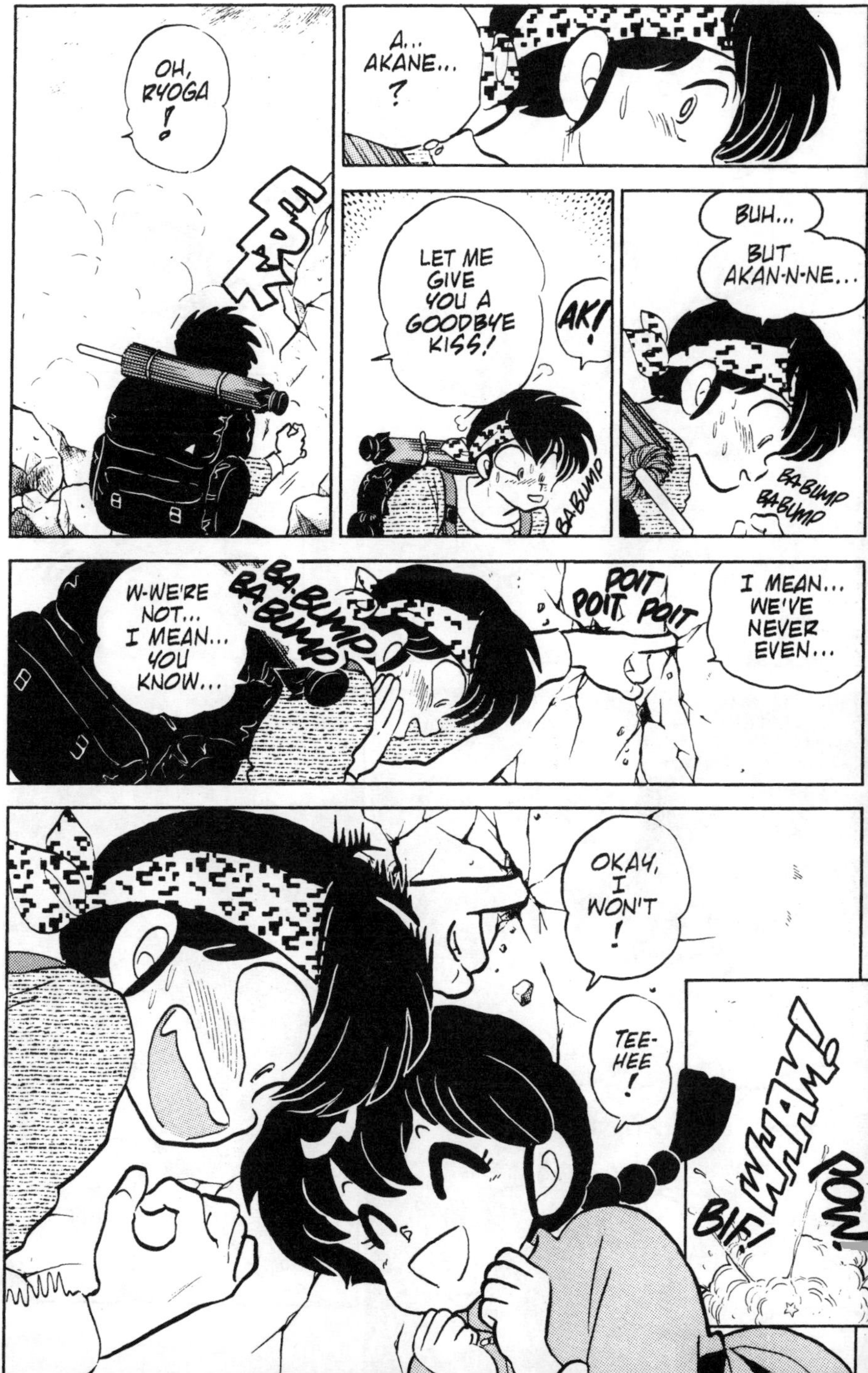
OH, RYOGA!
A... AKANE...?
LET ME GIVE YOU A GOODBYE KISS!
AK!
BA-BUMP
BUH... BUT AKAN-N-NE...
BA-BUMP BA-BUMP
W-WE'RE NOT... I MEAN... YOU KNOW...
BA-BUMP BA-BUMP
POIT POIT POIT
I MEAN... WE'VE NEVER EVEN...
OKAY, I WON'T!
TEE-HEE!
BIF! WHAM! POW!

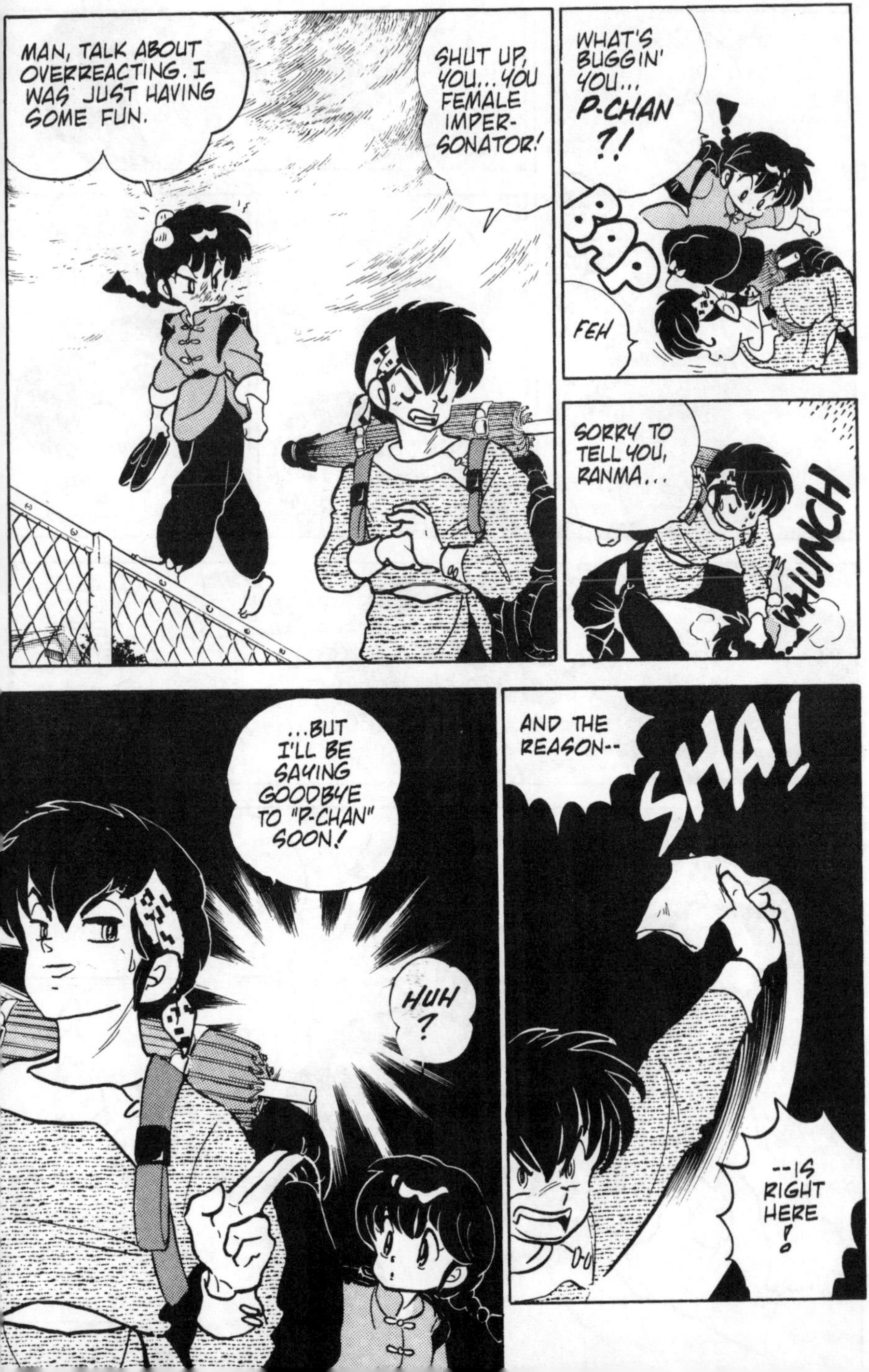
MAN, TALK ABOUT OVERREACTING. I WAS JUST HAVING SOME FUN.
SHUT UP, YOU... YOU FEMALE IMPER-SONATOR!
WHAT'S BUGGIN' YOU... P-CHAN ?!
BAP
FEH
SORRY TO TELL YOU, RANMA...
WHUNCH
...BUT I'LL BE SAYING GOODBYE TO "P-CHAN" SOON!
HUH ?
AND THE REASON--
SHA!
--IS RIGHT HERE !

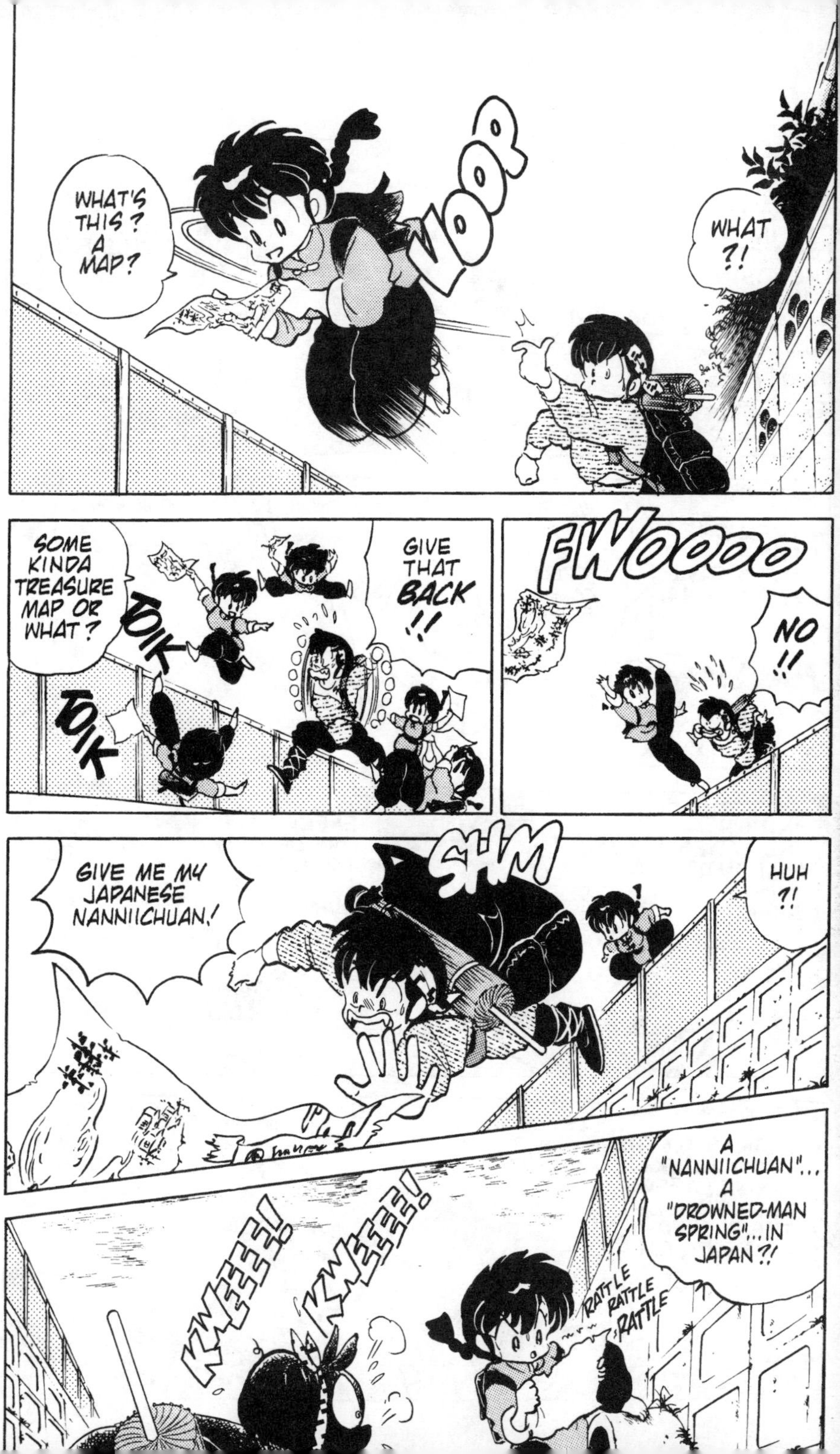
WHAT'S THIS? A MAP?
VOOP
WHAT?!
SOME KINDA TREASURE MAP OR WHAT?
TOIK
TOIK
GIVE THAT BACK!!
FWOOOOO
NO!!
GIVE ME MY JAPANESE NANNIICHUAN!
SHM
HUH?!
KWEEEE!
KWEEEE!
RATTLE RATTLE RATTLE
A "NANNIICHUAN"... A "DROWNED-MAN SPRING"... IN JAPAN?!

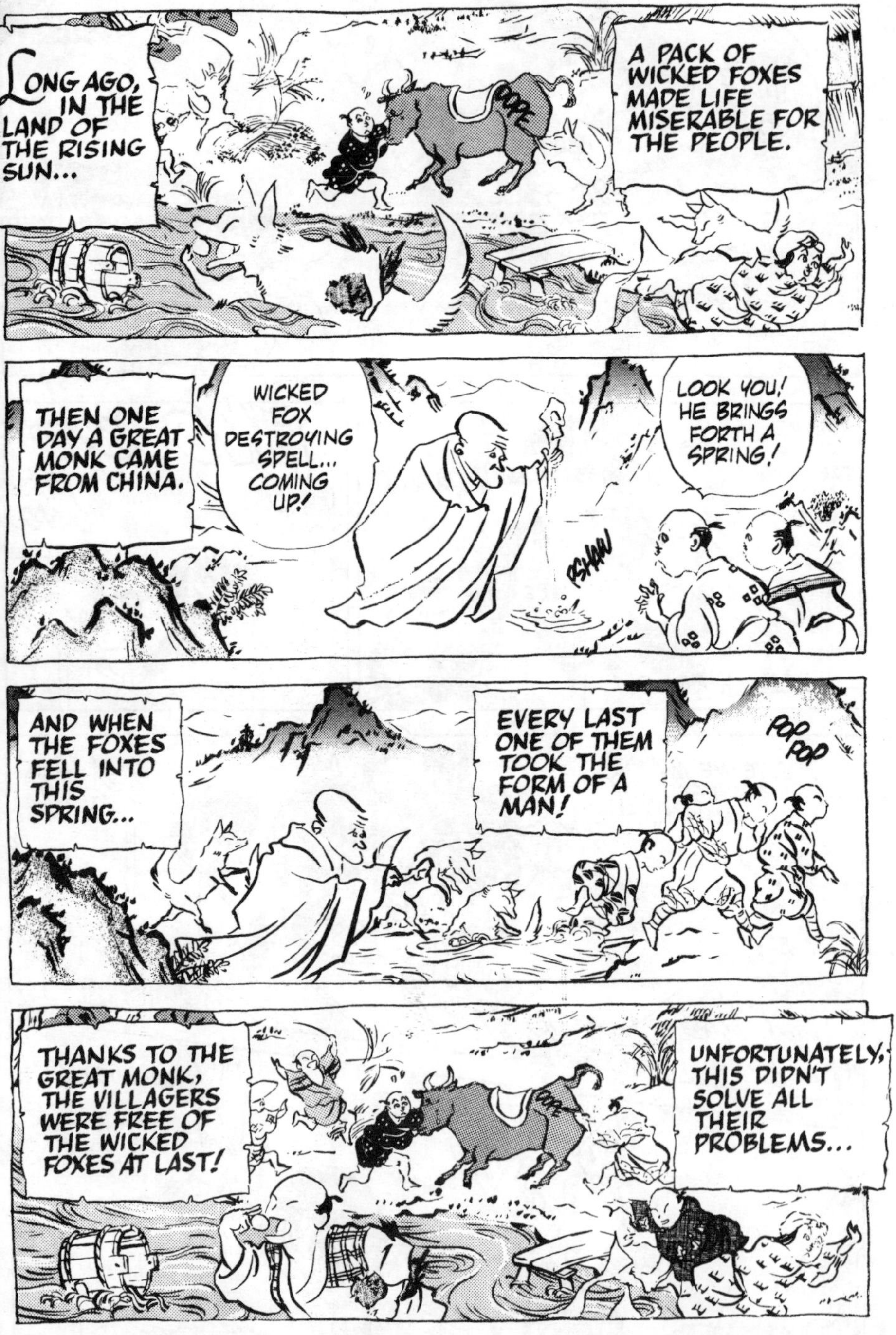
LONG AGO, IN THE LAND OF THE RISING SUN...
A PACK OF WICKED FOXES MADE LIFE MISERABLE FOR THE PEOPLE.
THEN ONE DAY A GREAT MONK CAME FROM CHINA.
WICKED FOX DESTROYING SPELL... COMING UP!
PSHAW
LOOK YOU! HE BRINGS FORTH A SPRING!
AND WHEN THE FOXES FELL INTO THIS SPRING...
EVERY LAST ONE OF THEM TOOK THE FORM OF A MAN!
POP POP
THANKS TO THE GREAT MONK, THE VILLAGERS WERE FREE OF THE WICKED FOXES AT LAST!
UNFORTUNATELY, THIS DIDN'T SOLVE ALL THEIR PROBLEMS...

IT...IT HAS TO BE! A MAGIC SPRING...THE NANNIICHUAN...

.....

SO, AS I SAY, I MUST BE GOING.

WAIT A SECOND, RYOGA!

PLOOSH

YOU?! HELP ME?! FORGET IT!

COME ON, I'LL TAKE YOU RIGHT TO THE PLACE!

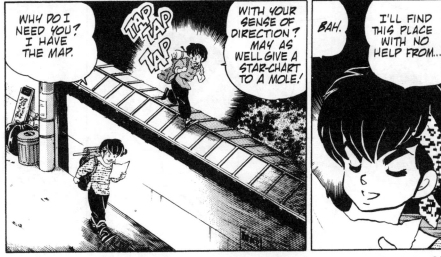

WHY DO I NEED YOU? I HAVE THE MAP.

TAP TAP TAP

WITH YOUR SENSE OF DIRECTION? MAY AS WELL GIVE A STAR-CHART TO A MOLE!

BAH.

I'LL FIND THIS PLACE WITH NO HELP FROM...

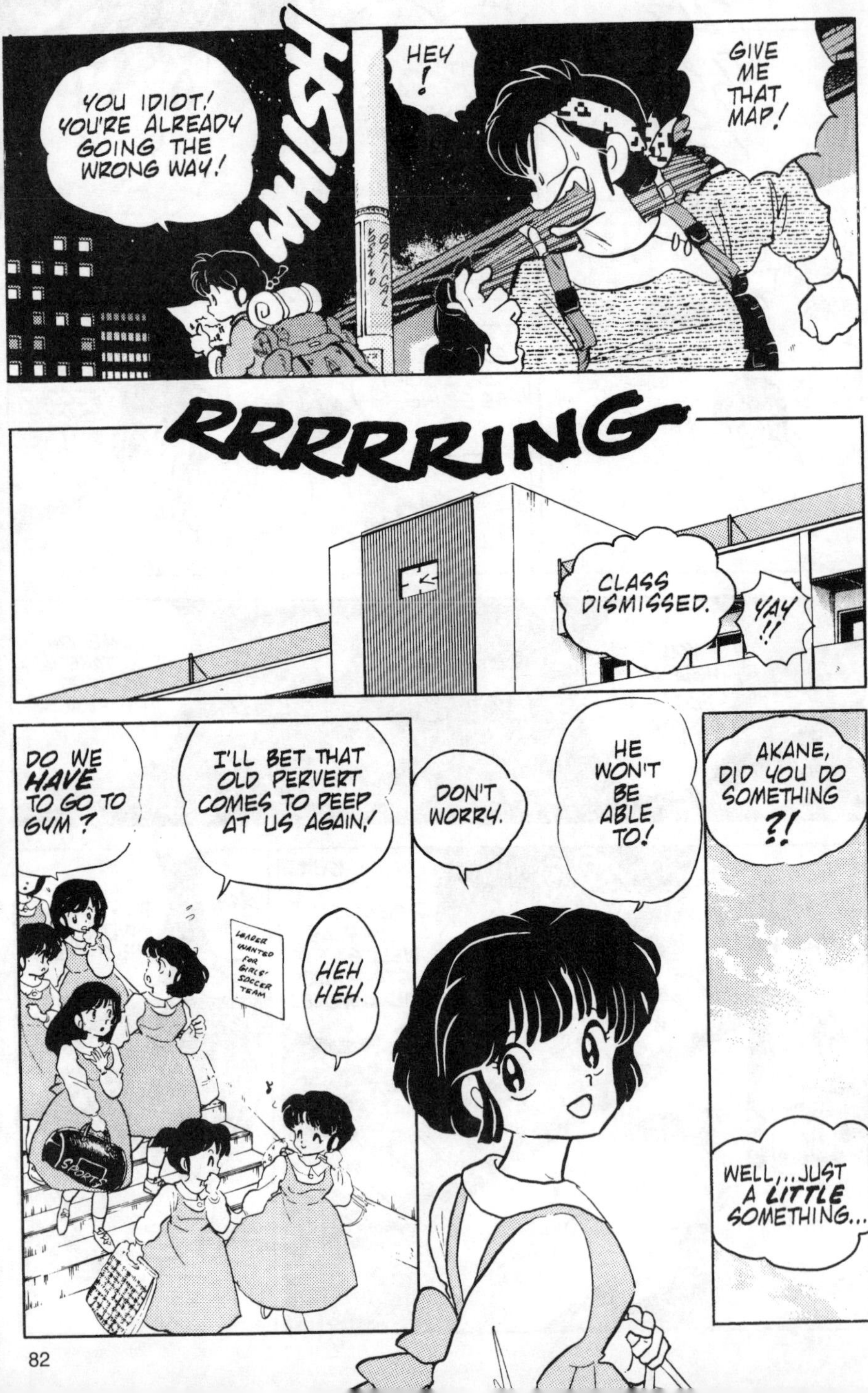
YOU IDIOT! YOU'RE ALREADY GOING THE WRONG WAY!
WHISH
HEY!
GIVE ME THAT MAP!
RRRRRING
CLASS DISMISSED.
YAY!!
DO WE HAVE TO GO TO GYM?
I'LL BET THAT OLD PERVERT COMES TO PEEP AT US AGAIN!
LEADER WANTED FOR GIRLS' SOCCER TEAM
SPORTS
HEH HEH.
DON'T WORRY.
HE WON'T BE ABLE TO!
AKANE, DID YOU DO SOMETHING?!
WELL,..JUST A LITTLE SOMETHING...

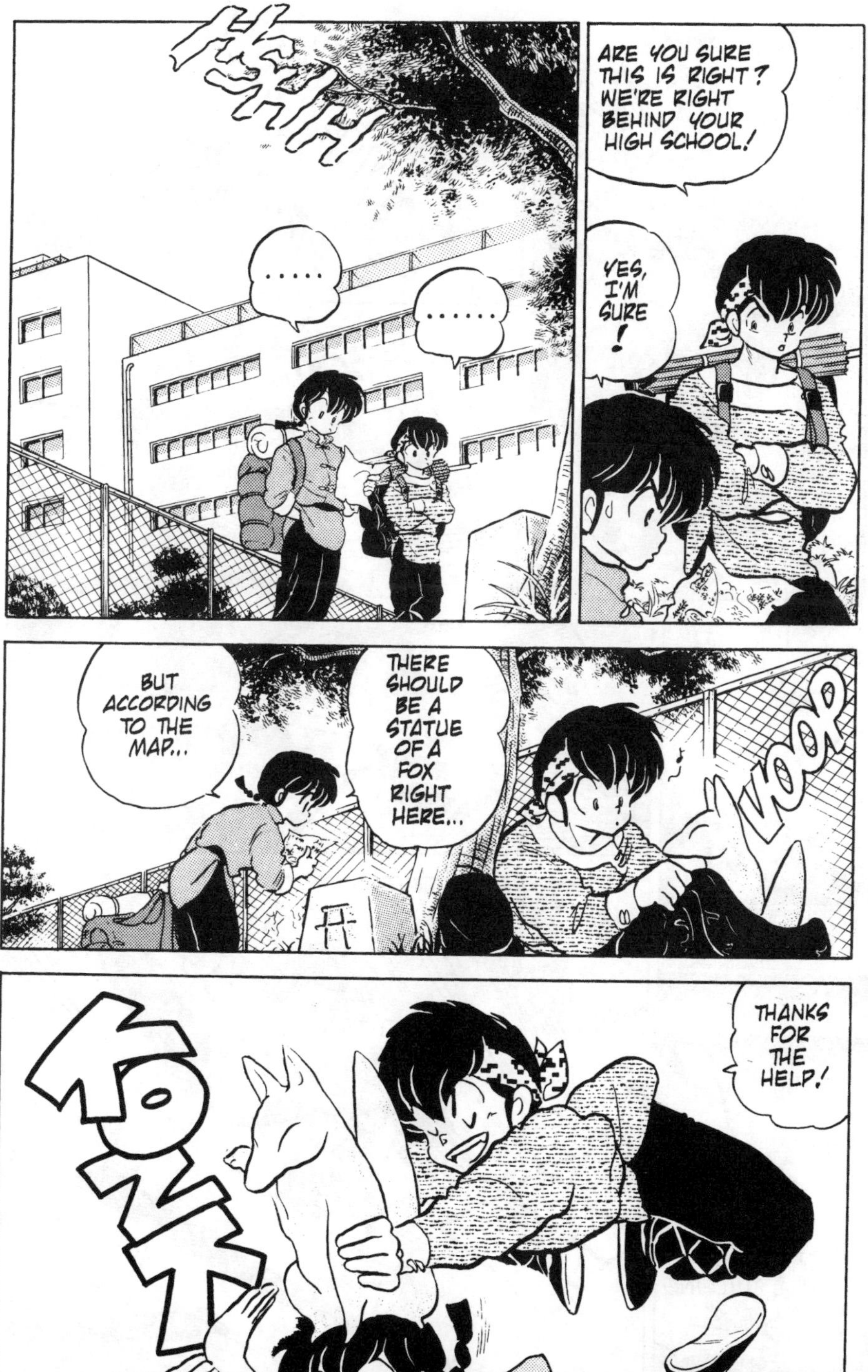
HSHH!
......
......
ARE YOU SURE THIS IS RIGHT? WE'RE RIGHT BEHIND YOUR HIGH SCHOOL!
YES, I'M SURE!
BUT ACCORDING TO THE MAP...
THERE SHOULD BE A STATUE OF A FOX RIGHT HERE...
VOOP
KONK
THANKS FOR THE HELP!

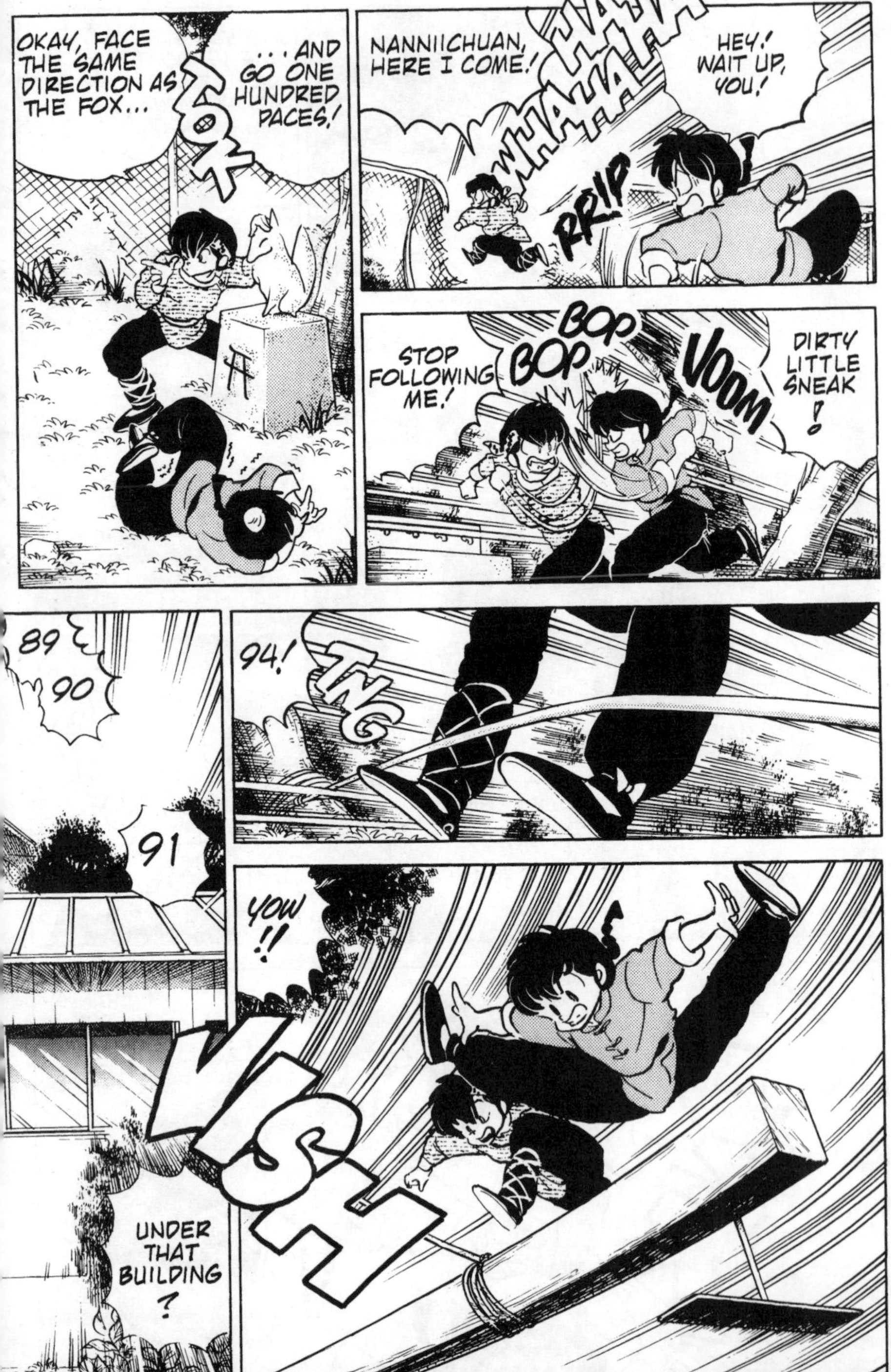

OKAY, FACE THE SAME DIRECTION AS THE FOX...
TOK
...AND GO ONE HUNDRED PACES!
NANNIICHUAN, HERE I COME!
WHAHAHAHA HAHAHA
HEY! WAIT UP, YOU!
RRIP
STOP FOLLOWING ME!
BOP BOP
VOOM
DIRTY LITTLE SNEAK!
89
90
91
UNDER THAT BUILDING?
94!
TNG
YOW!!
VISH

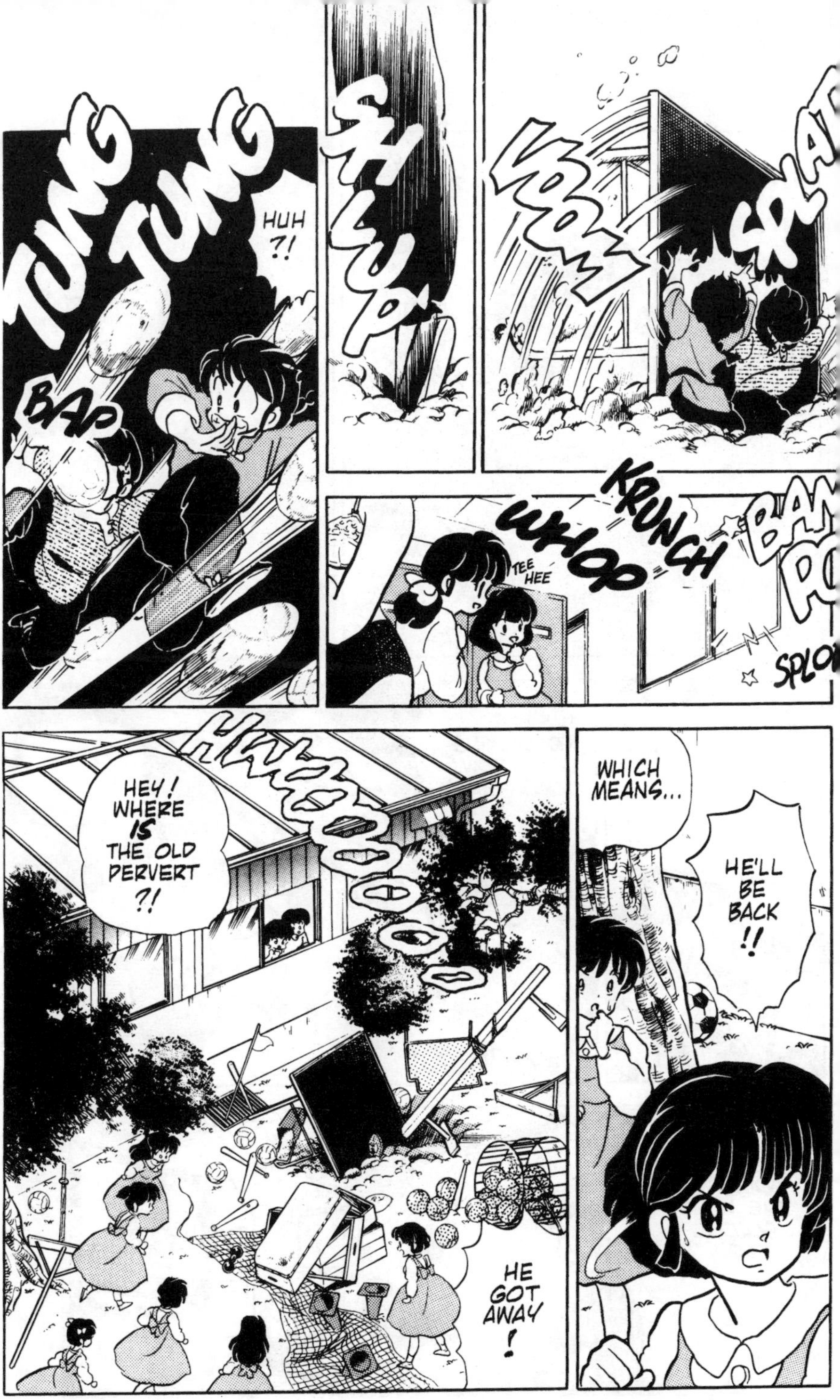
TUNG TUNG
HUH ?!
BAP
SHLUP
VROOM
SPLAT
TEE HEE
WHOP
KRUNCH
BAM
PO
SPLO
HYOOOOO
HEY! WHERE IS THE OLD PERVERT ?!
HE GOT AWAY!
WHICH MEANS...
HE'LL BE BACK !!

# PART SIX

# THE TROUBLE WITH GIRLS' LOCKER ROOMS

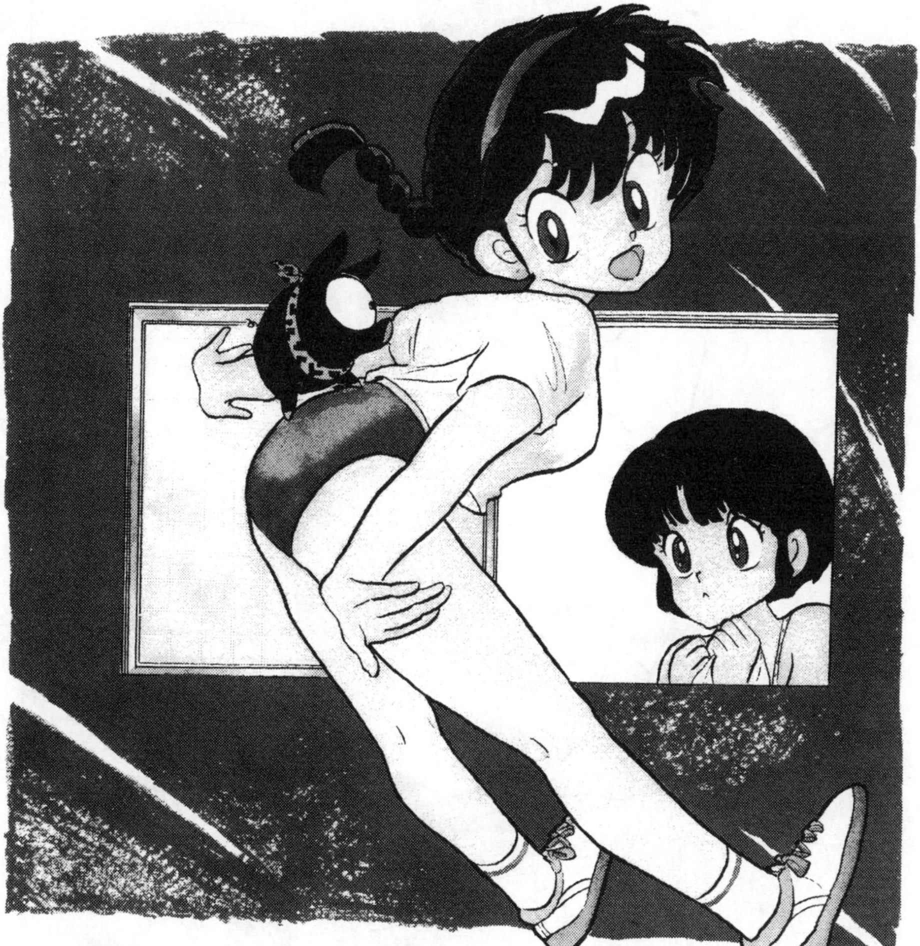

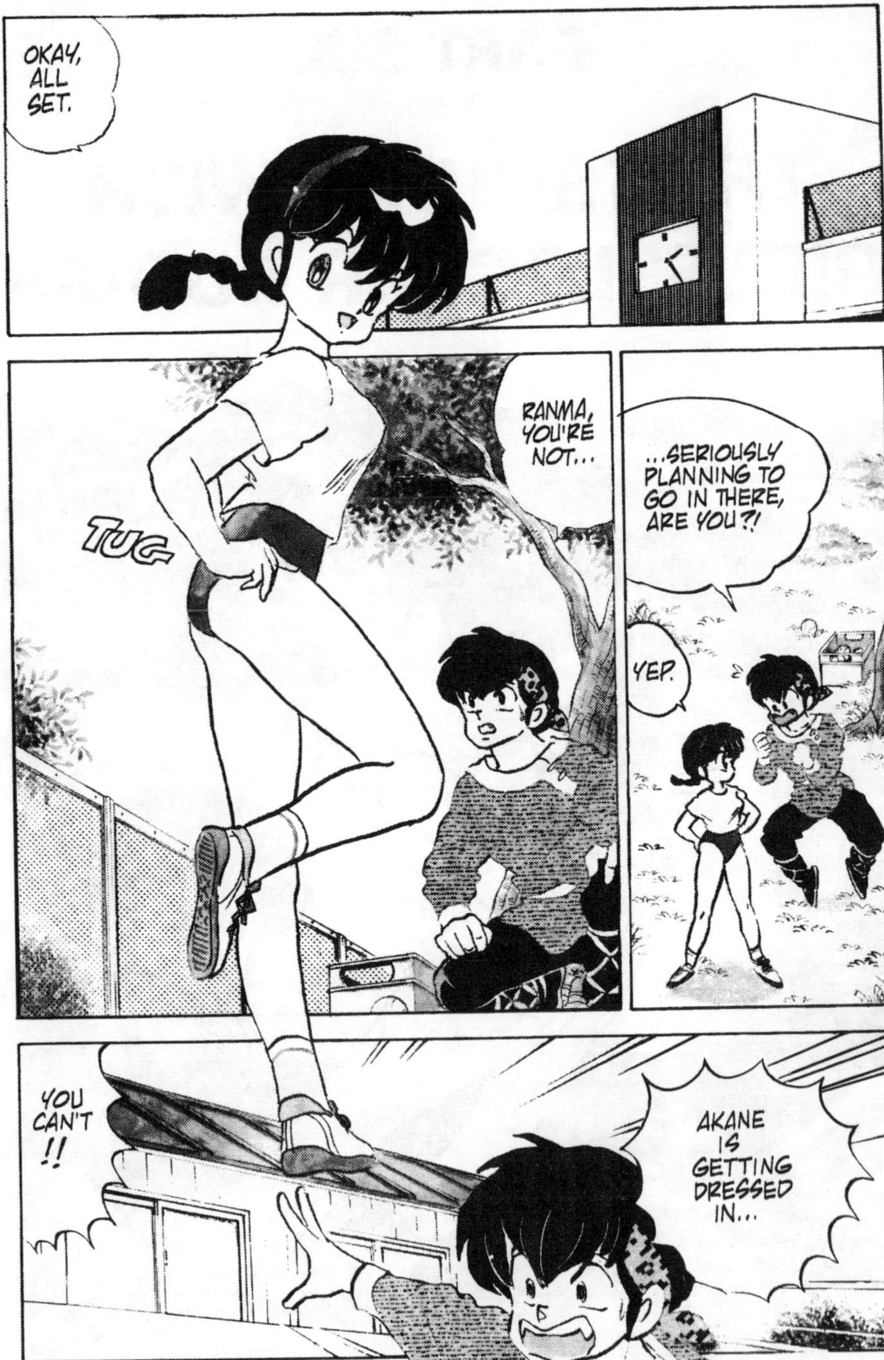
OKAY, ALL SET.
TUG
RANMA, YOU'RE NOT...
...SERIOUSLY PLANNING TO GO IN THERE, ARE YOU?!
YEP.
YOU CAN'T!!
AKANE IS GETTING DRESSED IN...

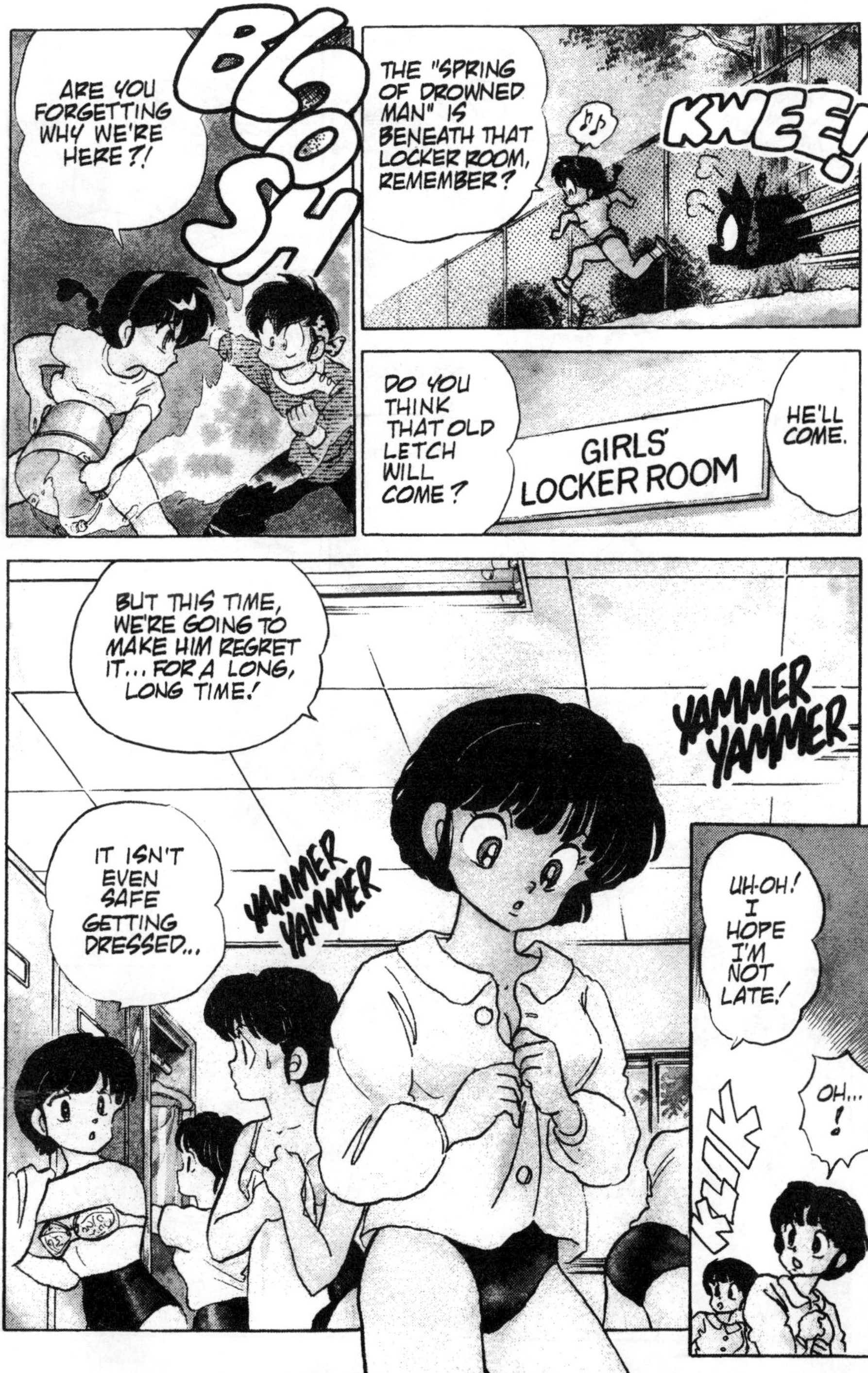
ARE YOU FORGETTING WHY WE'RE HERE?!
BLOOSH
THE "SPRING OF DROWNED MAN" IS BENEATH THAT LOCKER ROOM, REMEMBER?
KWEE!
DO YOU THINK THAT OLD LETCH WILL COME?
GIRLS' LOCKER ROOM
HE'LL COME.
BUT THIS TIME, WE'RE GOING TO MAKE HIM REGRET IT... FOR A LONG, LONG TIME!
YAMMER YAMMER
IT ISN'T EVEN SAFE GETTING DRESSED...
YAMMER YAMMER
UH-OH! I HOPE I'M NOT LATE!
KLIK
OH... !

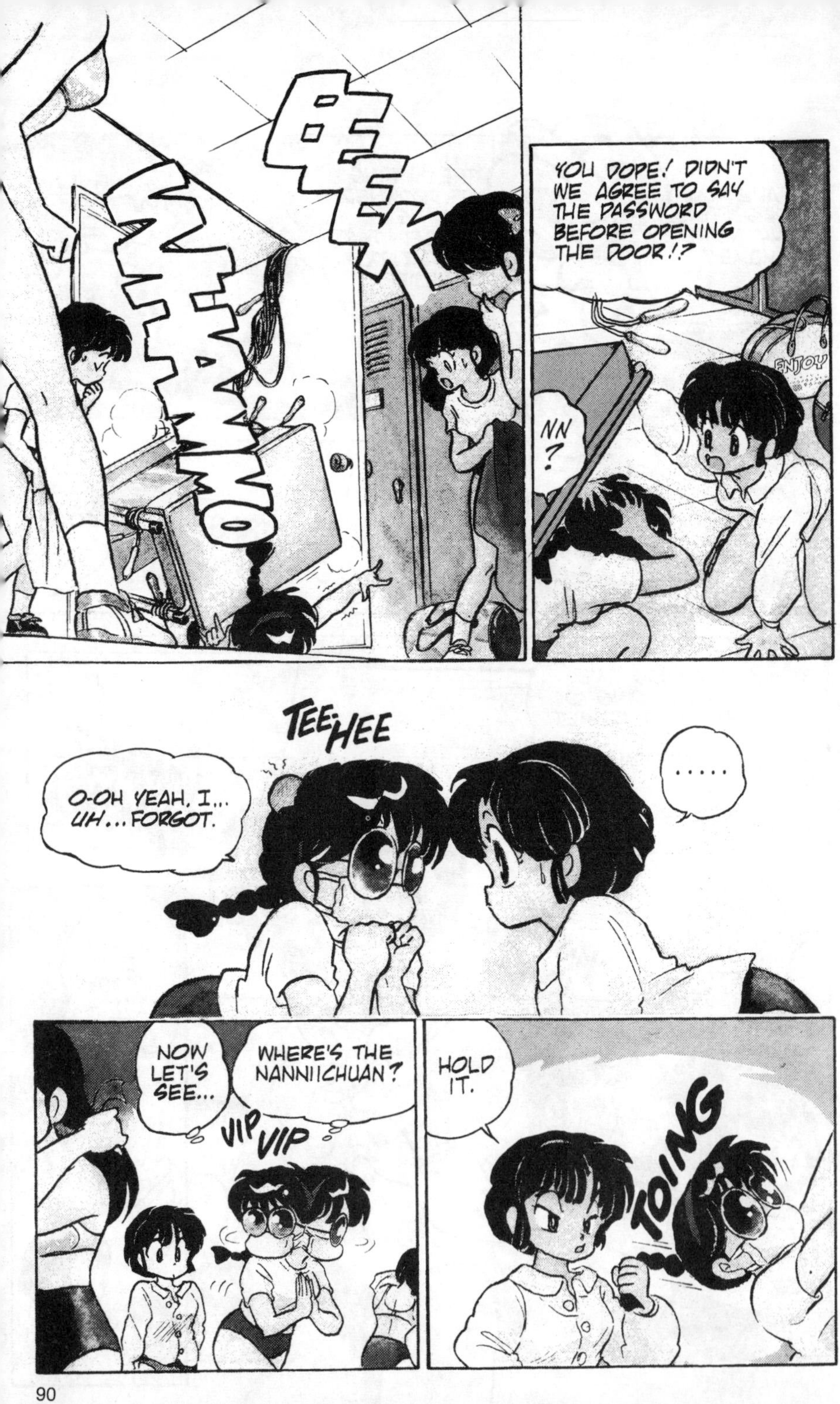
BEEK
WHAMMO
YOU DOPE! DIDN'T WE AGREE TO SAY THE PASSWORD BEFORE OPENING THE DOOR!?
NN ?
ENJOY
TEE-HEE
O-OH YEAH, I... UH... FORGOT.
.....
NOW LET'S SEE...
WHERE'S THE NANNIICHUAN?
VIP VIP
HOLD IT.
TOING

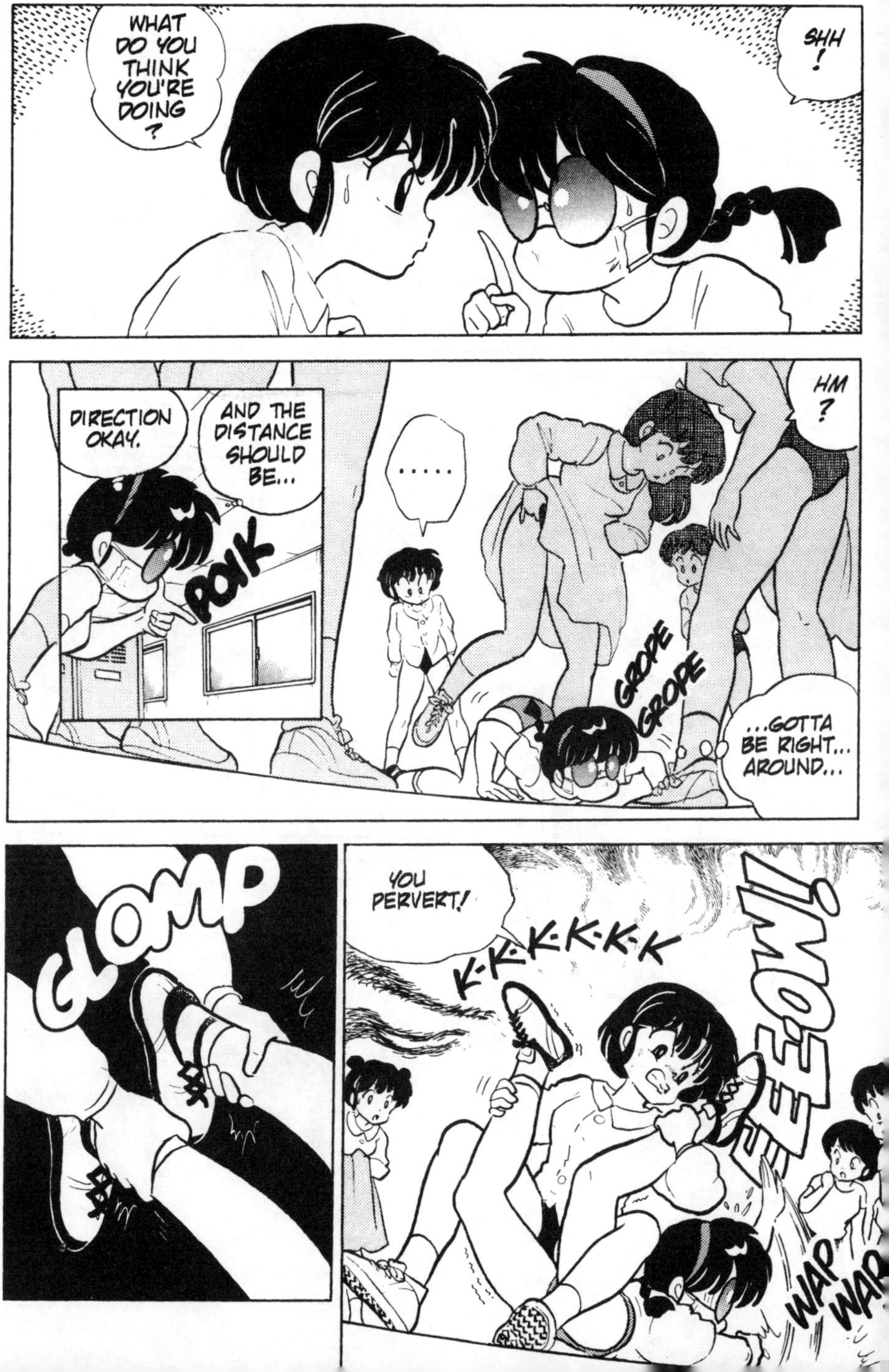
WHAT DO YOU THINK YOU'RE DOING ?
SHH !
DIRECTION OKAY.
AND THE DISTANCE SHOULD BE...
POIK
.....
HM ?
GROPE GROPE
...GOTTA BE RIGHT... AROUND...
GLOMP
YOU PERVERT!
K-K-K-K-K-K-K
EE-OW!!
WAP WAP

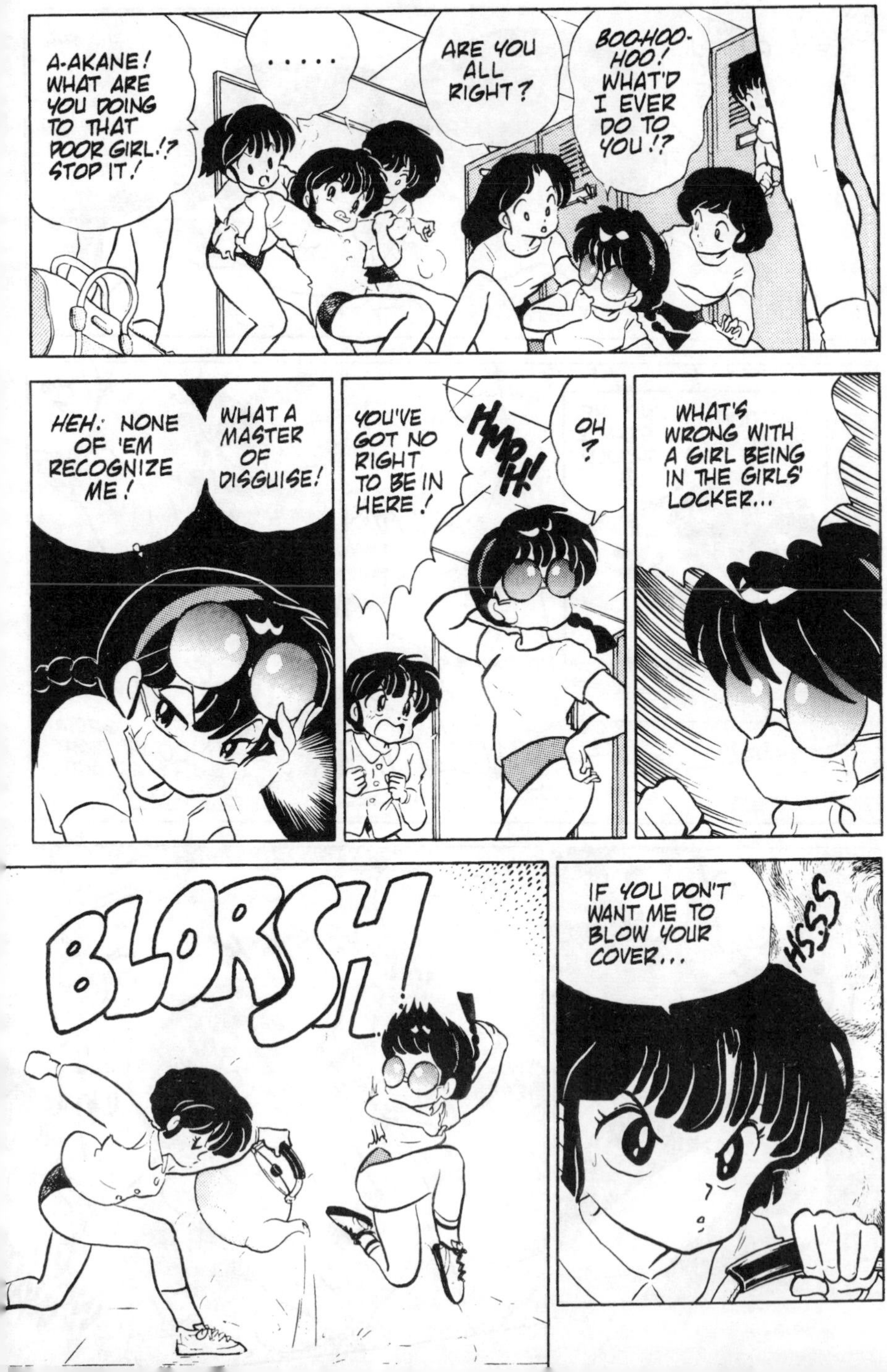
A-AKANE! WHAT ARE YOU DOING TO THAT POOR GIRL!? STOP IT!
. . . . .
ARE YOU ALL RIGHT?
BOO-HOO-HOO! WHAT'D I EVER DO TO YOU!?
HEH: NONE OF 'EM RECOGNIZE ME!
WHAT A MASTER OF DISGUISE!
YOU'VE GOT NO RIGHT TO BE IN HERE!
HMPH!
OH?
WHAT'S WRONG WITH A GIRL BEING IN THE GIRLS' LOCKER...
BLORSH
IF YOU DON'T WANT ME TO BLOW YOUR COVER...
HSSS

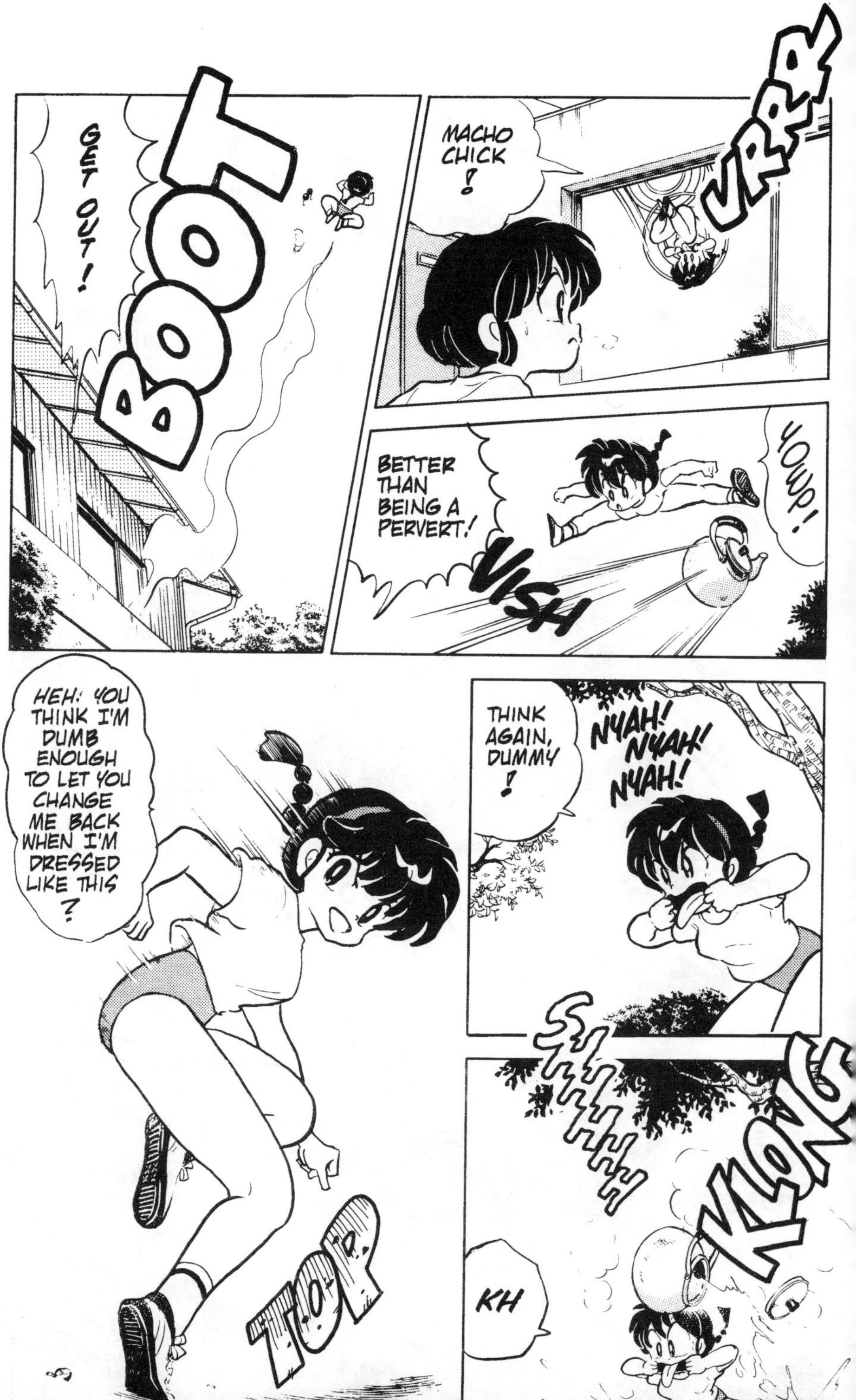

GET OUT!
BOOT
MACHO CHICK!
VRRR
BETTER THAN BEING A PERVERT!
VISH
YOWP!
HEH: YOU THINK I'M DUMB ENOUGH TO LET YOU CHANGE ME BACK WHEN I'M DRESSED LIKE THIS?
TOP
THINK AGAIN, DUMMY!
NYAH! NYAH! NYAH!
SHHHH
KLONG
KH

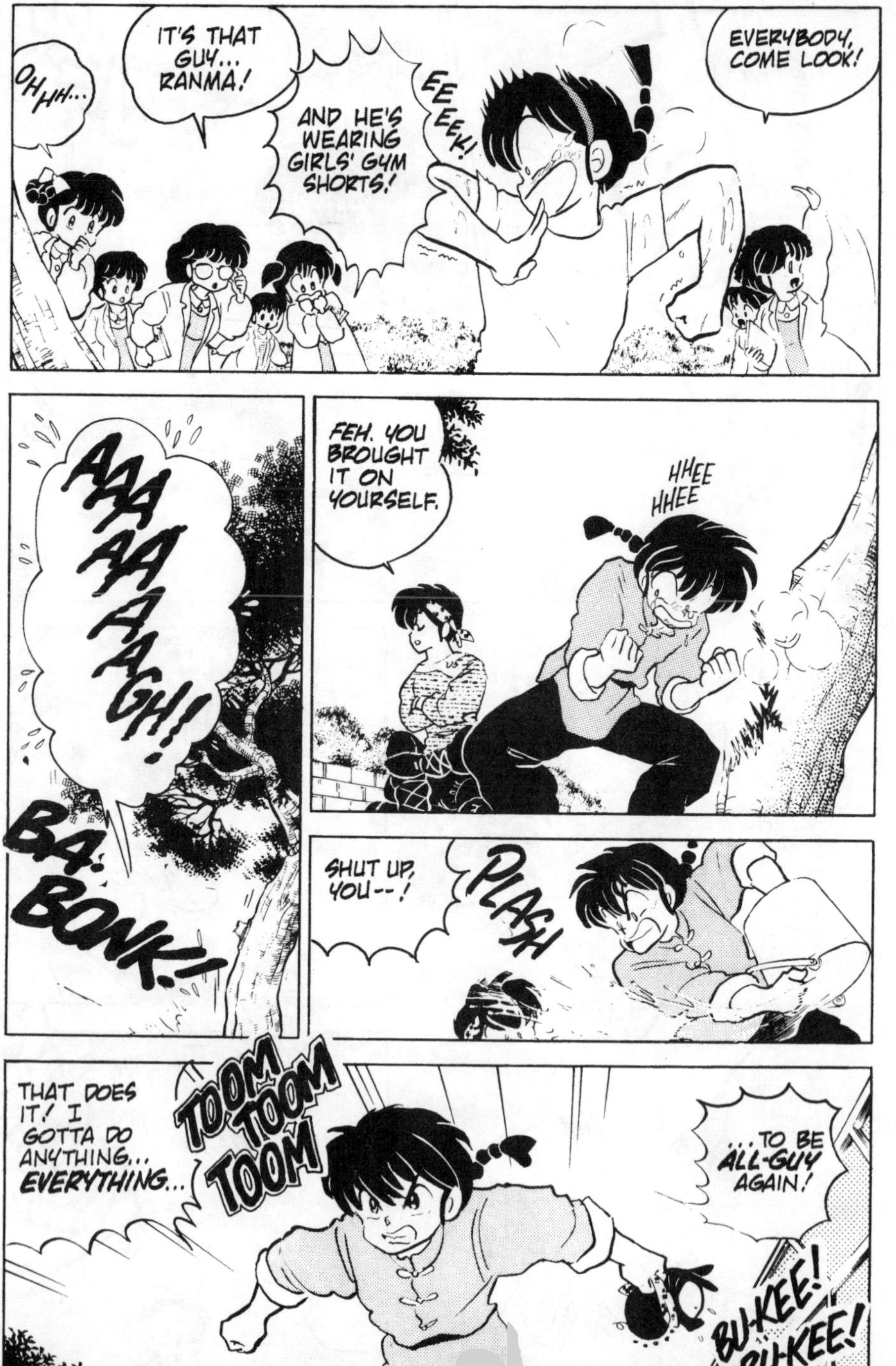
OHHHH...
IT'S THAT GUY... RANMA!
AND HE'S WEARING GIRLS' GYM SHORTS!
EEEEK!
EVERYBODY, COME LOOK!
AAAAAAAAAGH!!
BA-BONK-!!
FEH. YOU BROUGHT IT ON YOURSELF.
HHEE HHEE
SHUT UP, YOU--!
PLASH
THAT DOES IT! I GOTTA DO ANYTHING... EVERYTHING...
TOOM TOOM TOOM
...TO BE ALL-GUY AGAIN!
BU-KEE! BU-KEE!

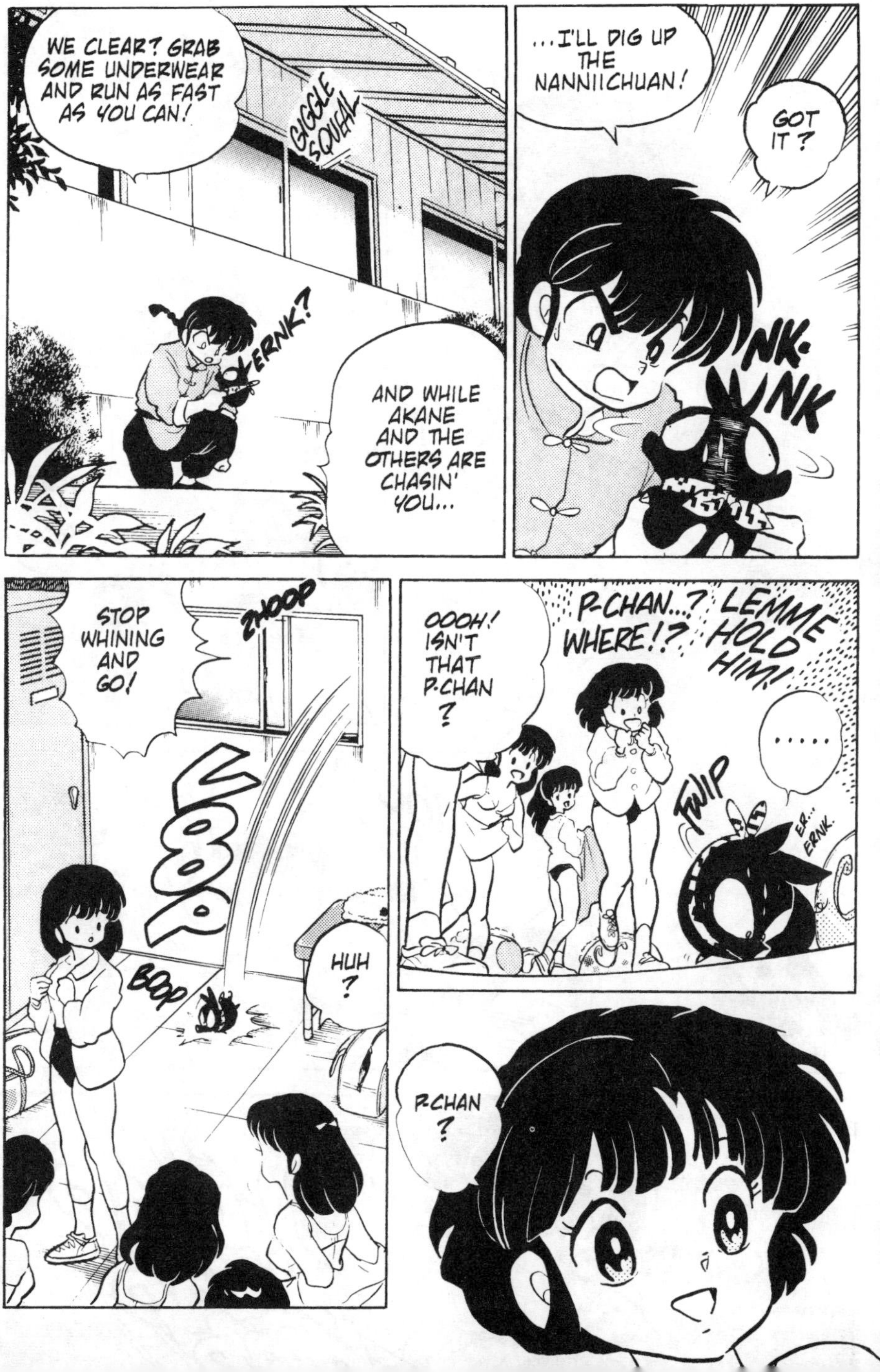
WE CLEAR? GRAB SOME UNDERWEAR AND RUN AS FAST AS YOU CAN!
GIGGLE SQUEAL
ERNK?
AND WHILE AKANE AND THE OTHERS ARE CHASIN' YOU...
...I'LL DIG UP THE NANNIICHUAN!
GOT IT?
NK-UNK
STOP WHINING AND GO!
ZHOOP
VOOOP
BOOP
HUH?
OOOH! ISN'T THAT P-CHAN?
P-CHAN...? WHERE!?
LEMME HOLD HIM!
.....
FWIP
ER... ERNK.
P-CHAN?

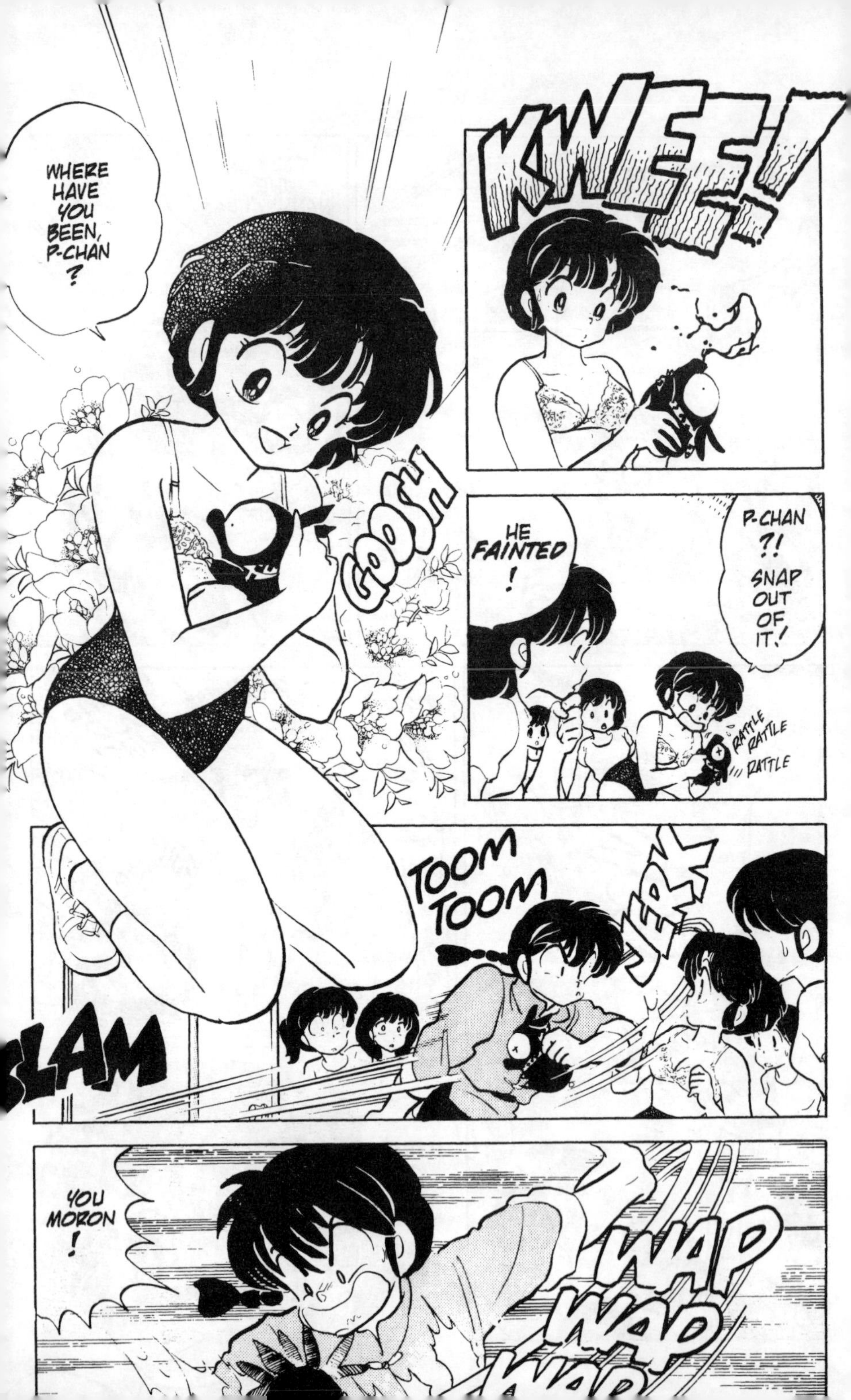
WHERE HAVE YOU BEEN, P-CHAN?
GOOSH
KWEE!!
HE FAINTED!
P-CHAN?! SNAP OUT OF IT!
RATTLE RATTLE RATTLE
SLAM
TOOM TOOM
JERK
YOU MORON!
WAP WAP

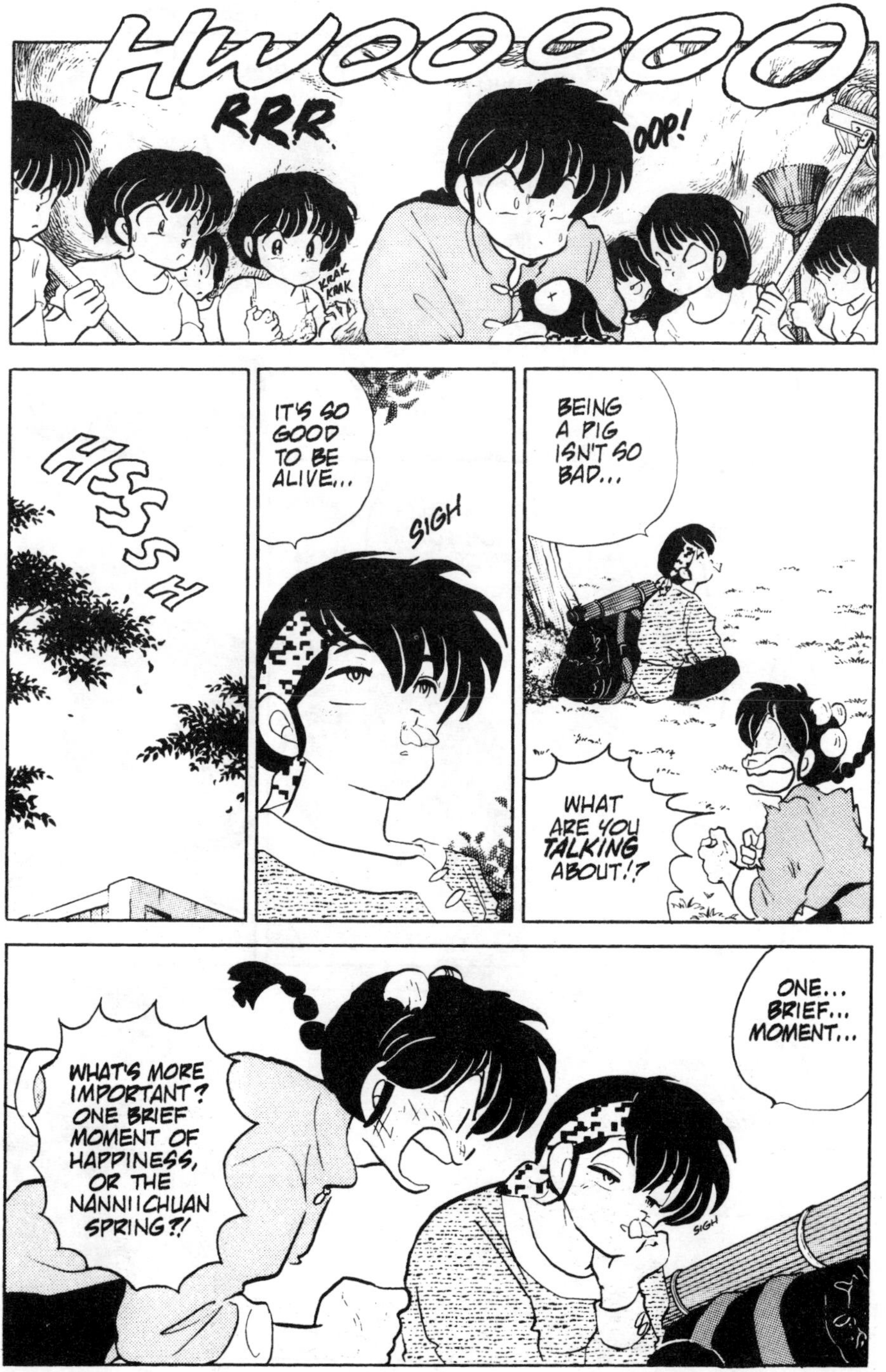

HWOOOOOO
RRR
OOP!
KRAK KRAK
HSSSH
IT'S SO GOOD TO BE ALIVE...
SIGH
BEING A PIG ISN'T SO BAD...
WHAT ARE YOU TALKING ABOUT!?
WHAT'S MORE IMPORTANT? ONE BRIEF MOMENT OF HAPPINESS, OR THE NANNIICHUAN SPRING?!
ONE... BRIEF... MOMENT...
SIGH

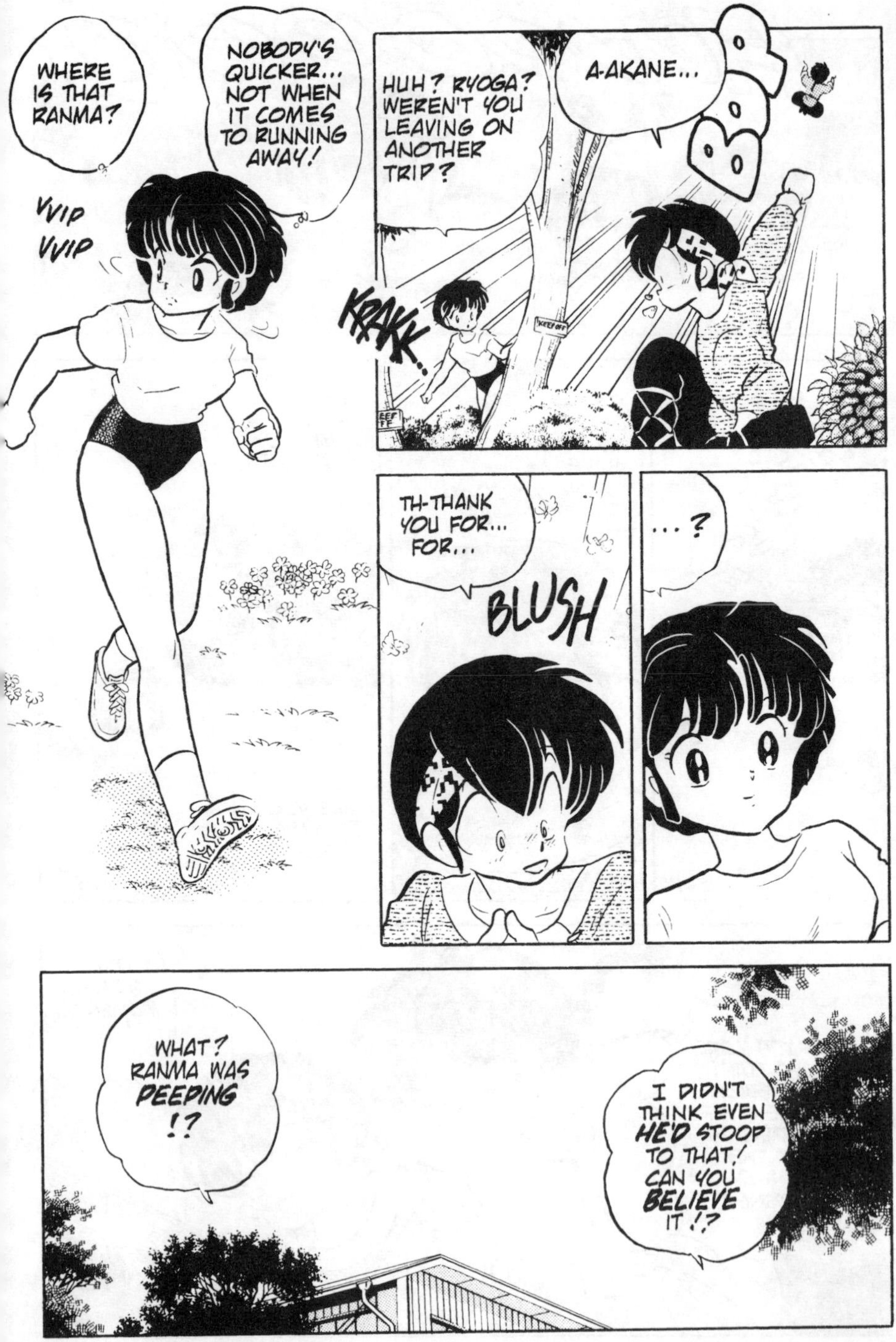
WHERE IS THAT RANMA?
NOBODY'S QUICKER... NOT WHEN IT COMES TO RUNNING AWAY!
VVIP VVIP
HUH? RYOGA? WEREN'T YOU LEAVING ON ANOTHER TRIP?
A-AKANE...
KRAKK
TH-THANK YOU FOR... FOR...
BLUSH
...?
WHAT? RANMA WAS PEEPING!?
I DIDN'T THINK EVEN HE'D STOOP TO THAT! CAN YOU BELIEVE IT!?

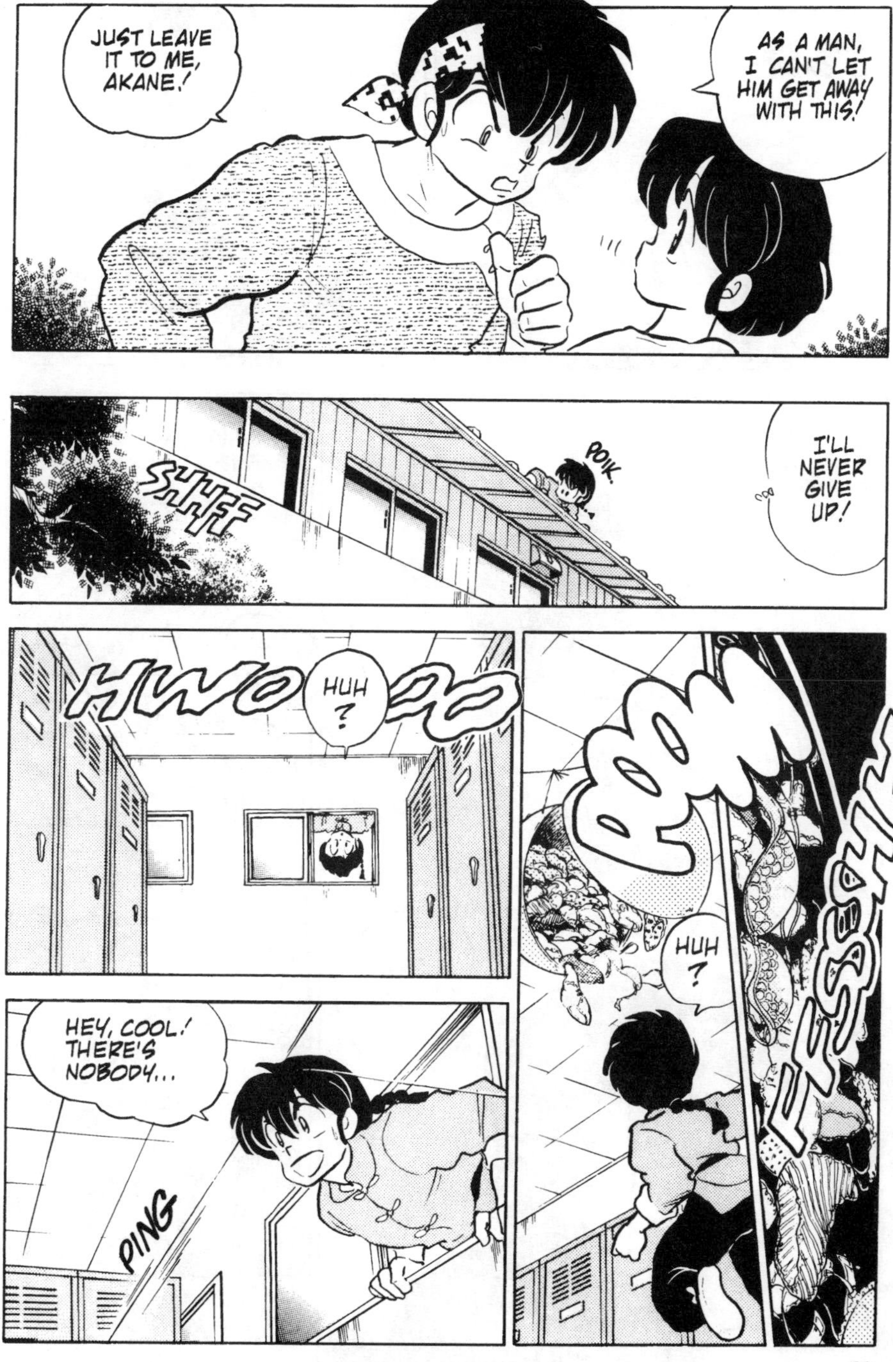
JUST LEAVE IT TO ME, AKANE!
AS A MAN, I CAN'T LET HIM GET AWAY WITH THIS!
SHFF
POIK.
I'LL NEVER GIVE UP!
HWOOO
HUH?
HEY, COOL! THERE'S NOBODY...
PING
BOOM
HUH?
FSSSHH

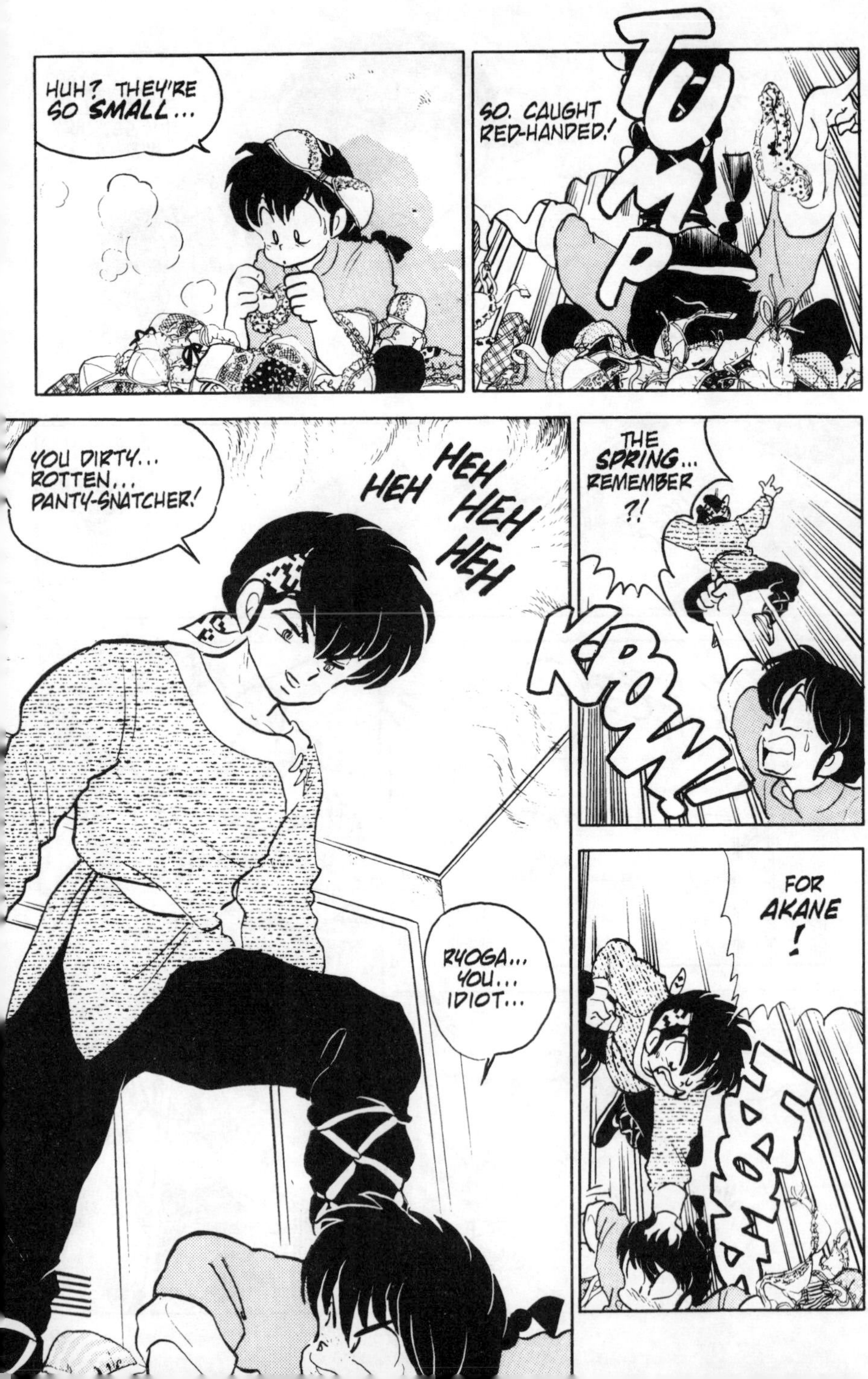
HUH? THEY'RE SO SMALL...
SO. CAUGHT RED-HANDED!
TOMP
YOU DIRTY... ROTTEN... PANTY-SNATCHER!
HEH HEH HEH HEH
RYOGA... YOU... IDIOT...
THE SPRING... REMEMBER ?!
KPOW!
FOR AKANE !
THOOMP

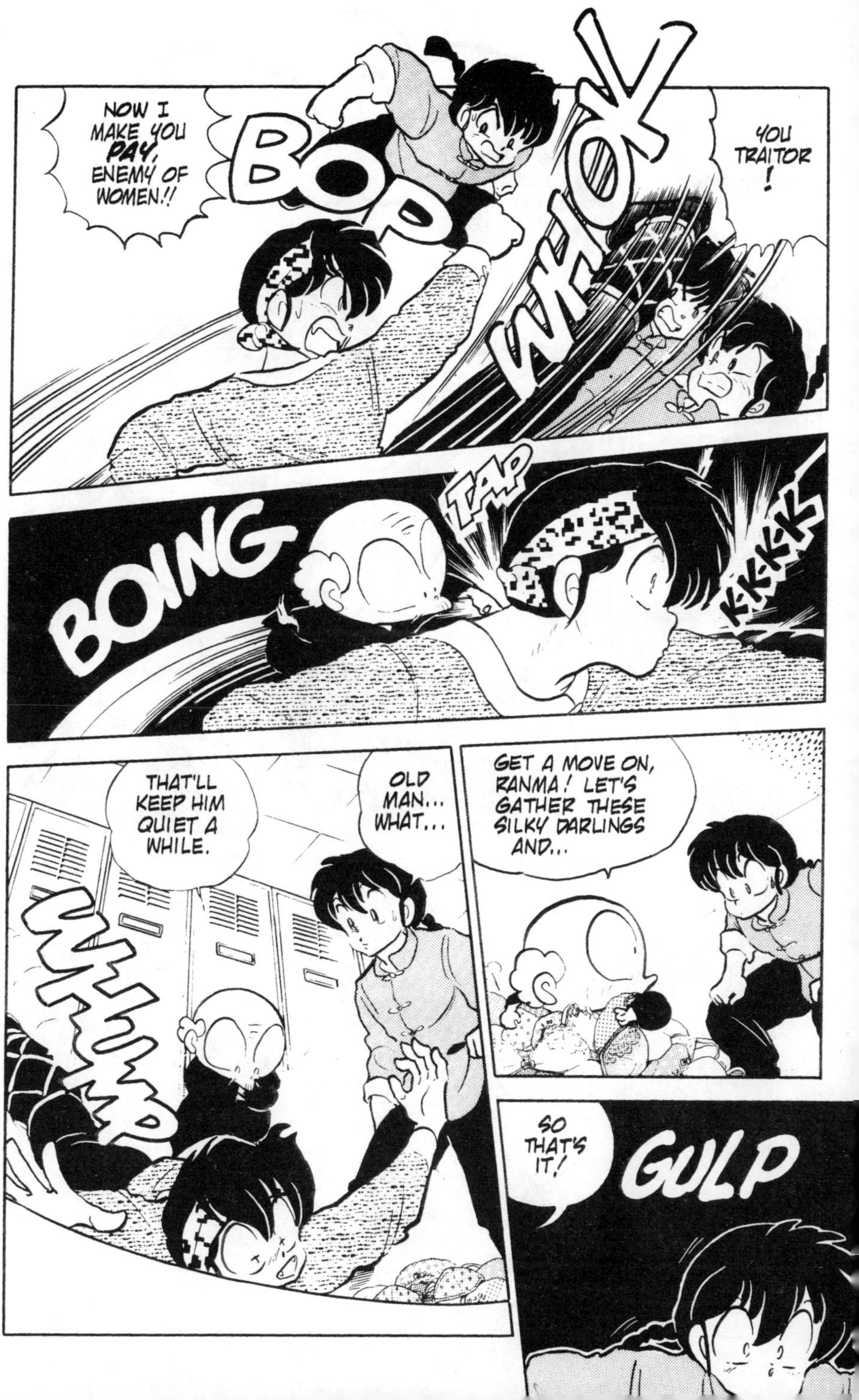
NOW I MAKE YOU PAY, ENEMY OF WOMEN!!
BOP
WHOK
YOU TRAITOR!
BOING
TAP
K-K-K-K
THAT'LL KEEP HIM QUIET A WHILE.
OLD MAN... WHAT...
WHUMP
GET A MOVE ON, RANMA! LET'S GATHER THESE SILKY DARLINGS AND...
SO THAT'S IT!
GULP

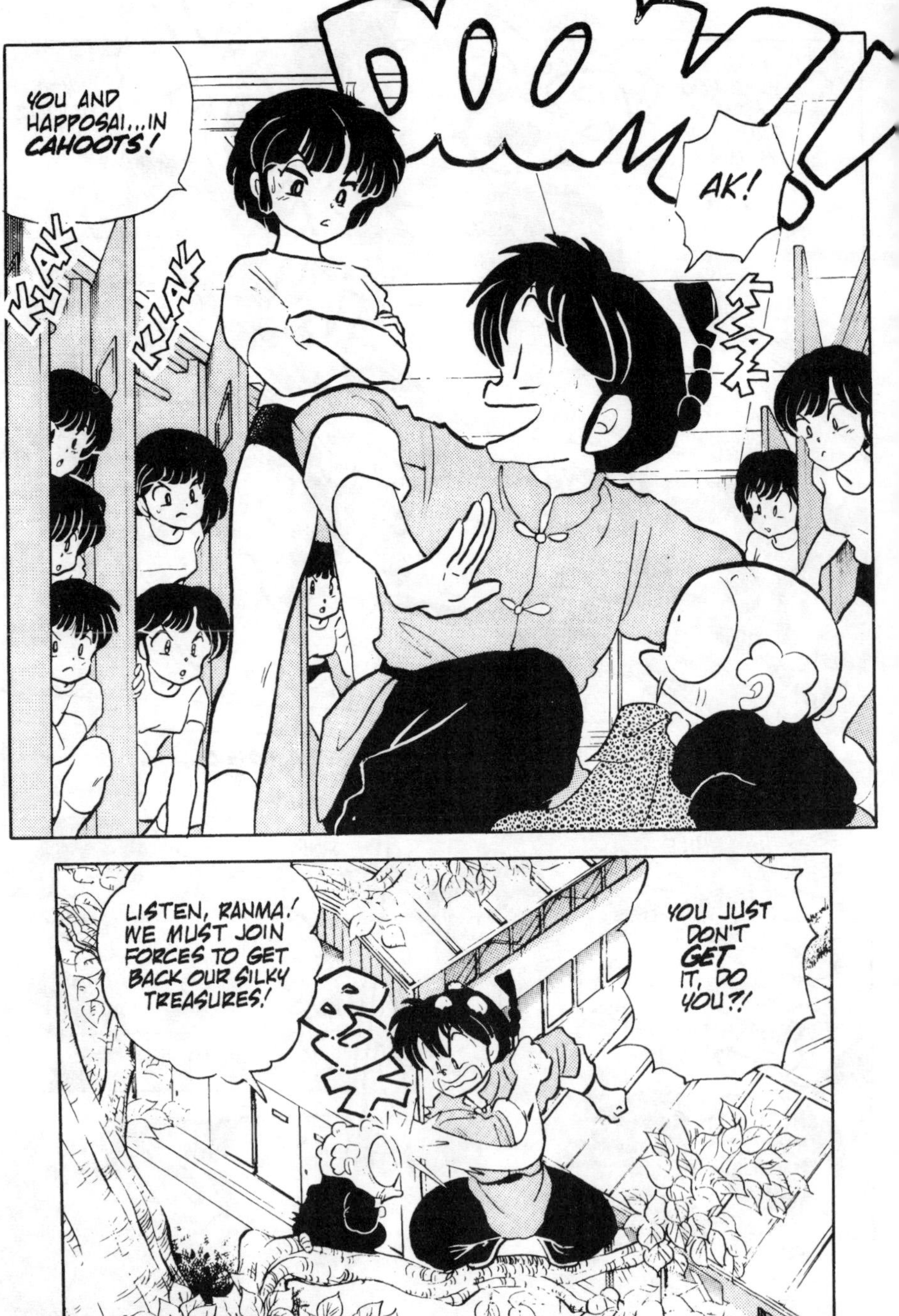
YOU AND HAPPOSAI...IN CAHOOTS!
KLAK
KLAK
DOOM!
AK!
KLAK
LISTEN, RANMA! WE MUST JOIN FORCES TO GET BACK OUR SILKY TREASURES!
YOU JUST DON'T GET IT, DO YOU?!

# PART SEVEN

# FROM THE SPRING, SPRINGS A MESSAGE

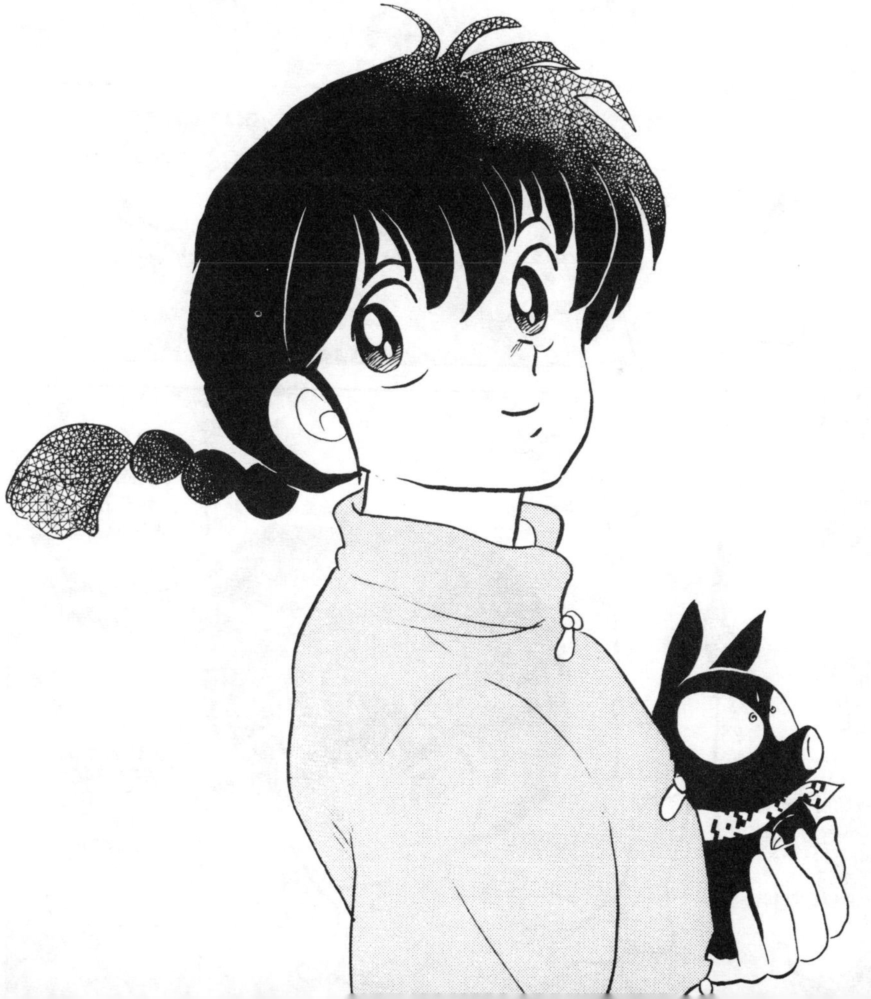

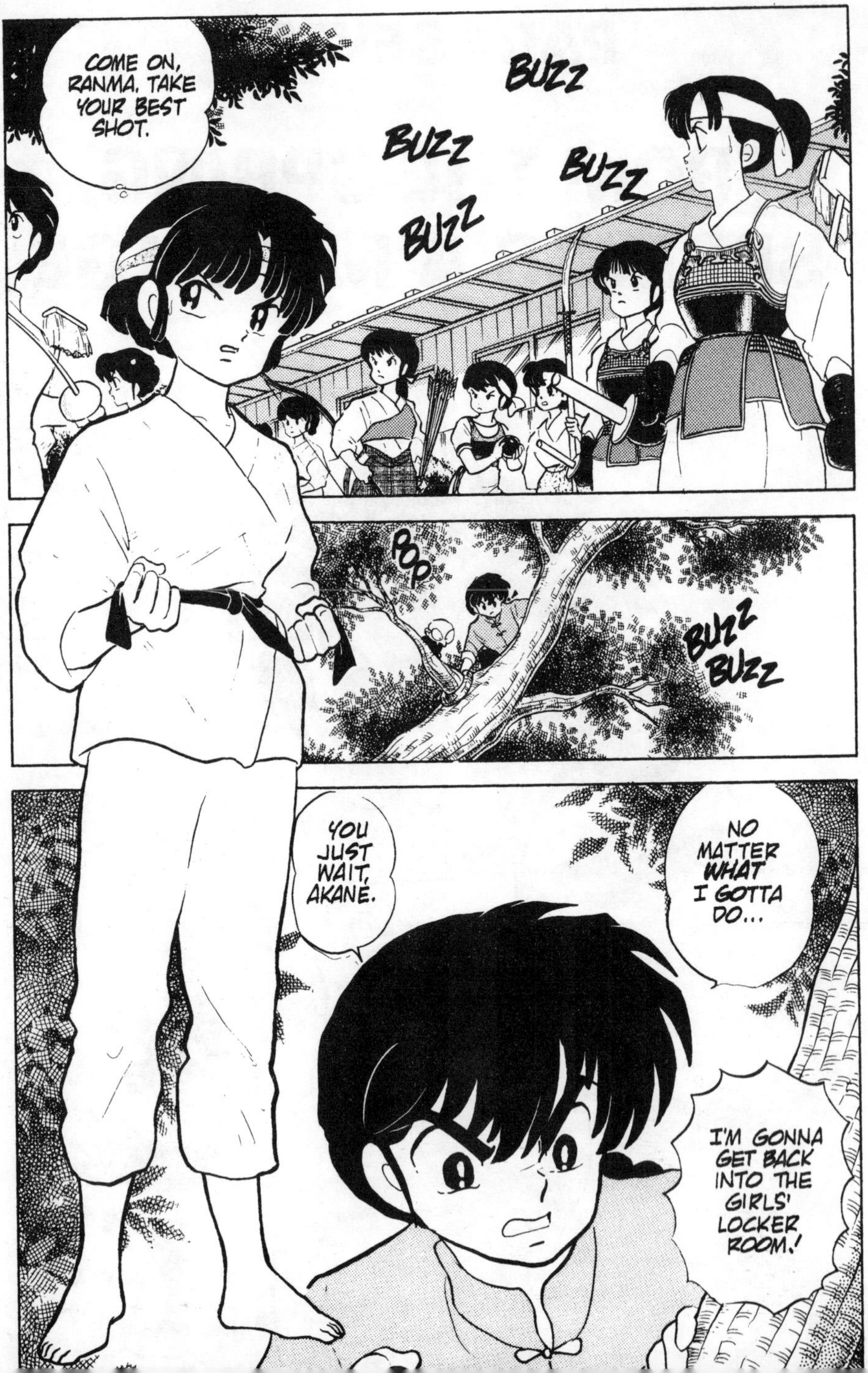
COME ON, RANMA. TAKE YOUR BEST SHOT.
BUZZ
BUZZ
BUZZ
BUZZ
POP
BUZZ BUZZ
YOU JUST WAIT, AKANE.
NO MATTER WHAT I GOTTA DO...
I'M GONNA GET BACK INTO THE GIRLS' LOCKER ROOM!

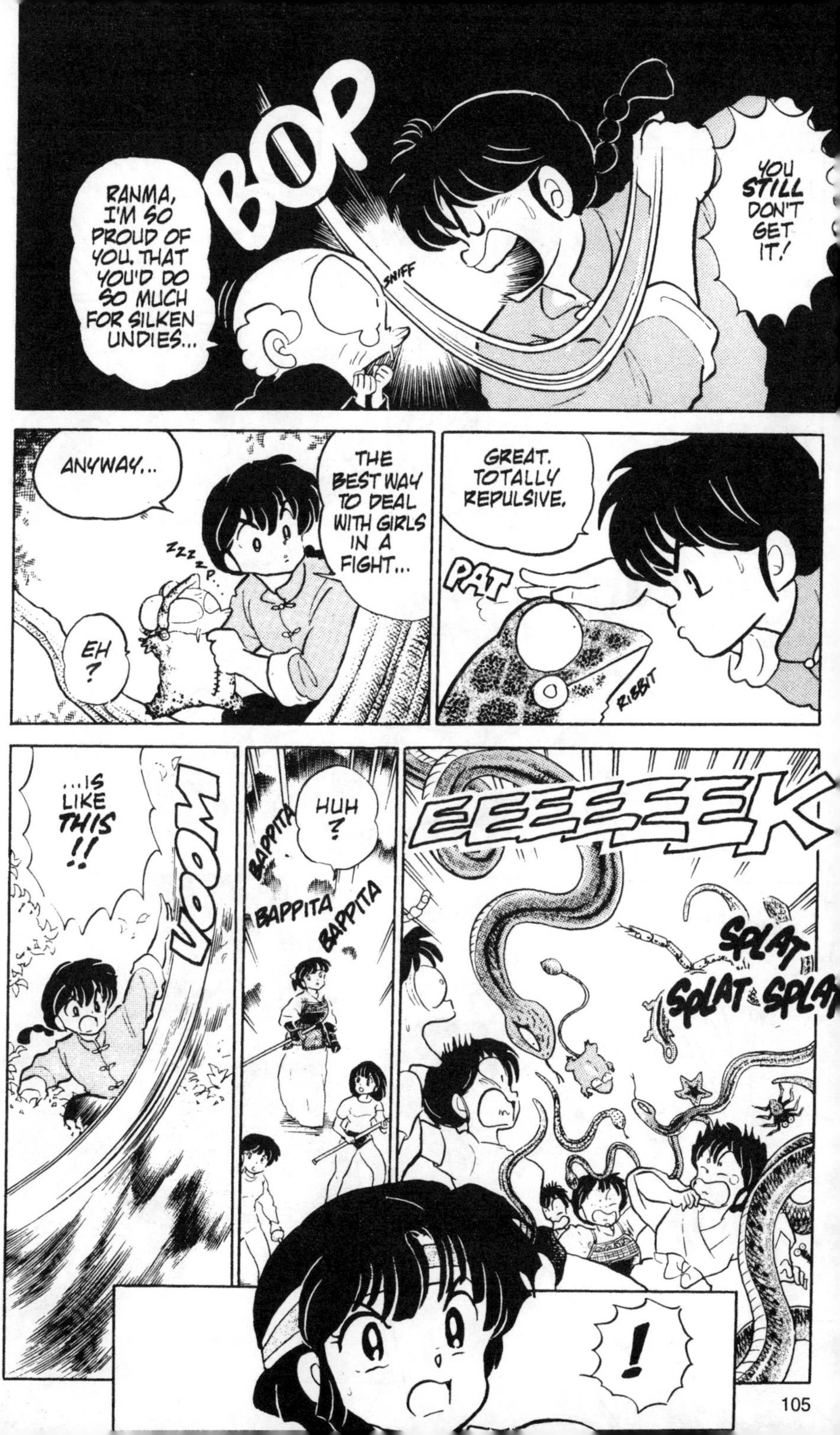
RANMA, I'M SO PROUD OF YOU. THAT YOU'D DO SO MUCH FOR SILKEN UNDIES...
BOP
SNIFF
YOU STILL DON'T GET IT!
ANYWAY...
ZZZZP...
EH?
THE BEST WAY TO DEAL WITH GIRLS IN A FIGHT...
GREAT. TOTALLY REPULSIVE.
PAT
RIBBIT
...IS LIKE THIS!!
VOOOM
BAPPITA
HUH?
BAPPITA
BAPPITA
EEEEEEEK
SPLAT
SPLAT SPLAT
!

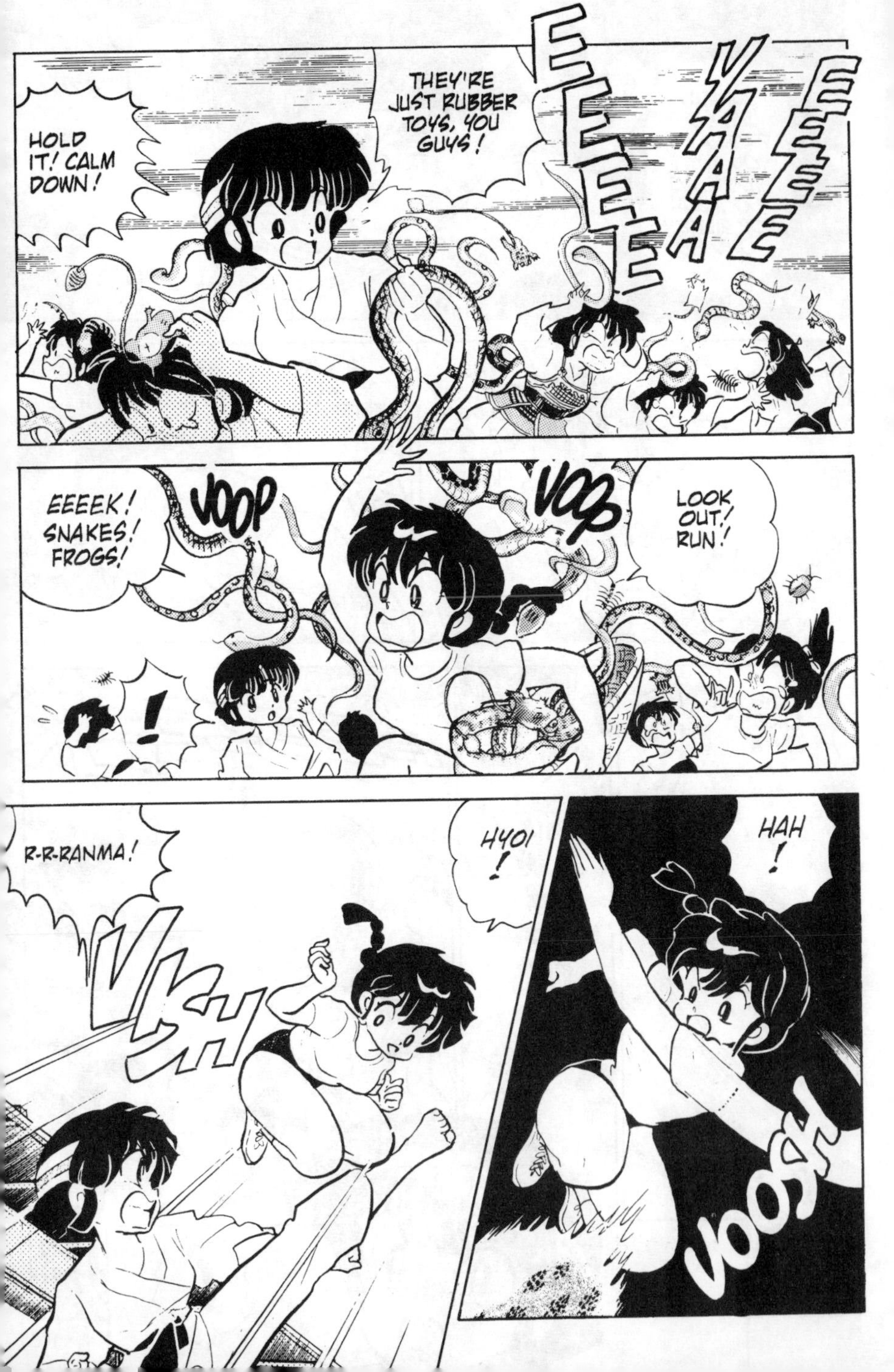
HOLD IT! CALM DOWN!
THEY'RE JUST RUBBER TOYS, YOU GUYS!
EEEEEE
YAAAA
EEEEE
EEEEK! SNAKES! FROGS!
VOOP
VOOP
LOOK OUT! RUN!
!
R-R-RANMA!
VISH
HYOI!
HAH!
VOOSH

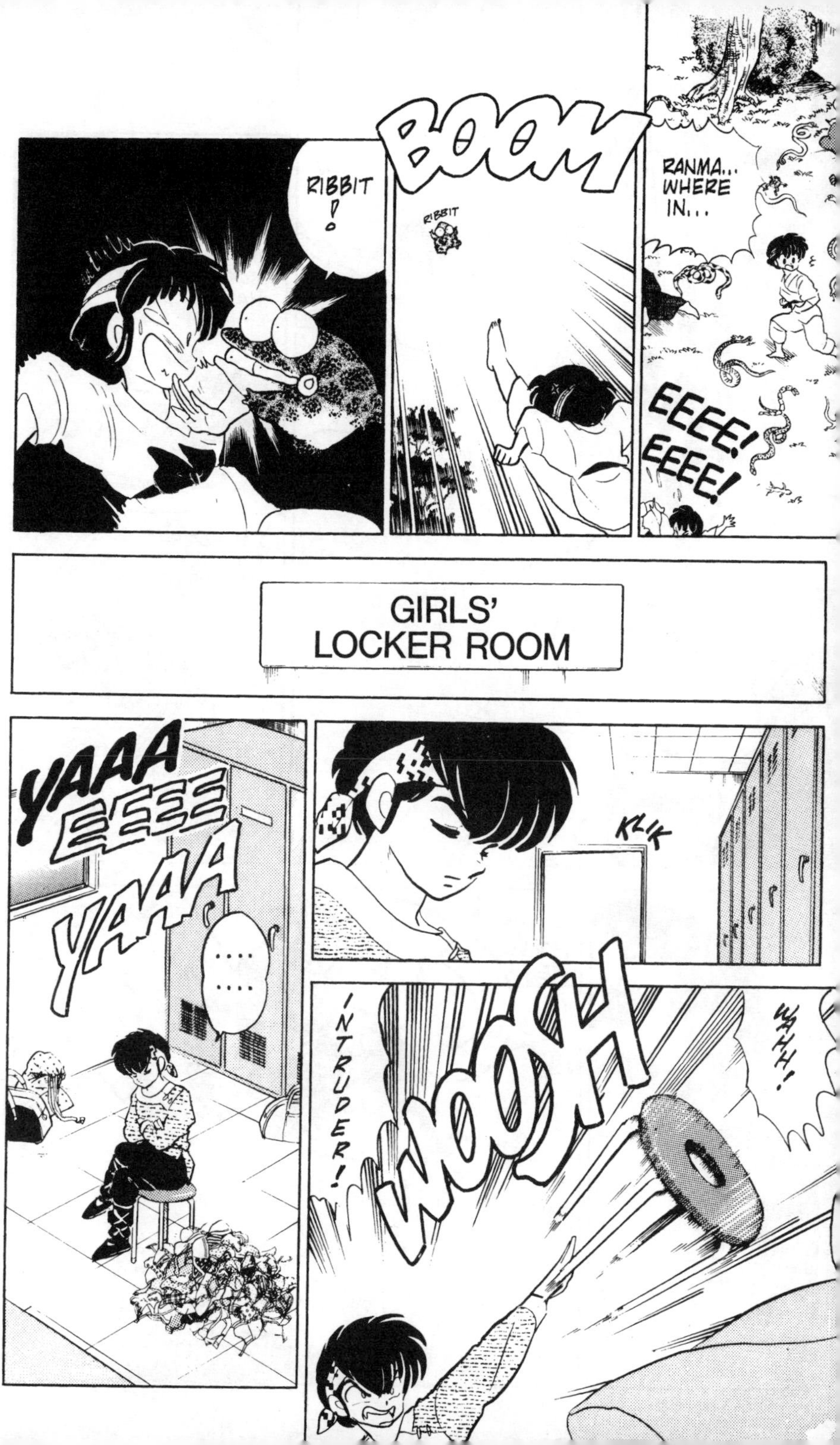
RIBBIT!
BOOM
RIBBIT
RANMA... WHERE IN...
EEEE! EEEE!
GIRLS' LOCKER ROOM
YAAA EEEE YAAA
....
....
KLIK
INTRUDER!
WOOSH
WAHH!

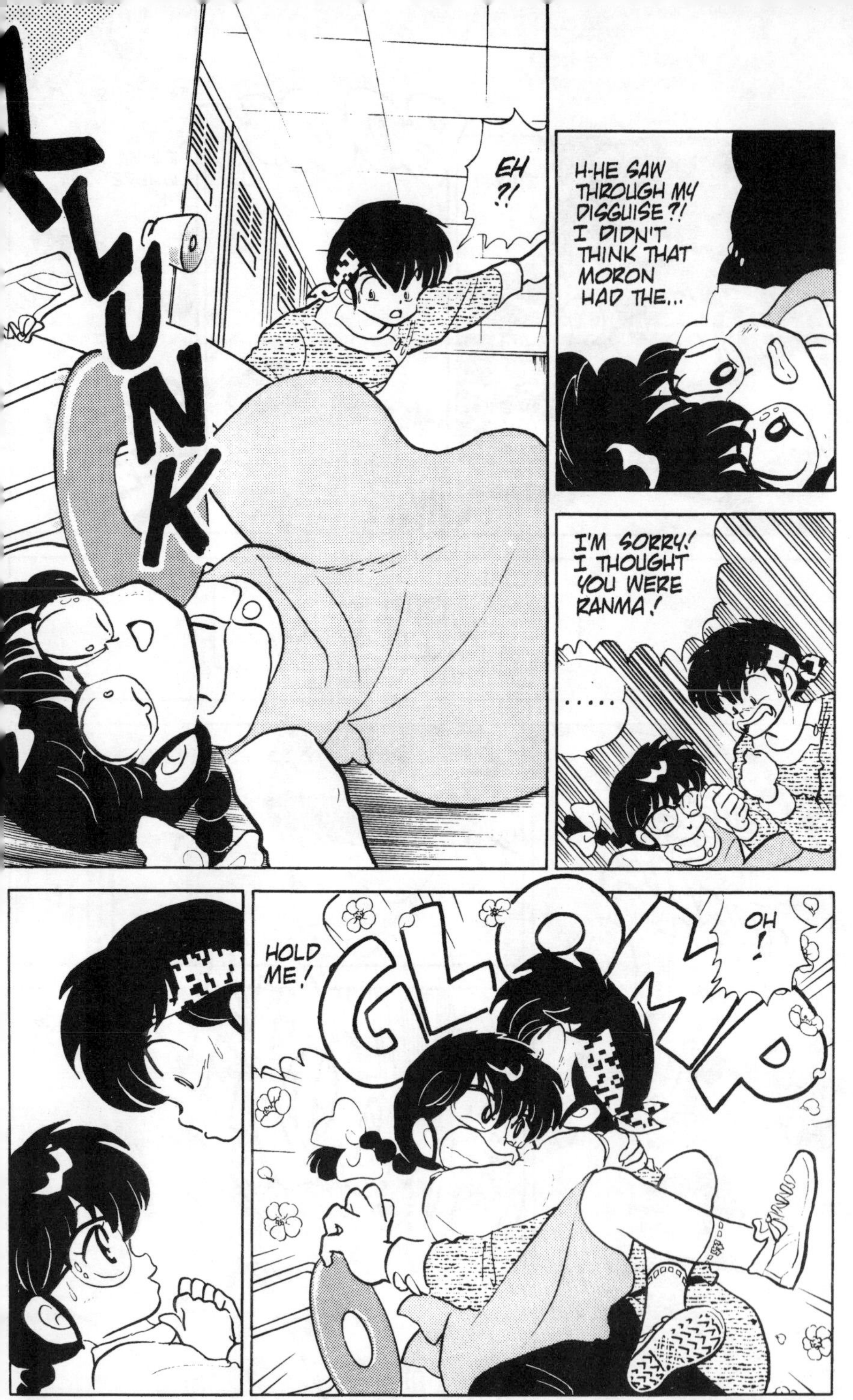
KLUNK
EH ?!
H-HE SAW THROUGH MY DISGUISE ?! I DIDN'T THINK THAT MORON HAD THE...
I'M SORRY! I THOUGHT YOU WERE RANMA!
.....
HOLD ME!
GLOMP
OH!

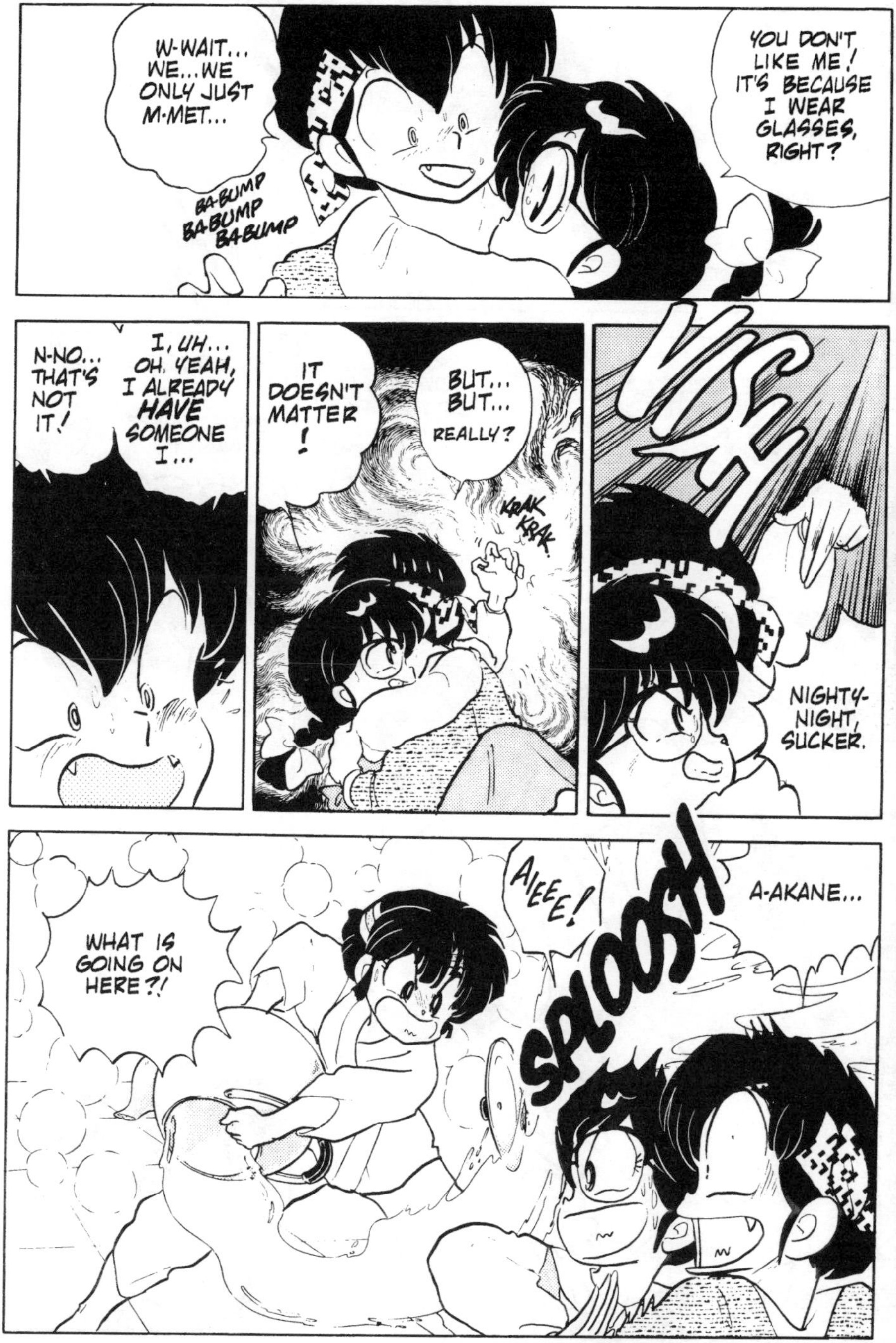
W-WAIT... WE...WE ONLY JUST M-MET...
BA-BUMP BA-BUMP BA-BUMP
YOU DON'T LIKE ME! IT'S BECAUSE I WEAR GLASSES, RIGHT?
N-NO... THAT'S NOT IT!
I, UH... OH, YEAH, I ALREADY HAVE SOMEONE I...
IT DOESN'T MATTER!
BUT... BUT... REALLY?
KRAK KRAK
VISE
NIGHTY-NIGHT, SUCKER.
WHAT IS GOING ON HERE?!
AIEEE!
SPLOOSH
A-AKANE...

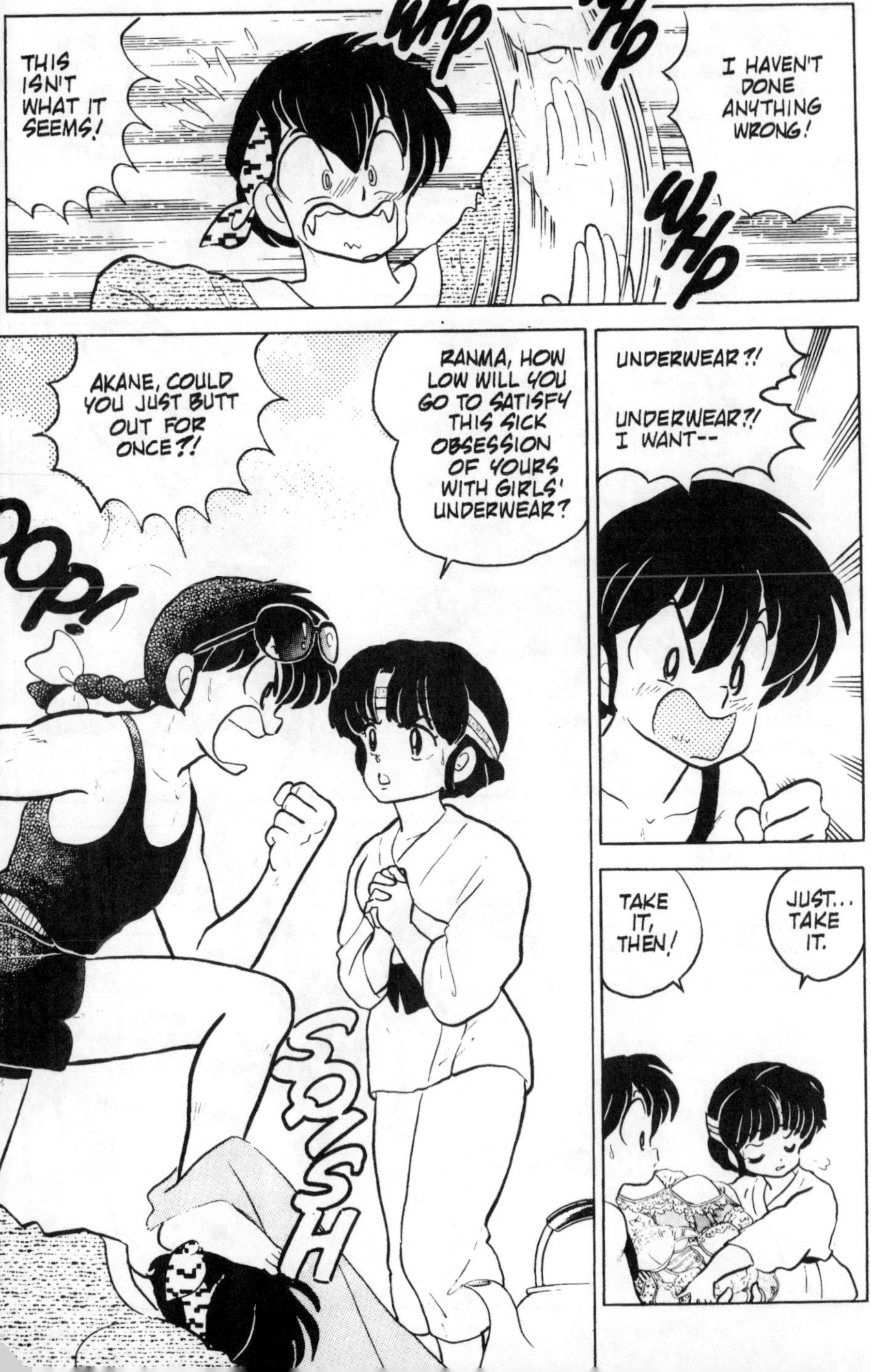
THIS ISN'T WHAT IT SEEMS!
WHP
WHP
WHP
I HAVEN'T DONE ANYTHING WRONG!
AKANE, COULD YOU JUST BUTT OUT FOR ONCE?!
RANMA, HOW LOW WILL YOU GO TO SATISFY THIS SICK OBSESSION OF YOURS WITH GIRLS' UNDERWEAR?
UNDERWEAR?!
UNDERWEAR?! I WANT--
TAKE IT, THEN!
JUST... TAKE IT.

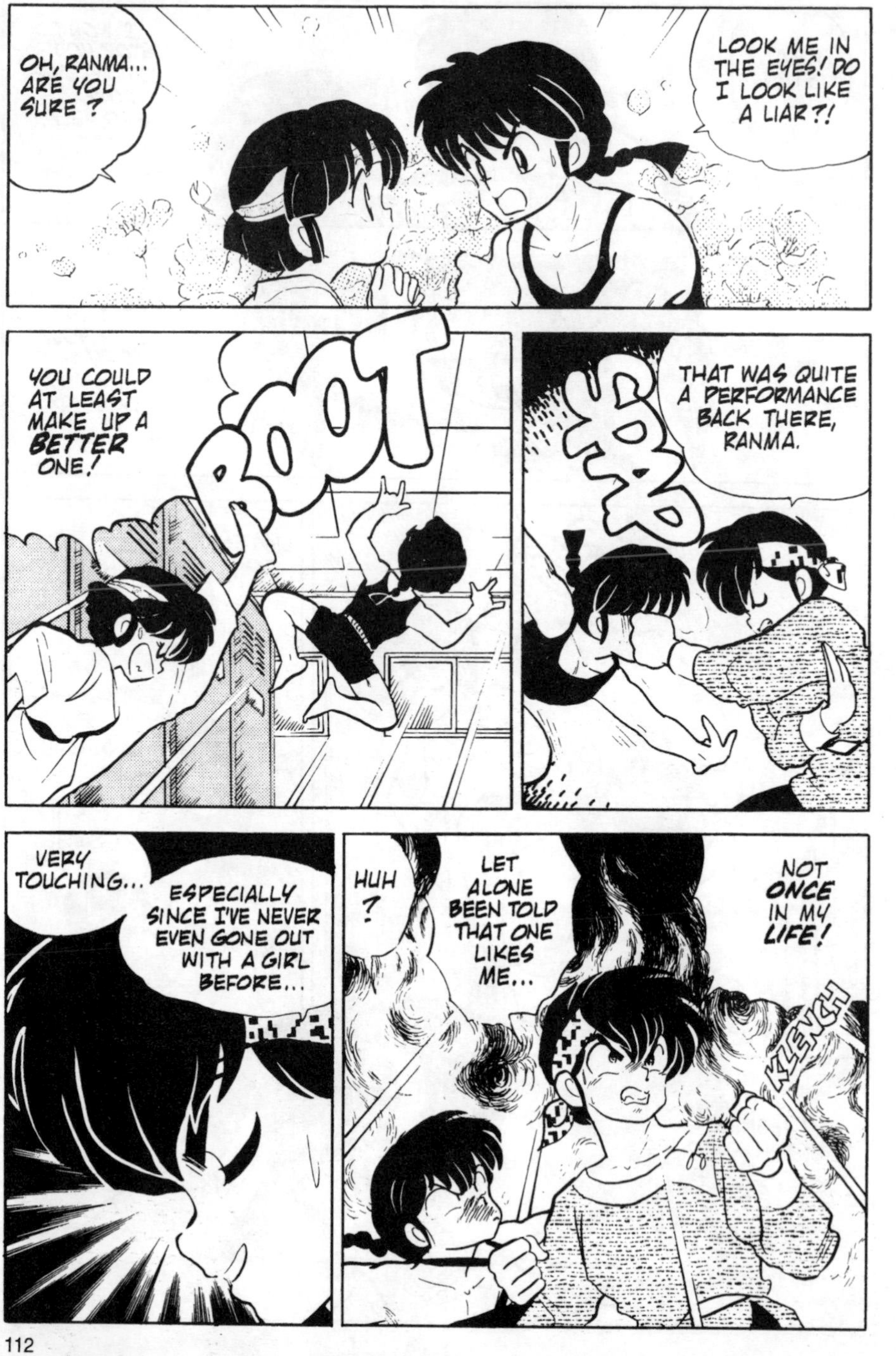
OH, RANMA... ARE YOU SURE ?
LOOK ME IN THE EYES! DO I LOOK LIKE A LIAR?!
YOU COULD AT LEAST MAKE UP A BETTER ONE!
BOOT
SCRAP
THAT WAS QUITE A PERFORMANCE BACK THERE, RANMA.
VERY TOUCHING...
ESPECIALLY SINCE I'VE NEVER EVEN GONE OUT WITH A GIRL BEFORE...
HUH ?
LET ALONE BEEN TOLD THAT ONE LIKES ME...
NOT ONCE IN MY LIFE!
KLENCH

RYOGA, IS THAT TRUE?

WHY WOULD *YOU* HAVE A MAP TO THE NANNIICHUAN...?

WHY...?

RYOGA, CAN IT BE...?

GASP!

BRRR

SHE...

SHE KNOWS...!

...YOU BROUGHT THAT MAP JUST FOR RANMA?!

OH, RYOGA, YOU'RE SO UNSELFISH!

SIGH

LUCKY FOR YOU SHE'S THICK AS A BRICK, EH, P-CHAN, OL' PAL?

PAP PAP

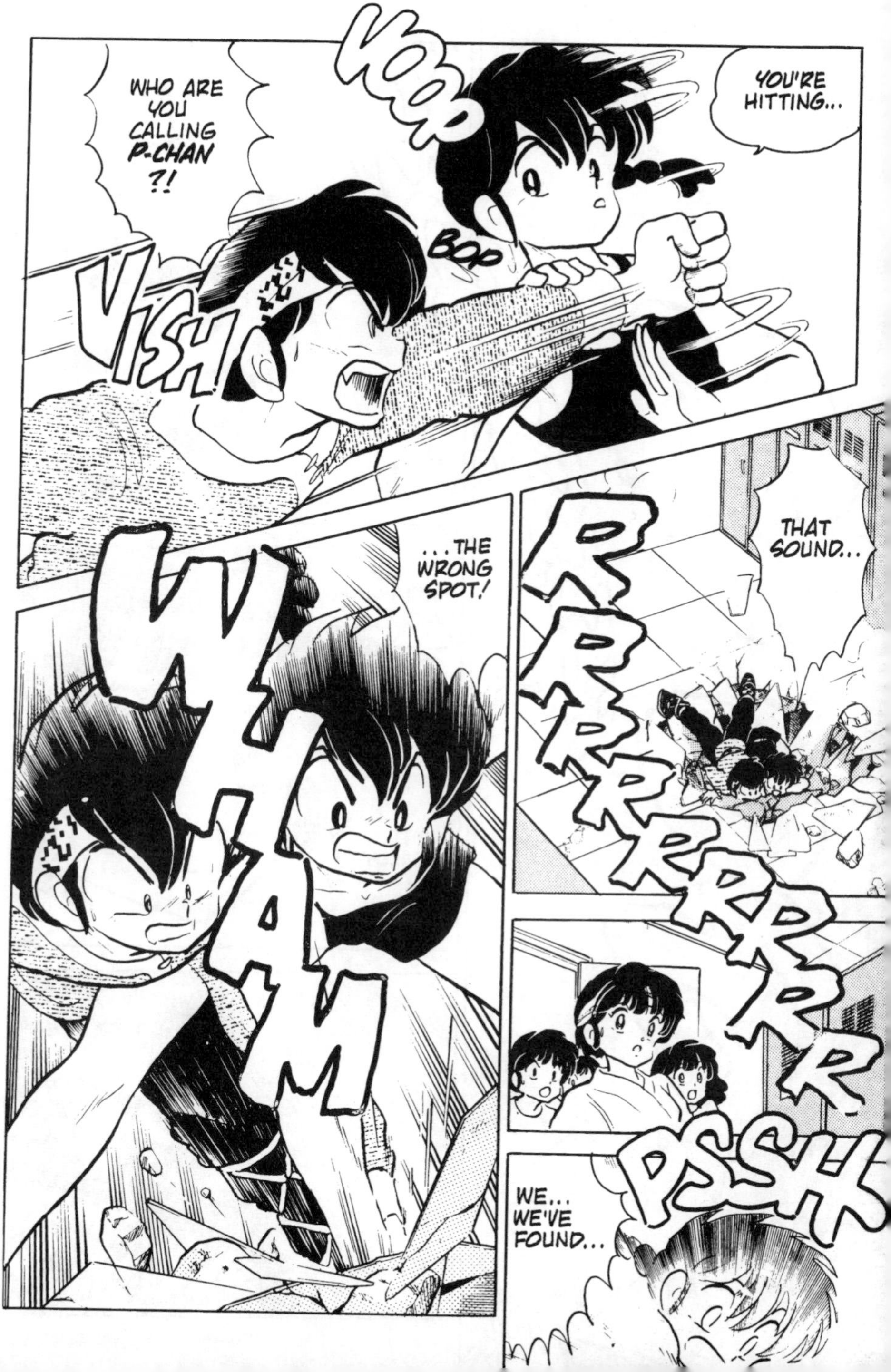

WHO ARE YOU CALLING P-CHAN ?!
VOOP
YOU'RE HITTING...
BOOP
VISH
...THE WRONG SPOT!
WHAM
RRRRRRRRRR
THAT SOUND...
WE... WE'VE FOUND...
PSSH

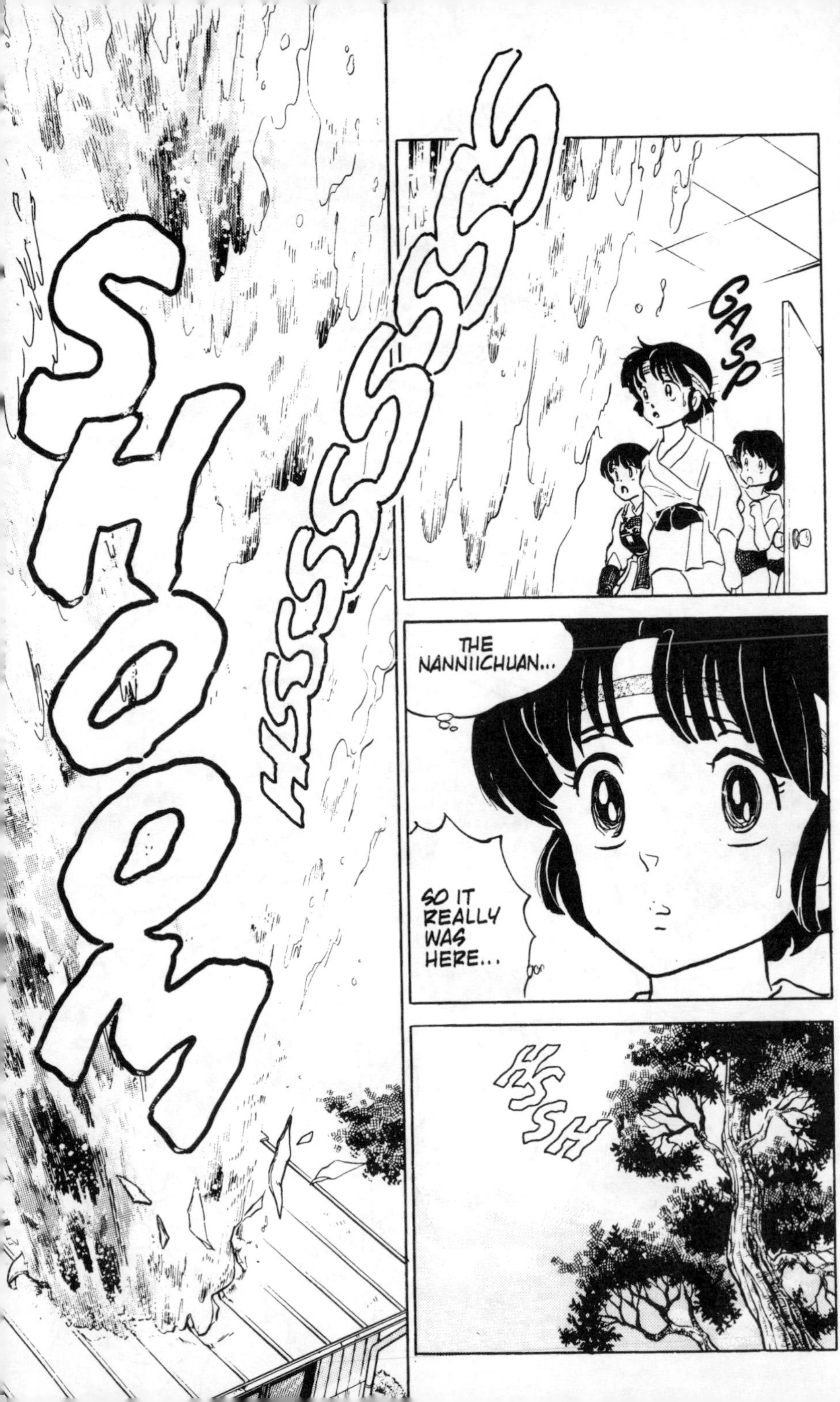
SHOOM
HSSSSSSSS
GASP
THE NANNIICHUAN...
SO IT REALLY WAS HERE...
HSSH

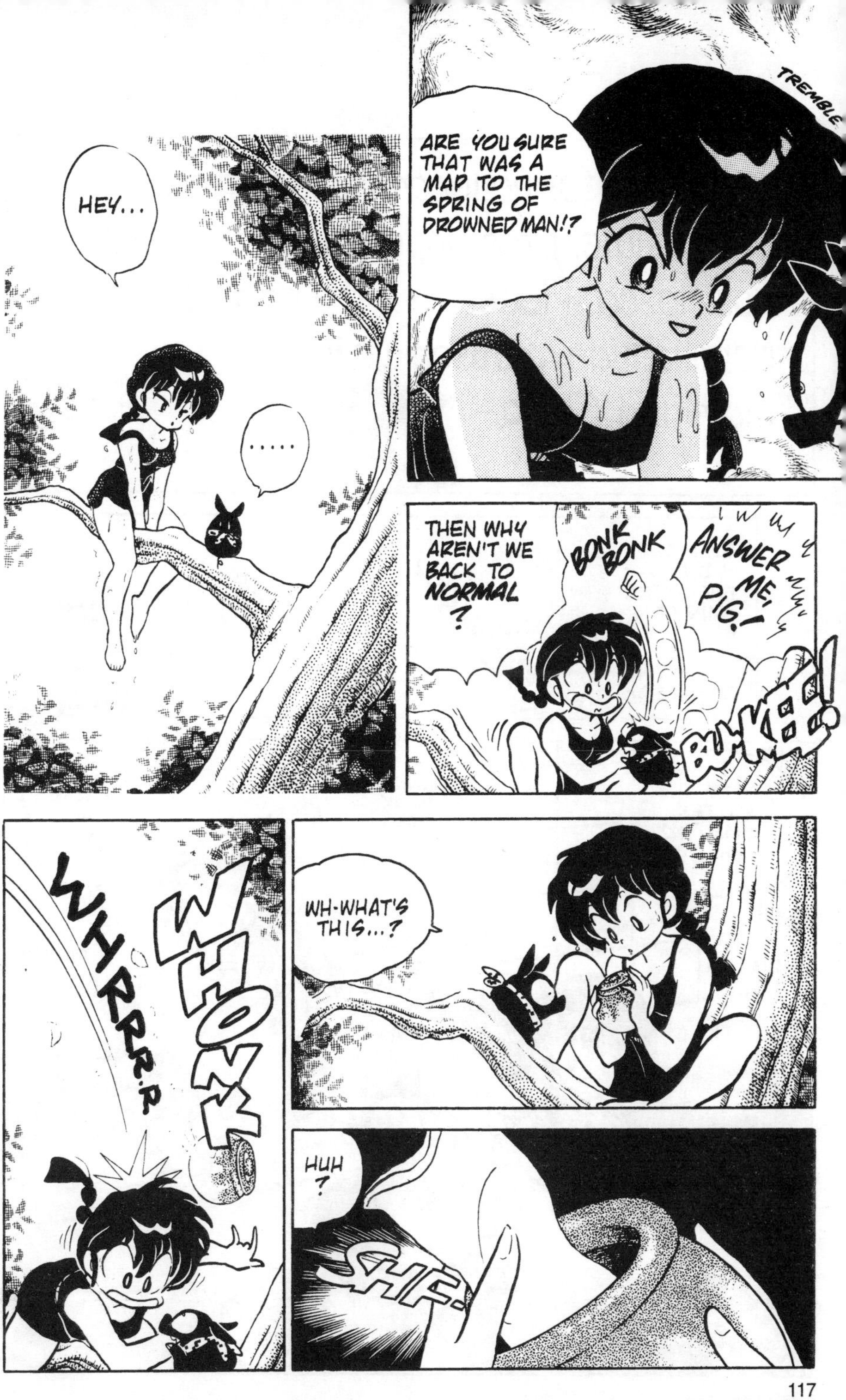
HEY...
......
TREMBLE
ARE YOU SURE THAT WAS A MAP TO THE SPRING OF DROWNED MAN!?
THEN WHY AREN'T WE BACK TO NORMAL?
BONK BONK
ANSWER ME, PIG!
BU-KEE!
WHIRRR.R
WHONK
WH-WHAT'S THIS...?
HUH?
SHF..

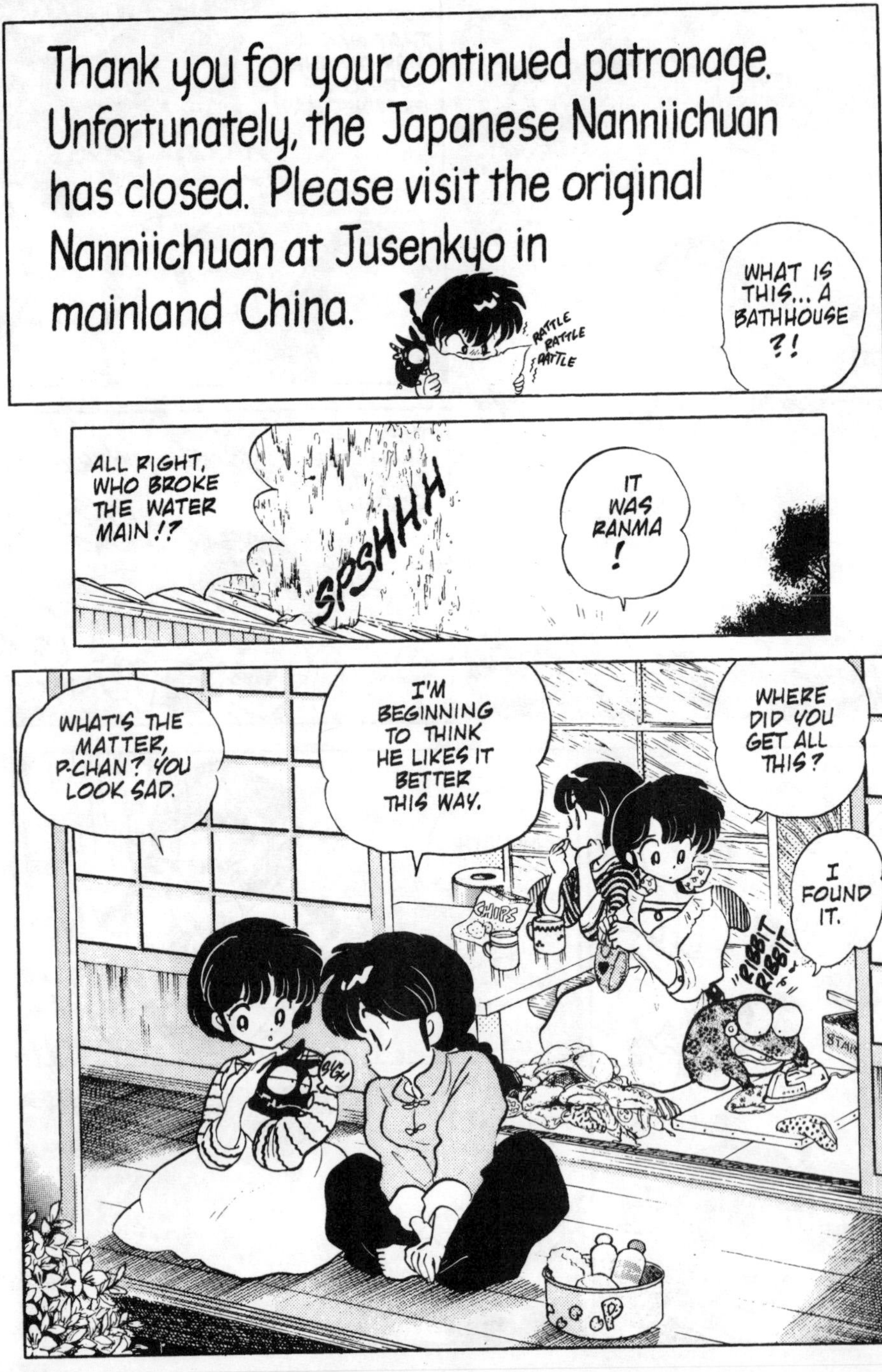
Thank you for your continued patronage. Unfortunately, the Japanese Nanniichuan has closed. Please visit the original Nanniichuan at Jusenkyo in mainland China.
RATTLE RATTLE RATTLE
WHAT IS THIS... A BATHHOUSE ?!
ALL RIGHT, WHO BROKE THE WATER MAIN !?
SPSHHH
IT WAS RANMA !
WHAT'S THE MATTER, P-CHAN? YOU LOOK SAD.
I'M BEGINNING TO THINK HE LIKES IT BETTER THIS WAY.
SIGH
CHIPS
WHERE DID YOU GET ALL THIS?
I FOUND IT.
RIBBIT RIBBIT

# PART EIGHT

# THE WAY THE COOKIE CRUMBLES

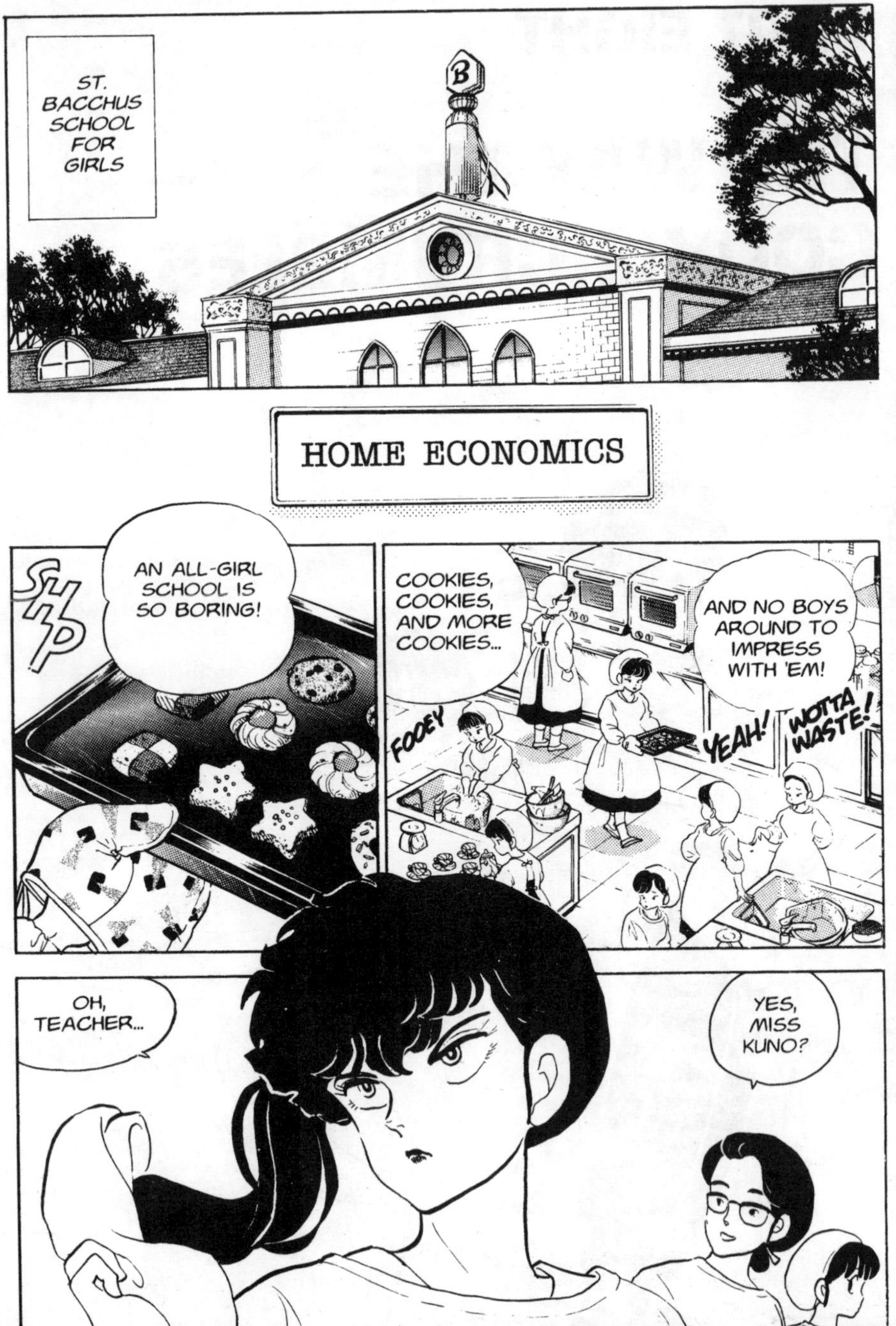
ST. BACCHUS SCHOOL FOR GIRLS
HOME ECONOMICS
SHP
AN ALL-GIRL SCHOOL IS SO BORING!
COOKIES, COOKIES, AND MORE COOKIES...
FOOEY
AND NO BOYS AROUND TO IMPRESS WITH 'EM!
YEAH!
WOTTA WASTE!
OH, TEACHER...
YES, MISS KUNO?

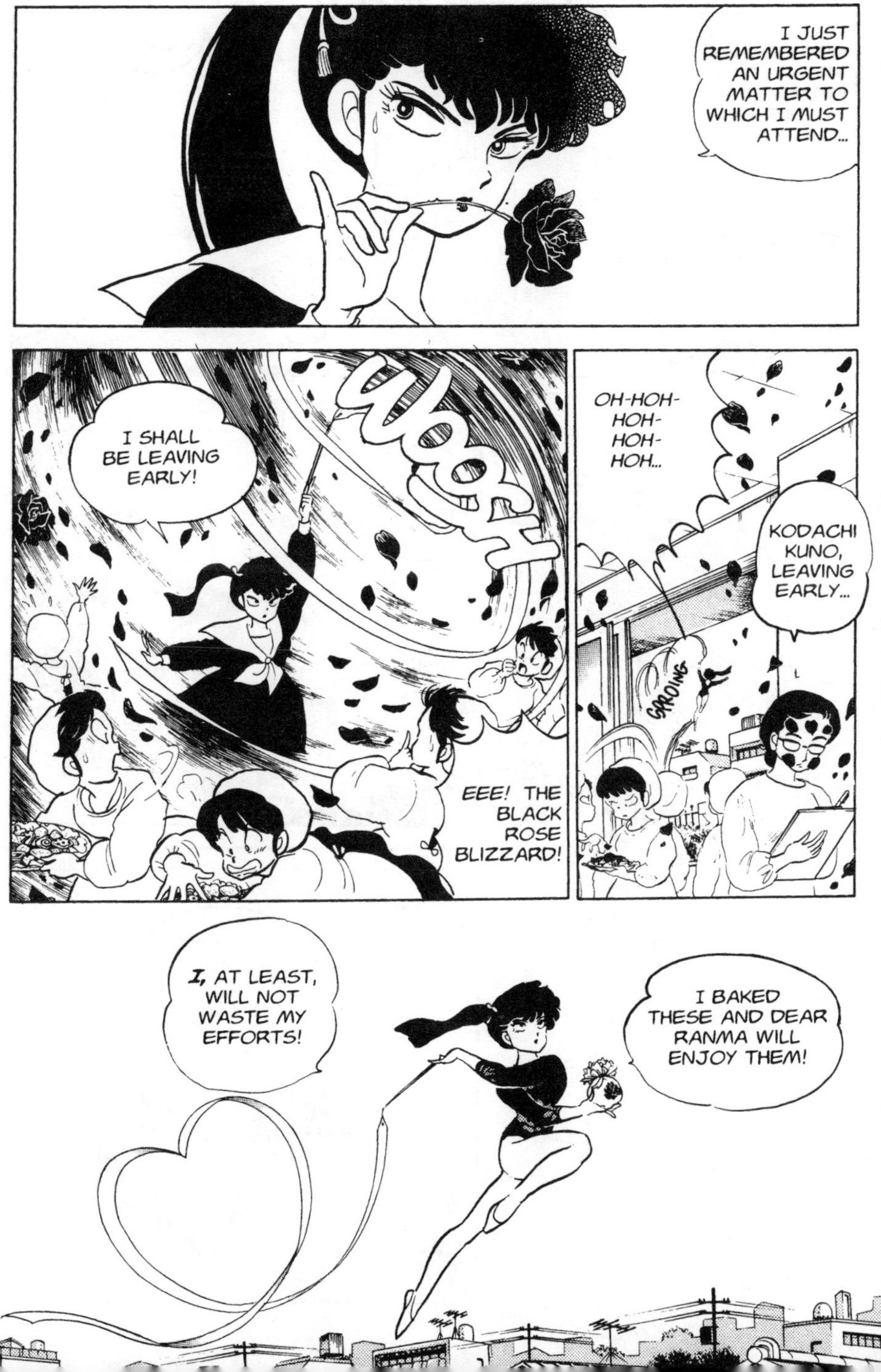
I JUST REMEMBERED AN URGENT MATTER TO WHICH I MUST ATTEND...
I SHALL BE LEAVING EARLY!
WOOSH
EEE! THE BLACK ROSE BLIZZARD!
OH-HOH-HOH-HOH-HOH...
KODACHI KUNO, LEAVING EARLY...
SPROING
I, AT LEAST, WILL NOT WASTE MY EFFORTS!
I BAKED THESE AND DEAR RANMA WILL ENJOY THEM!

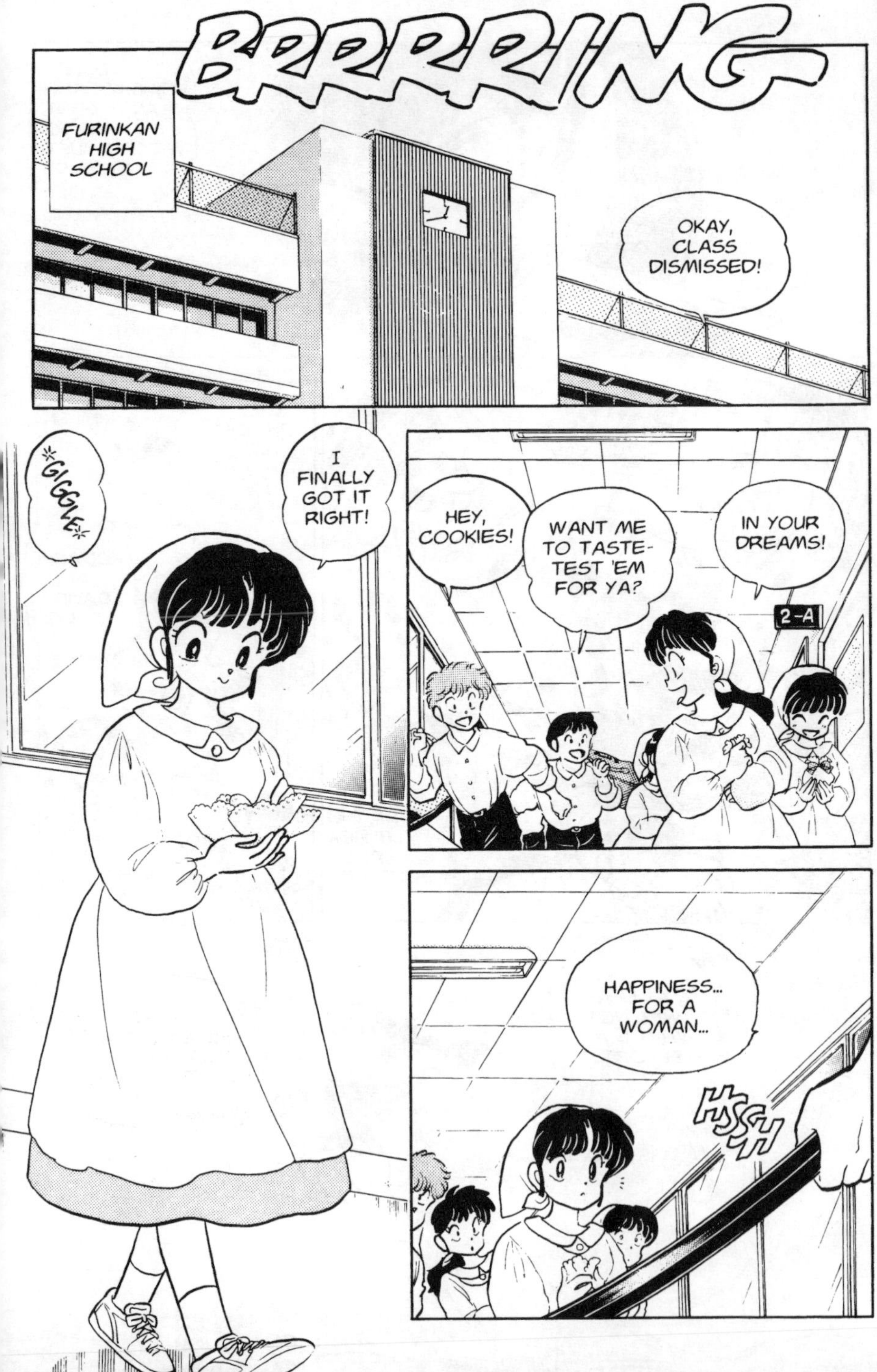
BRRRRING
FURINKAN HIGH SCHOOL
OKAY, CLASS DISMISSED!
*GIGGLE*
I FINALLY GOT IT RIGHT!
HEY, COOKIES!
WANT ME TO TASTE-TEST 'EM FOR YA?
IN YOUR DREAMS!
2-A
HAPPINESS... FOR A WOMAN...
HSCH

123

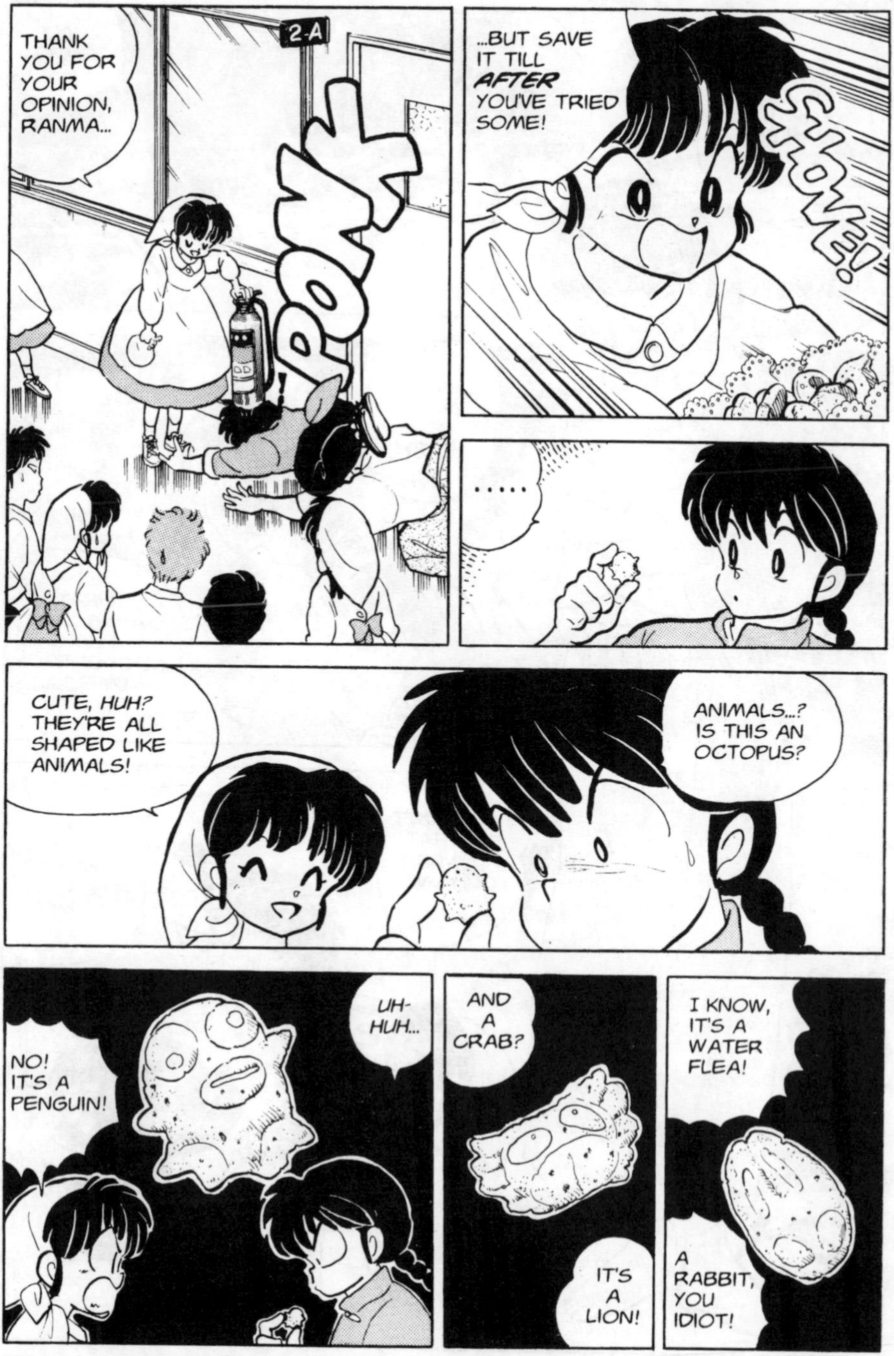

THANK YOU FOR YOUR OPINION, RANMA...
POW
2-A
...BUT SAVE IT TILL *AFTER* YOU'VE TRIED SOME!
SHOVE!
.....
CUTE, HUH? THEY'RE ALL SHAPED LIKE ANIMALS!
ANIMALS...? IS THIS AN OCTOPUS?
NO! IT'S A PENGUIN!
UH-HUH...
AND A CRAB?
IT'S A LION!
I KNOW, IT'S A WATER FLEA!
A RABBIT, YOU IDIOT!

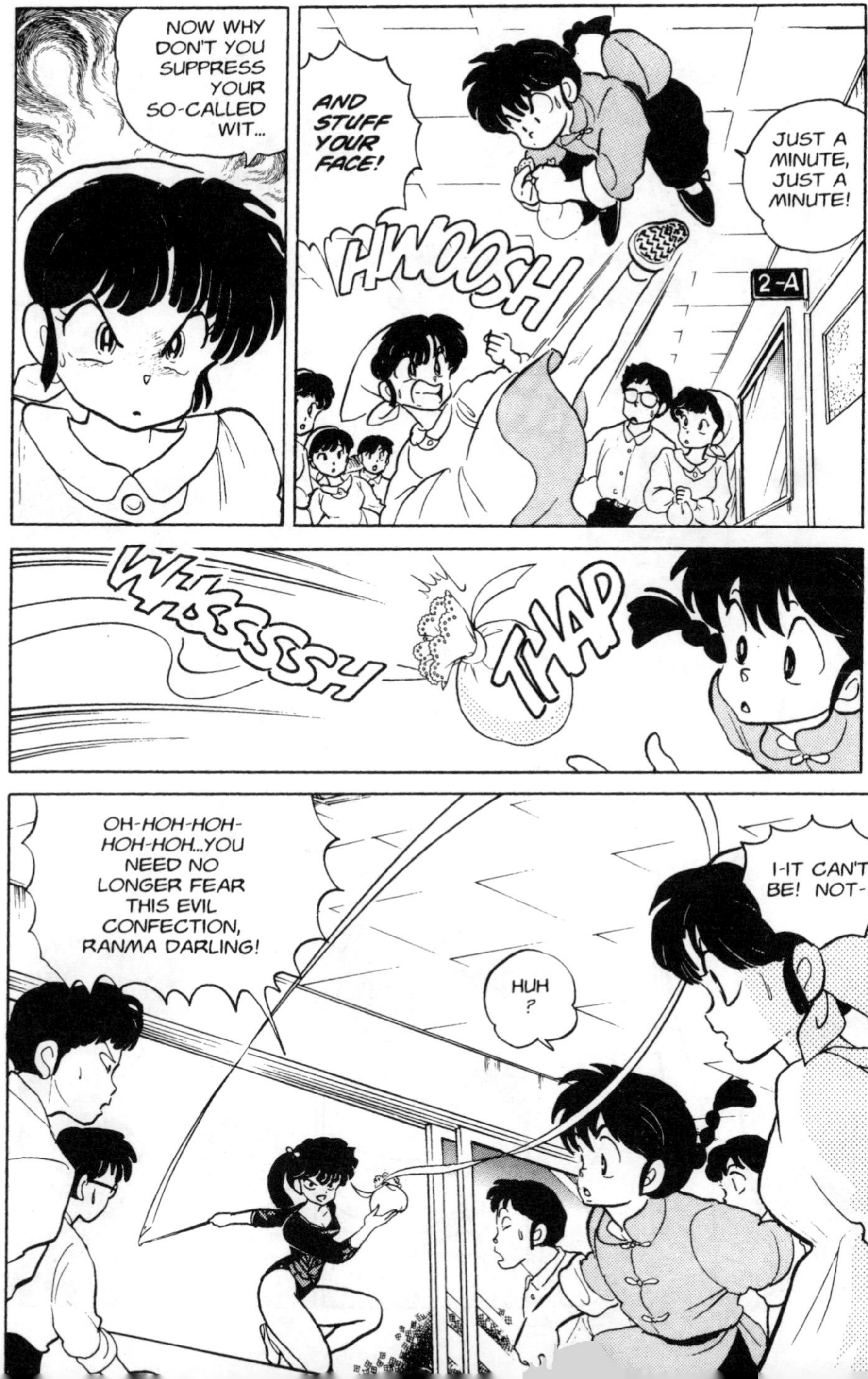
NOW WHY DON'T YOU SUPPRESS YOUR SO-CALLED WIT...
AND STUFF YOUR FACE!
HWOOSH
JUST A MINUTE, JUST A MINUTE!
2-A
WHOSSSH
THAP
OH-HOH-HOH-HOH-HOH...YOU NEED NO LONGER FEAR THIS EVIL CONFECTION, RANMA DARLING!
HUH?
I-IT CAN'T BE! NOT--

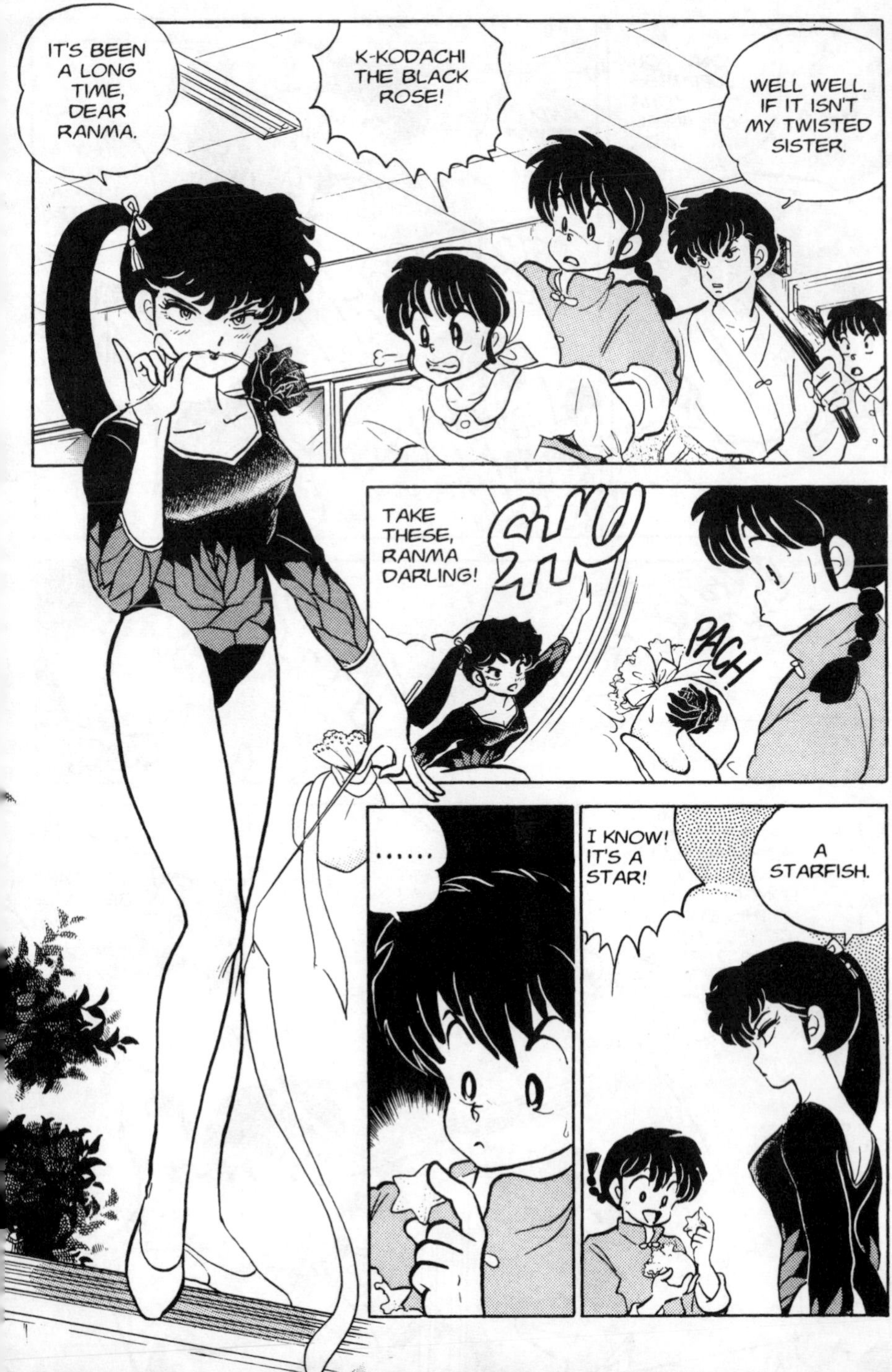
IT'S BEEN A LONG TIME, DEAR RANMA.
K-KODACHI THE BLACK ROSE!
WELL WELL. IF IT ISN'T MY TWISTED SISTER.
TAKE THESE, RANMA DARLING!
SHU
PACH
......
I KNOW! IT'S A STAR!
A STARFISH.

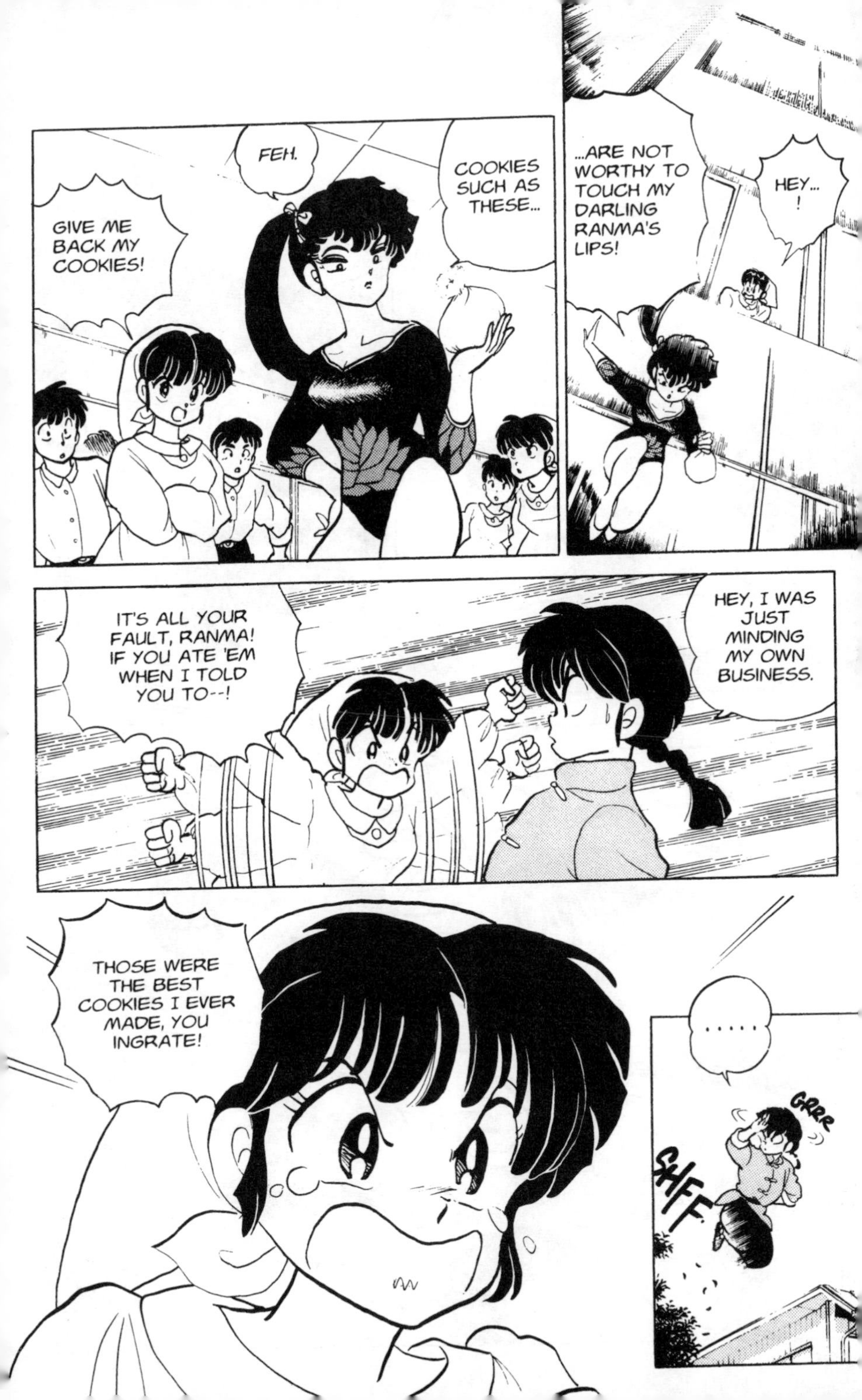
GIVE ME BACK MY COOKIES!
FEH.
COOKIES SUCH AS THESE...
...ARE NOT WORTHY TO TOUCH MY DARLING RANMA'S LIPS!
HEY... !
IT'S ALL YOUR FAULT, RANMA! IF YOU ATE 'EM WHEN I TOLD YOU TO--!
HEY, I WAS JUST MINDING MY OWN BUSINESS.
THOSE WERE THE BEST COOKIES I EVER MADE, YOU INGRATE!
.....
GRRR
SHFF

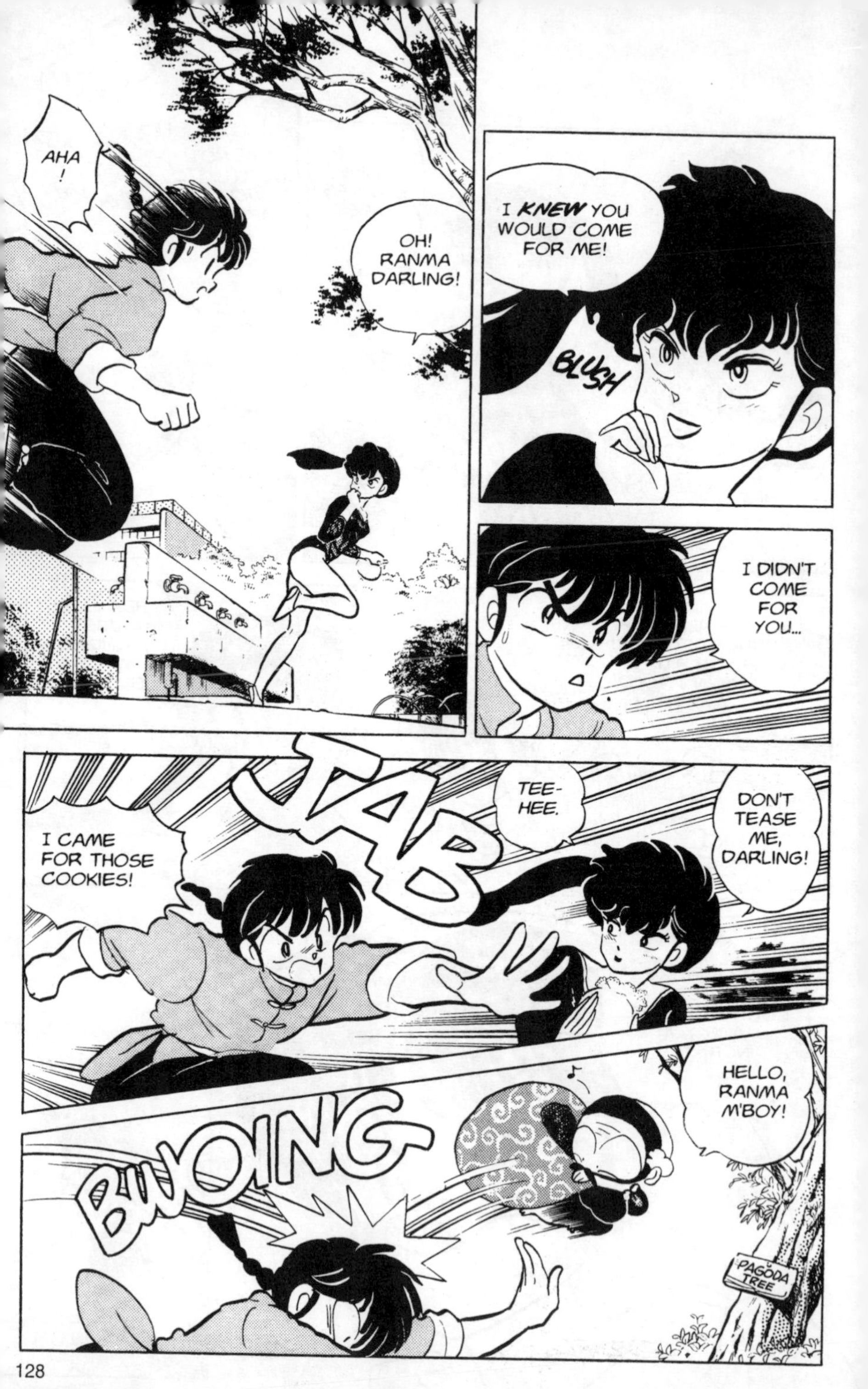
AHA!
OH! RANMA DARLING!
I KNEW YOU WOULD COME FOR ME!
BLUSH
I DIDN'T COME FOR YOU...
I CAME FOR THOSE COOKIES!
JAB
TEE-HEE.
DON'T TEASE ME, DARLING!
BWOING
HELLO, RANMA M'BOY!
PAGODA TREE

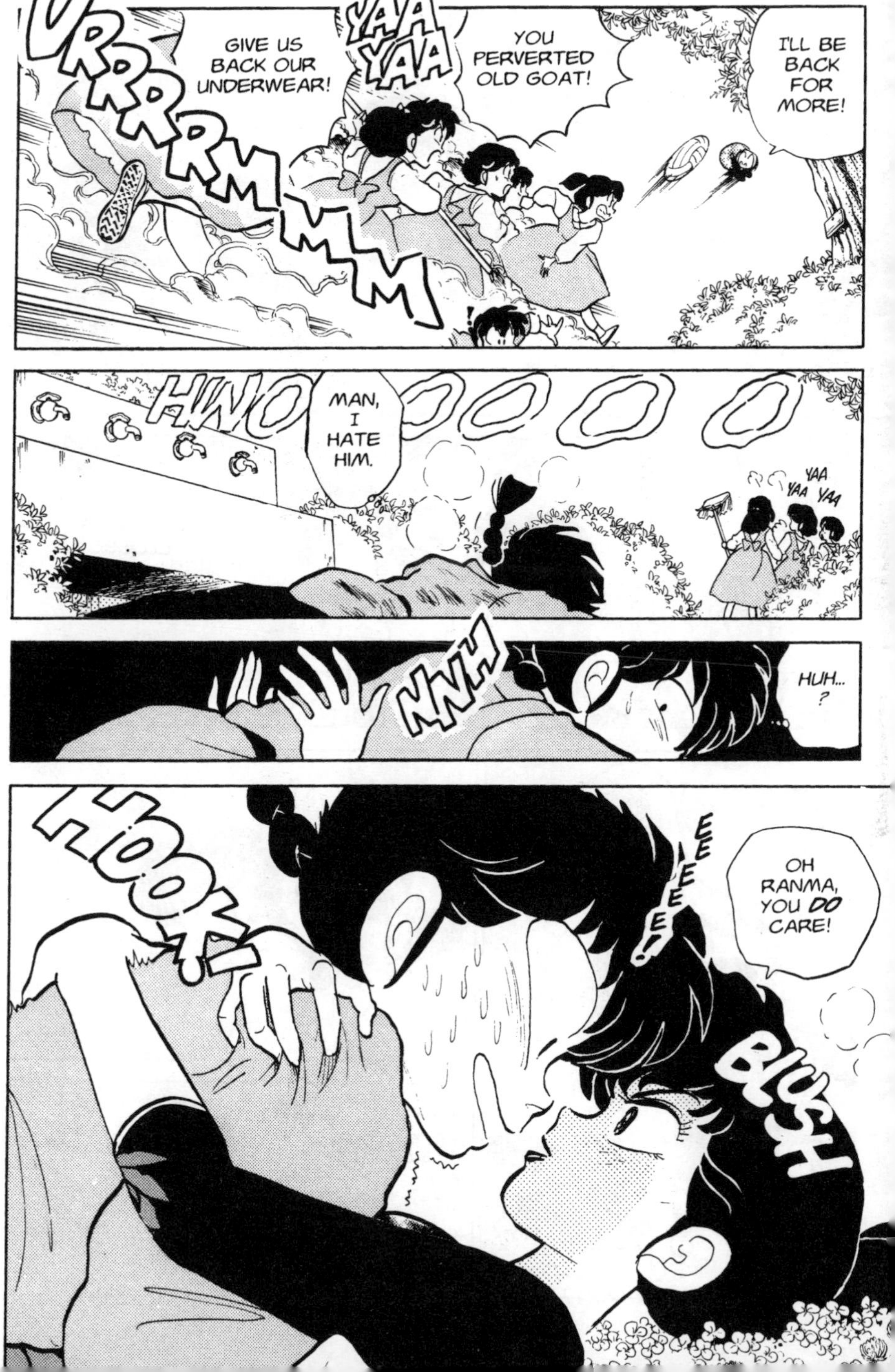
VRRRRMMMM
GIVE US BACK OUR UNDERWEAR!
YAA YAA
YOU PERVERTED OLD GOAT!
I'LL BE BACK FOR MORE!
!
HINOOOOOOO
MAN, I HATE HIM.
YAA YAA YAA
NNH
HUH... ?
HOOK!
EEEEE!
OH RANMA, YOU DO CARE!
BLUSH

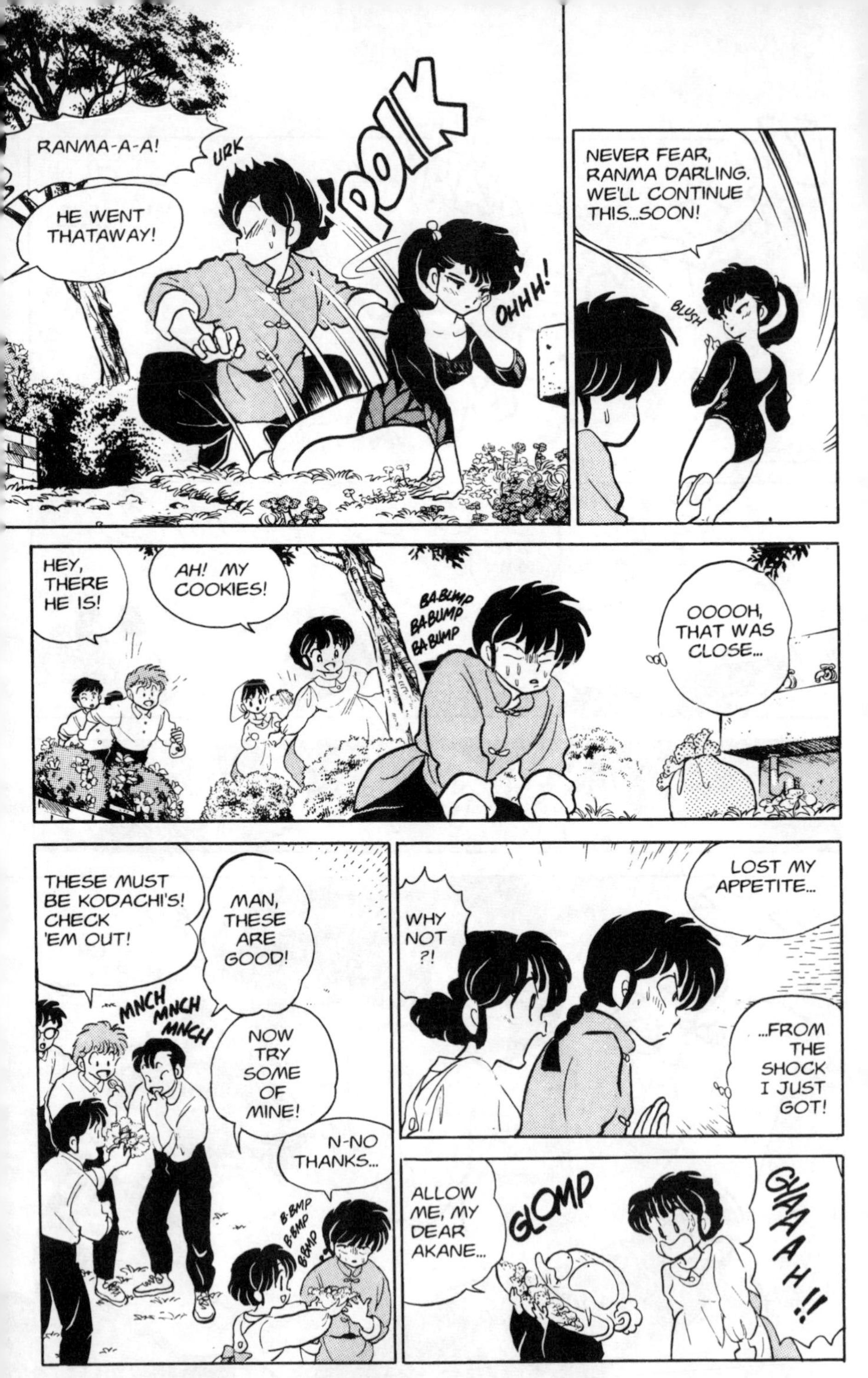

RANMA-A-A!
HE WENT THATAWAY!
URK
POIK
OHHH!
NEVER FEAR, RANMA DARLING. WE'LL CONTINUE THIS...SOON!
BLUSH
HEY, THERE HE IS!
AH! MY COOKIES!
BA-BUMP BA-BUMP BA-BUMP
OOOOH, THAT WAS CLOSE...
THESE MUST BE KODACHI'S! CHECK 'EM OUT!
MAN, THESE ARE GOOD!
MNCH MNCH MNCH
NOW TRY SOME OF MINE!
N-NO THANKS...
B-BMP B-BMP B-BMP
WHY NOT ?!
LOST MY APPETITE...
...FROM THE SHOCK I JUST GOT!
ALLOW ME, MY DEAR AKANE...
GLOMP
GHAAAH!!

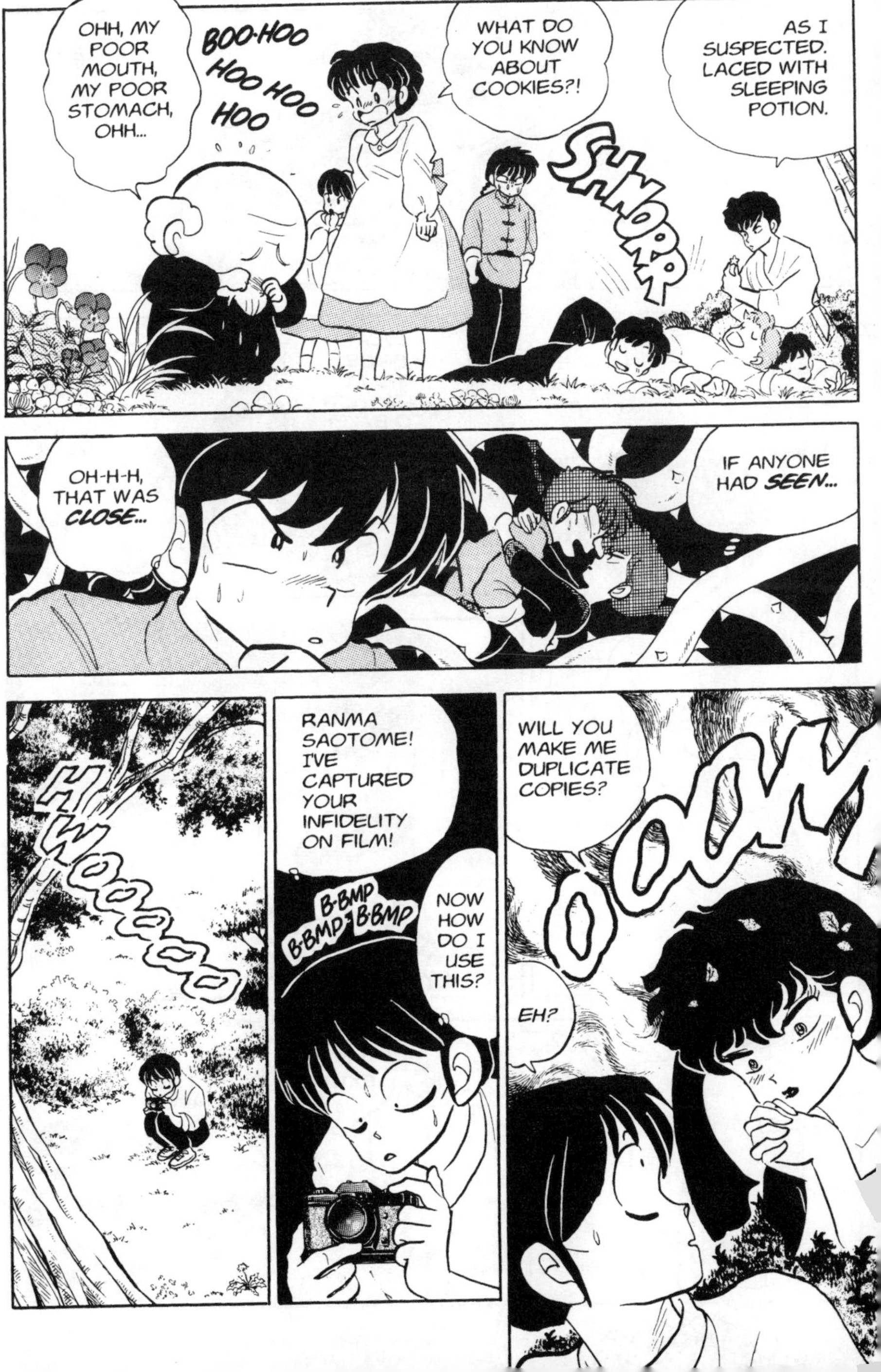
OHH, MY POOR MOUTH, MY POOR STOMACH, OHH...
BOO-HOO HOO-HOO HOO
WHAT DO YOU KNOW ABOUT COOKIES?!
AS I SUSPECTED. LACED WITH SLEEPING POTION.
SHNORR
OH-H-H, THAT WAS CLOSE...
IF ANYONE HAD SEEN...
HWOOOOOO
RANMA SAOTOME! I'VE CAPTURED YOUR INFIDELITY ON FILM!
B-BMP B-BMP B-BMP
NOW HOW DO I USE THIS?
WILL YOU MAKE ME DUPLICATE COPIES?
OOOM
EH?

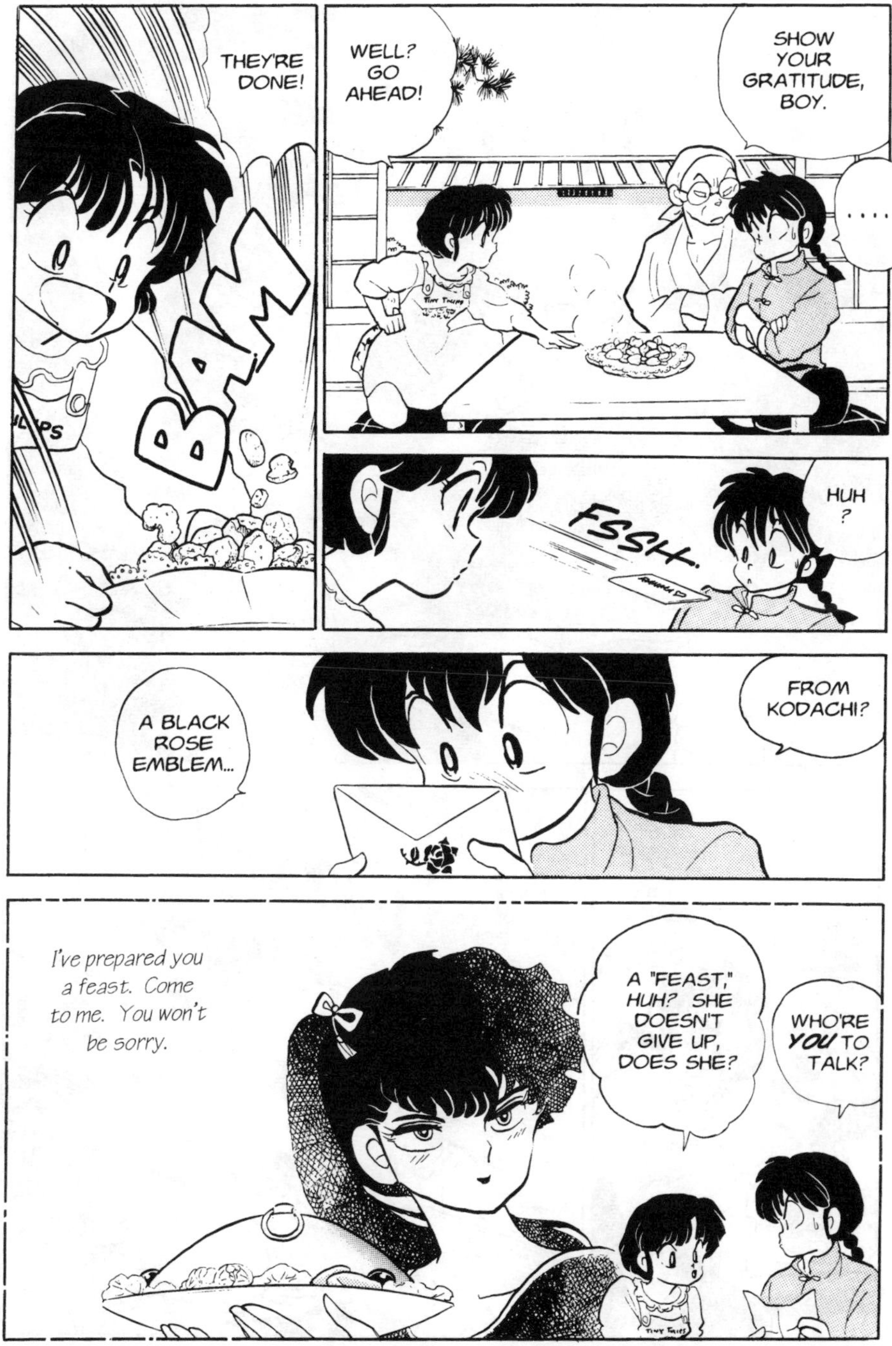
THEY'RE DONE!
BAM
WELL? GO AHEAD!
SHOW YOUR GRATITUDE, BOY.
.....
FSSH
HUH?
A BLACK ROSE EMBLEM...
FROM KODACHI?
I've prepared you a feast. Come to me. You won't be sorry.
A "FEAST," HUH? SHE DOESN'T GIVE UP, DOES SHE?
WHO'RE YOU TO TALK?

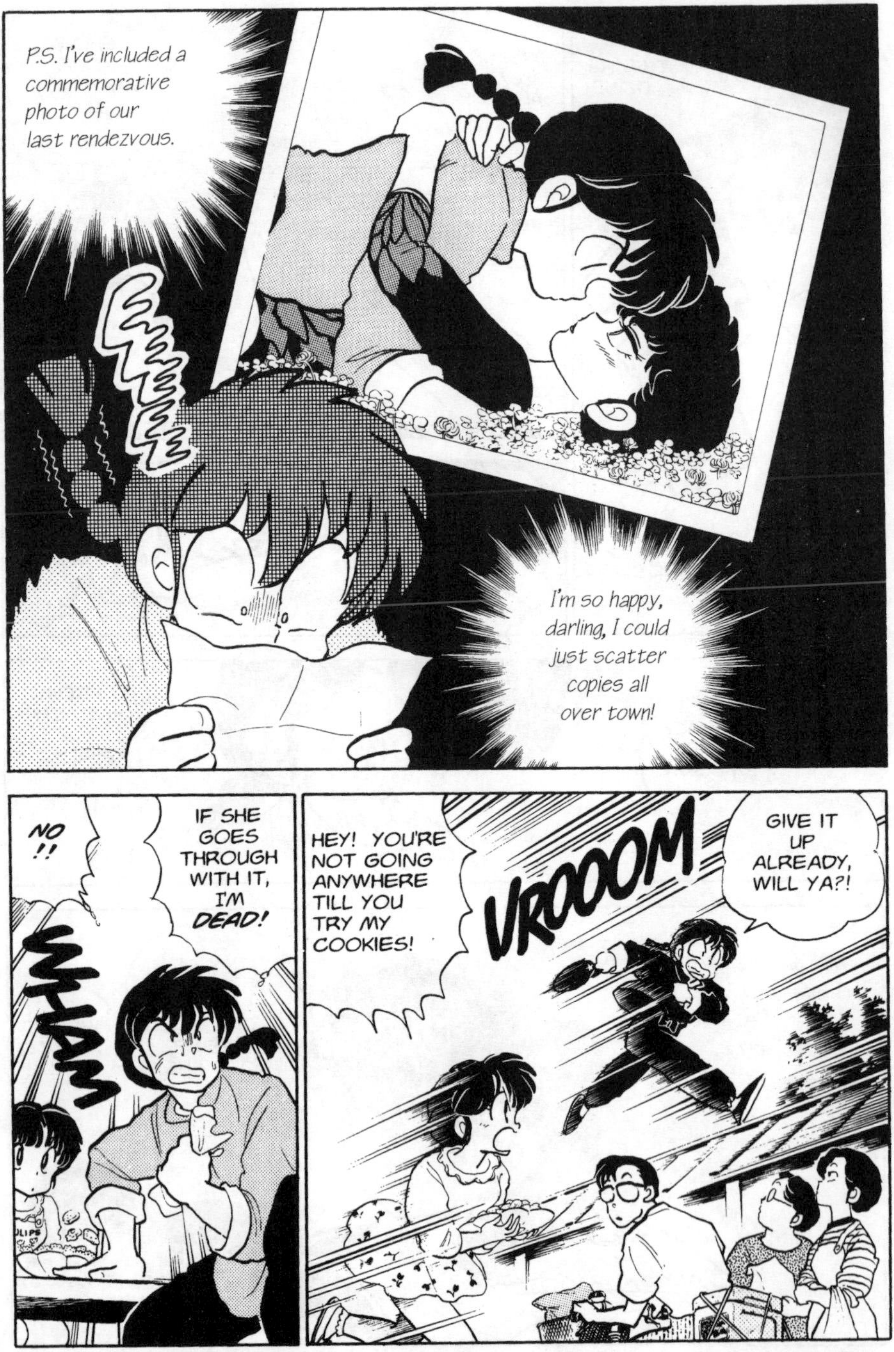
P.S. I've included a commemorative photo of our last rendezvous.
I'm so happy, darling, I could just scatter copies all over town!
NO!!
IF SHE GOES THROUGH WITH IT, I'M DEAD!
WHAM
HEY! YOU'RE NOT GOING ANYWHERE TILL YOU TRY MY COOKIES!
VROOOM
GIVE IT UP ALREADY, WILL YA?!

# PART NINE

# NEGATIVE FEELINGS

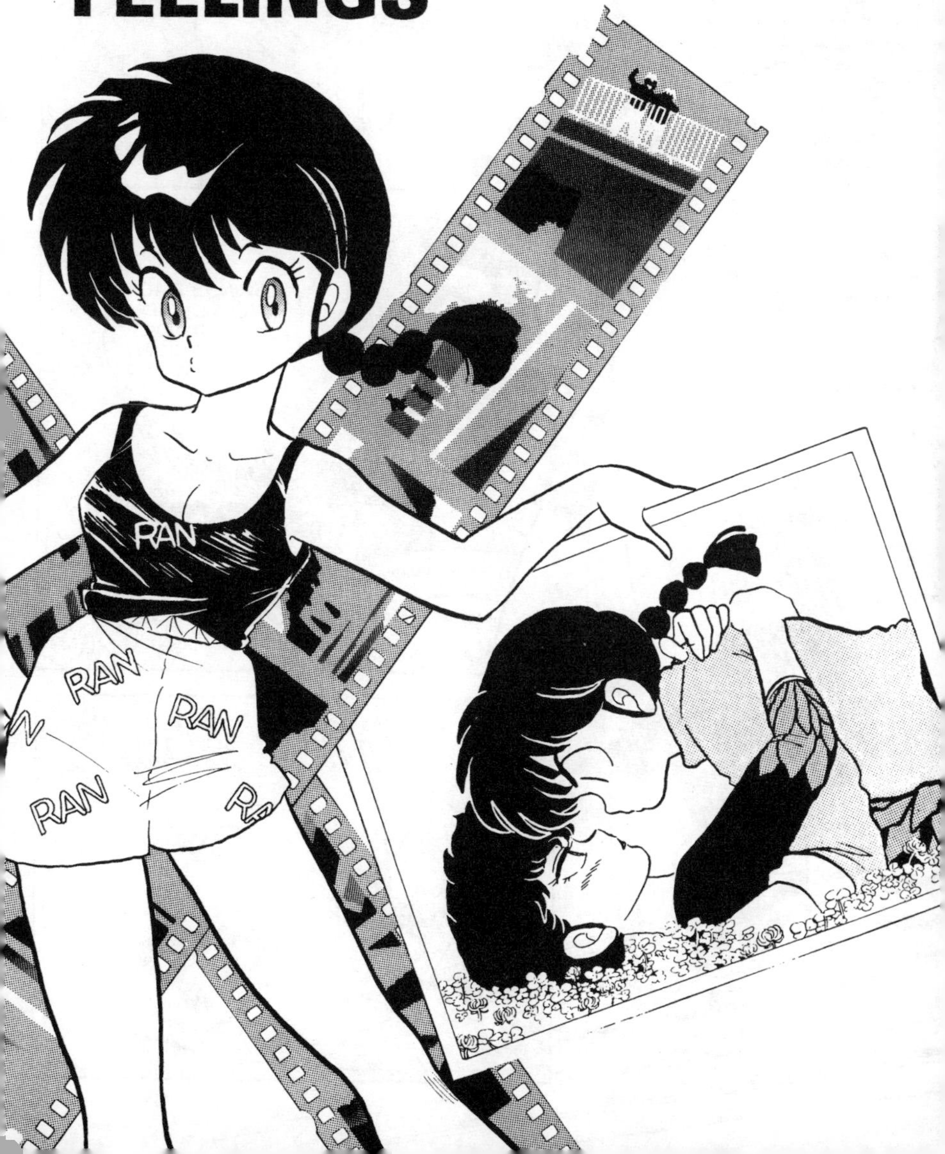
RAN
RAN
RAN
RAN

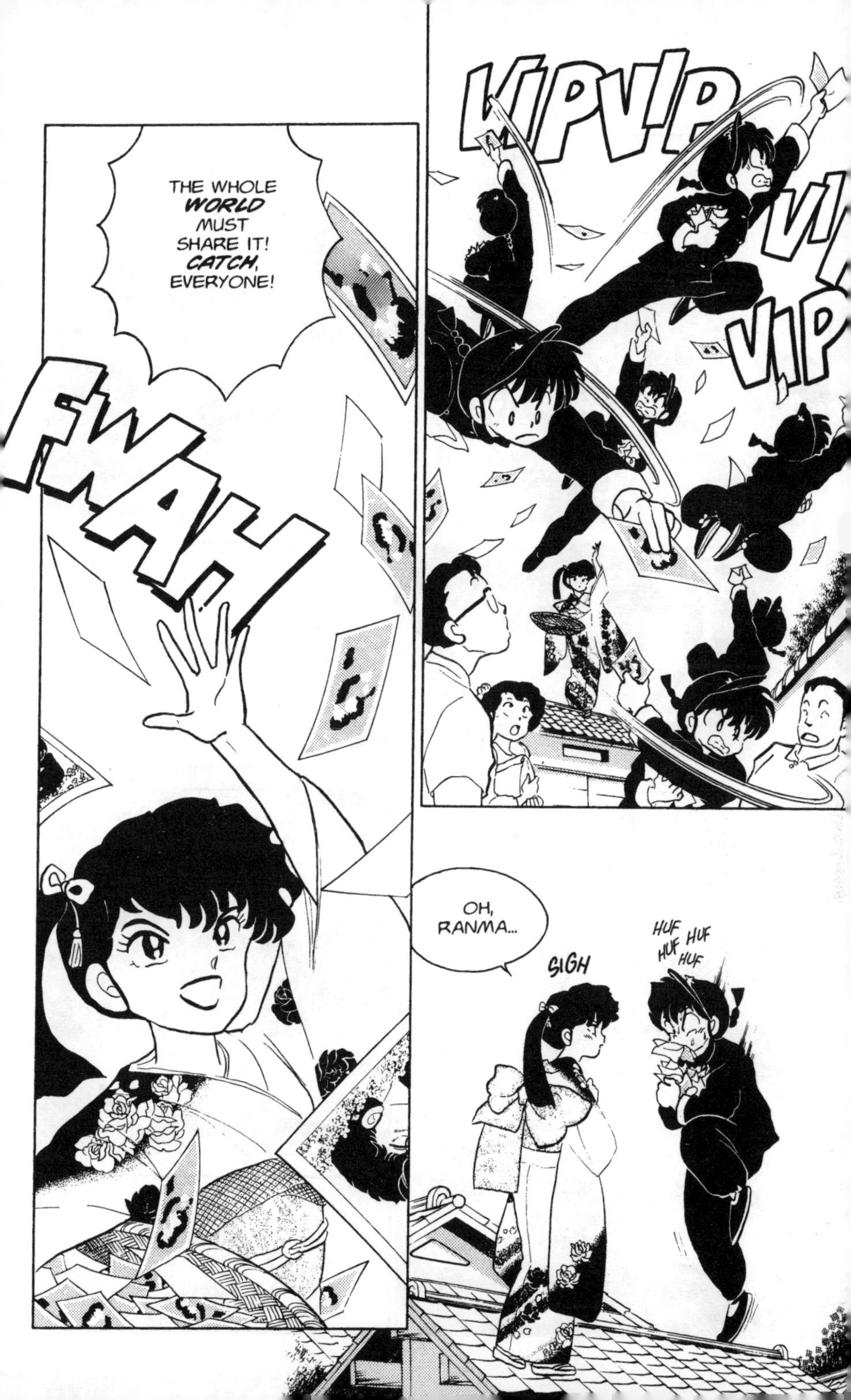
THE WHOLE *WORLD* MUST SHARE IT! *CATCH*, EVERYONE!
FWAH
VIPVIP
VI
VIP
OH, RANMA...
SIGH
HUF HUF
HUF HUF

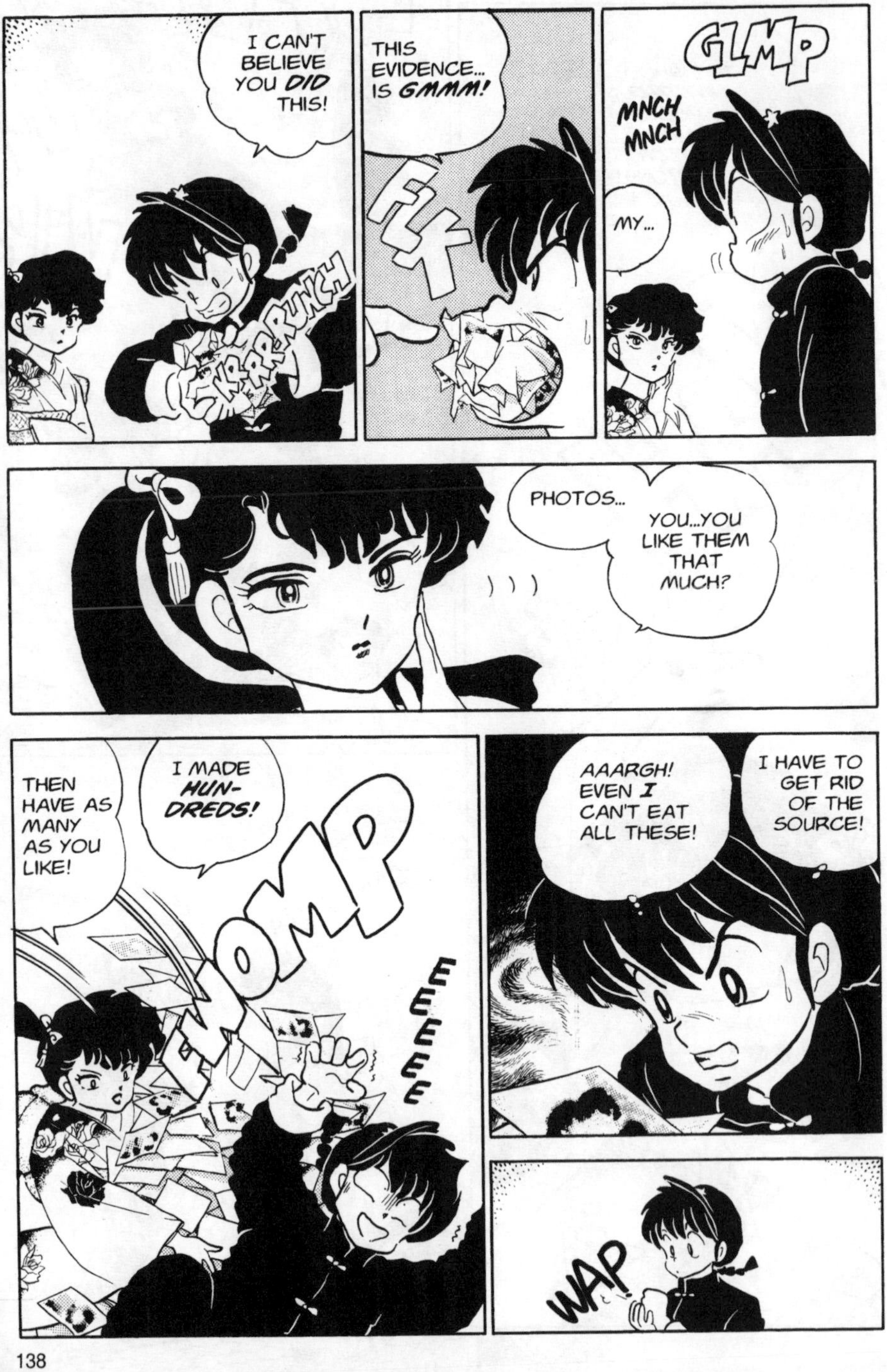
I CAN'T BELIEVE YOU *DID* THIS!
SKRRRUNCH
THIS EVIDENCE... IS *GMMM!*
FLIT
GLMP
MNCH MNCH
MY...
PHOTOS...
YOU...YOU LIKE THEM THAT MUCH?
THEN HAVE AS MANY AS YOU LIKE!
I MADE *HUN-DREDS!*
WOMP
EEEEEE
AAARGH! EVEN *I* CAN'T EAT ALL THESE!
I HAVE TO GET RID OF THE SOURCE!
WAP

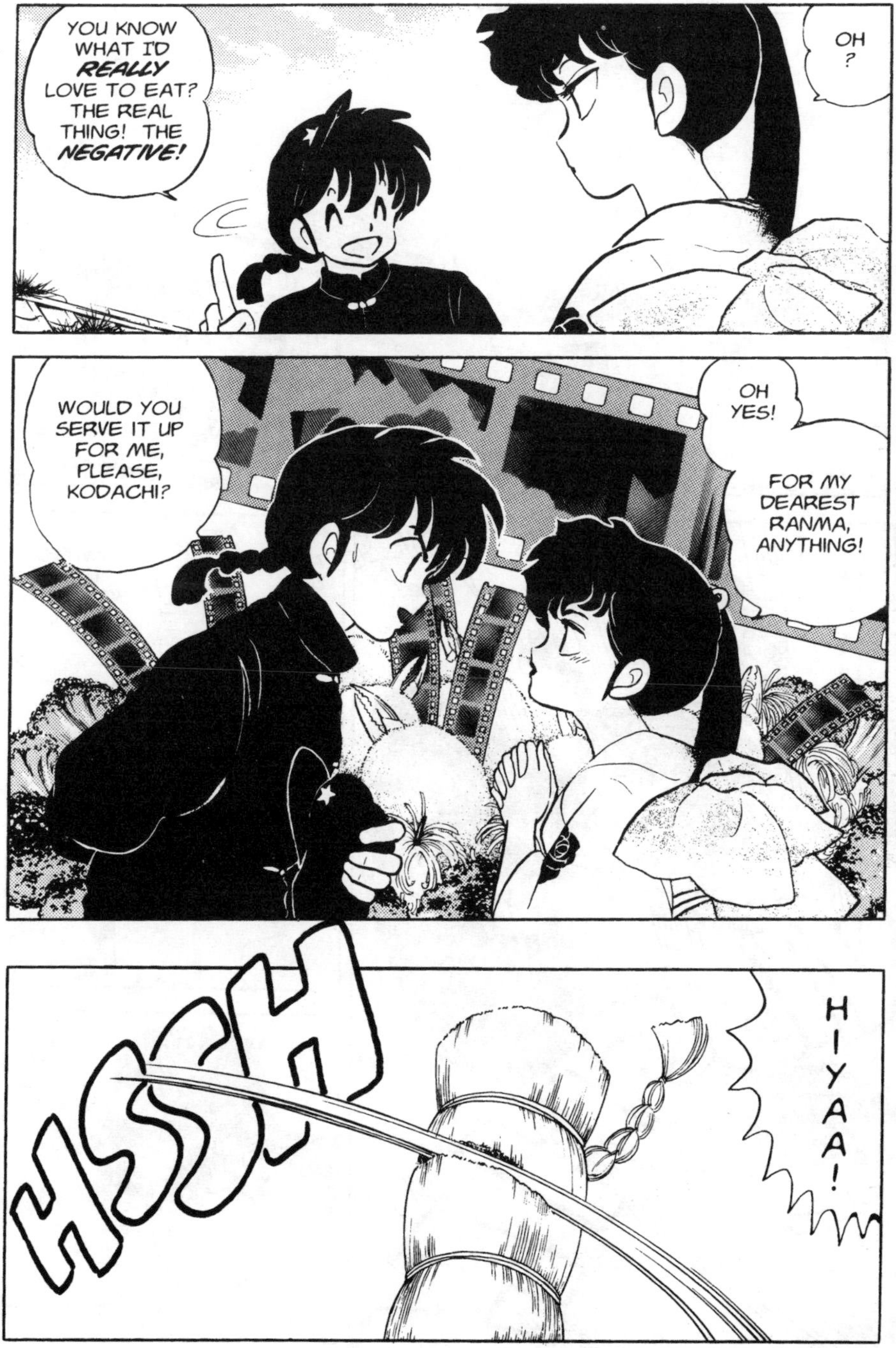

YOU KNOW WHAT I'D **REALLY** LOVE TO EAT? THE REAL THING! THE **NEGATIVE!**
OH ?
WOULD YOU SERVE IT UP FOR ME, PLEASE, KODACHI?
OH YES!
FOR MY DEAREST RANMA, ANYTHING!
HSSH
HIYAAA!

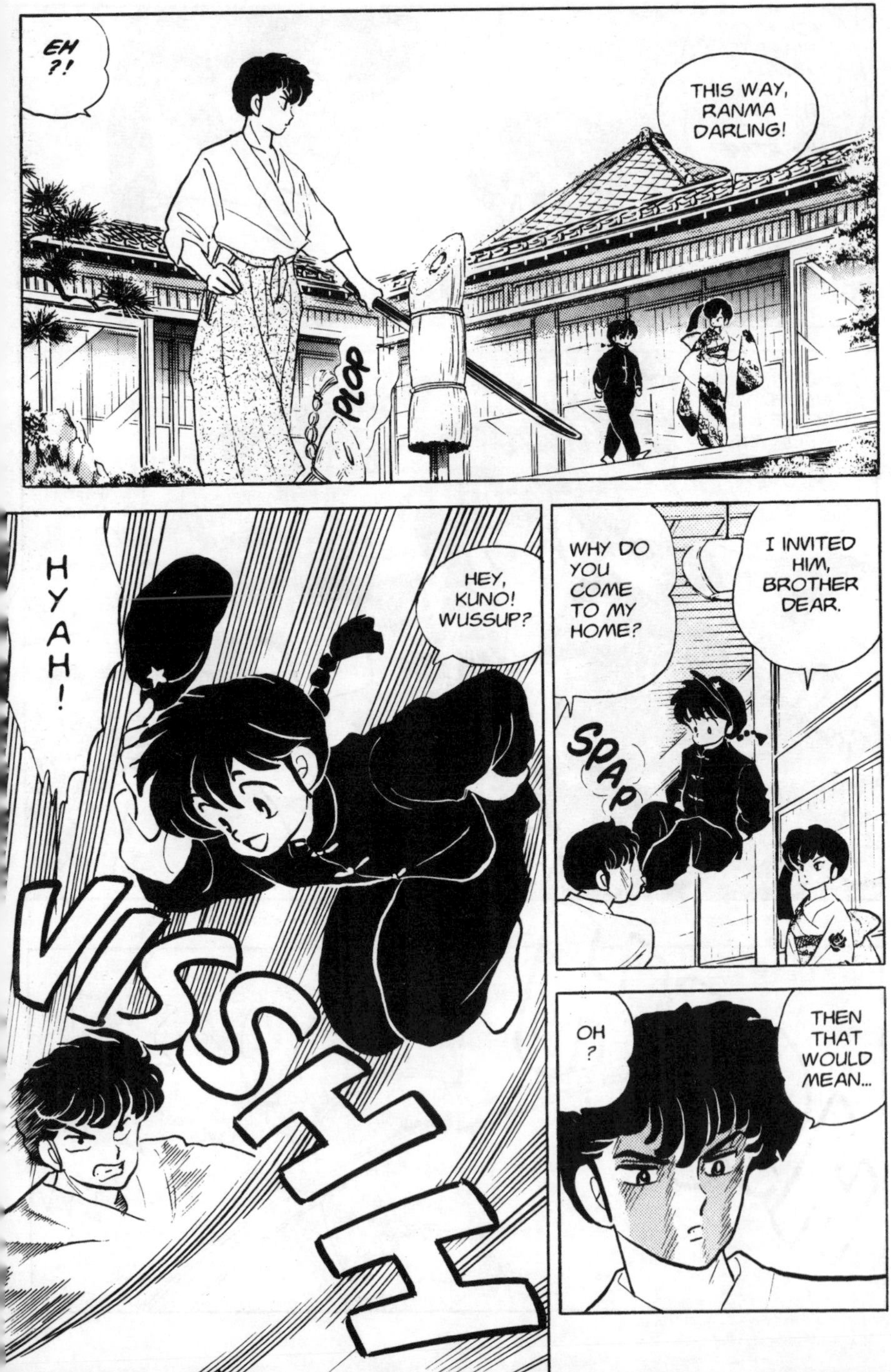
EH ?!
THIS WAY, RANMA DARLING!
PLOP
HYAH!
HEY, KUNO! WUSSUP?
VISSSH
WHY DO YOU COME TO MY HOME?
I INVITED HIM, BROTHER DEAR.
SPAP
OH ?
THEN THAT WOULD MEAN...

141

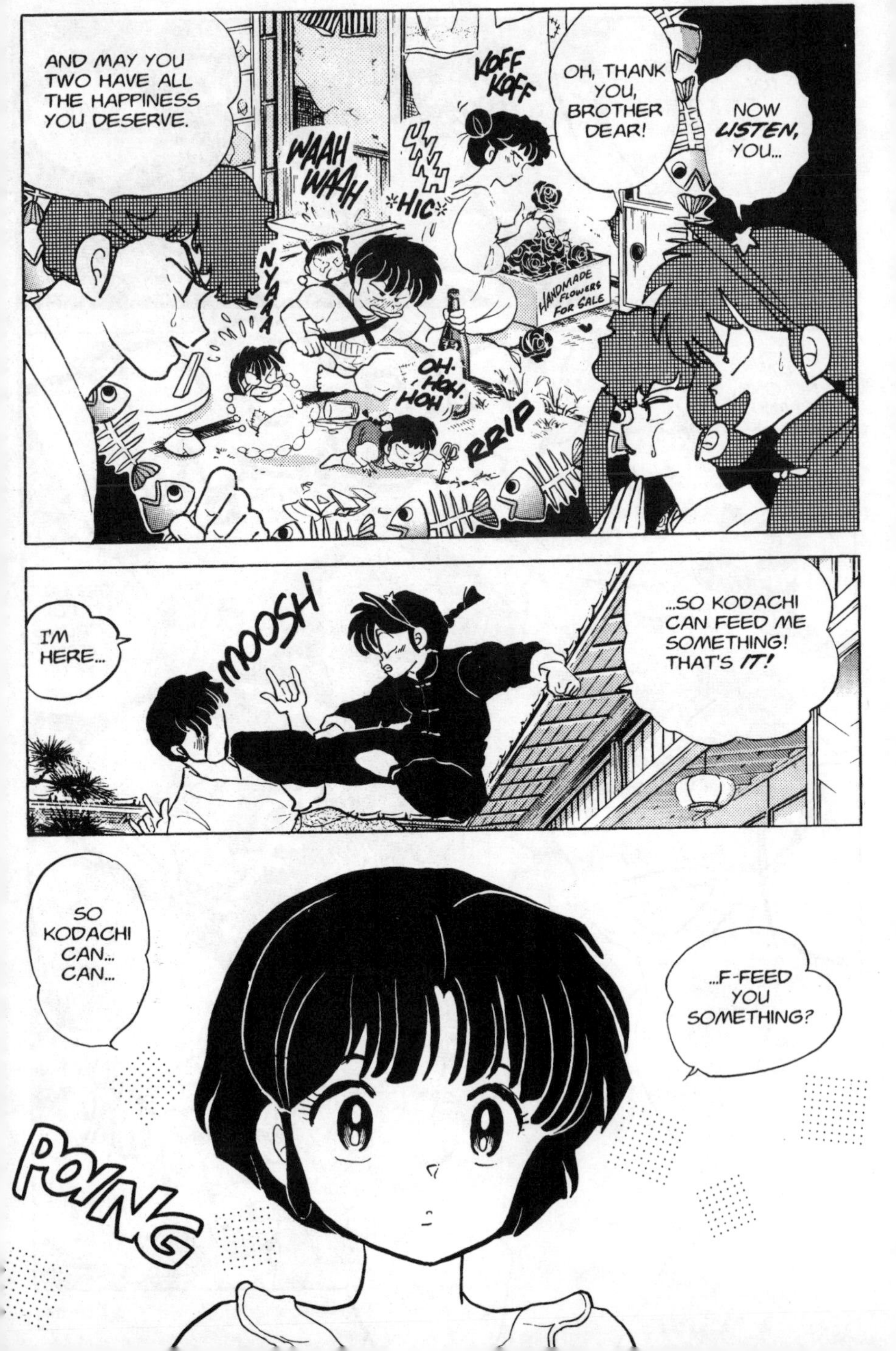
AND MAY YOU TWO HAVE ALL THE HAPPINESS YOU DESERVE.
KOFF KOFF
OH, THANK YOU, BROTHER DEAR!
NOW LISTEN, YOU...
WAAH WAAH
UWAH
*HIC*
NYAAA
HANDMADE FLOWERS FOR SALE
OH. HOH. HOH.
RRIP
I'M HERE...
MOOSH
...SO KODACHI CAN FEED ME SOMETHING! THAT'S IT!
SO KODACHI CAN... CAN...
...F-FEED YOU SOMETHING?
POING

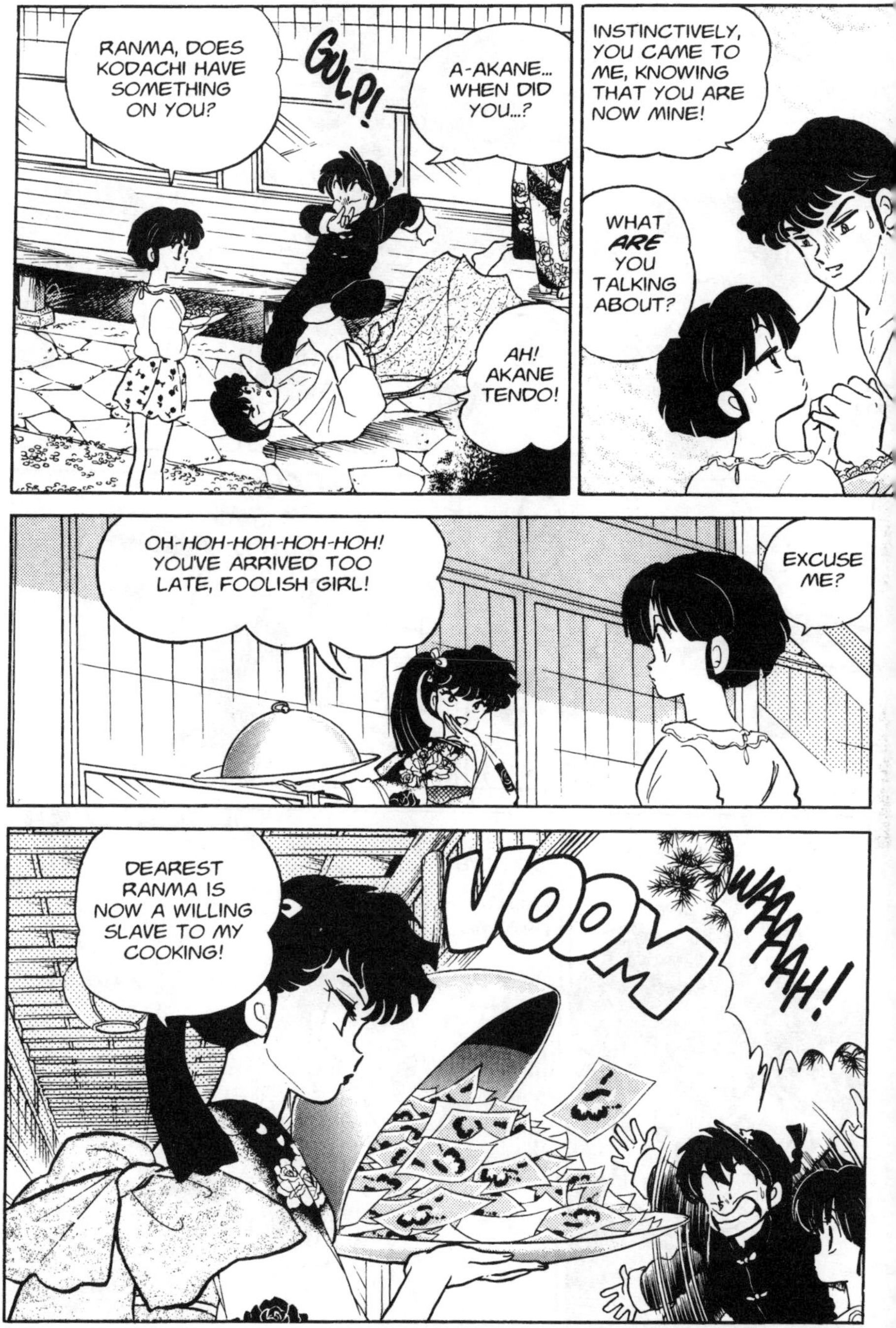
RANMA, DOES KODACHI HAVE SOMETHING ON YOU?
GULP!
A-AKANE... WHEN DID YOU...?
AH! AKANE TENDO!
INSTINCTIVELY, YOU CAME TO ME, KNOWING THAT YOU ARE NOW MINE!
WHAT ARE YOU TALKING ABOUT?
OH-HOH-HOH-HOH-HOH! YOU'VE ARRIVED TOO LATE, FOOLISH GIRL!
EXCUSE ME?
DEAREST RANMA IS NOW A WILLING SLAVE TO MY COOKING!
VOOM
WAAAAAH!

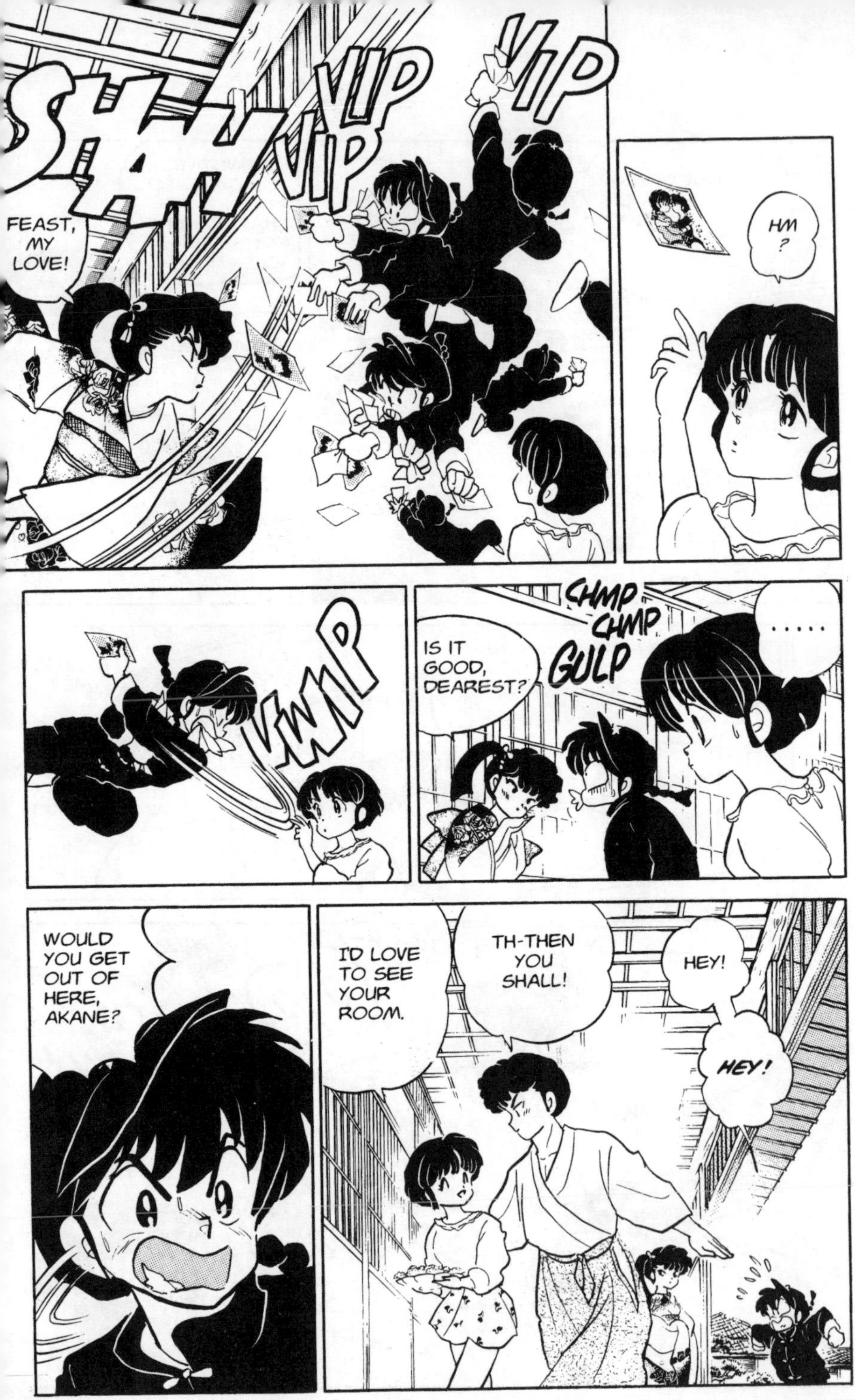
SHAH
VIP
VIP
VIP
VIP
FEAST, MY LOVE!
HM?
VWIP
IS IT GOOD, DEAREST?
CHMP CHMP GULP
......
WOULD YOU GET OUT OF HERE, AKANE?
I'D LOVE TO SEE YOUR ROOM.
TH-THEN YOU SHALL!
HEY!
HEY!

WHATEVER'S IN THAT PICTURE MUST BE *GOOD*...OR *BAD*.

AND HE *REALLY* THINKS I'M JUST GOING TO GO HOME?

NOW, MY DEAR RANMA...

WILL YOU GO FETCH THE NEGATIVE FOR ME?

FOR YOU?! *ANYTHING!*

YOU'LL FIND IT IN THE COLLAR OF MR. TURTLE, WHO LIVES IN MY POND.

VROOOM

HAH!

ONCE I GET MY HANDS ON THAT NEGATIVE...

I AM *GONE!*

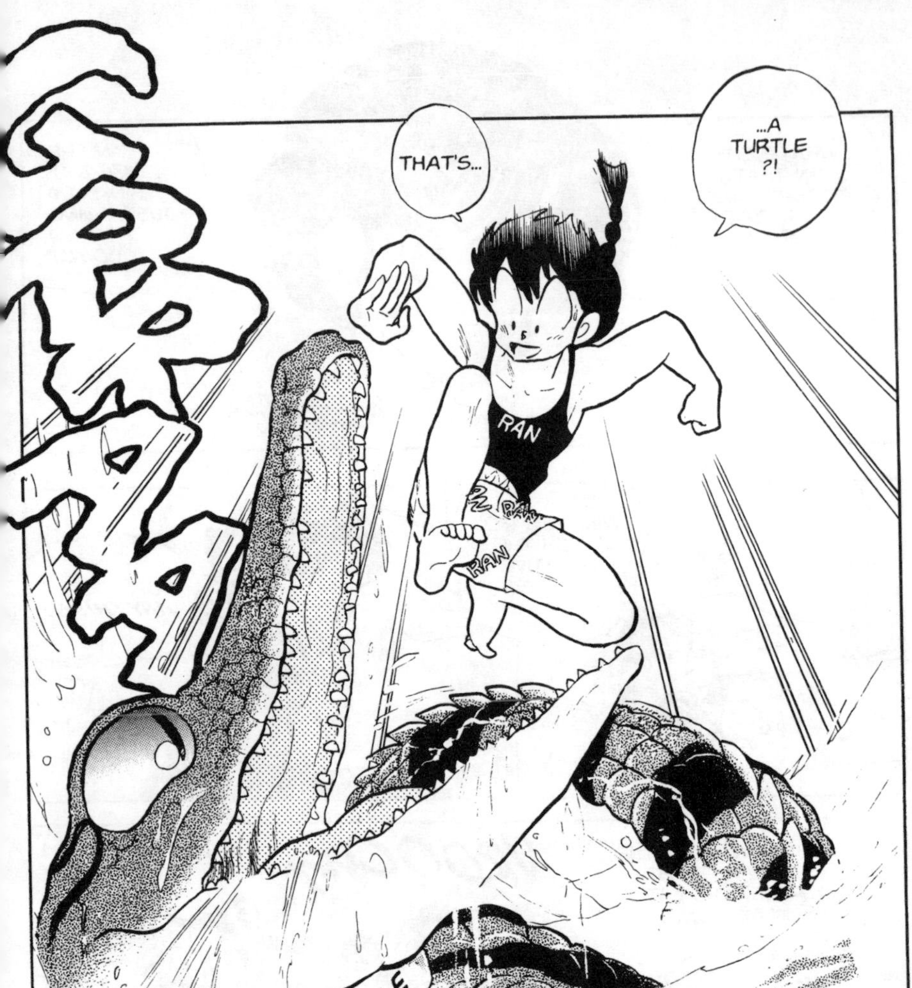
THAT'S...
...A TURTLE ?!
RAN
MR. TURTLE

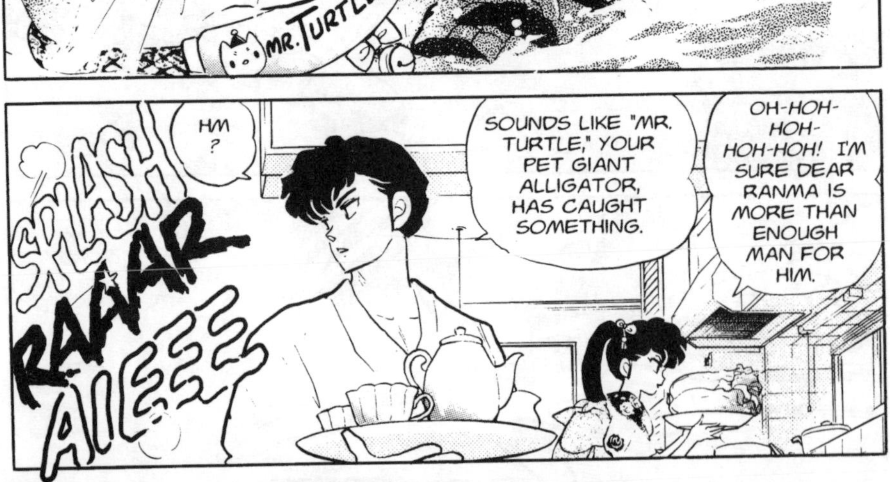
SPLASH
RAAAR
AIEEE
HM ?
SOUNDS LIKE "MR. TURTLE," YOUR PET GIANT ALLIGATOR, HAS CAUGHT SOMETHING.
OH-HOH-HOH-HOH-HOH! I'M SURE DEAR RANMA IS MORE THAN ENOUGH MAN FOR HIM.

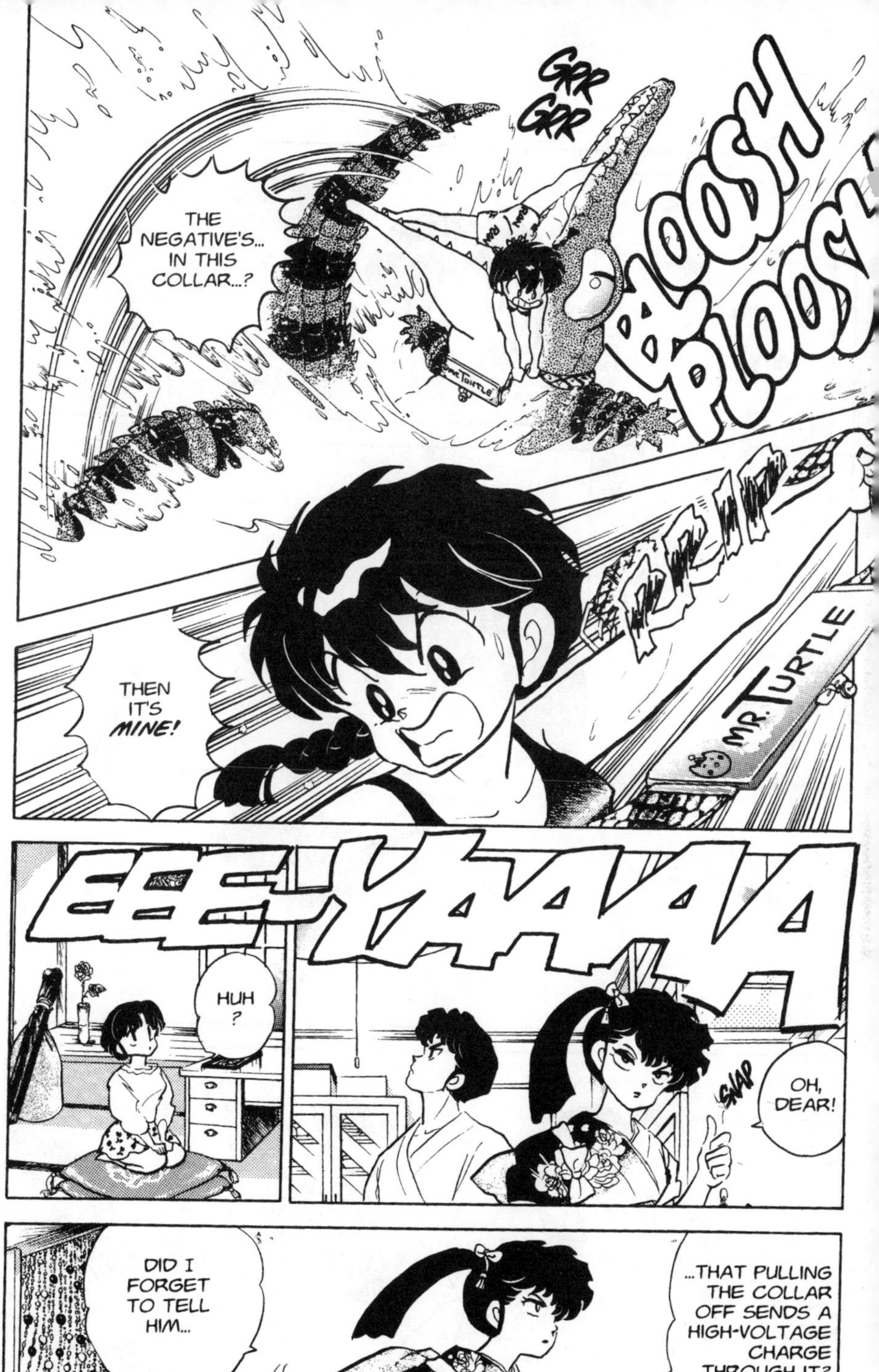

GRR GRR
THE NEGATIVE'S... IN THIS COLLAR...?
BLOOSH PLOOSH
THEN IT'S *MINE!*
MR. TURTLE
EEE-YAAAA
HUH ?
SNAP
OH, DEAR!
DID I FORGET TO TELL HIM...
...THAT PULLING THE COLLAR OFF SENDS A HIGH-VOLTAGE CHARGE THROUGH IT?

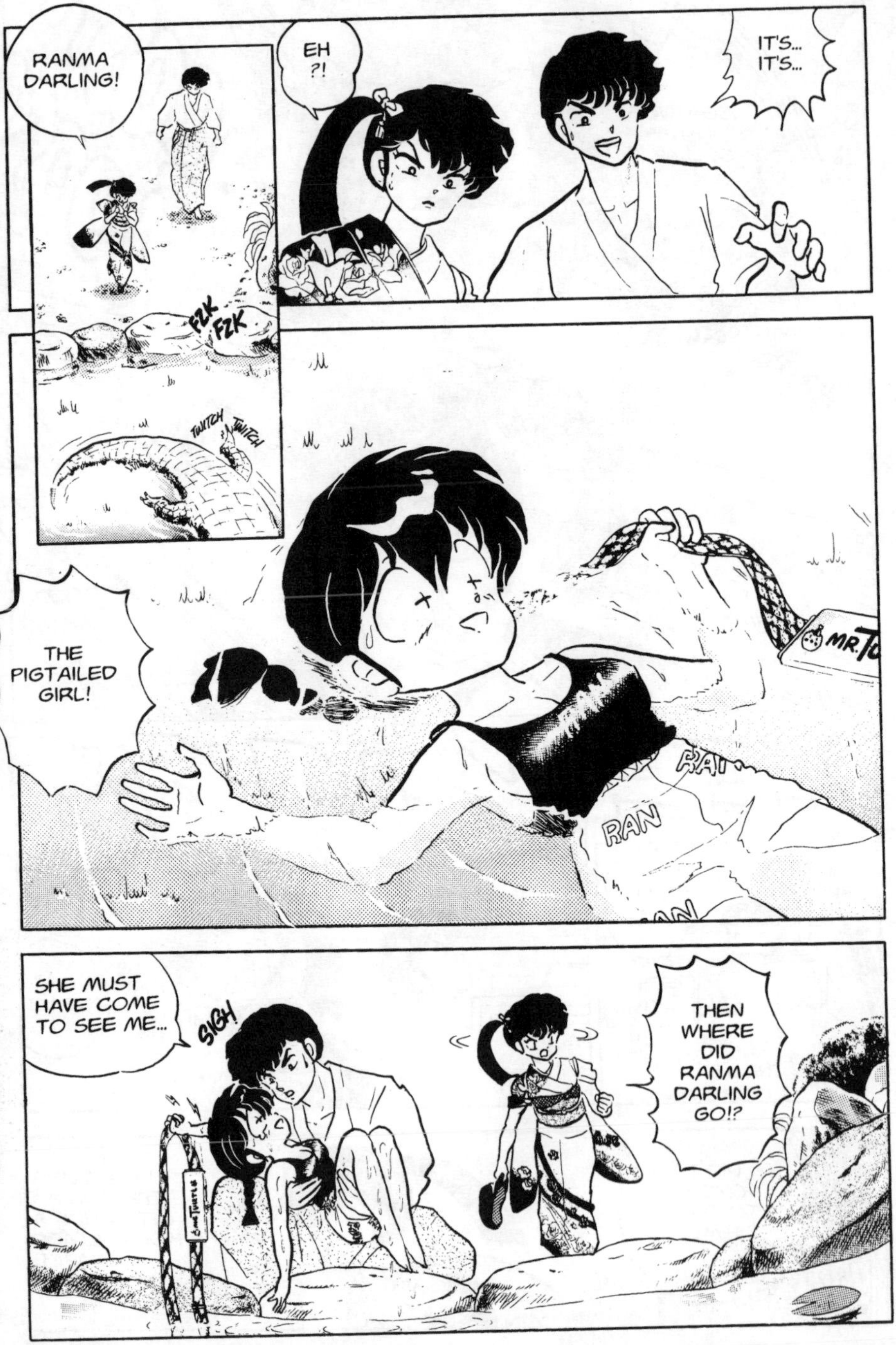
RANMA DARLING!
FZK FZK
TWITCH TWITCH
EH ?!
IT'S... IT'S...
THE PIGTAILED GIRL!
RAN
SHE MUST HAVE COME TO SEE ME...
SIGH
THEN WHERE DID RANMA DARLING GO!?

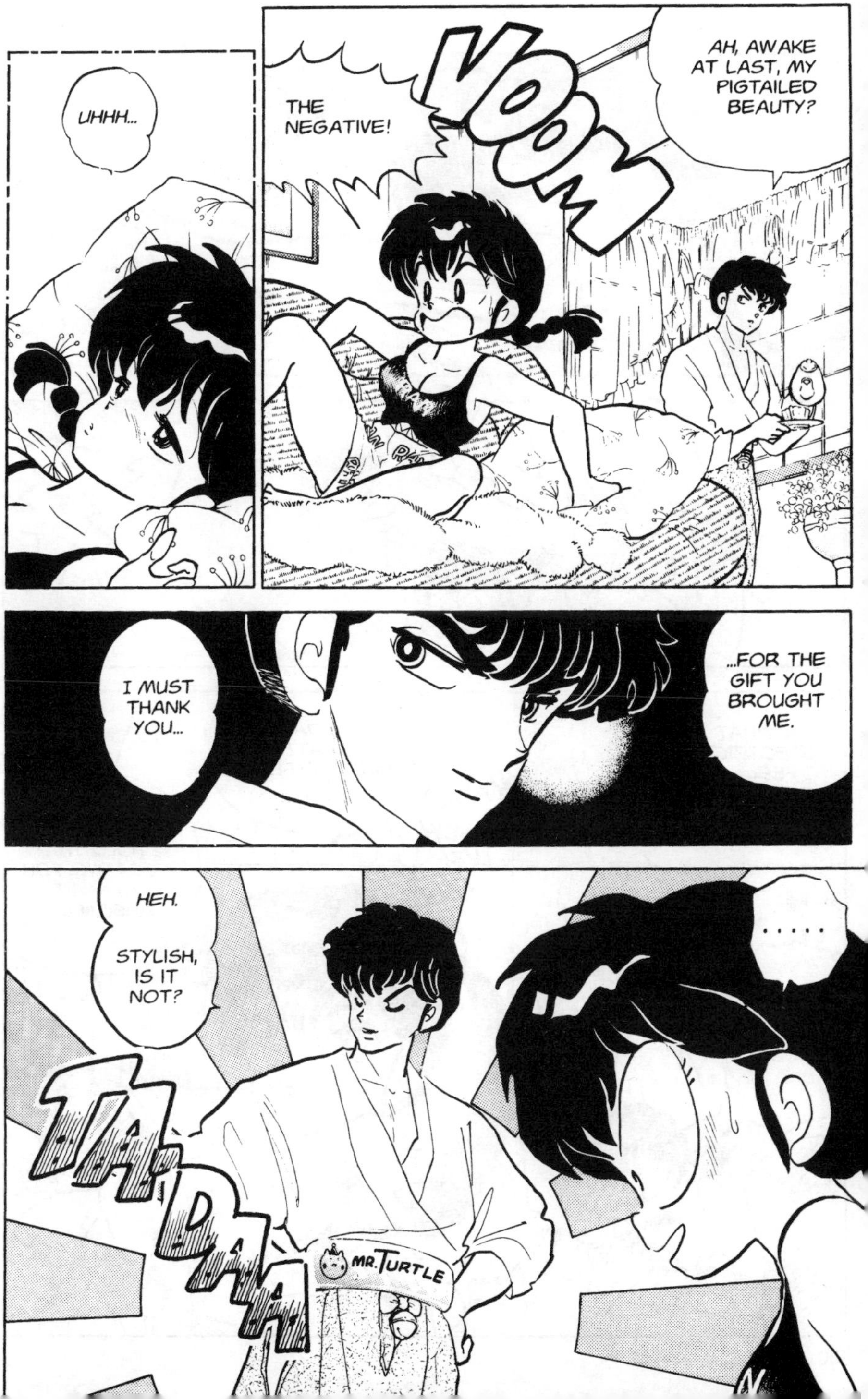
UHHH...
THE NEGATIVE!
VOOOM
AH, AWAKE AT LAST, MY PIGTAILED BEAUTY?
I MUST THANK YOU...
...FOR THE GIFT YOU BROUGHT ME.
HEH.
STYLISH, IS IT NOT?
.....
TA-DAAA
MR. TURTLE

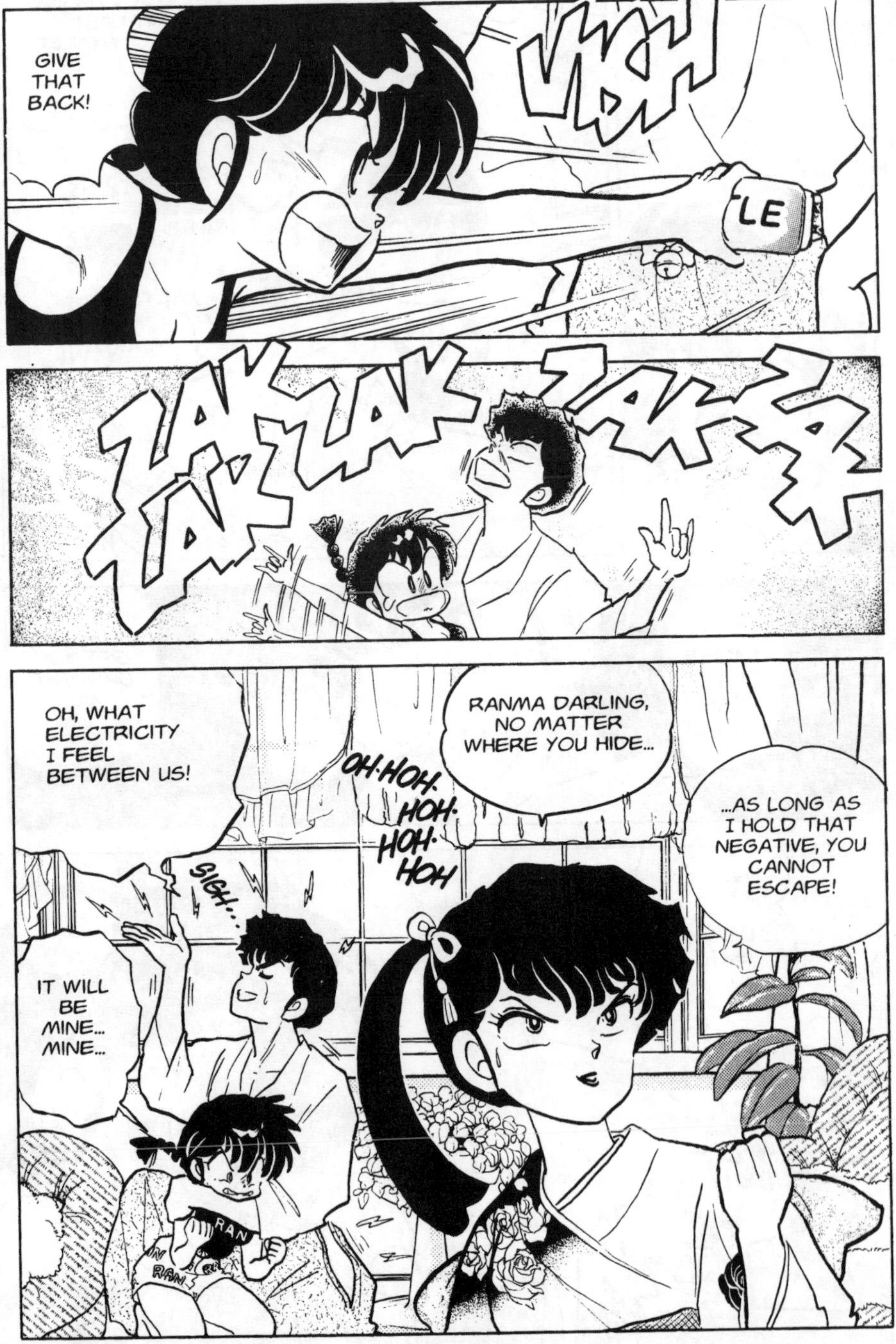
GIVE THAT BACK!
LE
ZAK ZAK ZAK ZAK ZA
OH, WHAT ELECTRICITY I FEEL BETWEEN US!
RANMA DARLING, NO MATTER WHERE YOU HIDE...
OH·HOH· HOH· HOH· HOH
...AS LONG AS I HOLD THAT NEGATIVE, YOU CANNOT ESCAPE!
SIGH...
IT WILL BE MINE... MINE...
RAN
RAN

# PART TEN

# TAKE ME OUT TO THE BATHTUB

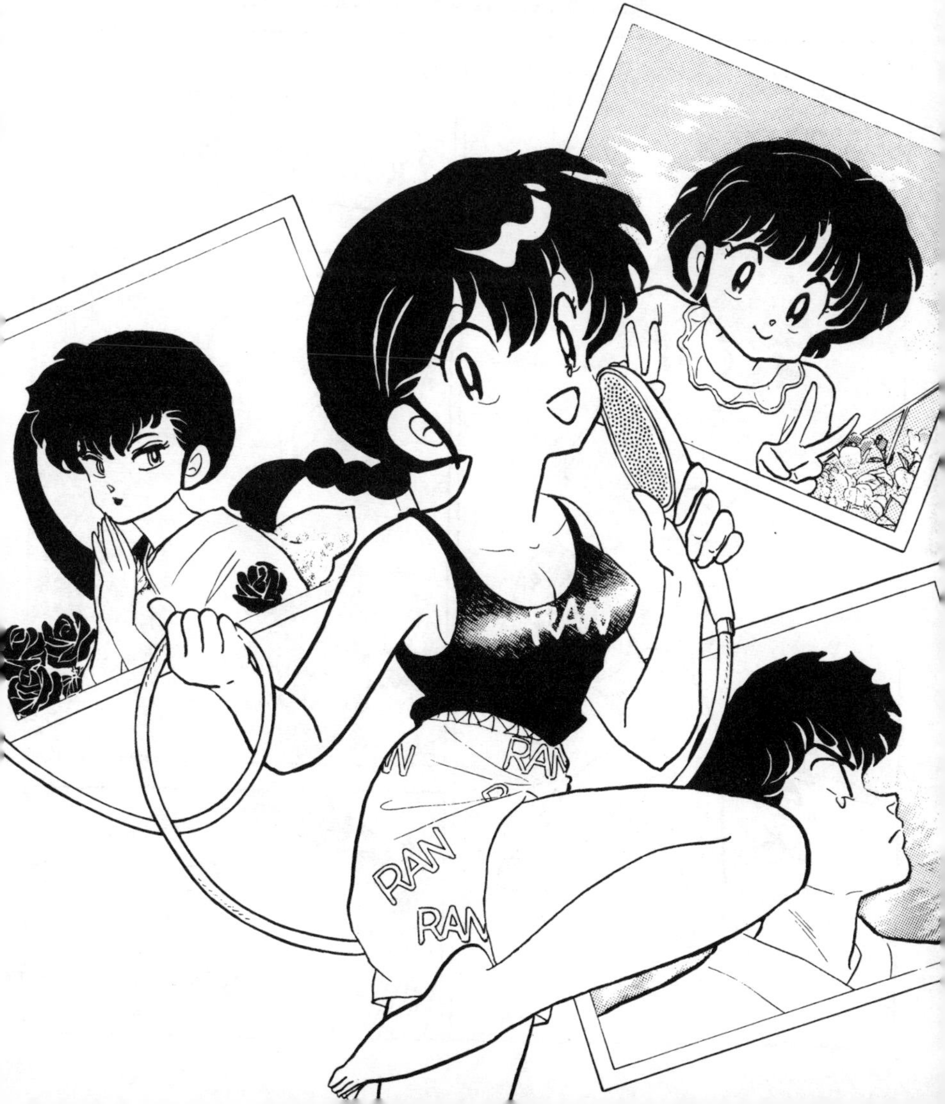
RAN
RAN
RAN
RAN

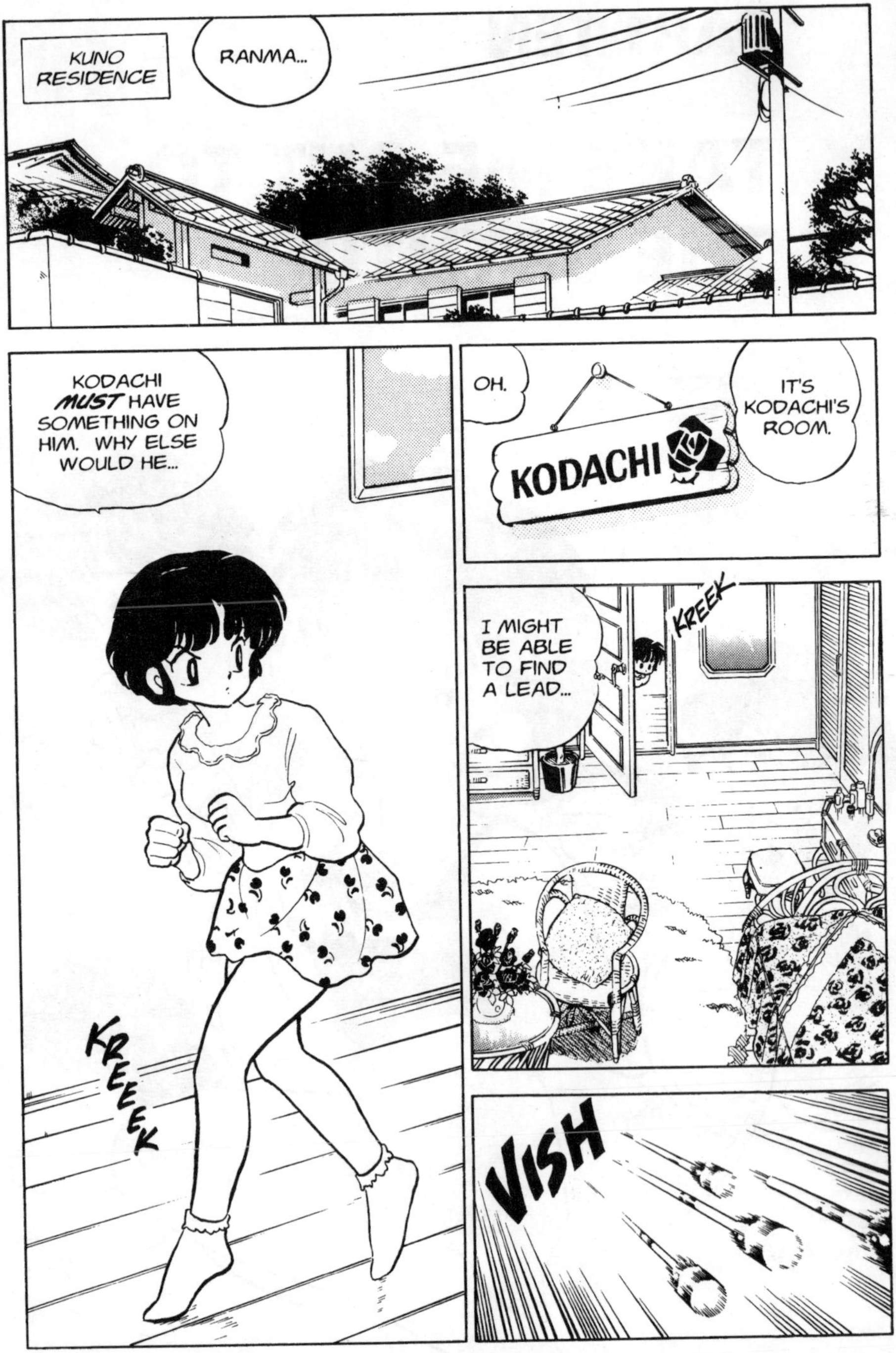
KUNO RESIDENCE
RANMA...
KODACHI MUST HAVE SOMETHING ON HIM. WHY ELSE WOULD HE...
KREEEEK
OH.
KODACHI
IT'S KODACHI'S ROOM.
I MIGHT BE ABLE TO FIND A LEAD...
KREEK
VISH

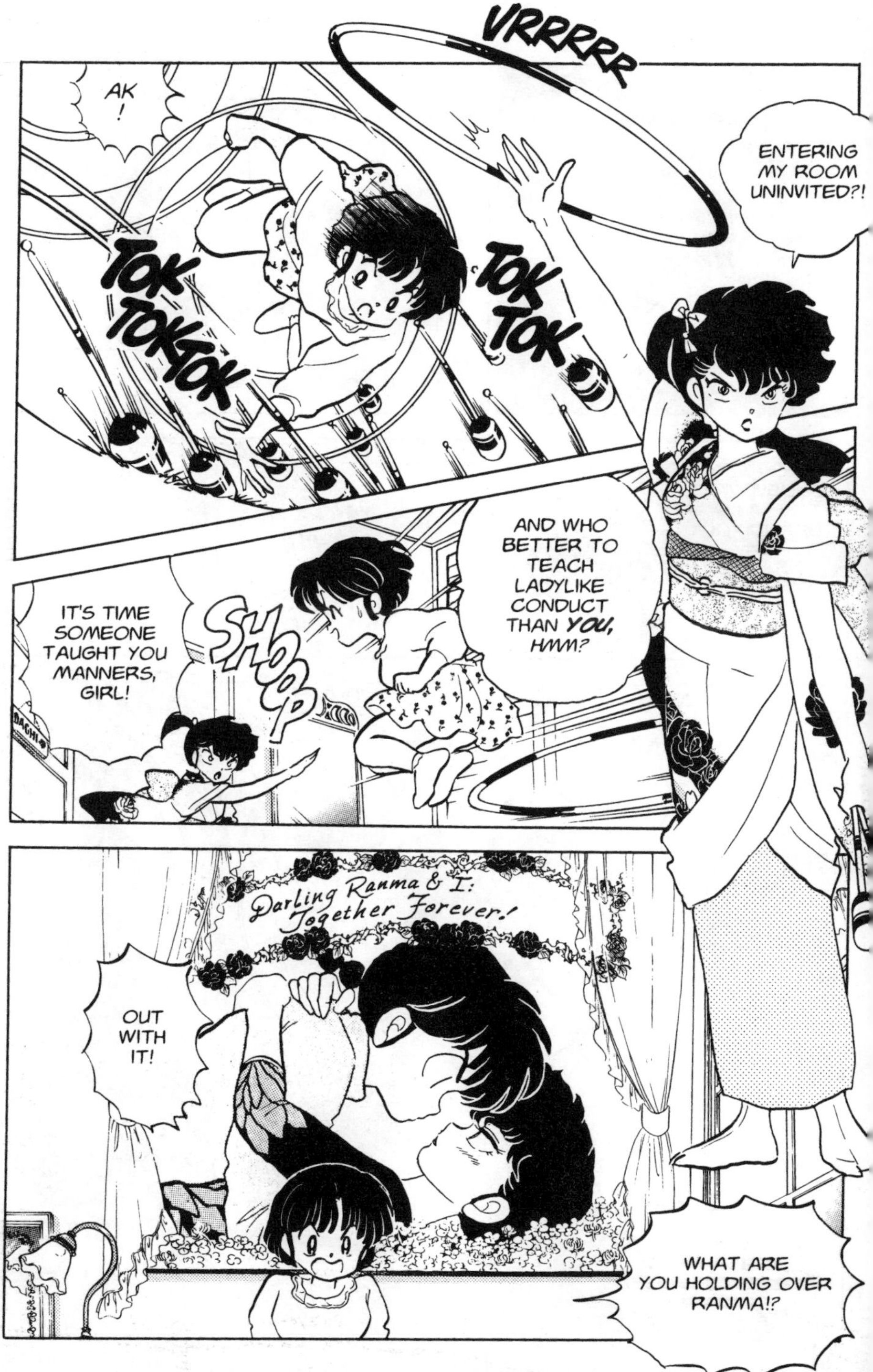
AK!
VRRRRR
TOK TOKTOK
TOK TOK
ENTERING MY ROOM UNINVITED?!
IT'S TIME SOMEONE TAUGHT YOU MANNERS, GIRL!
SHOOOP
AND WHO BETTER TO TEACH LADYLIKE CONDUCT THAN YOU, HMM?
Darling Ranma & I: Together Forever!
OUT WITH IT!
WHAT ARE YOU HOLDING OVER RANMA!?

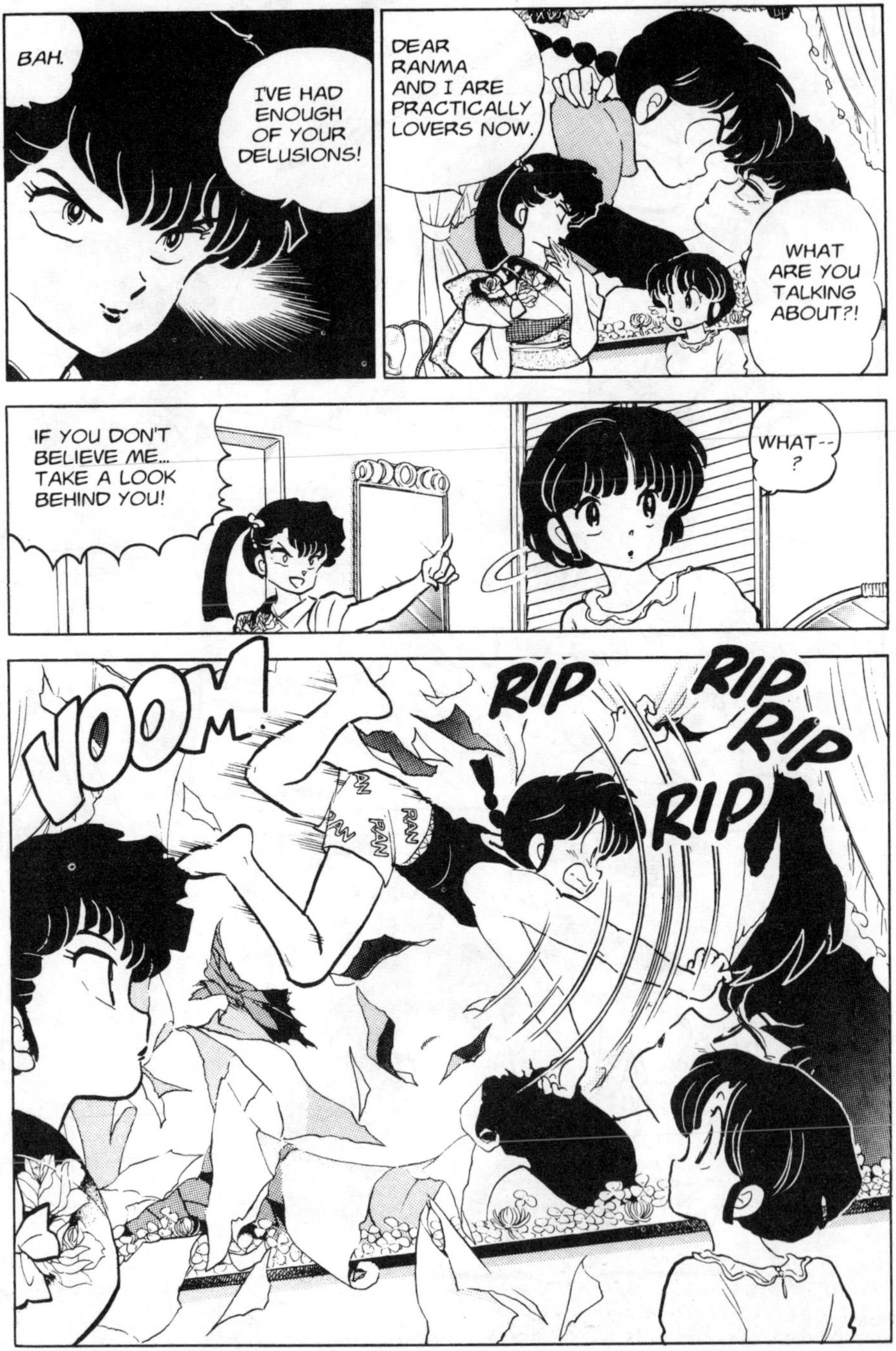
BAH.
I'VE HAD ENOUGH OF YOUR DELUSIONS!
DEAR RANMA AND I ARE PRACTICALLY LOVERS NOW.
WHAT ARE YOU TALKING ABOUT?!
IF YOU DON'T BELIEVE ME... TAKE A LOOK BEHIND YOU!
WHAT-- ?
VOOOM
RIP
RIP RIP RIP
RIP

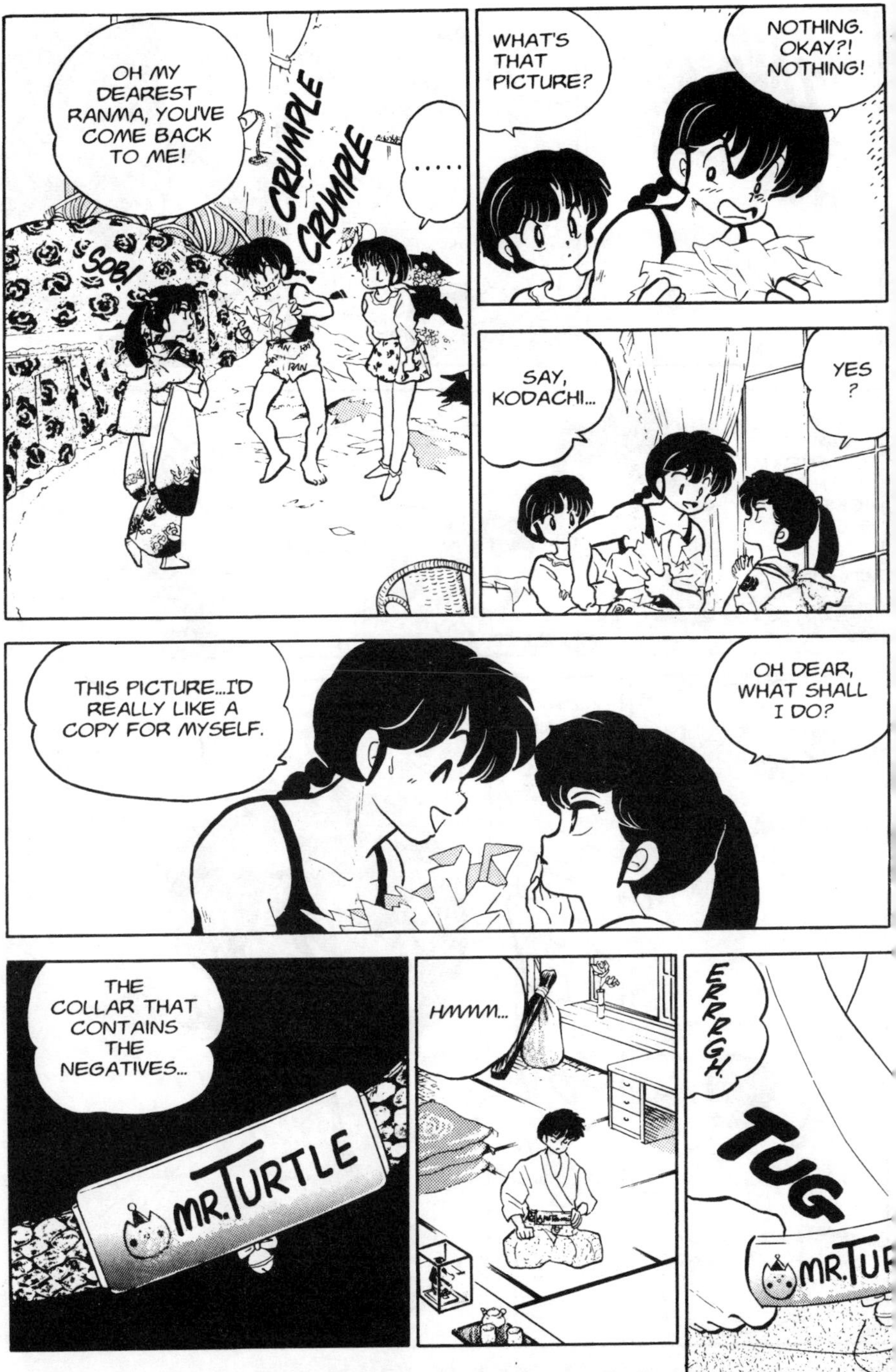
OH MY DEAREST RANMA, YOU'VE COME BACK TO ME!
CRUMPLE CRUMPLE
......
SOB!
WHAT'S THAT PICTURE?
NOTHING. OKAY?! NOTHING!
SAY, KODACHI...
YES?
THIS PICTURE...I'D REALLY LIKE A COPY FOR MYSELF.
OH DEAR, WHAT SHALL I DO?
THE COLLAR THAT CONTAINS THE NEGATIVES...
MR.TURTLE
HMMM...
ERRRGH.
TUG
MR.TUR

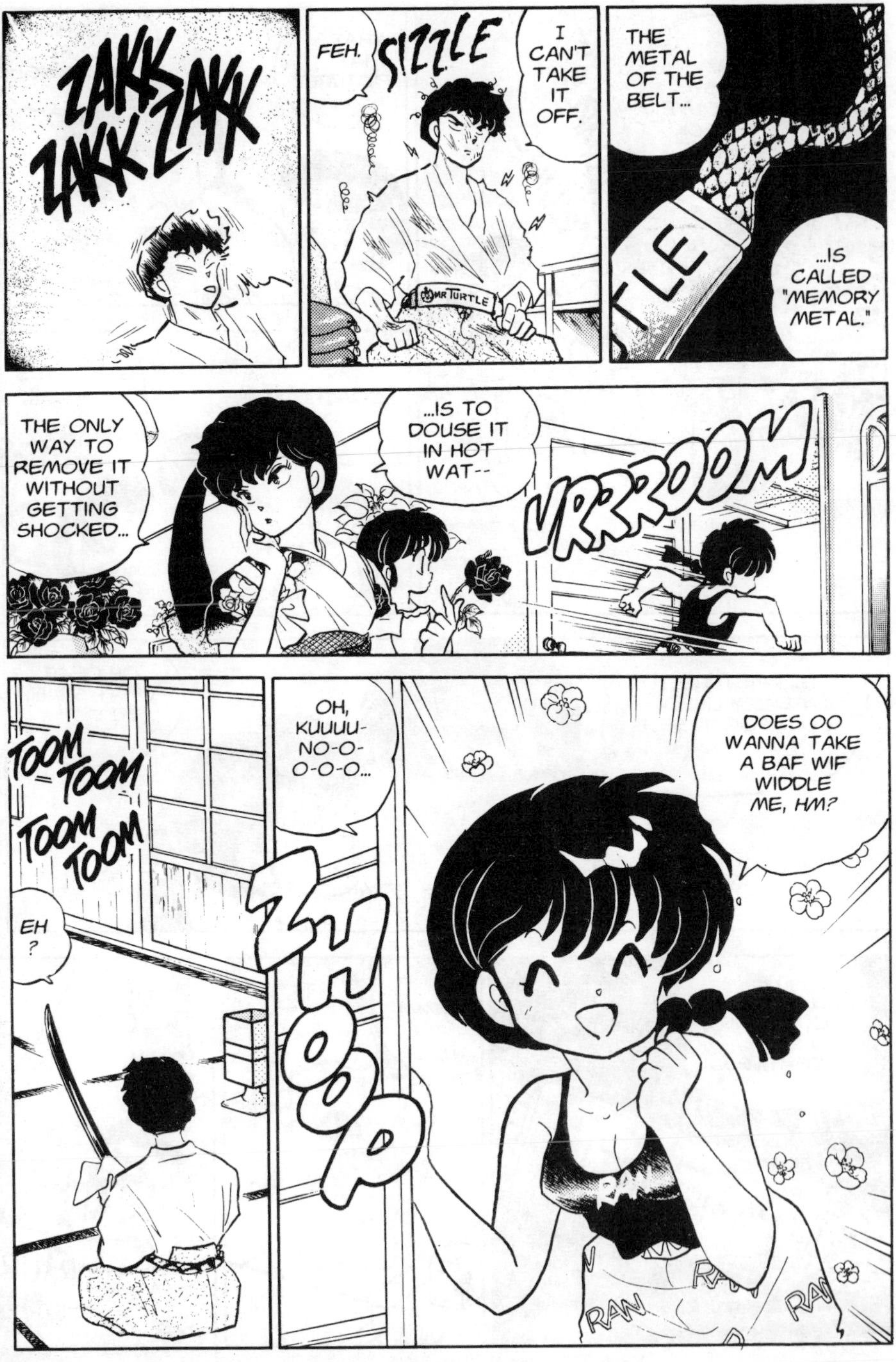
ZAKK ZAKK ZAKK ZAKK
FEH.
SIZZLE
I CAN'T TAKE IT OFF.
MR TURTLE
THE METAL OF THE BELT...
...IS CALLED "MEMORY METAL."
THE ONLY WAY TO REMOVE IT WITHOUT GETTING SHOCKED...
...IS TO DOUSE IT IN HOT WAT--
VRRROOM
TOOM TOOM TOOM TOOM
EH ?
OH, KUUUU-NO-O-O-O-O...
ZHOOOP
DOES OO WANNA TAKE A BAF WIF WIDDLE ME, HM?

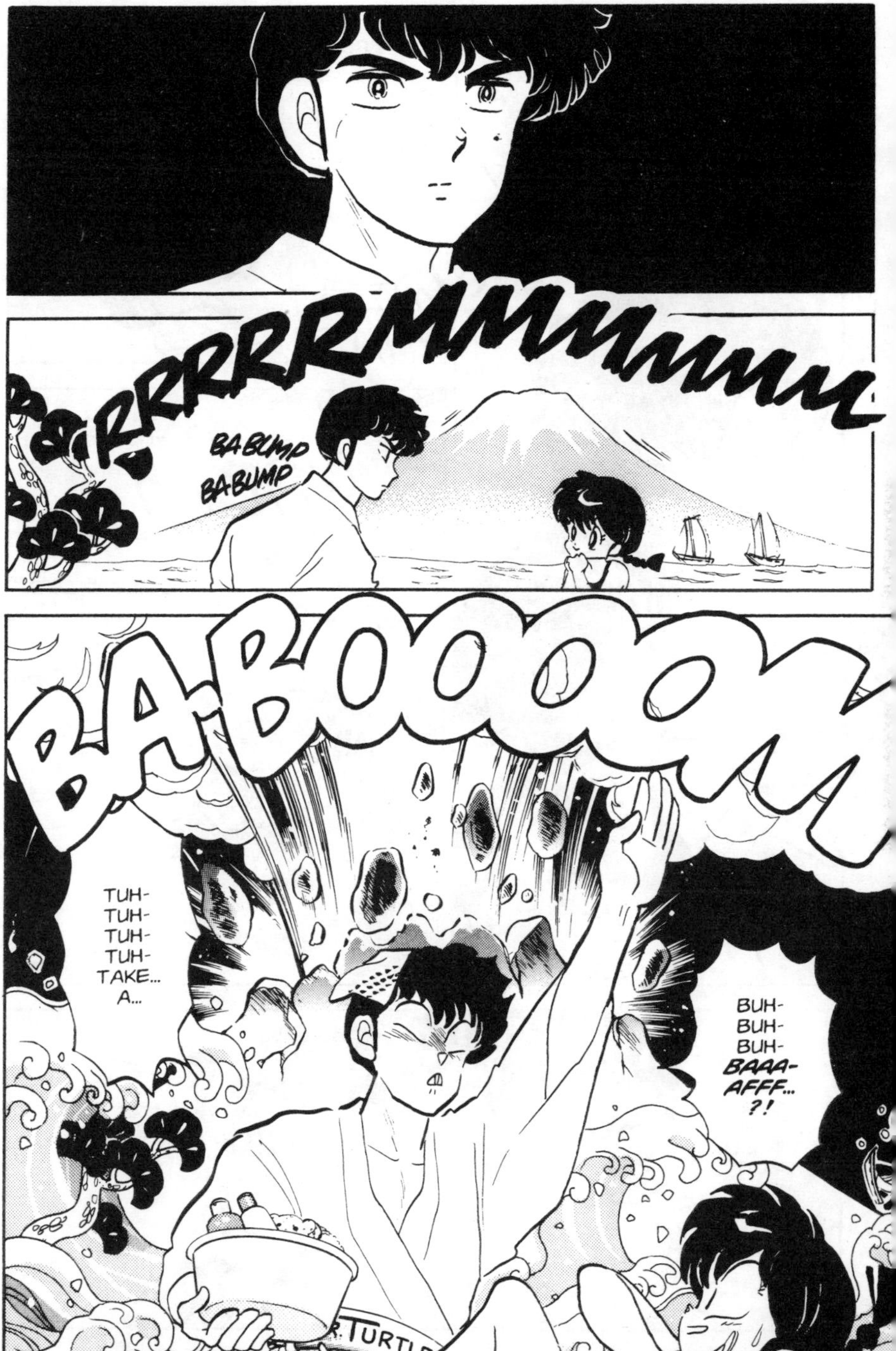
RRRRRMMMMMMM
BA-BUMP
BA-BUMP
BA-BOOOM
TUH-
TUH-
TUH-
TUH-
TAKE...
A...
BUH-
BUH-
BUH-
BAAA-
AFFF...
?!
R. TURTLE

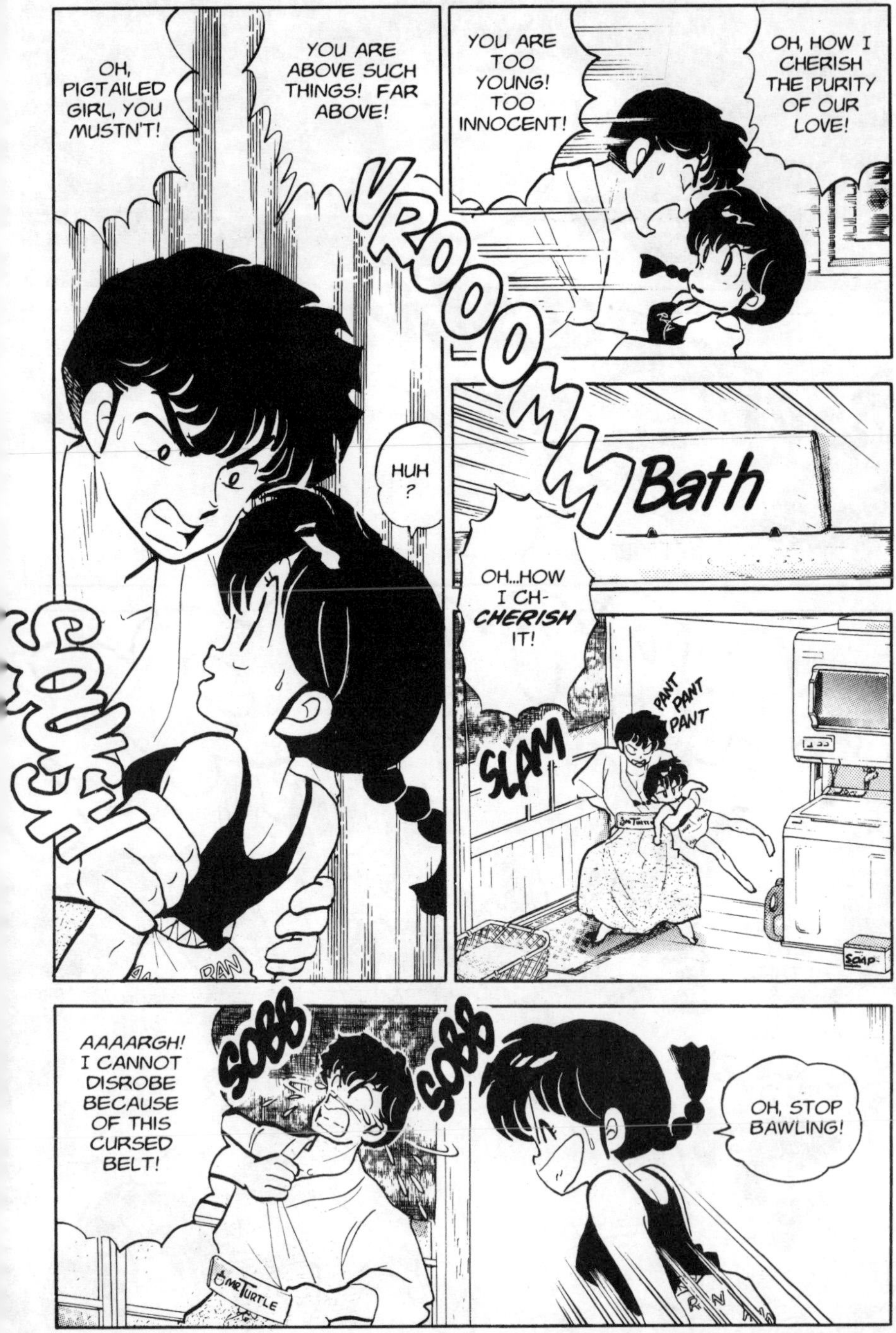
OH, PIGTAILED GIRL, YOU MUSTN'T!
YOU ARE ABOVE SUCH THINGS! FAR ABOVE!
VROOOMMM
HUH?
SQUNCH
YOU ARE TOO YOUNG! TOO INNOCENT!
OH, HOW I CHERISH THE PURITY OF OUR LOVE!
Bath
OH...HOW I CH-*CHERISH* IT!
PANT PANT PANT
SLAM
SOAP
AAAARGH! I CANNOT DISROBE BECAUSE OF THIS CURSED BELT!
SOBB SOBB
OH, STOP BAWLING!

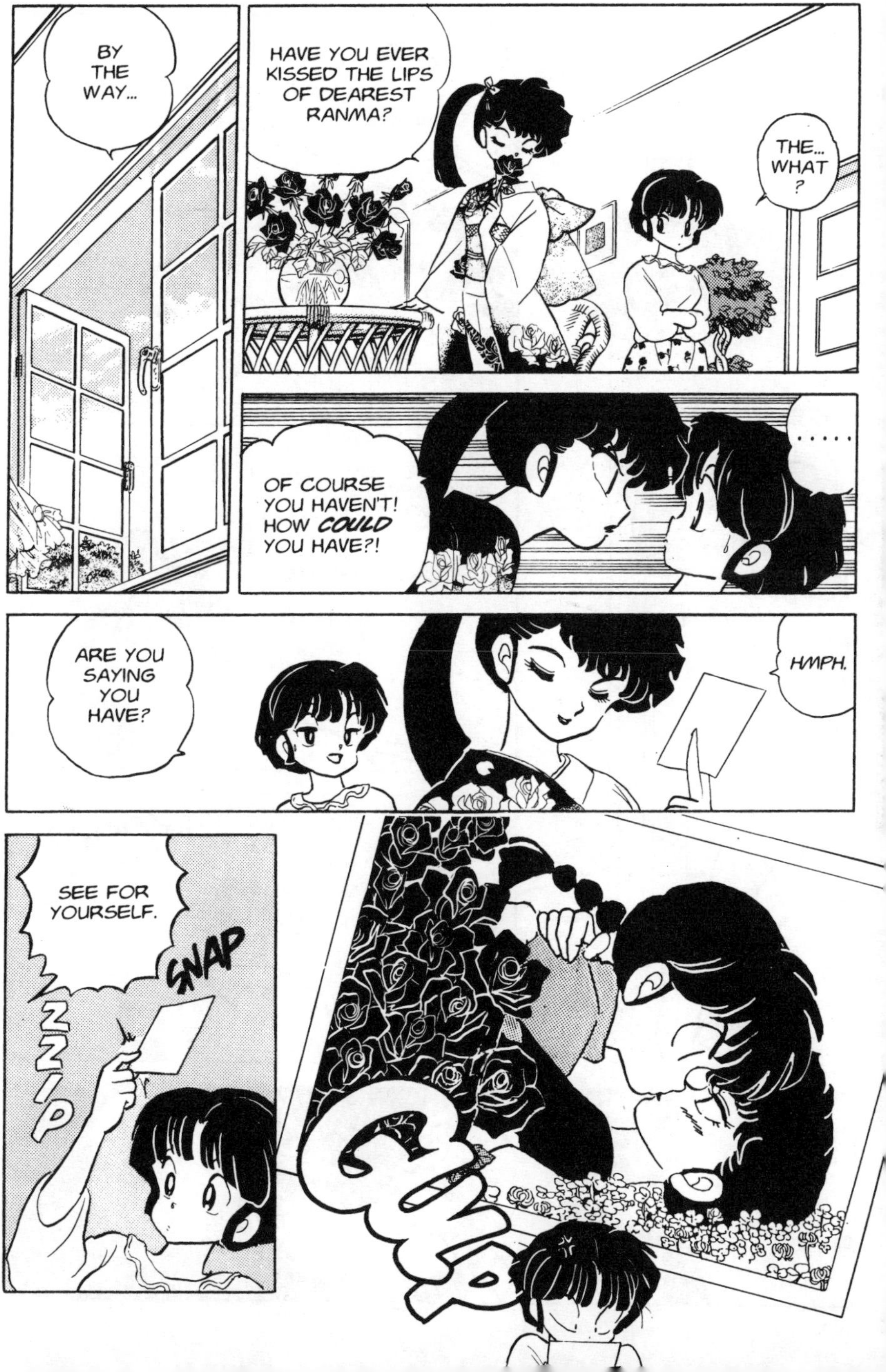
BY THE WAY...
HAVE YOU EVER KISSED THE LIPS OF DEAREST RANMA?
THE... WHAT?
OF COURSE YOU HAVEN'T! HOW **COULD** YOU HAVE?!
......
ARE YOU SAYING YOU HAVE?
HMPH.
SEE FOR YOURSELF.
SNAP
ZZIP

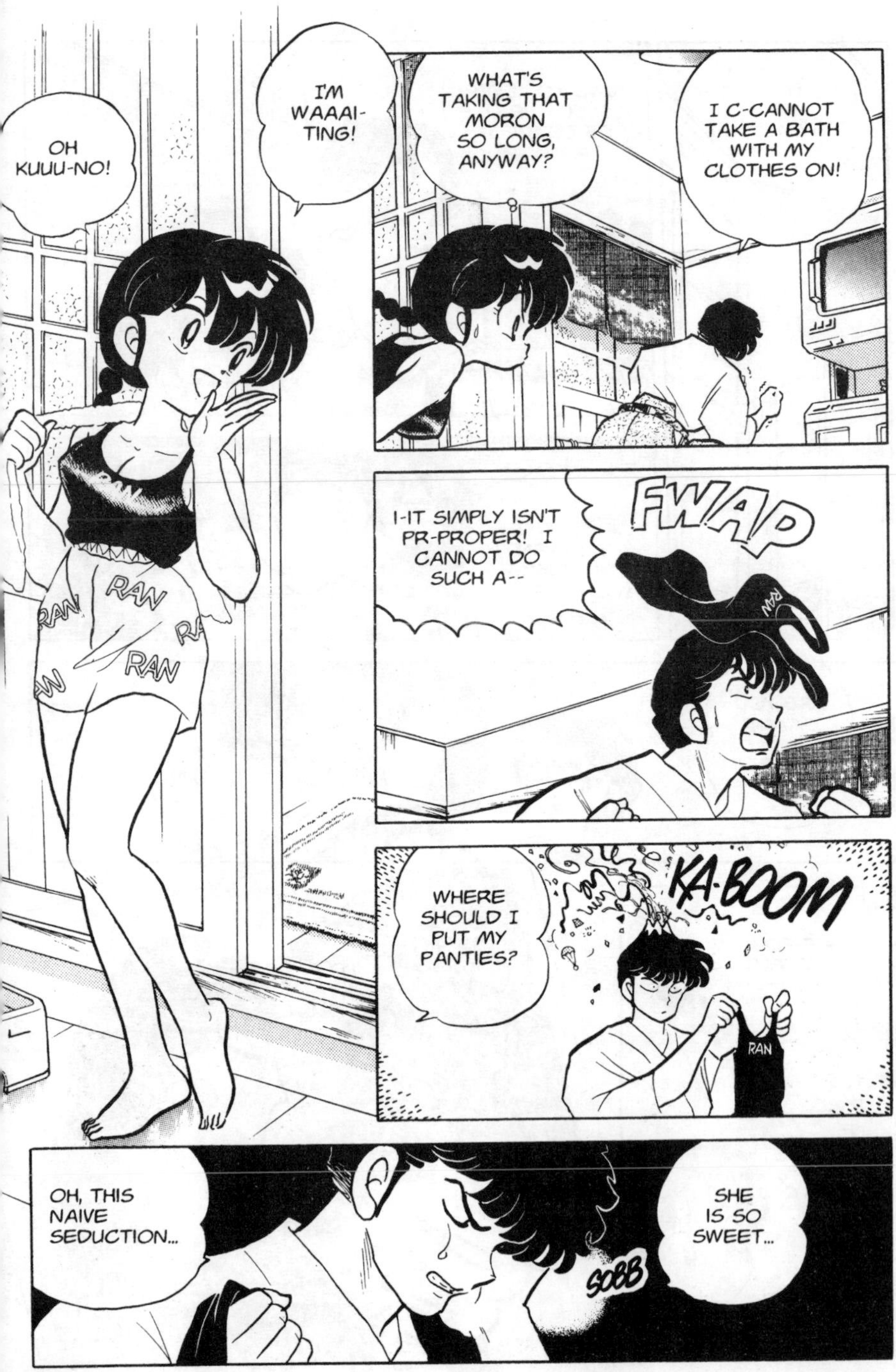
OH KUUU-NO!
I'M WAAAI-TING!
RAN RAN RAN RAN RAN
WHAT'S TAKING THAT MORON SO LONG, ANYWAY?
I C-CANNOT TAKE A BATH WITH MY CLOTHES ON!
I-IT SIMPLY ISN'T PR-PROPER! I CANNOT DO SUCH A--
FWAP
RAN
WHERE SHOULD I PUT MY PANTIES?
KA-BOOM
RAN
OH, THIS NAIVE SEDUCTION...
SOBB
SHE IS SO SWEET...

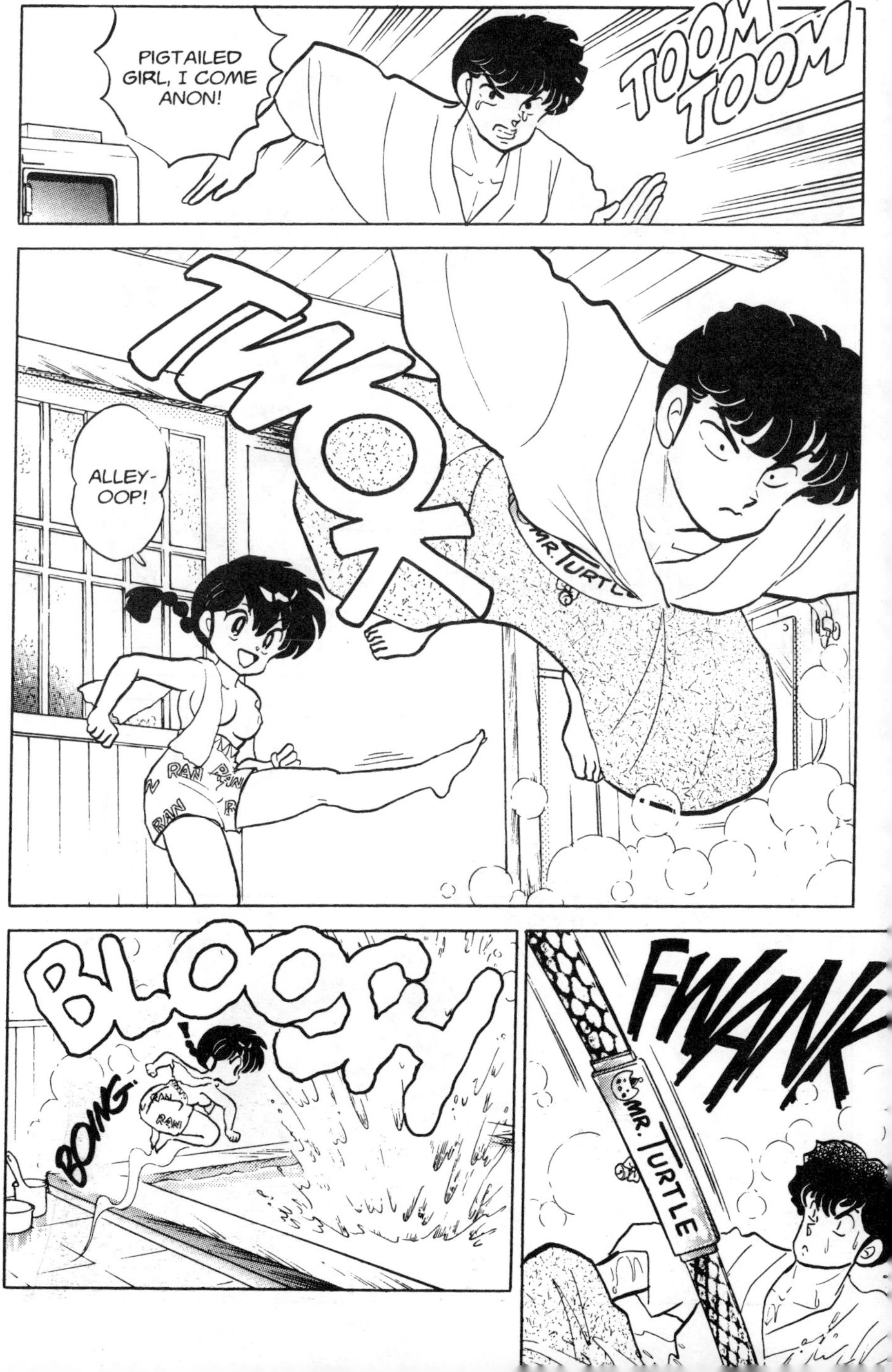
PIGTAILED GIRL, I COME ANON!
TOOM TOOM
ALLEY-OOP!
TWOK
MR. TURTLE
RAN RAN RAN
BLOOSH
BOING
FWANK
MR. TURTLE

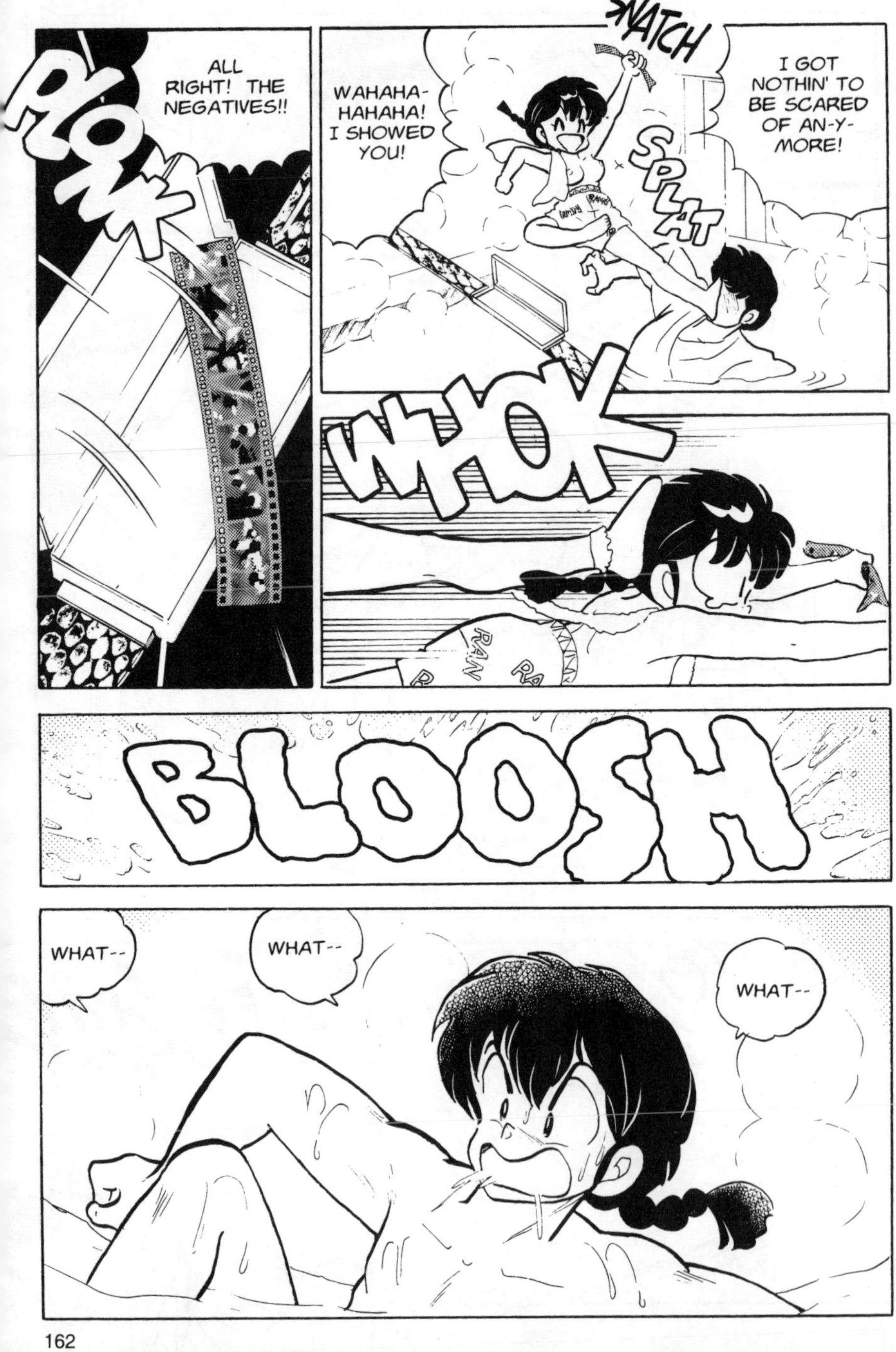
PLOMK
ALL RIGHT! THE NEGATIVES!!
SNATCH
WAHAHA-HAHAHA! I SHOWED YOU!
I GOT NOTHIN' TO BE SCARED OF AN-Y-MORE!
SPLAT
WHOK
BLOOSH
WHAT--
WHAT--
WHAT--

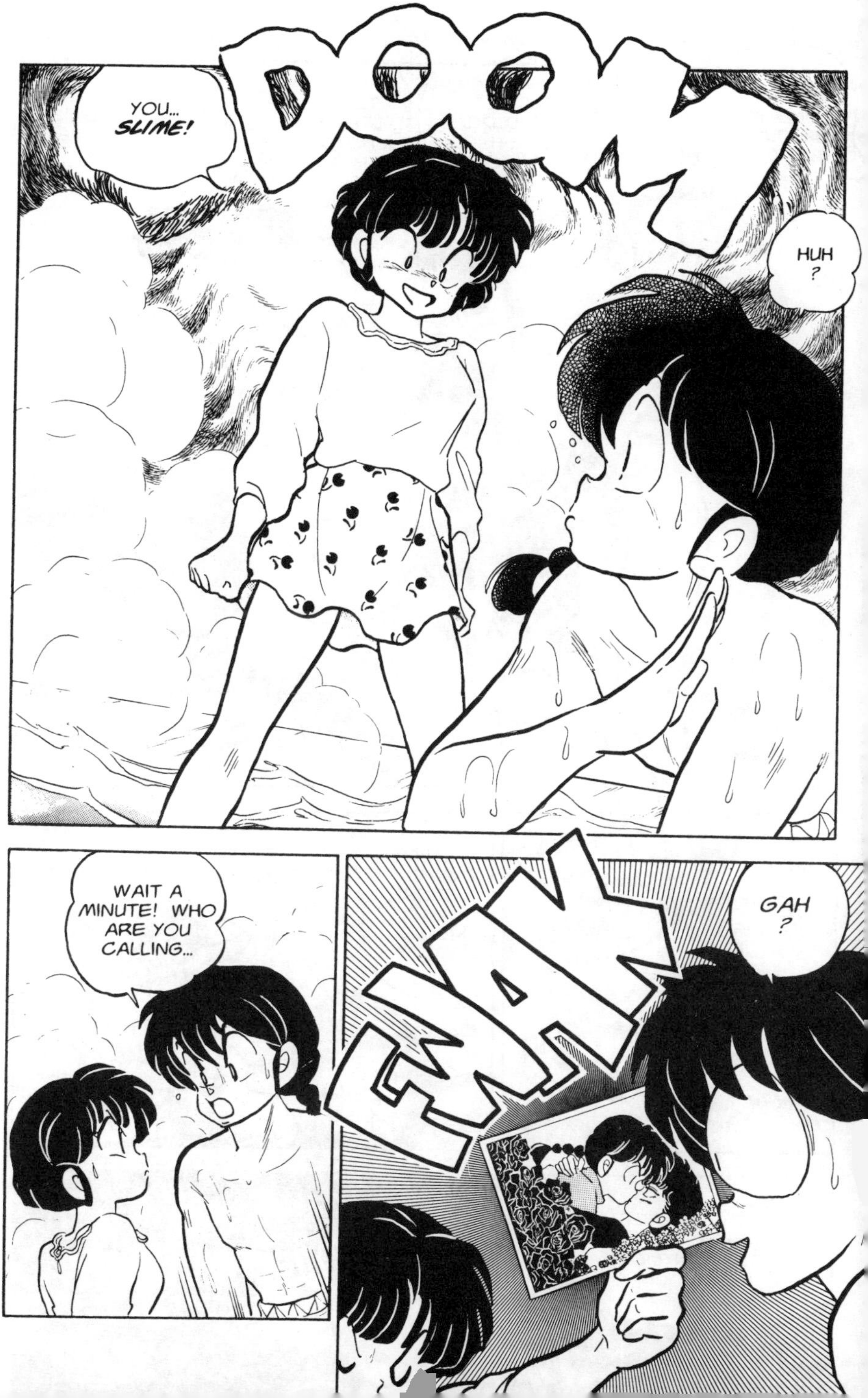
YOU... SLIME!
DOOM
HUH ?
WAIT A MINUTE! WHO ARE YOU CALLING...
GAH ?

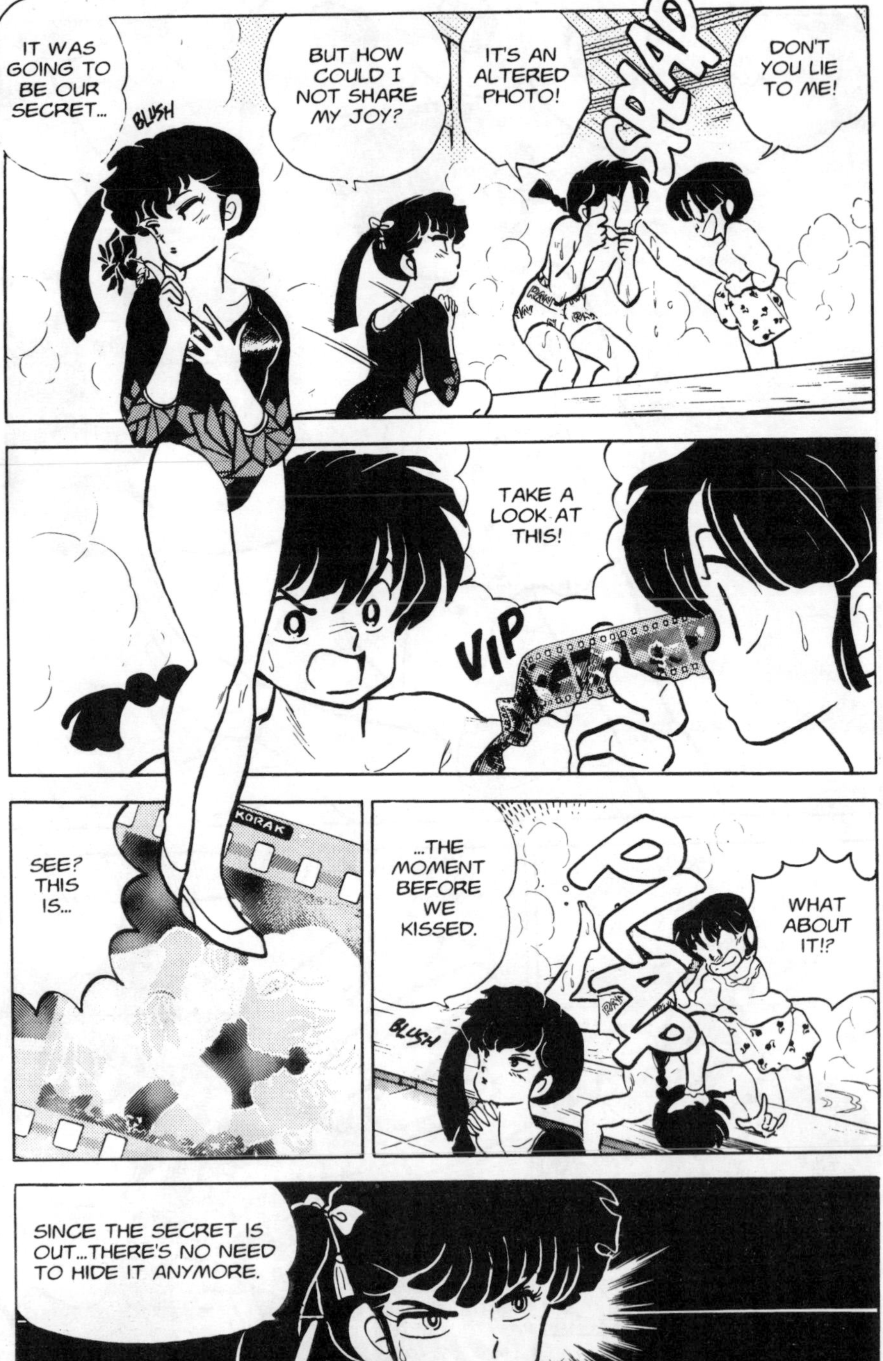
IT WAS GOING TO BE OUR SECRET...
BLUSH
BUT HOW COULD I NOT SHARE MY JOY?
IT'S AN ALTERED PHOTO!
SPLAP
DON'T YOU LIE TO ME!
TAKE A LOOK AT THIS!
VIP
SEE? THIS IS...
KORAK
...THE MOMENT BEFORE WE KISSED.
PLAP
WHAT ABOUT IT!?
BLUSH
SINCE THE SECRET IS OUT...THERE'S NO NEED TO HIDE IT ANYMORE.

COME!

LET US KISS BEFORE THE ENTIRE WORLD!

PSSHH

HEY! THAT'S COLD!!

NOOOO--!!

GLOMP

KISS ALL YOU WANT.

SHHHHHH

OH, PIGTAILED GIRL...

BLORSH

LITTLE WITCH! WHERE DID YOU HIDE MY DARLING RANMA!?

YOU WOMANIZER!

SNAP

VIP

KLONG

OH, SAVE ME, KUNO, SAVE ME!

PLOP

ARE YOU TAKING HER SIDE?!

SURELY YOU WON'T TURN AGAINST ME FOR AKANE?!

GLOMP

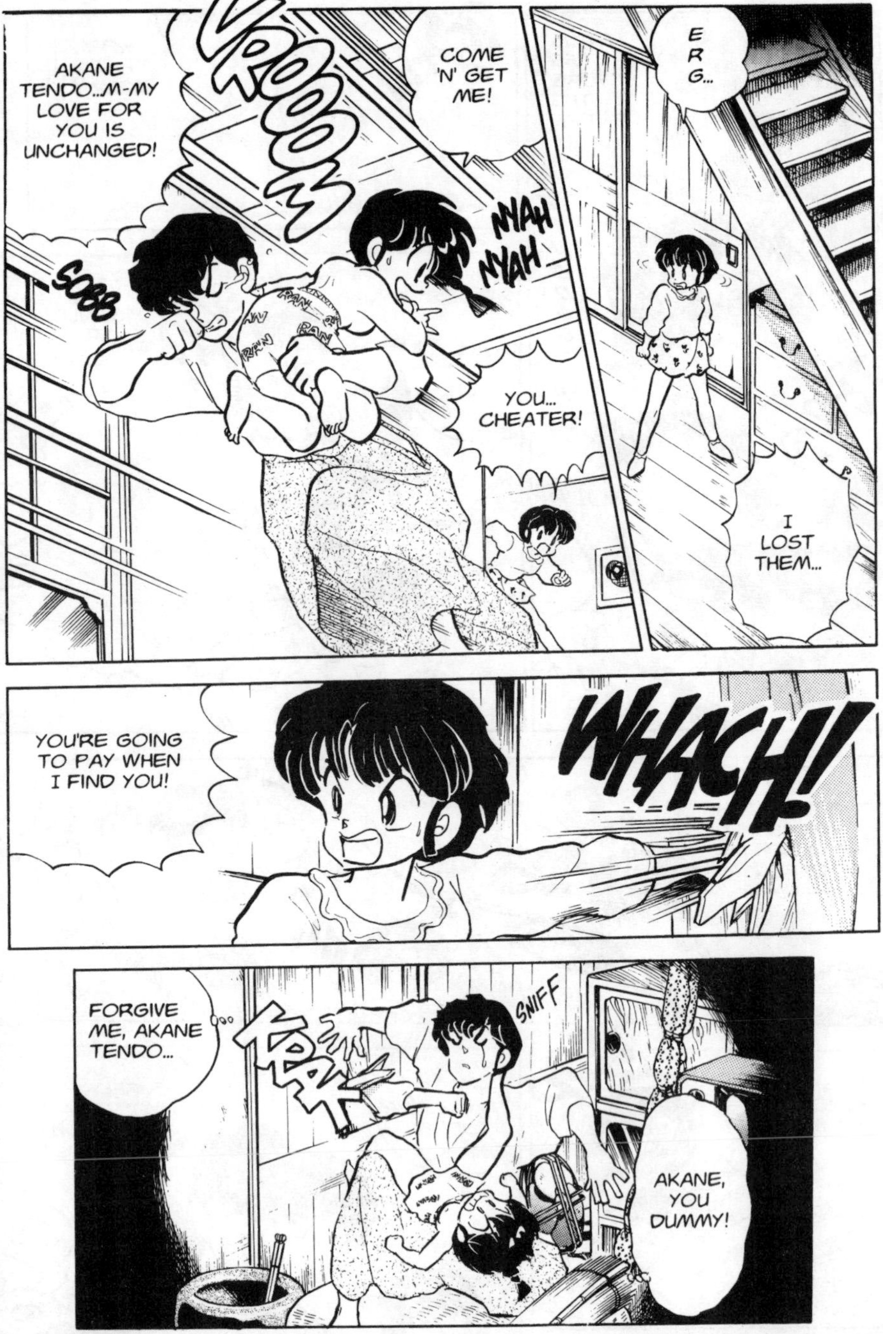
AKANE TENDO...M-MY LOVE FOR YOU IS UNCHANGED!
VROOOOM
SOBB
COME 'N' GET ME!
NYAH NYAH
YOU... CHEATER!
ERG...
I LOST THEM...
YOU'RE GOING TO PAY WHEN I FIND YOU!
WHACH!
FORGIVE ME, AKANE TENDO...
KRAK
SNIFF
AKANE, YOU DUMMY!

# PART ELEVEN

# ...I ATE THE WHOLE THING

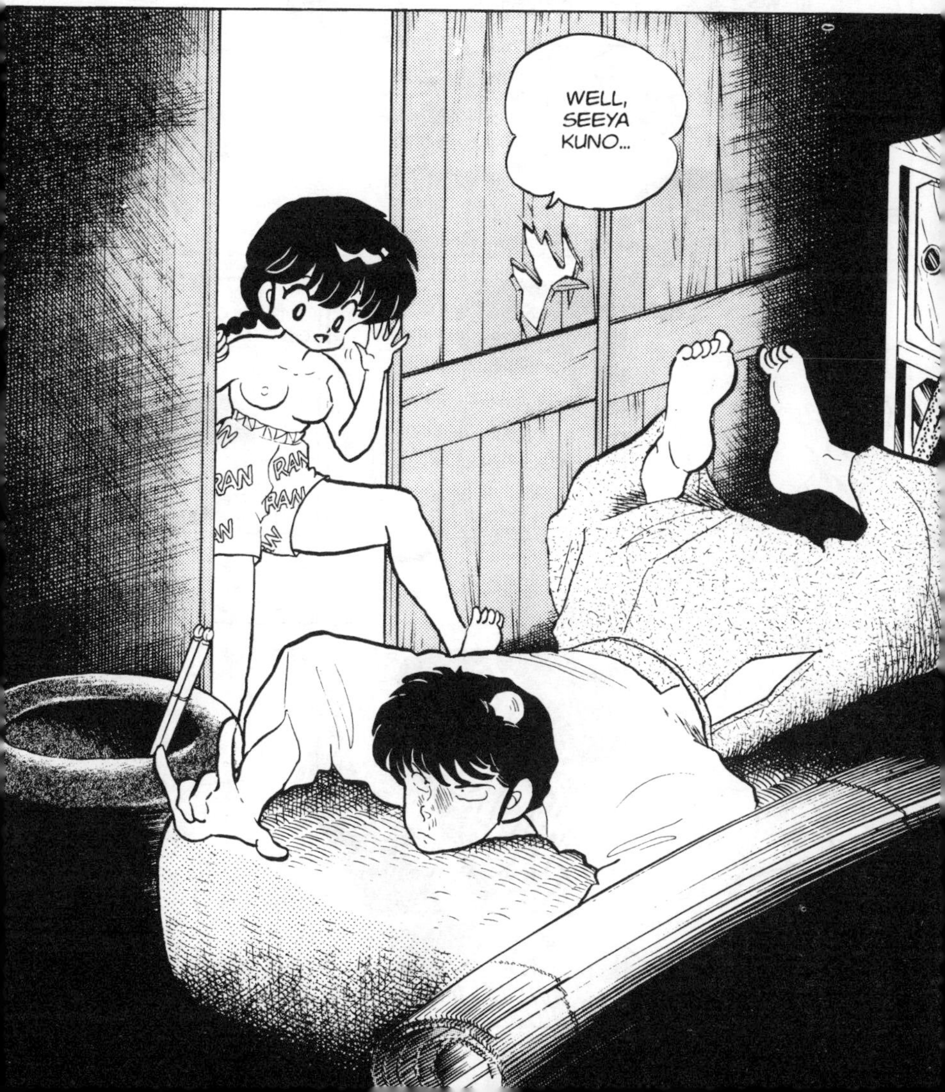
WELL, SEEYA KUNO...
RAN RAN RAN RAN

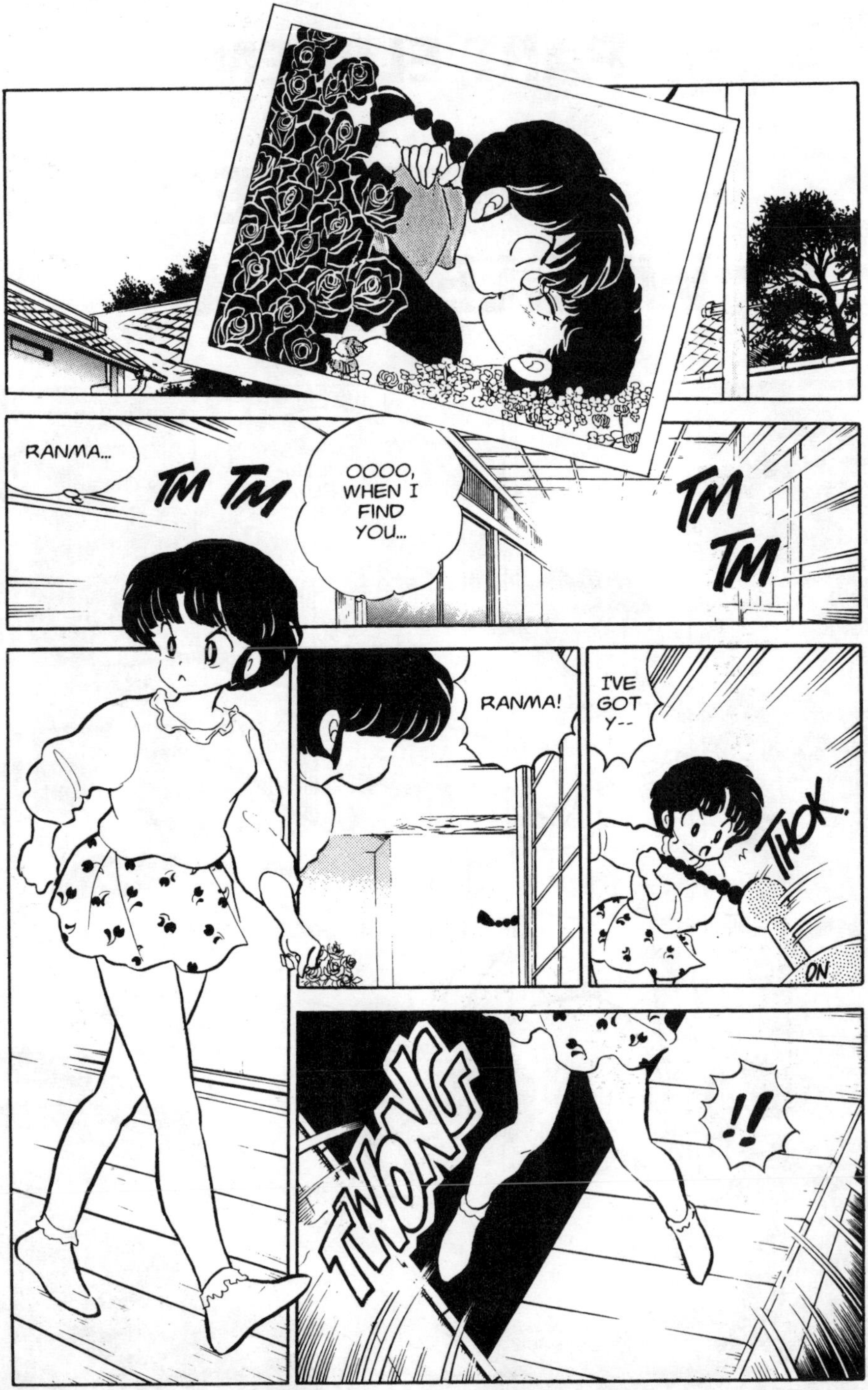
RANMA...
TM TM
OOOO, WHEN I FIND YOU...
TM TM
RANMA!
I'VE GOT Y--
THOK
ON
THONG
!!

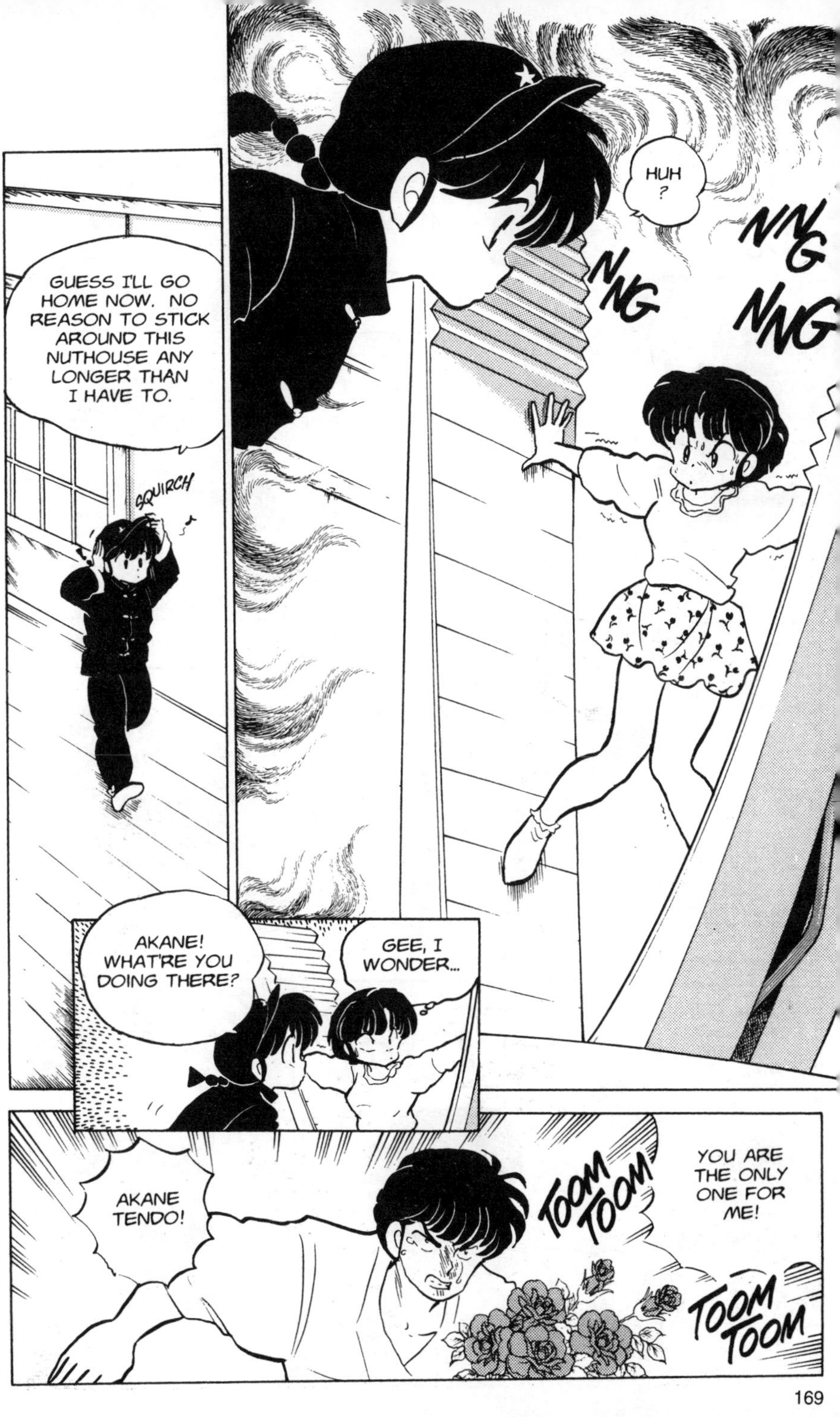
GUESS I'LL GO HOME NOW. NO REASON TO STICK AROUND THIS NUTHOUSE ANY LONGER THAN I HAVE TO.
SQUIRCH
HUH?
NNG
NNG
NNG
AKANE! WHAT'RE YOU DOING THERE?
GEE, I WONDER...
AKANE TENDO!
TOOM TOOM
YOU ARE THE ONLY ONE FOR ME!
TOOM TOOM

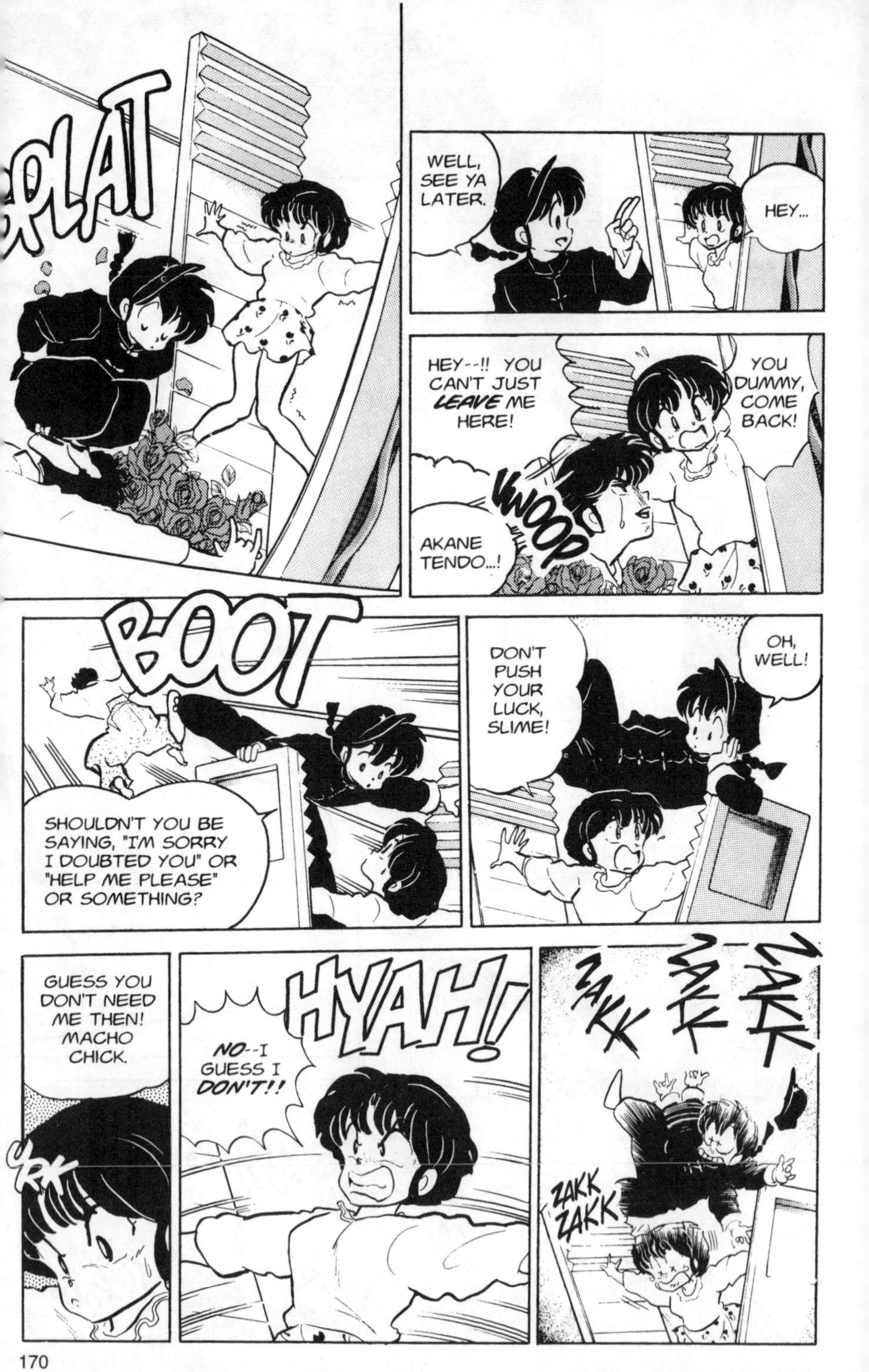

PLAT
WELL, SEE YA LATER.
HEY...
HEY--!! YOU CAN'T JUST LEAVE ME HERE!
YOU DUMMY, COME BACK!
VWOOOP
AKANE TENDO...!
BOOT
SHOULDN'T YOU BE SAYING, "I'M SORRY I DOUBTED YOU" OR "HELP ME PLEASE" OR SOMETHING?
DON'T PUSH YOUR LUCK, SLIME!
OH, WELL!
GUESS YOU DON'T NEED ME THEN! MACHO CHICK.
HYAH!
NO--I GUESS I DON'T!!
ZAKK ZAKK ZAKK
ZAKK ZAKK

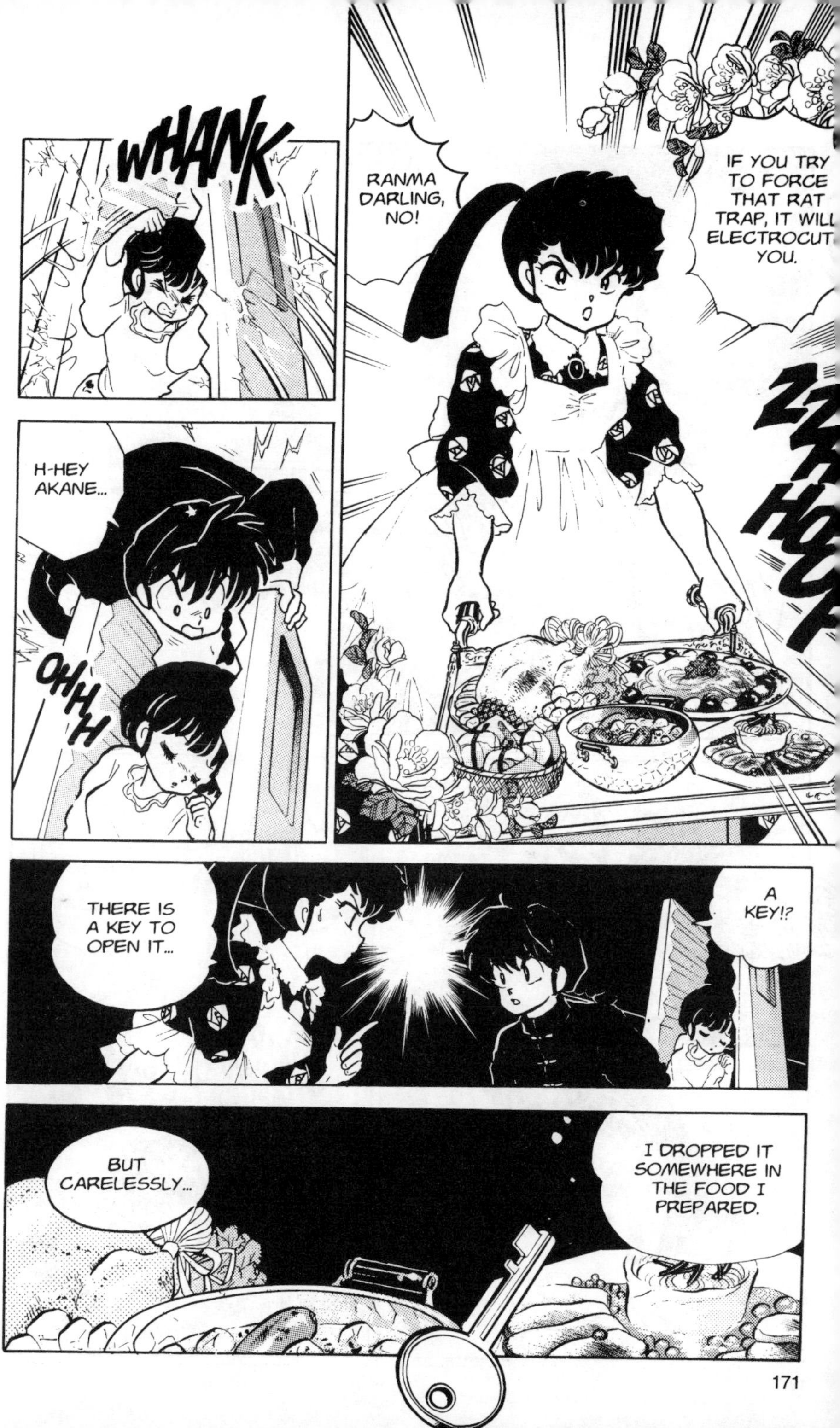

WHANK
H-HEY AKANE...
OHHHH
RANMA DARLING, NO!
IF YOU TRY TO FORCE THAT RAT TRAP, IT WILL ELECTROCUT YOU.
THERE IS A KEY TO OPEN IT...
A KEY!?
BUT CARELESSLY...
I DROPPED IT SOMEWHERE IN THE FOOD I PREPARED.

OHOHOHOHO! THE FOOD ISN'T POISONED, RANMA DARLING!

GLUMP GLUMP

SPLAP

IS IT TO YOUR LIKING?

GLUMP GLUMP
GLUMP GLUMP
GLUMP

UUUH...

SIZZLE
SIZZLE
SIZZLE
SIZZLE
SIZZLE

LUH-*HIII*-STEN, YUH-*HOO*...

YUH-*HEAH?* WHA-*AAT?*

PHEW

YOU KNOW, JEALOUSY PAST A CERTAIN POINT STOPS BEING CUTE.

*WHAT!?*

WHIRRRR

DON'T BE *STUPID?!*

WHY WOULD I BE JEALOUS OVER A...A...

WHY SO MAD THEN?

POIK POIK
POIK
POIK

WHAT DO YOU CARE WHOSE COOKING I EAT?

HUH? HUH? HUH?

.....

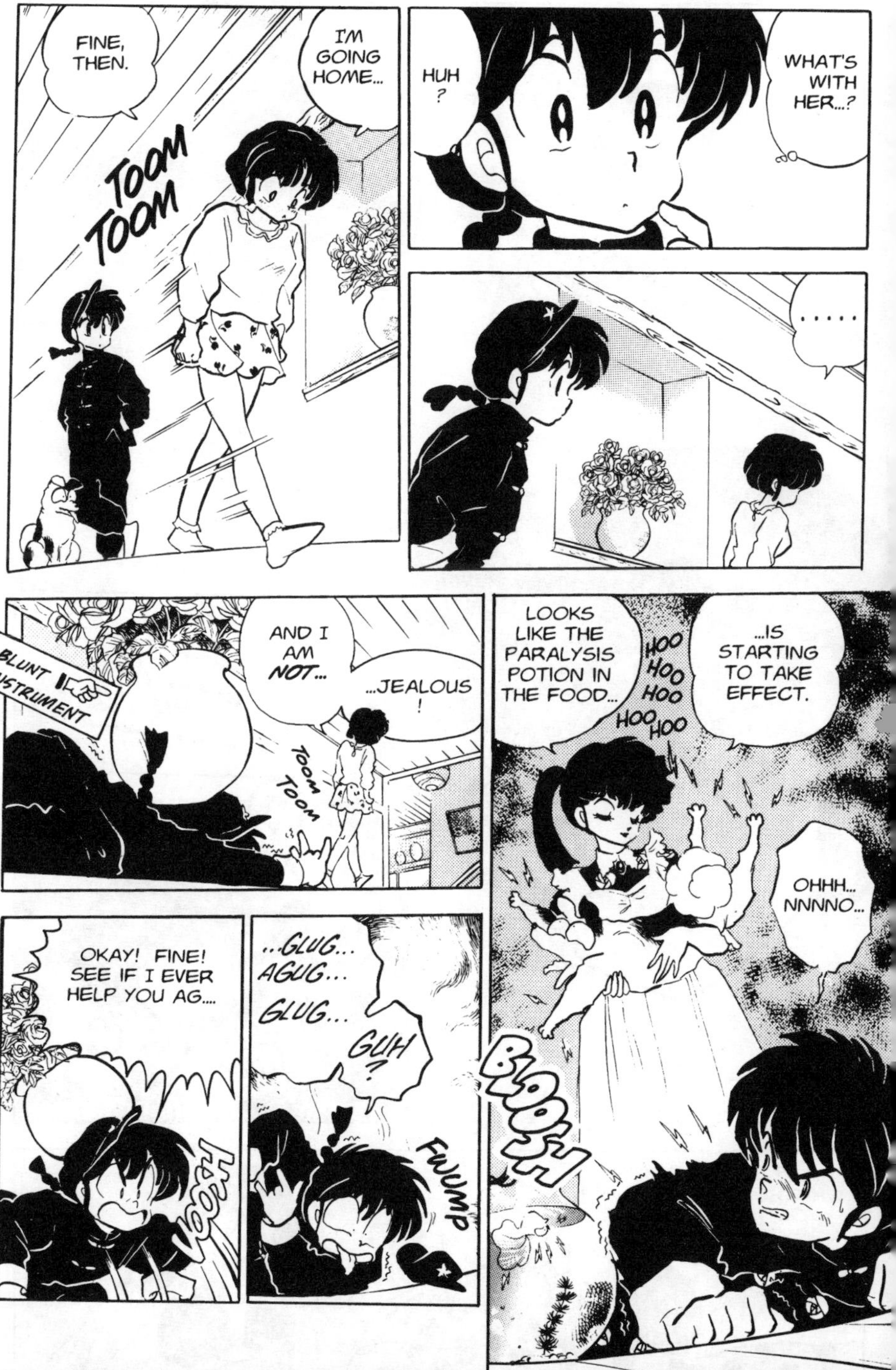
FINE, THEN.
I'M GOING HOME...
TOOM TOOM
HUH?
WHAT'S WITH HER...?
......
BLUNT INSTRUMENT
AND I AM NOT...
...JEALOUS!
TOOM TOOM
OKAY! FINE! SEE IF I EVER HELP YOU AG....
...GLUG... AGUG... GLUG...
GUH?
FWUMP
LOOKS LIKE THE PARALYSIS POTION IN THE FOOD...
HOO HOO HOO HOO HOO
...IS STARTING TO TAKE EFFECT.
OHHH... NNNNO...
BLOOSH

SIMPLE, DEAR RANMA. WE WILL NOW MAKE THAT FALSIFIED PHOTO...A REALITY!

NO WAY!

HOO HOO HOO HOO HOO HOO

SPROING

"FALSIFIED PHOTO"...?

RIGHT. I KNEW IT ALL ALONG...

I CAN GET OUT OF--

RRRG

MR. TURTLE

ZAK ZAK ZAKKA ZAKKA

OHOHOHOHO, HAVE YOU FORGOTTEN?

THAT BELT IS MEMORY METAL!

NOTHING WILL OPEN IT BUT HOT WATER!

MR. TURTLE

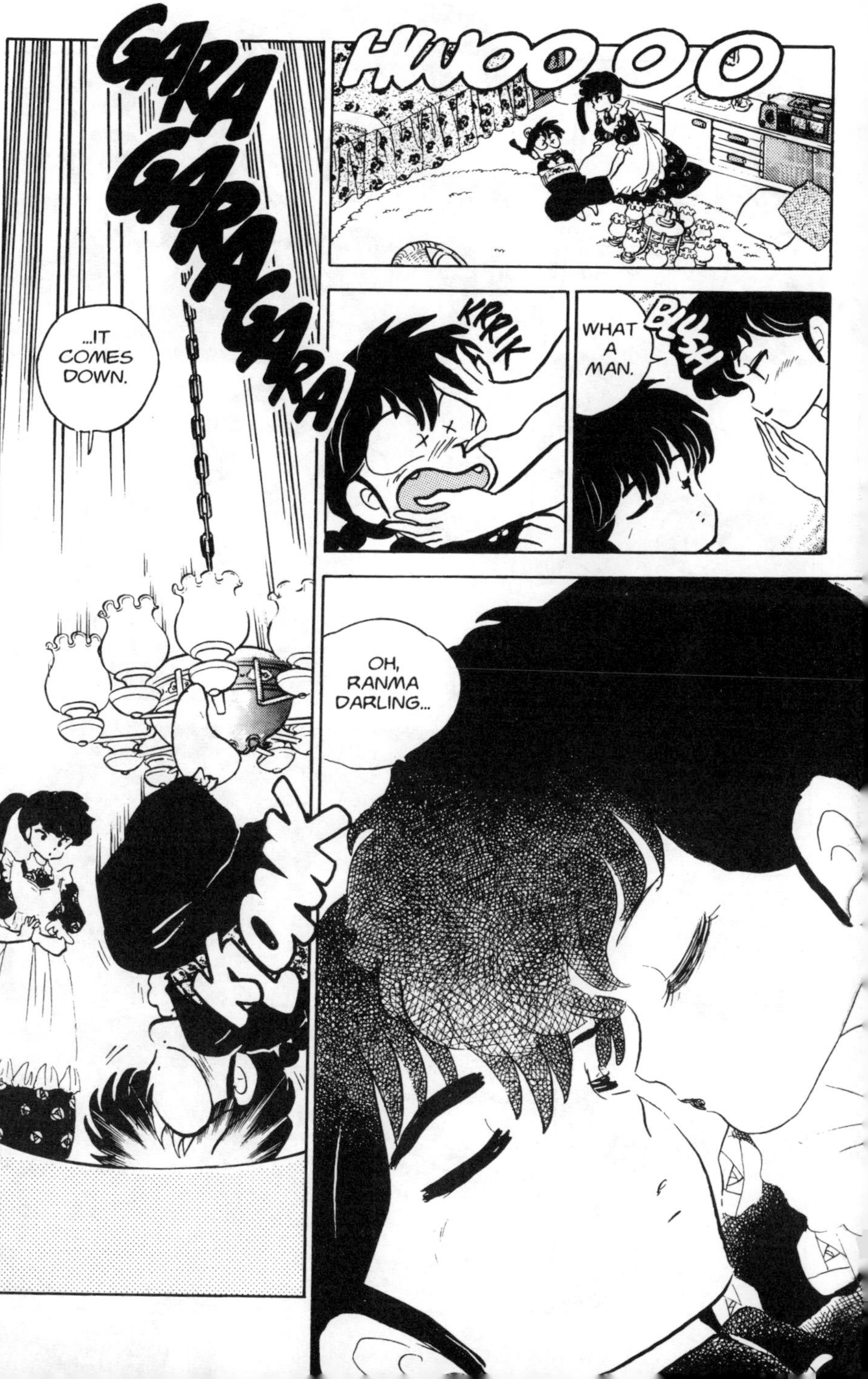
GARA GARAGARAGARA
...IT COMES DOWN.
HWOOOOO
KRRIK
WHAT A MAN.
BLUSH
KONK
OH, RANMA DARLING...

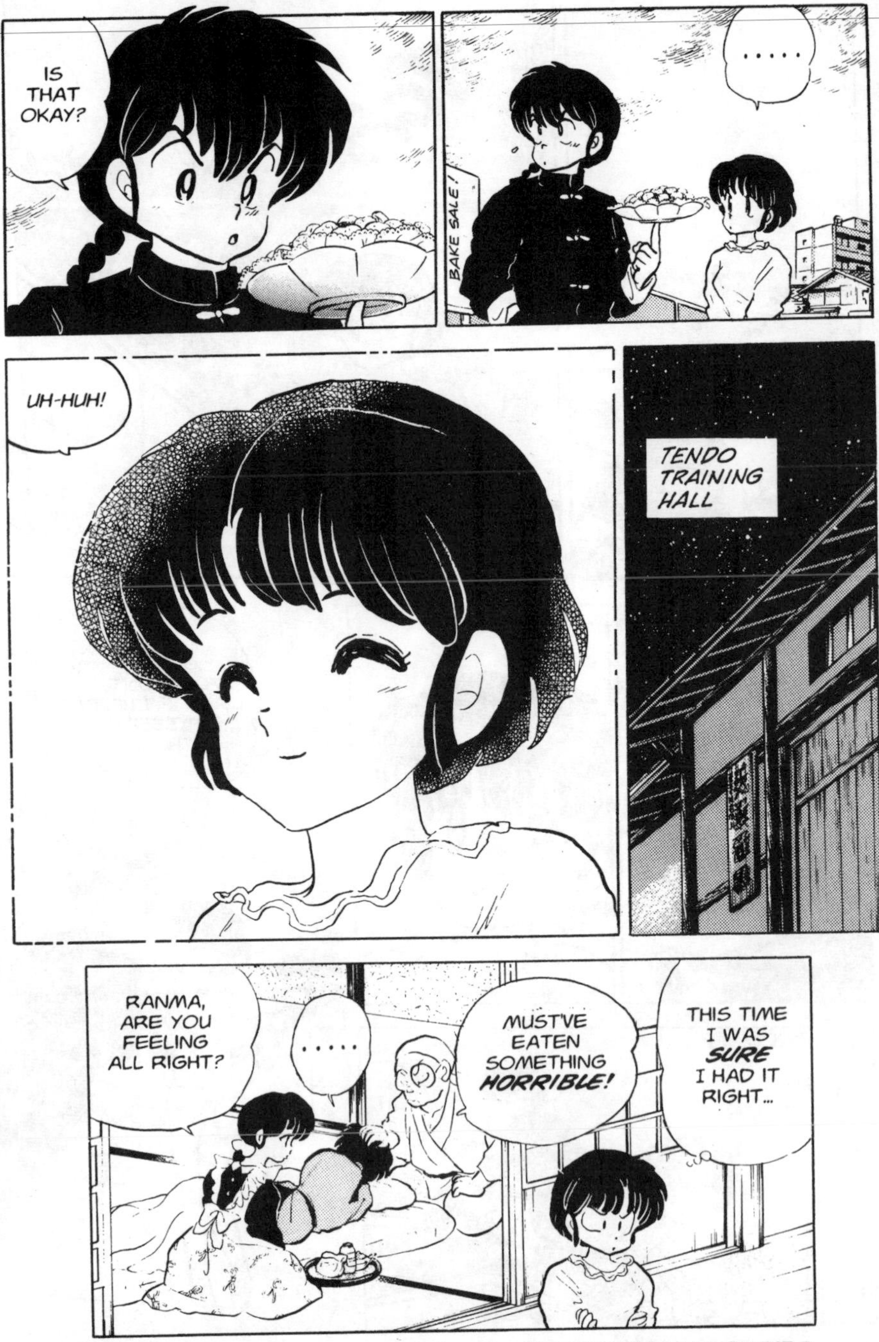
IS THAT OKAY?
BAKE SALE!
......
UH-HUH!
TENDO TRAINING HALL
RANMA, ARE YOU FEELING ALL RIGHT?
......
MUST'VE EATEN SOMETHING **HORRIBLE!**
THIS TIME I WAS **SURE** I HAD IT RIGHT...

END OF RANMA 1/2 VOLUME 7.

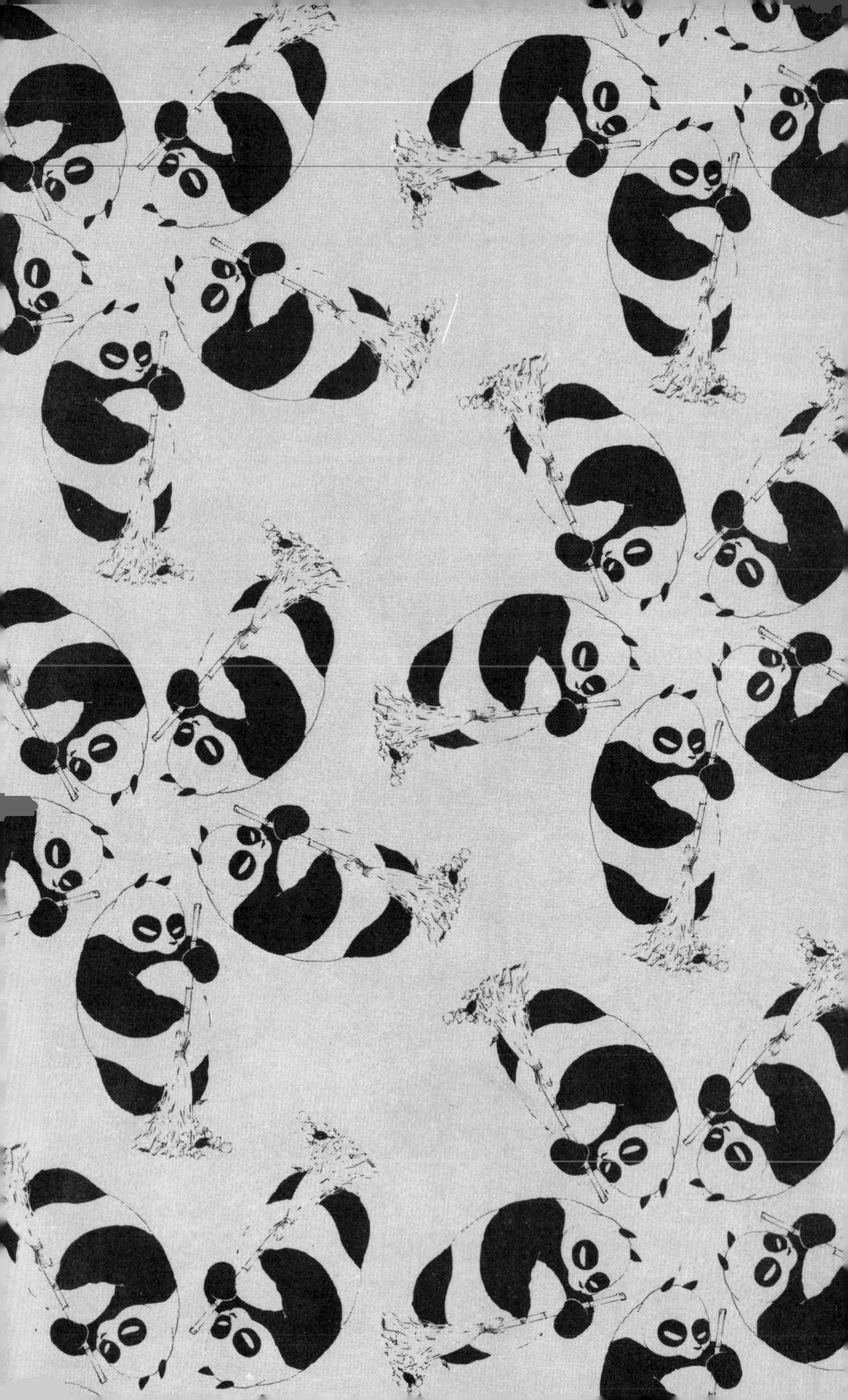